Hannah -

Grainger
County
Tomatoes

Hope you enjoy the book!

Other books by Nick Allen Brown

Field of Dead Horses
(HARROWOOD BOOKS, 2012)

The Astronaut from Bear Creek
(HARROWOOD BOOKS, 2015)

What Lies Inside
(HARROWOOD BOOKS, 2021)

Grainger County Tomatoes

A Novel
by
Nick Allen Brown

Harrowood Books
2021

Trade Paperback Edition
ISBN-13   978-0-915180-59-2
ISBN-10   0-915180-59-6

10 9 8 7 6 5 4 3 2 1

First Publication (eBook): October, 2020
First Paperback Publication: June, 2021

Harrowood Books
3943 N Providence Road
Newtown Square, PA 19073
800-747-8356
harrowood@verizon.net

PRINTED IN CHINA

For more than a century, farmers in Grainger County, Tennessee have produced the most flavorful tomatoes in the world. Climate, soil and shared knowledge between farmers contribute to the sweet, acidic and tangy flavor of each and every tomato grown.

This book is dedicated to the past and present farmers who have worked tirelessly in pursuit of perfection.

Chapter 1

1951 Grainger County, Tennessee

Arthur Humes steered his 1946 Studebaker Skyway Champion into his client's gravel driveway. As he pulled in, he could see four parked cars that left little room for his coupe. Just as he cut the engine, he looked out the passenger side window and saw three coonhounds playing in the front yard. Their tails wagged carelessly as they bounded toward a juniper tree. Opening the driver's door, Arthur planted his Oxford shoes on the gravel driveway and stood up with his tweed sport coat in hand.

As he walked, he shoved his arms through the sleeves while switching his dark brown leather briefcase from one hand to the other. Once his coat was on, he held the briefcase in his right hand as he took long, casual strides in the wiry shade of the juniper. The coonhounds eyed Arthur, ready to bark and announce his presence. It was March and the weather was unusually mild. *The Farmer's Almanac* for that year had predicted that oddity, forecasting more sun and less cloud cover.

When one of the three coonhounds decided the man was of no consequence, it lunged at the other two. They playfully pawed, swatted, and gnawed at one another before collapsing onto the soft grass, rolling around in a lank pile. Arthur adjusted his tie as he stepped up on the front porch of a rather large home that had belonged to his client, Thaddeus Campbell.

When Thaddeus died, he was wearing overalls, a winter coat, and work boots. He was found by one of his workers lying face down in the dirt after he had collapsed from a heart problem that finally took its toll. The worker was a thin black man named Runt, and when he happened upon Mr. Campbell, he called out his name and clapped his hands.

"Mista Cam'bull? You ai'right Mista Cam'bull?" With no response, Runt sprinted to the main house to call for help.

Arthur Humes arrived at Mr. Campbell's house the day of his funeral. He could hear voices coming from inside when he opened the front door.

Upon entering, he saw wives, husbands, and children dressed in either black suits or dresses. Arthur knew what they were. Many months ago, his client had painted a very clear picture of what would be in his house on the day of his funeral. Scavengers. Some were nephews, some were cousins. All were opportunistic vultures that dreamt of inheriting the farm. The land would be rented, and the house would be sold.

The husbands and wives stopped talking when their eyes fell upon the man who entered through the front door wearing a nice, cream-colored tweed suit and holding a briefcase. Arthur averted his eyes from his client's family as he closed the front door and walked toward the kitchen. Glazed looks came from the husbands and curious expressions appeared on the wives' faces. While the children went back to what they were doing, the hard-soled shoes of the husbands and wives thunked on the wood floor until they entered the kitchen. Now tapping on tile with each step, they stopped in their tracks as they watched the well-dressed man set his briefcase on the large, wooden kitchen table. He unlatched and opened the briefcase, removed a stack of documents and set them aside. Arthur looked up at the gold diggers.

"Sir, may I ask who you are?" a husband asked. The skin around his eyes wrinkled with curiosity, and his hands rested on his hips.

"I'm Arthur Humes. My client is Mr. Campbell."

"Mister? Are you an attorney?"

"Yes, sir." Arthur replied. The husbands and wives watched as Arthur picked up a paper and cleared his throat. He looked at the words and began to read, *"To my family,"*...the wives took in a deep breath while the husbands held theirs. Is this the reading of the will? They thought. Is it this easy? One wife grabbed her husband's hand and muttered under her breath in excitement, "Oh, God" as Arthur began reading:

> *"Dear family,*
> *Thank you for coming to my funeral and the reading of this*
> *will. My attorney will be executing my final wishes, and at*
> *this time I respectfully request that this house be vacated.*
> *Please see yourselves outside until further notice."*

Confused, but hanging onto the promise of a small fortune, they abided by their uncle's wishes. They asked a few questions before leaving, but were given short, unsatisfactory, and frustrating answers only a skilled attorney could deliver. Once the family members scattered about on the front lawn, Arthur strolled over to the phone that hung on the kitchen wall. With a small piece of paper in his left hand, he read the phone number and used his other hand to operate the rotary dial. The signal from Campbell Farms traveled through a telephone exchange and down a series of telephone poles for almost three miles, reaching Werthan Farms. *Ring. Ring.*

"Hello?"

"Mr. Norman Werthan?" Arthur asked.

"Yes."

"Mr. Werthan, my name is Arthur Humes and I am an attorney. My client, Mr. Thaddeus Campbell had taken ill many months ago, and his doctor explained that he should set his affairs in order as his heart was causing him an array of problems."

"Okay."

"Did you know he had passed?"

"Yeah, I heard," Norman replied as he rolled his eyes.

"I am currently at his home on Washburn Road, and as part of him setting his affairs in order, I have been asked to read his will aloud in your presence."

"My presence?" his face scrunched in instant confusion.

"Yes, sir."

"What for?"

"I am instructed to read it only when you are present at his home."

"I'm not coming to his house. You come here if you want to read it. Besides, what did he leave me? Pig manure?"

"Sir, I am not able to tell you what is in the will over the phone. I am under Mr. Campbell's roof, per his instructions, and I must ask you politely to be present upon reading the will." Arthur said. Norman Werthan exhaled and shook his head, ready to hang up.

"I don't have time for this. I have a pretty good idea as to what is in the will so, I'll just say 'no thank you.'"

"Sir, I can guarantee you that you do not know what is in this will." Arthur responded. It wasn't the words that intrigued Norman, but his tone. He certainly had his attention.

"Okay. Fine."

"Can I expect you in ten minutes?"

"That or less."

Outside Mr. Campbell's house, the husbands and wives spoke

about Mr. Humes near the juniper, speculating as to how the estate would be divided up. The wives asked questions, and the husbands answered as best they could.

"Why would he ask us to go outside?" a wife asked.

"He's an attorney. He has to prepare the papers and get everything in order. That's what attorneys do."

"Why doesn't he come outside?" another wife asked.

"Isn't it obvious? The man needs a table."

From the back of the small group was a wife who wore brand-new, black dress shoes. Her skirt and blouse were perfectly pressed, and a brand-new cardigan hung on her thin frame. No one was paying her much attention, but when she did finally speak she chose a brief lull in the conversation.

"What if the estate isn't divided up equally?" she asked with one hand on her hip, the other near her mouth where she had been chewing on a polished fingernail. Everyone's imagination ignited with the thought of getting a bigger piece of the pie. Suddenly, she removed her polished fingernail from her mouth and turned to look at what sounded like a vehicle approaching. The rest of the husbands and wives turned their heads to see a 1940 Ford half-ton pickup truck park at the end of the driveway. On the side of the truck in faded letters read: *Werthan Farms.* When Norman exited the truck, he looked up at the husbands and wives who were staring him down. One husband started walking his way with a look of disbelief.

"Excuse me, sir. Are you Norman Werthan?"

"Yep."

"Well, you just get out of here. You ain't got no business being here, you lousy ol' coot." a husband said. Norman ignored him and kept walking while another husband shouted in his direction.

"Go home, you barn burner!"

"Yeah, barn burner, get out of here!" A wife added. The tallest of the husbands took a step out from under the wiry shade of the juniper as Norman took a step on the front porch.

"Mister, you're gonna get a face full of knuckles if you go in there," the husband said as he quickly rolled up his sleeves. Norman ignored him. With a turn of the doorknob, he went inside and closed it behind him. In fact, he slammed it. The wives scoffed at Norman's rudeness, and the husbands were dumbfounded and perplexed, especially the tallest husband with his rolled-up sleeves.

"Well, how do ya like that?" he said with a secret sigh of relief.

Chapter 2

"Hello?" Norman hollered out. He heard a rustling coming from the kitchen and the knocking of dress shoes on tile, then the thunking sound of shoes on hardwood floors. After several steps, a man in a shirt and tie appeared from around the corner.

"Mr. Werthan?" Arthur asked as he reached out his hand for a gentlemen's handshake.

"Yes, sir," he responded as he gripped Arthur's hand. Looking around the home of Thaddeus Campbell, he saw tasseled rugs on hardwood floors, lace curtains that decorated the windows and an upright piano that had been placed against the wall. Near the piano was a small table with an old tabletop tube radio resting on a knit doily. It wasn't what he expected.

"It's nice to meet you. You appear to be the same age as Mr. Campbell."

"I'm sixty-two. Two years younger."

"I see. Well, if we could, let's go into the kitchen. We'll have a seat in there." Before following Arthur, Norman turned and put his hand on the deadbolt. *Click.* He peered through the lace curtains and looked at the husbands and wives standing under the juniper before he followed Mr. Humes into the kitchen.

"Now, I have been instructed to read you a letter that pertains to the will. I have it right here."

"I didn't know he was sick."

"Yes. It had something to do with his heart not beating properly. It weakened over time. Poor fellow." Arthur said as he took a seat while Norman eased into a wooden chair next to the large, custom built table. He could see a pitcher of iced tea on the kitchen counter and next to it, an empty glass. It seemed that Mr. Humes had made himself at home.

"I'm ready, I guess," said Norman.

"Good. The letter which I will give you a copy for your records states the following and is written by myself and is dictated word for word as instructed by my client Mr. Thaddeus Edward Campbell, Jr." Arthur put his glasses on and shifted his weight to one side as he crossed his right leg and began reading.

"Norman Werthan, you are a knob and a moron, and I am unable to contain my utmost displeasure that you didn't die before I did. I assure you that in no way because of my death have you one-upped me, and the fact that you are an insufferable drip gives me assurance and peace knowing that it is I who one-upped you every day of my life."

Arthur began to chuckle while Norman rolled his eyes and shook his head. Arthur broke from the letter and looked at Norman. "So sorry."

"Is that it?"

"No, there is more. It gets less offensive I assure you," His smile was wiped away by Norman's irked expression. Feeling a little uncomfortable, Arthur shifted his weight once again, uncrossed his leg and found his place in the letter and continued.

"While my disdain for you is clear, and your death soon after mine would cause those who knew you to surely express a deep

resounding joy, I have nowhere to turn, but to the one who I am unable to tolerate."

"Where is this going? Do I really need to be here for this?" Norman interrupted. Arthur chuckled once more. "Again, accept my apologies. I do find this humorous to say the least." Arthur picked up where he left off.

"In short, I need your help. Even though your parents should have given you up at birth,"

...a deep resounding laugh came from Arthur. His face, hidden by the paper, jostled and moved up and down, while Arthur for the third time, apologized and continued reading,

"You were born with an understanding that only a real man of Grainger County can fully comprehend. In the end, I suppose we see eye-to-eye on how best to grow a tomato."

The insults weren't anything new. Trading verbal blows was an annual pastime at the yearly Baptist Labor Day picnic. There were also a handful of physical altercations over the 55 years they knew each other. Norman could easily believe that T.C. (as he was known around town) would request him to be present at the reading of his will, so he could be berated one last time. T.C. asking him for help was out of character. In mid-thought, Arthur continued.

"I have a proposition for you. I need you to travel and visit my niece and nephew, Samuel and Elizabeth Campbell. I am certain they aren't standing out on my front lawn waiting for a hand out. As of this writing, they were last seen in Marion,

*North Carolina. I need you to ascertain if Samuel is fit to take
on the operations of the farm. See if he knows anything about
growing tomatoes and rotation crops. He did own a small
tomato farm at one point. If you feel he is up to it and can meet
the high standards of a Grainger County tomato farmer, please
relay the info to Mr. Humes."*

"Why would he think I would even help him?"

"He has instructed me to compensate you. I am managing his
entire estate, and you will be paid for your time. If you can give
me a few more paragraphs, you'll see how this will work."

"Fine," said Norman. Arthur continued.

*"The only reason I think Samuel and Elizabeth would be good
for the farm is that Samuel comes from a line of tobacco and
tomato farmers. I hear he has a strong work ethic and has an
interest in farming. He just might fit the bill. If, however, you
feel that Samuel isn't fit to take over my farm, please inform
Mr. Humes. I will pay you for your time and discernment. If
you want to have nothing to do with this situation, my farm
will go to auction and will more than likely be owned by a
donut, whose only goal is money. Without your help, the highest bidder could easily grow turds on vines and sell them next
to your Gold Heirlooms at market. Know that my ultimate goal
is to prevent my wretched, unessential family from getting this
farm. They don't even know what a tomato is or what it should
taste like. While your horse face isn't welcome in my home, your
assistance in this matter is, and it will benefit Grainger County."*
Arthur said as he set the paper down on the table.

"There are plenty of other farmers around here that can do
this nonsense. I just don't understand why he is asking me."

"I am only allowed to say so much, Mr. Werthan. There are things I am privy to that I cannot say per my client's instructions. I suppose though, it would be okay for me to let on that Mr. Campbell did admire your tomatoes. He spoke of other things he was fond of, such as your knowledge and aptitude, but really if I say anymore I would be breaking an agreement."

"So, he didn't hate me?"

"He did think that you were the only one who could grow tomatoes like he could. Considered you a threat for some reason. He also mentioned that younger farmers don't respect crops like the older folks."

"I can understand that."

"He also mentioned something to the effect that you wouldn't really be helping him as much as making certain the farm didn't go to someone who didn't fully understand tomatoes."

"Good to know. Look, I'm not interested. I don't even know why I came."

"You don't even want to know what he would pay?"

"No. Thanks anyway. Good meeting you." Norman said as he stood up and walked out of the kitchen and headed toward the foyer. Before he reached the door, he thought about his tractor. It needed a new clutch. He thought about the leaking roof in his house. He was tired of putting pots and pans around his home when it rained. Money could fix those things. *What was T.C. offering?* Norman walked back into the kitchen.

"Just out of curiosity, how much is he offering?"

"Glad you asked. Two hundred dollars."

"Why so much?"

"He explained to me that money would be the only way you would even consider helping him."

"When would I get paid?"

"As soon as you let me know if Mr. Samuel Campbell is worthy."

"Can I take a day or two to make up my mind?"

"Of course," Arthur said with a grin. Norman left the kitchen and unlocked the front door. He stepped out on the porch while the man with rolled up sleeves came out from under the juniper and approached him.

"Hey, fella, you wanna tell me why you're in my uncle's house? In case you didn't know, he wasn't very fond of you."

"What business do you have here, huh?" A smaller husband shouted. His sleeves were still at arms length and he seemed satisfied shouting from a distance. Norman avoided them all as they continued to ask questions. He quickly made it to his truck and opened the door to the cab. Before sitting in the driver's seat, he looked at the husbands and wives following him from a distance. Instead of talking, Norman yelled as he rattled off a few names.

"Big Rainbow, Sunset Girl, Hillstacker Gold." He waited for them to respond. The husbands and wives stood puzzled in their tracks. "Well?" Norman asked.

"Well what?" Sleeves retorted.

"What did I just say?"

"I don't rightly know," Sleeves said as he turned around to an equally puzzled audience for help. Norman growled at them as he sat down in the cab of his truck. He started the engine and drove out onto the road.

"What's Hillstacker Gold?" Sleeves asked.

I don't know was the response that came in either verbal or facial expressions from the other husbands and wives.

Chapter 3

After two days of deciding what to do, Norman had concluded that two hundred dollars would not only fix his leaking roof, but he could also pay for the repairs on his tractor and have a little money left over. While Norman could easily afford these things, he liked the thought that by making a simple trip, his enemy would pay for the things he'd rather not spend his money on.

He called Arthur and explained that he would make the trip to Marion.

"Do you have a pencil?" Arthur asked. "I have the last known address of Samuel Campbell."

"I do. Just a second please," Norman said as he grabbed a pencil. He looked around for something to write on and quickly scrounged for a piece of paper. After digging through the trashcan, he came up with an opened envelope. The name on the return address read: *Paty Lumber Company,* and the top was frayed and torn from Norman tearing it open. If his wife were around, she would have said, *"Use a letter opener, Dear. We're not apes."*

Norman flipped the envelope over and wrote on the back with a short pencil that bore his teeth marks from tax preparation frustration. Once Norman wrote down the address, Arthur hurried off the phone with a parting thought. "Don't say anything

about the inheritance. That's my part. All you need to do is discern if he is a good candidate."

Once on the highway to Marion, Norman thought about
Thaddeus Campbell and what a nuisance he was to him for most
of his life. Now, he was doing T.C. a favor even if he was being
paid for his efforts. *Hopefully,* Norman thought, *this young Samuel
loves tomatoes and has a passion for being a tomato farmer.* His job
would be done, and he could collect his two hundred and move
on. Even if Samuel turned out to be a bust, Norman would still
collect his money. Either way, his time wouldn't be wasted.

The drive began shortly after 9:00 A.M. At noon, he pulled
over at a rest stop and unpacked a sandwich and crackers from
his lunch box. After eating, and drinking water from a thermos,
he got back on the highway and arrived in the town of Marion
right at 1:20 P.M. After driving around for five minutes, not
knowing where to start, he stopped at a Sinclair filling station.

An attendant came out from the garage dressed in navy-blue
pants, a white button-up shirt with a navy-blue tie and an official
Sinclair zippered jacket. The weather in Marion wasn't freezing,
but cold from the constant breeze. His uniform was common to
all Sinclair attendants as was his friendly demeanor. He bent
slightly near the driver's side of Norman's truck with his hand
on the roof for balance and a smile on his face.

"Can I do ya for?"

"Fill up and a Coca-Cola, please." The attendant immediately
walked back inside his station while Norman got out of the car
and fished out a few dimes from his pocket as he headed for the
phone booth. The attendant came out of the station with a cold
glass bottle of Coke in his right hand. Holding it high above his
head, he yelled in a helpful tone.

"Sir, your Coca-Cola!"

"Just put it on the hood. I'll be back in a minute." Norman stepped inside the phone booth and opened the Marion phone book. He searched through a list of Campbells and easily found the number that matched the address Arthur Humes had given him. He inserted a dime and used the rotary dial.

Ring. Ring.

"Campbell residence," answered the voice of an elderly woman.

"Hello, I am looking to speak to Mr. Samuel Campbell," Norman said.

"May I ask who am I speaking with?"

"My name is Norman Werthan. I wanted to let Mr. Campbell know I was going to pay him a visit. I didn't want to stop by unannounced."

"Well, Mr. Werthan, I am so very sorry to inform you that Samuel passed away about eight months ago. Were you a friend of his?" Norman cocked his head back and looked up at the ceiling of the phone booth. He exhaled, as the thought of making phone calls before traveling several hours would have been a good idea. He righted his head and spoke as he tapped absent-mindedly with his index knuckle on the glass of the phone booth.

"No. I wasn't. Can't say I ever met him. I am sorry to hear of his passing."

"Is there something I can help you with?"

"No, no. Please accept my deepest sympathies," Norman offered and hung up the phone. He stood silent in the phone booth. His eyes scanned the scenery beyond the panes of glass while pondering if he should just go back home. Instead, he reached into his back pocket and retrieved his mangled envelope. He had written down Arthur's office number just in case.

Back in Grainger County, Arthur Humes was in his office and had just closed the door. He rushed to his chair and sat down behind his desk and slowly opened the top drawer, revealing a small box from a department store that looked like it might contain jewelry. When Arthur opened it, he removed not a ring nor a pocket watch, but a monocle. He inspected it with a smile and held it carefully, trying not to smudge the glass surface. He stood up and faced a mirror that hung on the wall and placed it under his right eyebrow. The monocle immediately fell, and Arthur tried again. He squinted, trying to keep it in place to no avail. The phone rang, and he quickly put the monocle back in the box and returned it to the top drawer before answering.

"Hello?"

"Hey, I'm in Marion."

"Mr. Werthan. How are things?"

"Not good. Samuel Campbell died six months ago."

"Oh, dear."

"I figured I would give you a call and make sure this was the end of the road before I head back home."

"Can you give me a minute please?"

"Sure," replied Norman. Arthur set the phone down and shuffled a stack of papers to make it sound like he was checking for something. Instead, he was thinking. If the farm went to an heir, it would have required a simple signature and a quick filing with the county. If the farm went to auction, he would have to manage the auction, work with land surveyors, approve the division of the tracts, schedule endless tax meetings with a CPA, and disperse taxed proceeds to the Ross Barnett gubernatorial campaign, per Mr. Campbell's instructions. Whether Arthur simply filed papers with the county or drudged through the arduous process of a lengthy estate auction, he would be paid the same. He slid the Campbell file in front of him and looked it over before he picked the phone up off his desk.

"Mr. Werthan?"

"Yes?"

"Mr. Samuel Campbell's wife is listed here as Mrs. Elizabeth Campbell. Can you see if she has any knowledge of tomatoes or what it takes to be a successful tomato farmer?" Arthur asked in a polite tone. Norman couldn't believe what he was hearing.

"A woman?" Norman asked.

"Yes, sir."

"Mr. Humes, you ever hear of a woman owning a tomato farm?"

"No, sir."

"Me, either."

"Since you are there, could you at least check?" Arthur asked in a manner that would now imply he was asking for a favor. Norman exhaled into the phone while he shook his head.

"Yeah, okay. I'll call ya if I have any problems," he said just before he used his weathered finger to push the lever down on the pay phone. The lever flipped back up as he removed his finger and deposited another dime.

Ring. Ring.

"Hello?" the same voice from before answered.

"Hi. This is Mr. Werthan again. Could you tell me where I might find Mrs. Campbell?"

"Is she in some kind of trouble? What is this about? Are you from the bank?"

"No ma'am. It's a legal matter."

"Doesn't surprise me. You'd probably find her up at Harris Clay in Spruce Pine. It's a big mining operation," the voice said as Norman used his chewed pencil to write down notes on the back of the tattered envelope.

Elizabeth

Harris Clay

Mining operation

Spruce Pine

"Why doesn't a legal matter surprise you?"

"The farm. When Samuel died, she couldn't make the payments. She lost the farm and took a job at Harris. Isn't that why you're calling?"

Lost the farm

"It is. Thank you for your help."

When he hung up the phone, he looked back at the attendant who was now cleaning his antenna out of boredom. Norman spoke under his breath. "For cryin' out loud. My antenna?" He fished around in his left pocket for payment and a generous tip while he crammed the envelope into his back pocket.

Chapter 4

Feldspar. A mineral found in many areas of the world that is used to manufacture ceramic tile, paint, electrical components, fiberglass insulation, glass jars and bottles. While it could be found across the globe, it happened to be most abundant in the small town of Spruce Pine, North Carolina. Harris Clay Mining Company was the largest producer of feldspar in the nation and widely known for posting paper bills in public buildings that read:

Top paying jobs

Housing is provided

Walk to general store and restaurant

In 1950, Elizabeth Campbell, 28, was standing in line with her ten-year-old daughter at the post office in Marion, NC. The words *Housing is provided* had caught her attention and only a short five weeks later, she found herself in Spruce Pine.

The jobs at Harris Clay weren't as plentiful for women as they were for men. When she arrived, she stood in a long employment line while holding a piece of paper with a long list of jobs printed on one side. Nearly every job was crossed out except for equipment house, mine shaft labor, and pulley operator. After choosing equipment house, she and her daughter, Claire, were sent to bunkhouse F3. The living quarters for the workers of Harris Clay were crudely constructed buildings. While it was called a bunkhouse, there weren't any bunks to sleep on. Instead, forty canvas cots were placed in each building. Forty uncomfortable, spine-stiffening, miserable cots that squeaked, cracked, and popped with every slumbering movement.

After living in Spruce Pine for seven months, Elizabeth felt like a veteran of the mining company. She knew how the pay structure was set up and that raises were impossible. She knew that once she had a job, she wasn't moving up. Housing was provided, but it wasn't adequate. If a worker wanted to save money, one would have to hide it in a coffee can and bury it outside.

The same day that Norman Werthan was driving to Spruce Pine, Elizabeth had just gotten off work after cleaning 142 pairs of gumboots and reconditioning 70 miners coats. As she walked to bunkhouse F3 in the damp mountain air, Elizabeth hurried past groups of filthy, tired men that were starting campfires and brewing strong coffee. The equivalent of heading to the bar after work, campfires with coffee and dirty jokes were commonplace at Harris Mining Company. Elizabeth had grown accustomed to the hoots and whistles from burly miners who ogled her thin frame and strawberry blonde hair as she walked back to her living quarters.

She reached her bunkhouse and opened the door to yelling and screaming. Elizabeth immediately rushed to where her cot was, finding her daughter, Claire, sitting quietly and cautiously watching the two women yelling. Finding her daughter safe, she turned her attention to the crowd that now formed around the two screaming women. Shirley Biggs was in the middle of the yelling which wasn't a surprise. Standing in front of Shirley was an older lady named Lexie. She was pale with short hair, a stark contrast to Shirley who was large and imposing. Lexie screamed at the giant.

"You were near my cot when I came in! My money is missing! You can't do this to me!" Lexie had been saving up like most women at Harris Clay Mining Company in order to leave and find a better life. Instead of using a secret hiding place, Lexie had foolishly stashed her money inside one of her shoes.

"I was looking for toothpaste. I don't need your money, besides you probably didn't have any to begin with. Not much anyway," Shirley defended.

"How would you know that if you didn't take my money?" Lexie retorted.

Nearly every female housed in bunkhouse F3 knew that Shirley Biggs took Lexie's money, but without anyone to stand up as a witness against Shirley, the money was as good as gone. Lexie would have to start over.

The door to the bunkhouse opened and an older woman stood in the doorway. She didn't live in F3, so the crowd around Shirley and Lexie turned their heads just as the old woman spoke.

"Mrs. Campbell? Is there a Mrs. Campbell here?"

During the altercation, Elizabeth had been holding Claire's hand. Not for comfort, but in case punches were thrown, and the two bodies of fighting women tumbled their way. With her motherly grip, Elizabeth could have easily pulled Claire out of their way. She had let go of Claire's hand briefly to move to one side and look at the woman standing in the doorway of the bunkhouse.

"I'm Elizabeth Campbell."

"There is a man out here that needs to see you."

Claire stood up next to her mother.

"I'm coming with you," Claire said as she kept her eyes on both Lexie and Shirley. She wasn't afraid of them, but she was cautious, preferring to avoid an accidental face full of knuckles.

Elizabeth had only three outfits to her name. The day Norman arrived, she was clothed in a dirty, long-sleeved white shirt and tattered navy-blue pants. The fabric of her left knee had worn away and her kneecap was exposed. Claire tucked her un-washed, shoulder length brown hair behind her ears and held her mother's hand once again.

Outside was a man wearing denim overalls and looking out over the mining operation. With his hands on his hips, he stared at the massive rock wall in which three mine shafts were dug into the side of a small mountain. He licked his lips as the mineral dust in the air gave him a salty taste in his mouth. His attention was directed to a thin woman and a young girl as they stepped down off the pine steps of bunkhouse F3.

"You, Elizabeth Campbell?"

"I am."

"Does it smell like pine in there?" Norman asked as he ges-tured to the interior of the bunkhouse behind Elizabeth.

"It probably did at one time. It doesn't smell like pine any-more," Elizabeth replied. Norman walked up to the bunkhouse and knocked on the wood.

"This place made completely out of pine?"

"I think so."

"These things burn faster than a fuse." Norman said with a voice of concern. "Hope no one smokes in there."

"I'm sorry?" Elizabeth asked with a confused expression on her pale, freckled face.

"Nothing. Forget it." Norman waved his hand as if he was swatting his thoughts out of the air. "My name is Norman Werthan. I'm from Grainger County, Tennessee, and I came here to see you."

"Why is that?"

"Well, it is kind of a long story. You got a minute?"

"My daughter and I were about to eat."

"Oh, well I guess I could wait."

"We go over to the diner. You can walk with us."

"That'd be fine."

As they walked, Norman asked about her husband and how he passed. The victim of hard work, Samuel Campbell had been in his field all day in the heat of July and developed a throbbing headache. He said aloud that he could feel his heart racing just before he collapsed in front of Elizabeth and Claire.

By the time Norman was up-to-date on the last eight months, they were standing at a walk-up window at the rear of the HC Diner. Employees handed out baked potatoes through a small window to a line of frugal, Harris Clay miners. Each spud was wrapped in newspaper and sold for ten cents each. Norman opted out of the plain potato and asked more questions.

"What did you and Samuel farm?" he asked as Claire bought two potatoes.

"Mom, they're hot!" Claire said as she juggled and bounced the potatoes, attempting to alleviate the burning of her hands and fingers. Elizabeth quickly grabbed the bottom of her cotton shirt and held it out, letting Claire drop the hot potatoes into the makeshift pouch.

"We had cucumbers, cabbage, and sweet potatoes," Elizabeth said as she kept walking. As she spoke, Norman caught a glimpse of the front of the restaurant. It was built from pine with big windows in the front. He could see people sitting down and eating.

"You ever go in there?"

"Just on birthdays and such."

"Are potatoes all you eat for dinner?"

"Tonight, it is. Tomorrow they sell hash and bread."

"What do they serve inside?"

"Pretty much anything," Claire answered. Norman couldn't help but notice that they were both very thin and it appeared that food was a luxury for them.

"How 'bout we ditch the potatoes and go inside?"

"We can't afford it right now."

"I can. My treat. Besides, I am starving. Let's go inside."

Claire's eyes widened to the size of the potatoes. She looked at her mother who gave her a "shush". Elizabeth stopped and looked at Norman with a cautious look.

"Mr. Werthan, is this about my husband? Are you from the bank?"

"That's funny. Look at me. You think I'm that smart?" Norman said as he held out his hands and displayed his denim and dirty button-up shirt.

"You don't look like a banker." Elizabeth replied with a curious expression as if she was trying to figure him out.

"I have some questions about your farm," Norman said. To appear less threatening and more inviting, he playfully changed his tone, "May I buy you and your daughter dinner?" Elizabeth's curious expression dissolved as she grinned and nodded her head.

The menu was written out in pencil on worn index cards and placed between the salt and pepper shakers. Elizabeth slid a card out and looked at it with Claire. Hamburger, ham sandwich, mixed vegetables and cornbread was written on the front. On the back were three words: *Dessert—vanilla pudding.* After placing their order with the tired waitress, Norman looked at Elizabeth and asked the question.

"What do you know about growing tomatoes?"

"I have grown a few in my day, nothing more than a row or two for our table food. Samuel grew up on a tomato and tobacco farm. When we bought our small farm, we decided on three crops that had a high yield and high return for our area. Then it all went to the bank."

"How long did you own it?"

"Four months."

"So, if I said Black Gold or Early Girl, do you know what types of tomatoes those are?" asked Norman. Elizabeth slightly cocked her head as she spoke.

"No. I can't say that I do. Why do you ask?"

Norman could only think that he had to go back home and tell Arthur that she wasn't a viable choice.

"No reason. Just curious about the farm."

"Why are you coming to see me? I am still unclear about that." Elizabeth asked just as the food arrived at their table. Norman took the interruption as a much-needed break from the conversation to come up with something other than the fact that this broke mother and daughter were so close to a small fortune and had lost it all.

"Well, I am so sorry to tell you that Samuel's uncle passed away recently."

"Samuel's uncle?"

"Yes."

"Old man Campbell? That's what Samuel called him."

"I suppose so. His name was Thaddeus Campbell. Back home he was known as T.C., among other things."

"I never met him. Are you related to me? Are you and T.C. kin?"

"No ma'am. No relation," he answered, holding back the truth about T.C. being a hemorrhoid. While Norman ate a ham sand-wich, the girls on the other side of the table ate cornbread, a ham-burger, and a plate full of vegetables. Elizabeth and Claire dug into their food like they were making up for past meals they had missed. While Norman was all but ready to hit the road and get back home, his mind had drifted to the pine bunkhouse.

"When I came to the door to ask for you, I heard yelling."

"Yeah. That isn't uncommon around here. Every once in a while, money or property goes missing."

"Why is that?"

"There isn't any law enforcement here for one, and there isn't anywhere to put your things, so you have to hide your money and hope no one finds it."

"Do you hide your money?"

"Of course. We are trying very hard to get out of here." Elizabeth said as she looked at Claire. "Aren't we?"

"How's that?" Norman asked. "How do you get out of here?"

"We don't eat much, as you can see. We save our money rather than spend it."

"Since you have to hide your money, are you afraid someone will find it?"

"Not really. I sneak out in the middle of the night. I hide it outside."

Elizabeth continued to talk and explain their plan for leaving. It seemed that she was planning on a fall escape, so to speak, October or November maybe.

"How much money have you saved up?"

"Forty-two dollars."

"What's it take to get out of Dodge?"

"Sixty or seventy. We need bus tickets and money to stay at a motel."

"Where you headed?"

"Georgia or Florida. Not sure. We have time to think about it, but she's eleven going on twelve and we need to get her into a real school soon," she said as Norman reached into his pocket and counted thirty dollars. Norman thought that getting paid a little less and helping a woman and her daughter was a good exchange. Norman laid the money on the table in front of Elizabeth.

"Let's make it sooner than later," he said as he took a drink of water.

Thirty dollars. It was decent amount of money to Norman, but a life-changing amount to Elizabeth. She covered her mouth.

Tears began to collect in her eyes and she started to sob. "Hey there," Norman said. "No need for that," he whispered. Claire began to cry and hugged her mother. She hated sleeping on a cot. She hated her outdoor schoolhouse. The food was awful. Her mother was sad much of the time. Things were about to change.

Norman sat across from two crying girls and closed his eyes as he took a bite of his ham sandwich. Suddenly he felt a hand on his shoulder. Elizabeth had gotten up and sat next to Norman and wrapped her arms around him.

"Thank you. Thank you, Norman Werthan," she said in a pleasant and sincere voice. Norman started to reply while chewing a mouthful of food, and his face resembled a person who overheard someone cursing in church.

"For Pete's sake. No thanks required. Come on now, you shouldn't be crying. I'm just helping out a little," he stated as he removed her arms from around his neck. By now, the people eating in the restaurant turned to look at him. He smiled at them just as Elizabeth stood up.

"I'm sorry. You just don't know what this means to us."

"Sit back down. Go on. Have a seat," he said trying to get the stares and off-handed looks from the crowd to cease.

"I will pay you back. I promise."

"I don't need to be paid back. Just calm down," he said in a near whisper.

"We need this money. Don't get me wrong, but I don't feel right taking it."

Norman waved her off as he popped the last bite of his sandwich into his mouth. He chewed and continued to ignore Elizabeth. Then an idea came to him. He began to think that if somehow T.C. were able to look up from his place in the fiery depths of hell and see what he was about to do, he would be most displeased.

Chapter 5

Norman asked a waitress to use the phone in the restaurant. Without explaining it was long distance, he dialed the number to Arthur's office.

"Hello?"

"Hey, it's Norman."

"Do you have good news?"

"If she were to take the farm, how does this work exactly? Does she just get the farm forever?"

"Not at all. She must curate a single crop of tomatoes of no less than 40 acres and have it reviewed by two judges from the state fair."

"You mean people come all the way from Nashville to judge the crop?"

"Yes, sir."

"Seems a bit much."

"It's my client's instructions. The judges are compensated."

"What if she doesn't have the funds for hands and tools?"

"Mr. Campbell has left a hefty sum in a controlled account. Funds shouldn't be a problem."

"So, from seed to about eighty days, give or take?"

"I suppose that time frame is sufficient. To be honest, I'm not that educated in agriculture, but if I remember correctly I think Mr. Campbell has given a time frame of ninety days," Arthur replied. Norman did the math in his head. Seeds in the ground the first week of April plus eighty days meant the second week of July. Thaddeus Campbell could surely spare 90 days for a niece who was in need. Norman looked over at Elizabeth and Claire sitting and talking with excited expressions. They didn't know it yet, but their distant relative was about to provide much needed free shelter. Norman spoke with a tone of certainty.

"She can do that."

"Really? She knows a lot about tomato farming?"

"Absolutely. She was raised on a cucumber and tomato farm. When she got married they bought a tomato farm and worked it for years."

"Oh, wonderful!" Arthur said. "Could you bring her by tomorrow morning at eight to sign an agreement? She can go ahead and stay the night at the house. The backdoor is unlocked. When you come by tomorrow, I will pay you your end."

"Sure thing," Norman answered. Arthur ended the call with a smile on his face. His legal fee was secure. No additional work was needed. When he hung up the phone, he celebrated by removing the monocle from his desk drawer and walking up to the mirror on the wall. He carefully set it in his eye socket and squinted, attempting to keep it in place.

Norman took his seat at the table and sat with his arms crossed. He leaned forward, his weight on the table as he explained to Elizabeth that he was leaving for Rutledge, Tennessee and that she and Claire should go with him. Within fifteen minutes, Elizabeth had raided her cot, dug up her tin can containing forty-two dollars, and climbed into the small cab of Norman's truck. On the way to Rutledge, Claire sat next to the window while her mother sat in the middle next to Norman. Claire leaned on her mother's shoulder before falling asleep. While Elizabeth was just as tired, the excitement of escaping the mine kept her adrenaline at an all-time high. Norman talked with her as he navigated the highway in front of him.

"I have to tell you something, and I don't quite know how to say it."

"Well, it seems we have some time. No hurry," she said. Norman thought about how to explain the situation.

"Well, Samuel's uncle passed away, and he left someone his farm. The conditions of keeping the farm mean that they are to grow a minimum of forty acres and have it reviewed by agricultural judges. If the judges deem the crop worthy, the new owner gets to keep the farm."

"Wow. Do I know them? Are they kin?"

"Well, you see it was supposed to be Samuel."

"Samuel? Why?"

"Because he grew up on a tomato farm and isn't directly related to Mr. Campbell. Well, not immediate family anyway."

"Why does that matter?"

"Mr. Campbell was an old badger. He was cruel and extremely unintelligent, and he hated women, children, and animals."

"Goodness."

"T.C. hated his family and rightfully so. They're a bunch'a bad apples and scavengers. He wanted to make sure that they don't get the farm. I suppose he thought that Samuel was the most deserving and giving him the farm would ensure his immediate family members would be enraged."

"I see. So now that Samuel has passed, now what?"

"That's what I wanted to talk to you about," Norman said as he steered around a long curve in the highway. "I told the estate attorney that you know everything there is to know about farming tomatoes." Shock and surprise formed on Elizabeth's face as she gasped in disbelief.

"You mean an entire farm!" Claire shifted toward the window and kept her tired eyes shut before drifting back to sleep. "I have only grown a few vines. I don't know how to grow tomatoes! Especially forty acres!"

"You don't need to. Just stay at his house until July and then split. You don't have to grow a single tomato."

"I don't know. That seems dishonest."

"Your husband's uncle was a revolting moron and never did anything good while he was alive. At the very least, he could help someone in his death. You will get a bank account to take money from, and you'll get time to think about what you're going to do while staying in the comfort of his house, which is pretty big by the way."

"Am I taking the place of a relative who could do good with the farm? This doesn't seem right."

"The estate attorney said that if you don't work out then the farm goes to auction. Trust me. You should take advantage of this."

"Mr. Werthan, it's not like me to take advantage of anything."

"You took my money, didn't you?"

"I thought that was a gift."

"It was. And so is this. The biggest gift you're ever going to get. Now, I'm not going to push you into it, but frankly if you don't take this opportunity, you might as well go dig ditches," Norman said with a thick layer of irritability. Elizabeth could feel his annoyance and thought it to be well meaning. After a moment of silence, Elizabeth spoke up.

"So, I should live on the farm, decide what I want to do, and take money from Mr. Campbell?"

"Exactly," said Norman.

"I appreciate what you're doing for me, but I'm not sure about this."

"Like I said, I'm not going to push you."

When they arrived in Rutledge, it was past seven o'clock, a few hours before Norman's usual bedtime. He had decided to get her over to T.C.'s house and get home.

"I'm gonna drop you off at the house. The attorney said the backdoor is unlocked. I'll be by at seven forty-five in the morning to pick you up. We have to go see that attorney fella for you to sign papers or something."

"Mr. Werthan, I wanted…"

"Please, call me Norman."

"Norman, thank you for what you are doing for me. You have changed our lives."

"Yeah, I know. Can't help myself. You remind me a lot of my daughter. I wouldn't be able to sleep at night knowing you and that little girl were sleeping in that ridiculous pine box that could go up in flames at a moment's notice," Norman said as he looked for the driveway to Thaddeus's house. Elizabeth chuckled over his concern, though she knew it was valid.

Claire woke up and they said their goodbyes. When the passenger side door was opened, the chilled air greeted them along with three coonhounds that trampled over each other to see who was exiting the truck.

"Hey, puppies!" Claire said. Licking tongues, sniffing noses and excited whimpers came from the pack as Claire and Elizabeth exited. "Hi, doggies," Claire continued as she tried her best to pet each one. Their wet noses and licks could be felt on Elizabeth's hands.

"These dogs are crazy!" Elizabeth laughed just before she closed the passenger side door. The dogs jumped and pawed at the new arrivals all the way to the back porch.

Norman waited for a light to turn on in the house to ensure they got in okay. Once he saw the light, he backed out into the street and headed across town toward his farm.

Chapter 6

Elizabeth and Claire left the playful dogs outside and walked in through the backdoor into a dark room. A light switch was quickly found after Elizabeth swept the walls with her hand. She pushed the button and illuminated the kitchen. Standing on spotless white tile with a beautiful canary-yellow refrigerator on the opposite side of the room, Elizabeth and Claire's jaws dropped. To the right of the refrigerator was a white GE Airliner four-burner stove. Elizabeth's eyes scanned the kitchen, coming to a stop at the oversized, porcelain white, kitchen sink. Neither a crumb nor a scuff or scrape could be found on the countertops. Claire remarked on the size of the kitchen table. It looked to have been hand crafted and stained. The appliances appeared to have been cared for with white gloves seemingly readied for a photo shoot for *LIFE Magazine*.

"Wow!" whispered Claire. Elizabeth covered her mouth in disbelief. "Everything looks brand new!" They took their shoes off to ensure that they kept the white tile clean. In the living room, they found hardwood flooring with floral patterned upholstered furniture. An upright piano was on the opposite wall and a small table with a tube radio was positioned next to a pair of floral-patterned chairs on either side. The lace curtains gave the room a classy and refined appearance.

"Mom?"

"Yes?"

"Is this ours? I heard Mr. Werthan talk about inheritance."

"No. It isn't ours." Elizabeth answered. *If only I knew how to grow tomatoes, it would be,* she thought.

"Who's is it?"

"He was your great uncle."

"What happened to him?"

"I don't know," she replied as she walked slowly toward a window and reached out her hand. She pulled gently on the lace curtains, feeling the craftsmanship between her fingers. Claire had walked over to the piano and played a single note. Elizabeth looked across the room and saw a door with a brass knob. She walked over to it and opened it thinking it was a closet. Instead of clothes, she found a small bedroom with a queen mattress.

"Claire! Look," she said as she covered her mouth and looked at a real bed with an old quilt covering the sheets on the mattress. They both sat on the edge and felt the slight bounce. The bed was plain and didn't have a headboard or end tables on either side. The absence of such luxuries went unnoticed. The bed held a promise of a good night's sleep, a luxury that was unfathomable only a few hours ago.

They next visited the dining room where a beautiful, polished table sat beneath a glass chandelier. Eight wooden chairs surrounded the table where Elizabeth could imagine a family sitting around it, while eating on a Sunday after church.

"Mom?"

"Yes?"

"What's in here?" Claire asked as she pointed at an unusual door in the dining room. It resembled an office door in a municipal building. The door had a deadbolt instead of a keyhole. A plate glass window in the door was beveled and frosted and appeared to be missing a name painted on the glass that was seen in so many public office buildings.

"I don't know. It's an unusual door."

"It's locked," Claire said as she tried the doorknob.

"Well, let's not bother with it. I'm sure it is supposed to stay locked."

The tour continued upstairs where there was one bedroom. Walking through a doorway, they found a queen-sized bed with a white comforter and fluffy lace pillows. Looking at her daughter, Elizabeth mouthed the words: Oh my God! Next to the bed was a door. Claire walked over and opened it expecting a closet and instead found a bathroom.

"Wow! Right next to the bed!"

Going from a cot in a room full of women to a large home with comfortable queen-sized beds overwhelmed Elizabeth to the point of tears. Instead of letting it get to her, she quickly wiped her eyes and joined in on the excitement with Claire.

"And we get to sleep on this?" Claire asked, unable to believe her luck. Elizabeth nodded with delight. "Can we stay for a week?" Claire asked.

"I think we get to stay until July."

"Really?" Claire replied with her infectious smile. She gazed upon the plush bed and thought of how dirty her clothes and hair were. "Mom? Can I take a bath?"

"We both need a bath, but you can go first."

Claire hurried into the bathroom and began turning the knobs by the faucet. The water flowed into the tub with a rush of clear water. Elizabeth took a seat in a rocking chair that was adjacent from the bed. She rocked gently and closed her tired eyes. Over the roaring of the water, she could hear Claire talk to herself.

"This is great!" With her eyes still closed, and rocking ever so slightly, Elizabeth smiled.

Chapter 7

While Elizabeth and Claire were getting settled in for their first night in Rutledge, across town there was a family preparing for a long night. Gordon Tyrell, 41, was pouring water into a glass jar and mixing Aerohalor Powder into the water with a metal spoon. Once the powder was dissolved, he carried the jar into the room of his twelve-year-old son, Harold Tyrell. A medical tent made of thick canvas material had been attached to the wall above Harold's bed and draped over half of his body. He was lying under the tent with his head propped up by three pillows. While the interior of the tent was dark, a small plastic window sewn into the canvas let in a little light and let Harold see part of his room in front of him.

The jar Gordon carried was inserted into a wooden box beside the bed. He moved a plastic tube to the inside of the jar and placed it in the water. A switch was flipped and the tube sucked the medicinal water into a vaporizer, and the mist emitted into the tent. Harold had been coughing hard enough to rupture blood vessels in his esophagus and spatters of blood had started to come up with each cough.

"Take it easy. Just try to breathe slow," Gordon said just as his wife, Annie, had come into the room with a box fan. She plugged it in and turned it on. The sound of the fan coupled with the vaporizer pump made it noisy enough to cause Gordon and his wife to raise their voice as they spoke. Annie placed her hand on Gordon's shoulder and spoke loudly over the noise.

"Go to bed, and I will come get you if I need you."

"I don't know. We might want to consider calling Dr. Talbot."

"We will if this persists, but for now I think you should get some rest."

"I'd rather not."

"Please."

"Will you stay awake? Keep your hand on his chest to feel him breathing?" Gordon said as if he was telling her and not asking.

"Yes. Of course. Just go to bed. You have to get up early anyway."

Gordon grabbed his son's hand and kissed it.

"Love you, buddy."

"Love you, too, Dad," Harold said which caused his cough to erupt and more blood speckled out of his mouth. Annie rushed to his side with a tissue. The blood was nothing new. He had gone through violent coughing fits his entire life. The canvas tent was only a year old and the one before that was made entirely out of plastic, which made Harold sweat profusely through the night due to heat retention.

While other kids in Grainger County were going to school, making friends, and playing stickball in the streets, Harold was restricted to his home. If his cough surfaced, he retreated to the tent. On a good day, he only had to be under the tent once. On a bad day, he was in bed from morning to night with a cough that would sear his esophagus and lungs.

Gordon left his son's room and closed the door behind him, dampening the loud rumbling of the electric motors. He walked down the hallway and into his own bedroom and closed the door.

After picking up his briefcase, he opened it up and laid it on the bed, flinging stacks of papers on the bedspread searching for a legal envelope. Worn and ruffled from being transported through the mail, the oft-used brown envelope with shredded edges had seen better days.

Gordon reached inside and pulled out a packet of information. On the cover, printed in black and white was a picture of a metal box about the size of a doghouse. Tubes and pipes jetted from the top and an electrical box was attached to the side. On the front of the metal box was a window to a small tank that held clear liquid. At the top of the first page were the words *Nebulizer for asthma and bronchial conditions.*

Three months earlier, Gordon learned of this device that could provide Harold's room with better, breathable air without a tent. The device could also be transported to a room built in the back of a classroom and give him the chance to attend school. While it offered a better future for Harold, its cost was unimaginable.

Instead of sleeping in separate rooms, Elizabeth and Claire opted to sleep in the same bed. Tired from the day and the excitement, Claire had already taken a hot bath, dried her hair as best she could and fell asleep on what was predetermined as her side of the comfortable, plush bed.

After her bath, Elizabeth had turned out the light on the beautiful handmade nightstand and laid down next to her daughter, feeling the support of the mattress underneath her tired and exhausted body. Her eyes were closed for nearly five minutes until they sprang open when she heard a door creaking downstairs as it opened. Elizabeth quickly sat up and listened. *Are the dogs play-*

ing outside, she thought. Unable to hear over her own heavy breathing, she held her breath. The sound of a creaking door coming to a close could be heard. Unsure of the layout of the house, her best guess was that it was the door to the back porch. Still holding her breath, Elizabeth began to panic when she heard quiet footsteps coming from downstairs.

Chapter 8

Elizabeth threw on her dirty clothes and took quiet steps down the stairs. *Was it Mr. Werthan? Did he come back?* The house was dark except for a small table lamp in the living room that illuminated a small corner with a dim bulb. Once she had two feet firmly planted at the very bottom of the stairs, she could hear someone in the kitchen. The sound of a refrigerator door opening made her think it might be Mr. Werthan.

She cautiously approached the kitchen as the thought of Mr. Werthan possibly stocking the refrigerator entered her mind. When she came into view of the kitchen, she quickly turned on the light and saw a very short black man in front of the refrigerator and screamed. While drinking cold water from a mason jar, the scream caused the man to choke on the water and drop the mason jar. He spun around and saw a thin, strawberry-haired woman wearing a dirty white t-shirt.

"Don't hurt us!" she yelled. At the same time Elizabeth uttered the words, the black man shouted,

"Don't hurt me!"

She put her hands out in front of her as if she was trying to protect herself from an oncoming car. The black man stood with his back to the canary yellow refrigerator with an expression of terror drawn across his face.

"What you doin' here?" The man yelled.

"Me? What are you doing here?"

"I work here," he said. Elizabeth relaxed her hands while the man was still pinned to the refrigerator.

"I'm kin to Mr. Campbell," she replied. The man's hands left the side of the refrigerator and went to his chest. He was breathing heavily, and he closed his eyes.

"You done scared the fire outta me," he said as he caught his breath.

"You work in the house?"

"No ma'am. I work the farm. I live in the hand quarters over yonder," he said as he continued to catch his breath. "I keep a jar of water in the fridge. I like cold water."

"Mom?" Claire yelled downstairs. The man jumped again as he clutched his chest.

"Go back to bed. Everything is alright."

"I'm so sorry. I didn't know ya'll were here."

Elizabeth looked down and saw that the man had dropped the mason jar and it had broken into many pieces.

"Don't move."

"What?"

"Don't move. There is broken glass everywhere."

"Oh, ok."

"I will find a broom."

"It's by the back door. Dust pan is there, too."

Once the broom and dustpan were located, Elizabeth spent several minutes sweeping around the man's feet and ensuring that all the glass was up off the floor. During this time, the man had finally calmed down. When Elizabeth was by the back door returning the broom, she had found a tin pail. After dumping the broken glass from the dustpan to the pail, she returned to the kitchen.

"I'm sorry I came in without knocking. I just didn't know anyone was here."

"It's fine. What is your name?" She asked. His stature was that of a twelve-year-old. She thought he might be taller than Claire but wasn't sure.

"Name's Runt. People call me Runt."

"I'm Elizabeth."

"Nice to meet you ma'am. I'll be going now."

"Did you get enough to drink?"

"I did. Yes, ma'am."

"That can't be your name. What's your real name?"

"I s'pose people call me Runt since I was a kid."

"What did your mother name you?"

"Ben. But I kinda got used to Runt."

"I see."

"You gonna keep me on even though you found me in the kitchen?" Runt asked. It was the first time the thought crossed Elizabeth's mind that Runt was keeping a jar in the refrigerator without the knowledge of T.C. Campbell.

"Do you have another jar?"

"No, ma'am," he replied. Elizabeth walked to a cupboard and opened two doors at once. Plates and bowls. While Runt looked on, she scooted to another set of cabinet doors and opened them. Inside were drinking glasses and spices. She reached inside and removed a clear drinking glass and took it to the sink. She filled the glass and spun around and opened the canary yellow refrigerator door and placed the glass on a shelf. Once she closed the door, she turned and looked at Runt.

"That's your new glass. Come in whenever you want to. Okay?"

"You sure?"

"Absolutely," she answered. Feeling thankful and appreciative yet uneasy about the circumstances, Runt shuffled toward the back door.

"I thank you. That is very nice of you, but I cannot accept."

"Why not?"

"I aim to have a job here. Employees don't go into the owner's house," he said as he got close enough to the door to reach for the doorknob.

"Runt?"

"Yes, ma'am."

"My daughter and I aren't here for very long. We will be leaving at some point, and I am in no position to employ anyone. However, you may stay at the hand quarters and drink from the cold glass in the fridge anytime you like and for as long as we are here."

"Thank ya, ma'am," he replied with a tone of voice that conveyed he wouldn't be taking advantage of her generosity. He spoke as he turned the doorknob. "I best be going then."

Chapter 9

Gordon Tyrell woke at dawn and immediately checked on Harold. He opened the door to the loud rumbling of the vaporizer and hurried to the bed and reached his hand under the tent. While Annie slept in the chair next to the bed, he quietly placed his hand on Harold's chest and felt him breathing. His eyes darted toward the glass jar that held the Aerohalor water and saw that it was getting low.

After Gordon made another mixture and replaced the glass jar, he reached his hand under the tent and felt Harold's chest move up and down as he breathed. He could hear the rattling in his chest as he exhaled. Gordon fell quietly to his knees and closed his eyes, praying to God that He would heal his son. Coming to tears, Gordon used the back of his hand to wipe them away as he ended the prayer and stood up. Annie turned in the chair trying to find a more comfortable spot but didn't wake up.

Leaving his house as the sun crested the horizon, he slid into the driver's seat of his 1948 Dodge pick-up and turned the engine over. He navigated to the main square and eyed a long stretch of parking spaces in front of Rutledge Savings and Loan. While the bank wasn't open yet, he knew that Roger Landry would be inside.

Knock. Knock. Knock.

"Hey, Roger? It's me. Can you open up?" Gordon yelled as he stared into a pane of glass with closed blinds blocking his view of the interior of the bank. The door was unlocked and opened by a man wearing a tan suit and an untied necktie.

"Thanks," Gordon said as he walked inside the darkened lobby while holding the large envelope underneath his arm. Roger spoke as he locked the door and lifted a section of the blinds to peer outside.

"Turns out that Mr. Campbell has a niece. She's gonna be taking over the farm." Gordon's reaction was similar to a train derailment.

"Dag gone it! It's supposed to be going up for auction!" he yelled as he paced the floor. Roger expected his boisterous reaction and calmly slid his hands into his pockets and strolled over to his desk as he replied.

"We all thought the auction was imminent. Everyone knows he hated his family." Roger sat down at his desk.

"She just gets the farm? That's it? Will she sell?"

"I don't know if she intends to work the land or not. The lawyer for the estate, Mr. Humes, said she doesn't get the farm free and clear though. She has to successfully grow a forty-acre crop and then she gets the farm."

"What? What kind of mess is this?" Gordon asked as his eyes squinted from confusion.

"I don't know," Roger said as he sat as far back in his chair as it would go. Not letting him rest, Gordon plopped the large envelope on Roger's desk and sat in the chair across from him. "Is that it?" Roger asked as he looked at the envelope.

"It's something like, twenty-thousand dollars." Gordon replied. Roger sat up in his chair and slid the black and white packet from the envelope. He looked at the image of the metal box about the size of a doghouse. The device looked as if only a trained physician could operate such a contraption. The tubes and pipes looked complicated and the window to a small tank that held clear liquid looked futuristic.

"Who has this kind of money?" Roger asked.

"Hospitals. It's designed for hospitals."

"So you can't even buy it?"

"I bet if I had the money they would sell it to me."

"What's it do?"

"Creates breathable air for Harold."

"So, if it costs that much, why are you trying to buy old man Campbell's farm?"

"I only need the farm for three months. Then I will sell it."

"And that will somehow afford you to buy this machine."

"Yes."

"You'd buy and then somehow sell the farm for twenty-thousand dollars more than you paid for it?"

"Something like that."

"You have a buyer?" Roger asked. Gordon ignored the question.

"Is she selling the farm, or is she trying to farm it?"

"I don't know. Mr. Humes called me last night to tell me the auction wasn't necessary."

"I can't believe this."

"Can't you mortgage the rest of your business for twenty, buy the machine and then pay us back overtime."

"I'm making payments on the first five thousand you lent me," Gordon replied as his head dropped and spoke like a scorned child. "I also owe a bank in Knoxville another five. I had to pay for hospital stays, Aerohalor medicine and all the home visits."

"All that was ten grand?"

"No. We also needed a new belt motor at the mill. Without it, I couldn't run the mill, and I had to pay some back payroll to my employees along with payroll taxes."

Roger continued to console Gordon as his plans were falling apart. He was puzzled that Gordon wanted to purchase the Campbell Farm for three months – a strange proposition and land transaction. *Why only three months?* Roger couldn't have guessed that it wasn't the farm that Gordon wanted, rather he was after what was buried beneath it.

Chapter 10

Elizabeth woke up to the sound of dogs barking near the house. Daylight was peeking through the lace curtains as she sat up and quickly remembered where she was. Sleeping soundly was a luxury she had long forgotten. The soft mattress in the master bedroom was so comfortable she had slept through the night without waking. She felt rested even though it was early.

Moving and shifting her body quietly out of bed, she walked over to a window. From up on the second floor she could see rows and rows of dirt mounds that seemed to stretch for miles. The farm was massive and the thought of planting forty acres seemed daunting—a task she wouldn't be able to complete no matter how much she liked the house.

Claire slept through her mother getting ready in the bathroom. A big mirror and a nice hot bath made the morning ritual a luxurious experience and the comfort did not go unappreciated.

Norman had arrived at 7:42 A.M. and could only hope she would be on time. At 7:45 A.M., Norman kept his eye on the front door until it opened. Three coonhounds rushed up to Elizabeth and frolicked around her as she approached the passenger side door. Once in the cab, she carefully closed the door making sure she didn't shut it on a floppy ear or a wayward tail.

"Good morning," Norman said.

"To you as well."

"You sleep okay?" He asked as he backed out of the driveway.

"I did. Best night of sleep in forever."

The casual conversation eventually turned into Elizabeth profusely thanking Norman for his gesture. He tried his best to wave her off, but his efforts were in vain. Driving faster and giving Elizabeth tips before going to see Mr. Humes seemed to help alleviate her incessant string of accolades. Norman was adamant that she let him do the talking when it came to the farm except she needed to ask Mr. Humes for one thing.

"Every respectable farmer worth his salt has a rotation book. Do you know about crop rotation?"

"Uh...it's planting other crops to help the soil?"

"Right. Rotation keeps the soil from being stale or stagnant. We all keep journals of our seasons although we don't ever call it a journal."

"No?"

"No. I don't know if Arthur knows that or not, but either way you ask him for the rotation book. It's the life-blood of the farm that book. It means so much to us that we usually lock it up." Elizabeth's thoughts drifted to the locked green door. *Is that where T.C. kept his rotation book?* "I tell you this so that you ask him for it first. You bring it up early in the conversation, but not too early. Got it? That way it makes him think you know what you are talking about."

"Got it."

Arthur Humes was standing in his office with the door closed. He had taken the lid off a cream-colored box and removed white tissue paper before reaching in and carefully removing a brand-new bowler hat. He turned and looked in the mirror as he placed it on his head. He then reached into his vest pocket and placed his monocle in his eye socket. He looked in the mirror to

the left of his desk and smiled at his appearance. He then turned
to a painting that hung on the wall that displayed his late father
who stood behind a wingback chair wearing a fine suit, a bowler
hat, and a monocle. Just as he turned back toward the mirror, he
heard the bell jangle above the door in the reception area. He
quickly placed the monocle back in his vest pocket and removed
the bowler hat. Arthur put it back gently in the box and covered
it with tissue paper before spinning around and hurrying to his
chair. His secretary knocked on the door.

"Yes?" he hollered. The door opened, and she escorted Mr.
Werthan and Mrs. Campbell inside.

"Come in," Arthur said with a smile. Norman made way for
Elizabeth to enter first. Upon walking in the office, Arthur gazed
upon her strawberry blonde hair and petite figure. She was
dressed in a linen shirt and a flowing skirt that she normally re-
served for a Sunday. Arthur introduced himself and offered her
a seat across from his desk. He shook Norman's hand never taking
his eyes off Elizabeth.

"Okay. We'll start with the reading of the will. This won't take
long as the instructions are simple and easy to understand."
Arthur began by removing a sheet of paper and holding it up to
his face. The temptation to use his monocle was present, but the
fear of it falling out was greater.

"Dear Samuel,"

Arthur started. He peered around the paper and looked at
Elizabeth. "Being Mr. Campbell's attorney I am accepting your
nomination under the power of attorney clause," he stated with
a smile and a nod before continuing. Elizabeth didn't quite understand but returned the smile and the nod.

"Please keep in mind that my ultimate goal is to keep my

immediate family from acquiring my farm. My second goal is to maintain the high standards of my farm. No one outside of Grainger County has the ability to grow a finer crop. My proposition to you is this. You must grow a minimum of forty acres of tomatoes. You will be given sufficient funds, tools and machinery. After ninety days, a panel of agricultural judges whom I have compensated, will travel from Nashville to my farm. Upon their approval, the farm and the entire estate will legally transfer to you. If the judges do not give their approval, the estate will go to auction."

When Arthur was finished, he set the paper down and smiled.

"Is that it?" Elizabeth asked.

"That's it," Arthur replied as he sat back in his chair.

"Forty acres will take quite a bit of money to pay the farm hands. What dollar amount are we talking here?" Norman asked, curious as to how it would all work.

"I believe the sum is just under nine hundred dollars," Arthur answered. Elizabeth's eyes widened, and her jaw dropped open for a brief moment and then quickly recovered. Norman nodded his head as if he was satisfied with the number. Arthur looked at Elizabeth who had suddenly remembered she was supposed to be a tomato farmer. He saw the look on her face change, causing him to be immediately concerned.

"Goodness. Is that not enough money?" asked Arthur with a puzzled look.

"Oh no," Elizabeth said thinking it was a lot of money and the amount took her by surprise. Upon her saying "Oh No," Arthur thought she meant that it was not enough money. Fearing that the arrangement wasn't adequate, and he might have to start an arduous process of calling land surveyors and auction houses, he tried to sell Elizabeth on an idea.

"My dear, in this file is not just a document, but an instru-ment. A 'legal' instrument. It can be changed and adapted to fit certain circumstances. In this case, if you feel that there isn't enough money, we can certainly increase it," he explained as he gently patted the folder on the desk in front of him. "Of course, within reason." Elizabeth, unable to speak watched as he opened the file and removed a pen from a holder on his desk. "If the amount is insufficient, what would be a more suitable amount for this venture?" he asked with a smile and his pen ready to make a change on the document. Norman could sense that Elizabeth was out of her element and took over.

"Twelve hundred," he chimed. "Twelve is more appropriate," Norman added as he looked at Elizabeth. Still in shock but aware of her awkwardness, she nodded and repeated Norman's state-ment.

"Yes. Twelve is appropriate."

"Twelve it is," Arthur said as he began to write in the amount. Norman shot a look at Elizabeth and shrugged his shoulders.

"Mr. Humes," Elizabeth said thinking that it was a good time to speak up and try to appear like an experienced tomato farmer.

"Yes, my dear."

"I would like to inquire about a rotation book."

"Oh, yes! Yes, of course." he replied as he searched through a stack of files and papers on his desk. Finding a large envelope at the bottom of the pile, he maneuvered it out from underneath the stack and opened the flap. He angled the envelope and allowed the contents to slide out onto his desk. Before him was a worn notebook, a set of keys, and a folded letter.

"Does she withdraw from the bank?" Norman asked while Mr. Humes handed her the notebook. She took it from his hands and held it in her lap.

"Actually, the city treasurer is handling that. I use him to disperse funds from a variety of trusts set up at the bank." Arthur explained. He then turned to Elizabeth. "You will simply visit Mr. Collins at his office in the courthouse or call him. Tell him the amount and where to send the check…and before I forget, Mr. Collins will also handle payroll. All of your hands will have to get their checks from him. There is a maximum of forty-five dollars a week per hand. I'm told that most farmers 'round here usually pay less, but it is up to you."

"What about cash for miscellaneous expenses?"

"Oh! Here," he replied as he opened his desk drawer and removed an envelope. He plopped it on the desk in front of Elizabeth as he pushed the bridge of his glasses up on his nose as he continued speaking, "That there is three hundred dollars in petty cash."

"Why so much?" Norman asked.

"It's what Mr. Campbell had in his cookie jar. I found it while making lemonade in his kitchen. We'll just make that part of the twelve hundred in expenses," Arthur said as he returned to the contents on his desk that had slid out of the large envelope. He picked up a folded letter and a set of keys. "Mrs. Campbell, I have two more things before we part ways. First, here are the keys to Mr. Campbell's truck. It is parked in the barn," he said as he handed her the keys. "The second thing is this, and I saved this for last as it is very important," Arthur said as his expression went from friendly to lawyerly. His eyes were focused and the lines around his mouth fell as he spoke in a serious tone. "In the house is a locked door. The door is downstairs in the dining room. It is painted green with a frosted glass window. You've seen it?"

"I have. Yes, sir."

"Do not open it. There is a lock on the door that only I have the key to. You are not to go near that door. The frosted glass window is not to be tampered with and should it break, even if by accident, this arrangement will be over. Now, upon the transfer of the deed to your name, I will gladly hand over the key to the green door, but only after the transfer of the estate is complete." Arthur said as he pointed his finger.

"What's behind the green door?" Norman asked. Arthur slightly turned his head and looked Norman in the eye. While he didn't verbally reply, Norman quickly understood that he wouldn't get an answer. Arthur looked back at Elizabeth.

"Do you understand?"

"I do."

"Great," he replied as he turned a piece of paper around and slid it in front of her. He set a pen down and gestured for her to sign the document. While she signed, Arthur looked at Norman and held up the folded letter. "Lastly, Mr. Werthan, your check. Before I give you the check, I am instructed to read you this letter from Mr. Campbell," Arthur said as he unfolded it and held it in front of his face. *"Norm, thank you for your assistance in this matter. Here is your check. Many years ago I was smoking a cigarette and fell asleep in the loft when the straw caught fire and burned my barn down. I was too embarrassed to say that I set my own barn on fire, so I told everyone you did it."* The second Arthur was finished reading the letter, his face cringed and braced before the dam broke. Norman stood up, his face instantly red from anger.

"You have to be kidding me!"

"Yeah, he said you would be mad at that one."

"The police questioned me for over a month. I've been called barn burner for over a decade!"

"He was a fickle fellow."

Arthur hid his smile in vain as he held the check in front of him. Norman grabbed it as he shook his head. Elizabeth was confused at the exchange but didn't speak up.

Arthur gave her a copy of the document she signed and saw them both to the front door as they left the office. As they walked down the sidewalk, Elizabeth asked Norman a question about the letter that made him so angry. From across the street Gordon Tyrell was sitting in his truck as he bit his fingernail and watched the strawberry blonde get into Mr. Werthan's truck. Once he was satisfied with knowing what she looked like, he turned the ignition over in frustration and drove off.

Chapter 11

Gordon Tyrell owned the only feed mill in Grainger County. His business supplied farmers with poultry, horse, pig and cattle feed. When Harold's asthma became worse as he grew older, Gordon was forced to mortgage half of his business to pay for medical bills, traveling expenses, and medication. For Gordon, when it rained, it poured as issues with his business surfaced at the worst possible time and machines had to be replaced.

While his business was functioning and generating revenue, the payments on the second mortgage left little for his family. Money was tight, and sleepless nights wore him down. The stress was enough to cause some of his hair to fall out which he would notice when taking a shower. The water would run down his face, carrying several strands of hair down his cheek and into his hands. He often broke down while sobbing into his cupped hands, always when he was alone and never around his wife or Harold.

When he heard of Mr. Campbell's death, he had remembered a rumor from when he was a child. Thaddeus Campbell hated banks. A victim of the Great Depression, Mr. Campbell kept his money in his house. The rumor began when the milkman delivered six bottles to the milk box on the Campbell's front porch and saw T.C. placing mason jars of money into a wheelbarrow. Keeping out of sight, the milkman watched as T.C. headed out into the fields.

The rumor circulated for weeks but soon dissipated and curiously no one had mentioned the rumor when T.C. passed. Two days after his death, Gordon had stopped by the Rutledge Savings and Loan and made small talk with a pretty brunette at the teller window. While writing out a check, he casually brought up the death of Mr. Campbell.

"*Too bad about ol' Campbell,*" *said Gordon.*

"*Yeah. I heard he passed.*"

"*I don't think he spent much money in his day. Bet his account here will be collected by his family up in Kingsport.*"

"*Probably. Campbell doesn't have an account with us though. We think he used a bank in Knoxville.*"

"*Oh. Guess I thought he would have been a local customer.*"

As far as Gordon was concerned, this confirmed the rumor. While he had many sleepless nights over his son's asthma and the mortgage on his business, the thought of Campbell's money buried in the ground somewhere on his farm brought a glimmer of hope.

Chapter 12

Norman drove his truck back to Campbell's farm. Elizabeth looked out over the fields that seemed to go on for miles out behind the house. Norman pulled the handbrake.

"Well, you're all set. Any idea where you and your daughter are headed next? Of course, you have time to figure all that out."

"Mr. Campbell, would you come out with me to the edge of that field over there?"

"Where?"

"Behind the house. The edge of the field."

"Well, I need to be..." Norman started to say as he looked at his watch.

"Just two minutes. Come look with me," she asked. Her voice sounded playful – a tone Norman hadn't heard since before his wife died.

"Okay. Two minutes," he said as he exited the truck. The cold air had warmed by nearly ten degrees since they'd left for Arthur's office that morning. They walked to the edge of the field and looked out over the rows of dirt that spanned over a hundred acres. When the coon dogs saw two people walking in the back-yard they scampered around them, licking their fingers and sniffing their shoes. Norman briefly scratched one of their heads. Even though it was warmer out, Elizabeth still had to wrap her arms around her torso to fight off the crisp air. Once the hounds greeted both Elizabeth and Norman, they bounded off as they chased a grasshopper.

"I like it here. I just wish I knew something about tomatoes."

"There is a lot of opportunity out there," he replied with his hands on his hips.

"What would it take for you to help me with this?"

"With what? Growing forty acres of tomatoes?"

"Yes."

"No," Norman said. He turned and looked at her. "I have my own farm to tend to. I don't think it would be a good idea to get it in your head that you can grow forty acres. It isn't going to happen. You don't know what it takes," he said. An annoyed and irritated old man had suddenly replaced the courteous and kind Norman Werthan. "The thought of you coming out here and trying to sow the land without any knowledge of how to grow a crop is offensive."

"I'm sorry, I didn't mean to…"

"We spend our lives perfecting the curating of tomatoes so don't think you can just throw seeds in the ground and hope for the best," he added just before he turned and walked back to his truck. Elizabeth followed and spoke in a pleading tone.

"Norman, I'm sorry. I didn't mean to offend you. I just like it here, and I hate to not even try, but I won't. I don't know anything about tomatoes. I'm sorry," He opened the door to his truck and hopped inside.

"I understand. Just bide your time here and move on. Good luck," Norman said as he closed the door and started the engine.

Just as he backed out of the driveway, another truck was slowing down on the main road. Elizabeth watched as Norman left and another truck pulled into the driveway. The driver parked and cut the engine. Seeing a new person on their land, the three coonhounds bounded off the porch and playfully sauntered up to Gordon Tyrell as he exited the cab of his truck with a big smile. Elizabeth returned the smile yet kept a curious expression.

"Hi there!" Gordon hollered out as he reached his hand down to pet the coon dogs.

"Hello," replied Elizabeth. She watched as the friendly man walked toward her. The dogs quickly lost interest and began playing all over each other in the grass.

"Do you own this farm?"

"Well, not sure if I'm staying," said Elizabeth as she avoided the question and shielded her eyes from the sun. The words were enough to cause genuine excitement in Gordon. He wanted to press further, but instead he kept to his plan.

"Well, my name is Gordon Tyrell, and my wife and I own the local feed company here in Rutledge. I just wanted to come by and express my sympathies for your loss. Is there anything we can do for you?"

"Oh. Well, thank you. I didn't really know my uncle and I just got here last night."

"I see. Are you and your husband farmers?" he asked. Thinking she should at least keep up appearances as she had just outright lied to an attorney, she decided to keep the lie going.

"I'm the only farmer here. My husband passed."

"Well, I am so sorry to hear that. My condolences. So you're selling then?"

"I think so. Probably in June."

"I see," Gordon replied. He continued the friendly small talk about supplying feed to farmers as to not reveal his true intentions. He politely ended the conversation and left in his truck. On the way back to the mill, all Gordon could think about was the money that might be buried in the fields.

Chapter 13

The morning that Elizabeth had gone into town with Norman to meet Mr. Humes, Claire woke up to a note that read: *Had to go into town with Mr. Werthan. Please do not leave the house. I will return shortly.* When Claire and Elizabeth vacated bunkhouse F3, they had grabbed their personal belongings. Claire's most valued possessions were in her pillowcase. Nearly two years ago, she was given a present from her mom and dad. When she unwrapped it, she discovered the present was a book titled: *Nancy Drew Mystery Stories – Nancy's Mysterious Letter.* She read it cover to cover in a matter of days and would re-read it often. On her eleventh birthday, she had asked for another Nancy Drew book. While it was difficult to find a book while living at Harris Clay Mining Company, Elizabeth searched two nearby shops to no avail before stumbling upon a flea market. After strolling by a table being tended to by an elderly woman wearing black-rimmed glasses, Elizabeth asked about her cardboard box full of used books. After flipping through the titles, a wave of joy and elation washed over her as she pulled out a copy of *The Mystery of the Tolling Bell.* Sadly, the book had many missing pages. While there were supposed to be 181 pages, the book only went as far as 106. Purchased for a penny, the book was wrapped in a handkerchief and given to

Claire who loved the book even though she didn't know how it ended. She would read both books over and over, sometimes reading her favorite paragraphs aloud to her mother.

In the books, Nancy Drew was always looking for a mystery to solve and in turn, so was Claire. The previous night, when Runt had entered the house and scared her mother, Claire had yelled downstairs. When her mother told her to go back to bed, Claire immediately ran to the window and stepped out onto the roof. She got down on her stomach and inched closer to the edge and hung her head over the side and looked through the window at her mother standing in the kitchen. If her mother were to be in danger, perhaps she could have helped. When it was apparent that the man wasn't a threat, Claire retreated inside the second-floor window and slid into bed.

Claire awoke to her mother's note and grabbed both Nancy Drew books off the nightstand. After pouring a glass of water, she walked out onto the back porch with a blanket and sat in a wooden rocking chair. With her legs pulled up to her chest, she read her favorite chapters in *The Mystery of The Tolling Bell* until her mother partially opened the back door and tilted her head through the opening.

"I thought I told you not to leave the house?" Elizabeth said with a smile.

"This is still part of the house."

"I suppose you are right." She walked out onto the porch and knelt beside the rocking chair.

"Can we go explore the farm now?" Claire asked as she closed the book with her index finger keeping her place.

"I thought we could go explore the town." Elizabeth said as she held up a pair of keys.

"What do those go to?"

"A truck in the barn. Wanna go check it out?" Elizabeth asked with a smile as she stood up.

The barn was located a half acre to the left of the house. Elizabeth used every muscle in her body to slide the massive barn door open. The corroded wheels rolled along the rusted track, screeching and squealing. Inside the barn was a tarp covering what looked like a truck. On the other side of the barn was a 1942 McCormick Deering Tractor.

"Wow! Can we ride that, too?" Claire asked as she pointed at the tractor.

"I don't think we should go near it," her mother answered. She recalled what Arthur said in his office, *"You will be given sufficient funds, tools, and machinery."* Seeing the tractor made her think that she did have everything she needed to make a go of raising forty acres, but since she didn't know where to begin, sadness replaced excitement.

"Can you help me remove the tarp?" Elizabeth asked. After a firm tug, a red 1937 Ford pick-up was revealed. The bed of the truck had been modified with a makeshift wooden fence that provided a wall on each side of the truck bed to maximize the height in which they could stack tomato crates.

"Can you drive this?" Claire asked as she knew it had been a long time since she drove anything.

"I think so."

They both hopped in the cab and Elizabeth turned the engine over. It took a couple miles of working the clutch and shifting to ignite her memory. Once on the roads of Rutledge, Elizabeth began to find the gears and navigated toward the town square. While Claire looked out the window, the excitement of the three hundred in petty cash and the rest of the money held by the city treasurer consumed Elizabeth's thoughts. The idea of twelve hundred dollars at her disposal seemed surreal. After a short ride in the truck, they pulled up in front of Shepard and Stowe

Mercantile. The store had two big windows on both sides of the entrance with hand painted lettering. The window on the left read:

Tools

Clothing

Shoes

The window on the right read:

Maple Syrup

Fresh Meats

Fresh Cheeses

"Looks like a nice general store." Elizabeth said.

"Can we get something to eat?"

"Well, since we are here for a couple months, we had better stock up. Just food though. No clothes or anything."

"We have enough money?"

"Um...I'm pretty sure we do. Remember, Norman gave us thirty dollars," she replied not giving into the temptation of telling her daughter about the money she had access to. She wasn't yet comfortable with the idea of using funds from the Campbell account or the stack of petty cash, so she decided it best to begin with the money she had saved at Harris Clay Mining Company.

Once in the mercantile, the aroma of country hams floated past their noses. The smell made their stomachs instantly crave a plate of mashed potatoes, green beans and a big slice of country ham. Elizabeth gave Claire instructions to find preserves and bread while she walked up to the clerk behind the counter. He wore a buttoned shirt, a white apron, and a pencil behind his ear. She asked a question in a hushed tone, so Claire could not hear her.

"Hello. Do you sell books?"

"We don't carry them, but we can order them," the clerk replied back in a lowered voice.

"Can you order Nancy Drew books?"

"Of course. We even have an order form. Want me to get you one?"

"Please do," she whispered. She waited only a brief moment until the clerk came out from behind the counter holding a leaflet. He spoke softly.

"This form has check boxes. If you fill it out, I can send it in for you. They are ninety-five cents for each book. Only a couple weeks for delivery."

Claire had found a mason jar of strawberry preserves but had yet to find the bread. When her mother walked up to her, she held the leaflet behind her back while smiling. Claire took notice of her expression.

"What?"

"I have been waiting so long to do this. I want you to know that you deserve it. You deserve this more than anything."

"What is it?" Claire asked. When her mother held out the form, Claire took it while holding the Mason jar in her right arm. Upon seeing the words *Nancy Drew and Order Form*, she set the jar on a nearby shelf. On the form were two columns. Twelve books were listed in column one and twelve books in column two. Twenty-four books were available and all she had to do was check a box next to the title she wished to read.

"How many can I get?"

"Let's start with six books," she replied with a big smile. "I noticed that there is a book on the list that you already have that you might like to finish," Elizabeth said. Claire looked at the left-hand column and saw the book titled: *The Mystery of the Tolling Bell* and smiled from ear to ear.

"When would they arrive?"

"The guy at the counter said a couple weeks. A very painful and looong two weeks," she replied with a grin. Even though Claire had attended a school at Harris Clay Mining Company,

Elizabeth considered Claire to be behind and could easily justify buying her six books as she loved to read. It was the best education she could get for now.

After making a rather large purchase at Shepard and Stowe that included a bag of dog food, they drove back to the farm. Elizabeth cracked eggs, made toast slathered with strawberry preserves, and cooked four slices of salted ham in a skillet. Over dinner, they talked about the comfortable bed upstairs, Nancy Drew, and what state they might move to in June. They cleaned their plates and slouched in their chairs while the gastronomic pain subsided after the excessive meal. Upon being able to move again, they fed the coonhounds by bringing them dog food in a tin dog bowl. The hounds pawed and whimpered to get their share while Claire and Elizabeth laughed at the floppy dogs fumbling over each other with wagging tails. Claire held a slice of ham in her hand and tore pieces off, feeding the pup that didn't get its fair share.

"Mom? Do you know their names?"

"No. I don't know."

"Does that man who lives nearby know?"

"Runt? Probably. I'll ask him next time I see him."

Later that night after Claire had gone to bed, Elizabeth walked out on the back porch and found the blanket Claire left on one of the rocking chairs. After getting comfortable, she fantasized a scenario where Claire went to school in Rutledge and came home to a farm that was producing fruitful crops.

Off in the distance, she could see a faint light. She squinted her eyes and thought it might be a house on the backside of the property. Then it occurred to her that it might be the hand quarters. Heading back into the kitchen, she rummaged through the drawers and found a red cloth napkin. She placed two pieces of toast and a slice of ham in the center of the napkin. Picking up the corners to form a pouch, she then grabbed Runt's water glass from the refrigerator. After putting on her shoes, she headed out toward the light while walking in the moonlight between the rows of dirt.

Chapter 14

After walking a quarter of a mile, Elizabeth reached the hand quarters, which strangely resembled bunkhouse F3. Instead of pine, the structure was built with cinder blocks. The exterior had been painted white long ago and had chipped in many places. As she approached the door, she could hear a scraping noise that repeated every second. She rapped on the door three times causing the repeated scraping sound to cease just before Runt answered the door.

"Mrs. Cam'bull!"

"Hello, Runt," she replied while holding out the red cloth napkin. "I brought you some food in case you were hungry, and I brought your water glass," she offered. Runt took the offerings taking to the water glass first, downing every drop of water there on the spot.

"Thank you, Mrs. Cam'bull. I needed that! Thank you kindly," he said as he backed away from the door and made way for her to enter. As she walked inside, she saw rows of metal bedframes with dirty mattresses on each frame. Only one mattress had sheets and blankets. Lanterns hung on nails throughout the building. Runt had lit only a few of them. The walls, ceiling, and even the shelves near the beds had been painted with whitewash and had been chipping away for years. The living conditions weren't great, but still better than the bunkhouse.

"I been sharpening tools, Mrs. Cam'bull. Been making them sharp for the next crew," he said as he set the drinking glass on an old, white painted shelf.

"You don't have to do that. I'm not sure what's going to happen to this farm."

"Well, it makes the time go by. Give me somethin' to do," he added with a nod and a smile that wrinkled the skin around his eyes.

"I understand. I would probably be doing the same thing," she replied as she took a seat on a bare mattress. When it became apparent that she was going to stay a moment, Runt took a seat on his bed that was neatly made with two thick wool blankets and opened the red napkin on his lap. She had questions to ask him but continued with the small talk as she sat on the adjacent bunk.

"Do you know the name of those three coon hounds that run around here?"

"Hmmm…I think one of them is named Scout, but I don't know which one. Mr. Campbell took 'em all huntin' from time to time. Heard him holler Scout a lot, but I don't think I heard the names of the others."

"That's okay."

"Is that what you came up here fo?"

"Well, I wanted to bring you some food and a glass of water, but I also wanted to ask you about tomatoes."

"Yes, Ma'am."

"What do you know about growing them?"

"Oh, not much I 'spose. Mr. Cam'bull handled almost everything. We just did the work."

"I wish I could find a way to make this farm work."

"Me, too, Mrs. Cam'bull! I need me a job!" Runt said as he slapped his knee and laughed. Elizabeth followed suit by offering a laugh of her own that she admitted in her head wasn't genuine.

Intending on having a real conversation, her smile turned to concern when she asked her next question.

"Do you know anyone we could get advice from?" she asked. Runt scratched his head in thought and shook his head no before he answered.

"I don't think so," he answered as he took a bite of cured ham.

"Who do you think is the best tomato farmer?"

"Well, that's easy. Irving Washington."

"Irving Washington? Who's that?"

"He a farm hand that knows more about tomatoes than anyone," he answered as he folded a piece of toast and shoved it into his mouth.

"Does he live around here?"

"Nope. He in prison," he replied with a mouthful.

"Prison? What is the best tomato farmer doing in prison?" she asked while Runt chewed his food.

"Well, it ain't real prison," his lips smacked as he continued answering her question. "He in a farmin' camp in Georgia. One of those slave camps."

"Slave camp?"

"That's what we black folks call it. The law gets ya for a minor infraction, usually a total lie. Then they put ya in a prison farm and keep you there until you either pay ya fine or work your fine off."

"How much is the fine?"

"Depends, but it usually doesn't matter. They keep addin' on fines for other infractions they make up along the way."

"So, the prisoners can't ever get out?"

"Sometimes folks get out, but it's a way for the state to get free labor and free produce which turns a profit. They don't want prisoners getting out. That's why they add more fines."

"Sounds like Georgia is cheating people out of their lives."

"Well, Tennessee and Alabama do it too. Especially Louisiana. I don't go to Louisiana."

"Do you know this man?"

"Irving? Yeah, I know 'em. I worked on his crew years ago on a small farm."

"Why is he the best?"

"He know more about crop rotation and sowing than anyone. Knows about cold weather crops and how to keep bugs from eating tomatoes and he ain't never had a crop not be fruitful. Never."

"You think if I somehow got him here he'd help me?"

"I think if you free the man, he'd give ya the best crop of tomatoes in Grainger County. Ain't nothin' worse than livin' on a prison farm."

"How do we find out what the fine is?"

"I s'pose call the prison and ask. You thinkin' you might pay it?" Runt asked as he wiped his mouth with the back of his hand. Elizabeth didn't answer immediately. She began pacing the floor and chewed on a fingernail while considering that there might be a real possibility of getting some help. She stopped pacing and looked at Runt.

"If I were able to afford his fine and he came here, you would have a job." Runt stood up and removed a ball cap off a shelf. He placed it on his head. "What are you doing?"

"Gonna make a phone call."

"To who?"

"The prison."

"It's nighttime."

"One thing I learned long ago is that prisons don't close. There is a phone booth down on the square," he replied as he removed a small tin from a nearby shelf and opened it. As he tipped the tin, a few nickels and dimes rattled and slid out into the palm of his hand."

"Can't you use the phone at the house?" she asked. Runt looked at her as if she just handed him another glass of water.

"That okay with you?"

"Of course," she said as she reached for his drinking glass on the shelf near his bed. "Let's go."

While Runt and Elizabeth were on their way to the main house, across town Gordon and his wife were in their son's room while Harold was having an asthma attack. Gasping for air as blood splattered from his mouth, Harold beat his own chest in hopes it would help him breathe. Gordon had the Aerohalor mixture knob at the maximum emission level.

"Easy. Real easy. Try to slow it down. I know it's hard. Slow down your breathing," Gordon said as he looked at his wife and nodded. She immediately left the room and phoned the doctor. When Dr. Burt Talbot's phone rang late at night, he would usually think Mr. or Mrs. Tyrell was calling and he was usually right. He kept a separate medical bag near the front door, ready for the call to rush to Harold's side.

Fifteen minutes after the phone call, Dr. Talbot arrived at the Tyrell's, let himself in the front door and rushed to Harold's bedside. He opened his medical bag while Annie was wiping blood from Harold's mouth. He handed Gordon an empty screw cap vial while paying full attention to Harold.

"Water. Half full," Talbot barked as Gordon took the glass vial and ran to the bathroom. "Bad one this time huh?" Talbot added as he grinned at Harold to lighten the mood.

"It started about an hour ago. Won't let up," Annie said. Gordon returned with the water. Dr. Talbot removed an opium powder from his medical bag that was in a small brown jar. He quickly measured a small amount and placed the powder into the vial with water. He then removed a folded piece of wax paper revealing a pre-measured amount of white caffeine powder in the folds. He poured the contents into the small vial and covered the opening with his finger and shook it vigorously. Once thoroughly mixed, he handed it to Harold who drank the contents.

Dr. Talbot removed a syringe from his bag and drew in 2.5ml of a steroid from a tiny-capped vial and quickly injected it into Harold's thigh. Harold knew it was coming. He had the shot before yet understood the temporary pain from the syringe was worth the relief that followed. Gordon rubbed his back and spoke softly to him.

"It's going to be okay. Just breathe easy."

"I'm hot," said Harold. Annie sprang into action and plugged in the fan.

Standing next to Elizabeth in the kitchen, Runt was on the phone. After speaking with the operator, he was transferred to a switchboard in Georgia who connected him to the Sugar Creek Prison Farm in Union County. When he finally got the right person on the phone, he asked about the fine for Irving Washington while Elizabeth waited patiently.

"One hundred and thirty-nine dollars?" Runt repeated as he looked at Elizabeth. "Okay. Thanks," he said before he hung up. "That's a lot of money, Mrs. Cam'bull. You got that much?" he asked. She thought once again of the twelve hundred dollars at her disposal and remembered she had three hundred dollars in petty cash in an envelope. Instead of sounding like the amount wasn't a problem, she came up with a reply that sounded like she could scrape it up and followed it up with a question.

"Runt, you want a job?"

"You bet I do."

"I'll pay you ten dollars to ride down to Union County with me."

"Ten dollars?"

"I need your help. I need a familiar face to help convince Mr. Washington."

"For ten dollars, I'll wash the truck too," Runt laughed. Elizabeth looked at the clock on the wall, which read 9:55pm.

"Let's leave in the morning. It'll take at least four hours to get there."

"Well, I wouldn't leave in the mornin'."

"Why?"

"Best be gettin' there in the evening. Go at the end of the day when the sun is down, and the guards be tired. Less chance of a problem."

"Okay. We'll leave after lunch then."

"Sounds good. G'night, Mrs. Cam'bull," he said as he headed toward the back door.

"If I'm gonna call you Runt, you gotta start calling me Elizabeth," she replied as she headed for the staircase. Completely out of view, and just before the back door closed, she could hear him holler out,

"You payin' me so, I'll call you whatever you want," he said with a laugh. As she headed up the stairs, she couldn't help but smile.

Chapter 15

When Elizabeth awoke the next morning, Claire was already out of bed. Thinking that she was on the back porch, Elizabeth took her time getting ready in the bathroom and reveled in the luxury of privacy and clean running water. Since she only had a few articles of clothing, she chose garments that would keep her warm in the cab of the truck on the way to Union County. She pulled a long sleeve shirt over her head and shoved her arms through the sleeves before slipping on a pair of tan pants made from heavy cotton.

Once downstairs she heard a noise coming from the dining room. When she walked in the room she saw Claire on the floor with a mirror in front of the locked office door that wasn't to be opened.

"Claire! What are you doing?"

"Trying to see what's in there!"

"Get away! Stand up and get away!"

"What's wrong?"

"Go to the back porch. Now!"

"Why are you yelling?"

"Hurry. Go now!"

Claire walked with her head down like a scorned dog. Her feet took quick strides through the kitchen and out onto the back porch. Claire felt her mother's hand on her shoulder guiding her to a wicker chair. She sat down as her mother stood over her and spoke with a tone in her voice she didn't use often.

"It's my fault for not making this clear. I apologize for yelling, but there is something you need to understand." Elizabeth explained the conditions of staying at the farm and stressed the importance of staying clear of the door.

"If that door is tampered with, we will be forced to leave."

"Why? What's behind the door?"

"I don't know. And I guess, I don't really care."

"Don't you want to know?"

"I heard of a man that might help us. If I can convince him to come here, I am going to try to grow forty acres of tomatoes."

"Really?"

"Yes, but if I am going to figure this out, I must go to Georgia and leave after lunch, so here are the rules. Do not leave this house while I am gone and you stay clear of the green door."

"Okay," Claire replied.

"I'm not kidding."

"I know. I promise," she replied with a nod. The berating ended with her mother releasing a deep breath. Elizabeth collected herself and went back inside. Claire spent the rest of the morning wrapped up in a blanket and a Nancy Drew book while Elizabeth paced in the kitchen preparing lunch and thinking about the possibility of growing 40 acres.

After sandwiches and a glass of milk, Elizabeth said her good-byes to Claire.

"I'm not going to say it again, but just stay clear of the green door."

"You just said it again."

"Also, last night, Runt told me that one of the dog's names was Scout but that was all he could remember."

"Scout?"

"Yep. You be good, I'll be back soon," she said as she kissed her on the cheek and headed around the side of the house toward the driveway. As she rounded the corner, she saw Runt hop in the bed of the truck. "Runt, why don't you ride up front with me?" she asked as she opened the driver's side door.

"Not sure I should be riding up front with a white lady through Tennessee and Georgia," Runt hollered as he hopped out of the bed of the truck. Elizabeth sat in the driver's seat and closed the door. She looked at him in the driver's side mirror.

"I see black folks riding with white people from time to time. I have questions, and I'd like the company. Plus, you're not a tomato."

"Well, it okay if I slouch down when people nearby?" he asked as he made eye contact with her in the side mirror.

"If they see you slouching, it will look suspicious."

"They won't see me," Runt said with a smile as he gestured to his stature.

Once on the road, the beautiful scenic drive whipped by while Elizabeth asked questions about Mr. Campbell and what it was like working for him. Runt shifted in his seat and kept on the lookout for white folks that might see him sitting in the front.

"Lots of farmers 'round here underpay their workers. Mr. Campbell would complain about the cost of help before he was forced to pay more."

"He was forced?"

"Lot of hands were leaving. He had to pay more to keep them."

"Why were they leaving?"

"Other farms in other counties were paying more."

"Oh, I see," replied Elizabeth. Up ahead in the oncoming lane, a car was approaching. Before the car even got close, Runt had ducked out-of-sight and continued speaking about the day when he got a pay increase.

During the trip to Union County, Elizabeth struggled to hear Runt's answers whenever his head was under the dash. She continued to ask questions about Mr. Campbell which led to Runt explaining the moment he found his boss's body in the fields. More questions followed.

Once in Union County, they arrived at Sugar Creek Prison Farm in the middle of the evening. Elizabeth drove past twelve-foot-high fencing that seemed to stretch for miles. Runt looked out the window in an attempt to spot Irving in the field. The workers were silhouetted against the setting sun, and their long shadows on the ground moved about as they tilled the soil and readied it for sowing.

"Can you slow down a minute?" Runt asked.

"Sure." Elizabeth slowed the truck down to a crawl. Runt scanned the fields and saw a few guards milling about near a section of the fence as they drove past. He slid down in his seat, keeping an eye on the field.

Further down the road, he recognized a man using a tiller attached to a horse.

"Oh! Stop for a second," he said in a whisper. Runt got out of the truck, checking for guards and saw none nearby. He got up to the fence and called out.

"Cole! Hey, Cole!" Runt said. The man turned around and took cautious steps near the fence.

"Runt? That you?"

"Yeah, where Irving at?"

"He near the greenhouse."

"Can you get 'em for me?"

"Yeah. Go up yonder and when you see a building with sheeting on it. Stop there."

"Ok," Runt whispered and got back in the truck. He watched

as Cole started toward the other end of the farm with a slight limp.

"Who was that?"

"Old friend. Said to stop when we see a greenhouse building with plastic sheeting on it," Runt replied as he looked toward Cole who was limping down the field. A moment later, Elizabeth spotted a framed building the size of a large shed covered in thin plastic. While the plastic wasn't quite see through, she could see the outline of people moving about inside.

"Park it here. Let's wait a second," he said as she pulled off the road and cut the engine. They could hear men working, tools clanging and the occasional shouting of one worker to another. Cole finally made it to the greenhouse and went inside. "Ok. Come on let's go."

"Where we going?"

"Just over to the fence here. He bringin' Irving out."

Elizabeth followed Runt's lead. When he exited the truck, he didn't shut the door, he kept it cracked open and Elizabeth copied his actions. After making their way to the fence, a middle-aged black man appeared from around the side of the plastic greenhouse. He was taller than six feet and wore a linen shirt with suspenders and brown pants that were filthy. His hair was unkempt, and his face was sweaty and splotched with dirt. Runt started in while wearing a curious expression.

"You 'memba me?" Runt whispered.

"How could I forget a midget like yourself, Runt. What are you doing here?" Irving whispered back.

"This lady wanna talk to you," he replied. Elizabeth jumped in, wasting no time.

"I have a farm in Grainger County. I need help and I will pay your fine and get you outta here if you help me." When Irving responded, he continued to keep his voice to a whisper.

"You gonna pay my hundred and thirty some odd dollar fine so's I will come work for you?" he asked as he looked around for a guard.

"Yes."

"When this gonna be?"

"Now. I will pay it now."

"What's the catch? Why me?"

"Runt says you're the best at growing a crop of tomatoes."

"Nah. I just care about it more than most folks."

"You gonna do it?" Runt asked Irving.

"I got a condition, and it's a deal breaker. Don't think you gonna like it," he added as his eyes continued searching for a guard.

"What is it?" Elizabeth asked.

"My momma and my daddy. They rent a house five minutes from here. I leave Georgia, they come with me."

"Done." Elizabeth said.

"Done? That quick? You must be in some kinda hurtin', lady," Irving said as he checked around again for guards.

"I am hurtin'. Don't mind if I say so."

"You gotta place for us to live and all that?"

"I do. Campbell Farms. Got living quarters and everything." Elizabeth replied. Irving looked at Runt.

"She got all the answers, huh?"

"So far," Runt shrugged. "What's your number?"

"Seventy-two," Irving responded just as the voice of a guard could be heard on the other side of the plastic sheeting. Irving dashed around the corner and walked back into the greenhouse. Runt turned to Elizabeth.

"We better hurry for we end up in there."

They quietly climbed into the cab of the truck and turned the engine over. She drove it to the front of the prison and parked the truck.

"I'm waitin' here. I know how these places run," Runt said as he slouched in his seat. "Don't use Irving's name. Just say prisoner seventy-two." Elizabeth nodded, got out of the truck and walked up to the front entrance which was nothing more than a tall, chain-linked gate. Two guards watched her as she approached. The guard who looked like he might be the result of a long history of inbreeding spoke up.

"What you doing here missy?" A dog in a cage nearby lifted its head and barked, which woke the other sleeping dogs in the cage.

"I'm here to pay a fine." she said raising her voice over the barking.

"Who you after?" he asked. When she responded, she looked at the dogs and took notice that they were bloodhounds. Lanterns hung on the outside of the metal cage.

"All I have is a number. No name," said Elizabeth. The guard unlocked the gate and allowed her to enter.

"You sure are a pretty thing to be out at a prison late at night with all the animals inside. Never know when one might get out." The guard leered at Elizabeth, but she didn't respond. "Go over to the window and ring the bell. Eloise will be with ya shortly." Once the dogs gathered she wasn't a threat, their barks ceased and were replaced with whimpers as they hadn't yet been fed their dinner.

Elizabeth approached a window that had been cut into the side of a small office building. A wire mesh covered most of the window. When she rang the bell, a tired woman named Eloise appeared. She was large, blonde and on the wrong side of fifty. The bow in her hair was much too big and made her look ridiculous instead of attractive.

"Help ya?"

"I am here to pay the fine for prisoner seventy-two."

"Ok." she said as she fished out a clipboard from a metal drawer on her right. She flipped a few pages on the clipboard and followed her finger across several boxed lines and found the amount. "One hundred and thirty-nine dollars and it's cash only," she said with an ornery smile. "You call earlier?" Elizabeth nodded as she reached into her pocket and took out the envelope of petty cash. She counted out denominations and slid the money under the wire mesh.

Inside the prison, Irving Washington had grabbed a burlap sack and began filling it with his sparse belongings. He then ran from the bunkhouse to the greenhouse. Inside, he found a few vines of tomatoes and plucked five off the vine and plunged them into the sack. Suddenly, a loud voice could be heard outside.

"Irving Washington! You're being released! Gather your belongings and report to the main gate."

After two gates were opened by two different guards, Elizabeth watched as Irving walked out of the shadows and into the lights that illuminated the parking lot.

Chapter 16

The guard that previously commented on Elizabeth's appearance when she first arrived, berated Irving as he walked away from the double entry gate.

"See you next week, Washington. That ain't even your real last name. We gonna double your fine next time. See you next week, won't I, Washington? See you next week!"

Ignoring the guard, Irving whispered to Elizabeth as she walked beside him toward the truck.

"We gonna go get my mama and daddy now?"

"Yes. Right now," she replied in a pleasant yet assertive tone.

"My name is Irving Washington. I don't know why you want me, but I thank ya for what ya did."

"I'm Elizabeth."

"You better tell me your last name. I can't be calling no white lady by her first name in public."

"Campbell. Elizabeth Campbell," she said now thinking of Runt calling her by her last name instead of her first. Irving looked up and saw a red 1937 Ford pick-up with Runt standing behind it. He opened the tailgate as they approached and climbed in the back.

"If it ah'right, I'm gonna ride in the back with Irving," said Runt. Irving looked at Elizabeth as he climbed into the bed of the truck.

"Take highway nineteen north until you see a burned down church. My folks' place is across the street from there."

At the same time Elizabeth was en route to pick up Irving's parents, Claire was back in Grainger County discovering which dog was named Scout. After saying Scout's name, a coon dog with a shiny brown coat approached her every time she said it aloud. She cupped its head in her hands.

"Is your name Scout? Is that your name? You are a smart doggie!" she said as she scratched around his ears. She decided the two other hounds needed names and gave the name Pepper to the dog that was peppered with spots and Blue to the dog with a bluish hue to his gray coat.

While Claire was making friends with the hounds, Elizabeth steered the truck along highway nineteen north until she saw a burned down church. Irving hollered out.

"See that house across the street? Pull up on the gravel drive there. I'll go inside," After following his instructions, Elizabeth brought the truck to a stop. Irving jumped out of the back and hurried inside with Runt following closely behind. Elizabeth waited for ten minutes in the dark with the engine off until the front door opened. An elderly black man waddled toward the truck. Following him was an elderly black lady who carried a suitcase in one hand and a table lamp in the other. The man approached the driver's side of the truck.

"Lady, you must have one wallop of a tomato problem," he said as he waddled closer to the window. "You spring my boy out of that slave camp?"

"Yes, sir."

"You have my gratitude," he said as he tipped his cap.

Elizabeth took notice that it wasn't an ordinary hat. It was a cap-tain's hat with a gold-plated anchor on the front.

"Well, it's me that really needs the help." Elizabeth said. The elderly woman had set the lamp and suitcase down on the ground and forcefully pushed her husband aside.

"Watch out now, you ol' dish!" the man shouted. The woman, paying him no mind, reached for the handle of the driver's side door and pulled it open. She looked at the thin white girl sitting in the seat and motioned for her to get out. When Elizabeth did, she was grabbed and quickly pulled toward the woman who gave her a warm and surprisingly strong hug.

"You did that for my boy. You don't know what you did for me. You hear? You are my angel, and I am in your debt." Elizabeth smiled and struggled to take in a breath of air. Inside the old rental house, Runt grabbed a floor lamp and a suitcase and headed out the front door. Irving was going through closets and looking in corners of the house for something. He went into the bath-room and looked in the bathtub. Nothing. He searched next to the stove and by the ice box. Unable to find what he was looking for, he hurried outside.

"Dad! Where's my trunk?" he hollered. His father turned around and looked back at his son standing on the front porch.

"It's by the back door with a towel over it," he hollered back. Irving quickly went inside to the back door and pulled a towel off of a small trunk that sat upright. Grabbing the leather handle, he picked it up off the ground and carried it as if he were a trav-eler lugging a large suitcase and running late for the train. The weight of the trunk caused him to lean to the right for balance as he carried it in his left hand. Runt set the floor lamp and a suit-case in the back of the truck while Irving hurried over with his heavy trunk and hoisted it up on the tail gate. Runt looked at Irving.

"Is that what I think it is?" asked Runt.

"Yep. I've thought about it every day," Irving replied as he put both hands on it and pushed it further into the bed of the truck. Elizabeth had watched the exchange and instantly became curious. On the way back to Rutledge, Runt, Irving, and Captain rode in the bed of the truck while Millie Washington rode up front with Elizabeth and called her an angel more than ten times before crossing the state line.

After playing with the dogs for some time, Claire eventually discovered if she picked up a stick, all three dogs immediately wanted it and would chase her around. Using the light that shone from the windows of the house, she ran laps around the farmhouse with the hounds chasing her. After several trips around, it dawned on her that there was a small wooden access door on the side of the house. Thinking it might lead her directly underneath the room with the green door, she ended the fun with the coon hounds and threw the stick out into the yard. The pups chased it into the darkness.

Instead of going to bed, Claire searched for a flashlight in the house before walking back outside to the wooden access panel. Getting on her hands and knees, she channeled Nancy Drew as she used her memory to find the underneath of the room with the green door. An earthen odor filled her nostrils as she crawled. The slats in the floorboards above her let in very little light between the separations. She hoped she could see into the room with the green door, even if a small glimpse. She crawled past spider webs thinking that Nancy Drew would have simply avoided them and would not have been afraid.

Once underneath what she thought to be the room with the

green door, she placed her flashlight up against the slats above her head. Inside the room, rays of light shot up from the separations and barely illuminated the room. Peering between the space of two floorboards, she could see white shelves and glass.

The sound of a door opening and footsteps on the hardwood floor above her made her think of her mother's return. Claire began to scramble out from underneath the house as quietly as possible and couldn't have known that her mother wasn't even in Grainger County.

Chapter 17

Claire reached the exit of the crawlspace and squeezed through the opening using her hands, elbows, and knees acquiring dirt and grass stains on her shirt and pants. She stood up, and immediately heard shouting. It wasn't her mother, it was a man's voice.

"There's someone here. A woman's clothes are upstairs and the bed ain't made." Claire crouched as she turned off her flashlight. She hurried to a window and looked into the dining room. A woman's voice could be heard shouting, but Claire couldn't see anyone.

"What is going on? Who would be staying here?" the woman said as she came into view from around the corner. Claire ducked and moved to the far-left side of the window. The woman was looking up the staircase and talking to someone out of view. Claire took mental notes. Blonde hair. White dress. Black belt. Red heels.

"I'm calling the police." She could hear a man say as he came into view at the bottom of the staircase. Brown pants. Brown hair. Blue button up shirt. Sleeves rolled up. The man walked into the kitchen and the woman followed behind him.

Claire moved to the front of the house and looked in the driveway. The car was a 1948 Chevrolet Fleetmaster, but all Claire knew was that it was a tan colored car with a silver stripe on the side. Upon hearing the calling of police, she considered for a moment of approaching the couple, then decided that Nancy Drew would stay out-of-sight and gain more information.

When Elizabeth finally drove in the driveway of the Campbell Farm, the headlight of the truck swept across a police car that was parked next to a tan Chevy.

Irving jumped out of the back of the truck, his shoes smacking the gravel. As he hurriedly approached the driver's side window, he tried to shake off the nervousness causing his arms and hands to tremble. He looked directly at his mother.

"Mamma, you get in the back with me and dad. Mrs. Campbell, if this police officer is here about me, tell him you dropped me off at the state line, you hear? He comes back here looking for me, I'm running, and you won't see me again! I ain't going back to that prison."

"I will go inside and see what this is about."

While Elizabeth got out of the truck and walked up to the house, Mrs. Washington was struggling to get in the back of the truck. Elizabeth could hear "Shhhhh" and "Keep quiet" coming from the truck behind her as she approached the front door.

When she walked inside, she saw a man and his wife in the living room standing next to a police officer.

"Are you the one staying here?" Sleeves asked.

"I am," Elizabeth replied.

"You are under arrest!"

Chapter 18

Claire had been hiding behind a bush when she saw her mother get out of the truck and walk inside. Instead of watching through the window, she hurried around to the back porch and quietly entered. Staying out of sight, she heard the man shouting.

"Officer, this woman is trespassing! I want to press charges!" said Sleeves. He had called for her arrest and to his dismay was met with stern eyes and deep, resounding tone of voice from the officer.

"Now hang on, just a minute," he said before turning to Elizabeth. "Can you please identify yourself?"

"I am Elizabeth Campbell, niece of Mr. Campbell."

"He had no such thing!" The wife said. The officer held up a finger to her to keep her quiet.

"Do you have proof?"

"I do," Elizabeth replied and left the room to go upstairs.

"This oughta be good," Sleeves said aloud as he crossed his arms. The officer had hoped she had proof so that he could kick these obnoxious people out of Mr. Campbell's house. When Elizabeth returned, she held in her thin fingers an unfolded, single piece of paper. When she handed it to the officer, he immediately took notice of the attorney letterhead belonging to Arthur Humes. When he read over the document, he handed it back to

Elizabeth and looked at Sleeves. With a slight grin, he said, "I'm gonna have to ask you both to leave."

"What!" he shouted. "Let me see that!" he yelled. Elizabeth took a step back and held the letter away from him.

"This is my letter. The officer reviewed it. Now please do as he says."

"Did that old farmer Werthan put you up to this? I'm gonna find out, and when I do, you're going to be in trouble."

"Now, you're both gonna have to leave or I'll have to arrest you both for trespassing."

The husband cursed at Elizabeth as the officer walked him and his wife out onto the front porch. Elizabeth closed the front door after thanking the officer and spun around.

"Claire!"

"Right here, Mom," she said from the kitchen. Elizabeth watched as her head appeared from around the corner.

"What did they say to you?"

"They never knew I was here."

"I guess we should start locking the doors. Or maybe changing the locks all-together."

"They were talking about the green door," said Claire. She watched her mother's face of concern turn to shock and outright fear.

"What?"

"They were saying something about the office with the green door being locked."

Elizabeth covered her mouth as she recalled what Mr. Humes had said. *"You are not to go near that door. The frosted glass window is not to be tampered with and should it break, even if by accident, this arrangement will be over."*

She hurried to the dining room and found the glass to be intact. She reached for the handle and found it to be locked.

"I'm going to the hardware store tomorrow. We need to protect this door."

Claire immediately felt guilty about crawling underneath the
house and trying to see what was in the room. She could see how
nervous her mother was and how much grief it gave her.

"Bring your flashlight," Elizabeth said as she headed toward
the front door. Claire removed the flashlight from her back pocket
and held it in her hand as she listened to her mother. "I am making a go at this. I want to keep this farm. You understand?"
Elizabeth explained as she looked Claire in the eye the entire time
to drive home her point. Claire nodded. "Despite what Mr.
Werthan said, I am going to try to raise 40 acres of tomatoes,"
Claire followed her mother out the front door and off the porch
toward the truck in the driveway. "When I went to Georgia, that
man Runt and I found someone who can help us. He is in the
back of the truck, and I want you to help in any way you can. Got
it?"

"Got it," Claire replied. Elizabeth stopped her just before they
reached the truck. She bent down and looked into her eyes. "I
have never wanted something so bad in my entire life. I want this
farm. It is a better life for you. It is a better life for me. I cannot
let this slip through our fingers. So, from here on out I want you
by my side learning from this man and listening to everything
he says. If we can help in any way to grow tomatoes, we will do
it and we will learn as we go. Understand?" she explained as her
eyes started to tear up.

"I understand," Claire replied.

"Okay."

Elizabeth opened the heavy tail gate. Claire turned her flashlight to four black people sitting and waiting nervously. She then
aimed the flashlight directly at the bed of the truck to keep from
blinding them.

"All clear," said Elizabeth.

"I heard the cars leave," Irving said.

"He's gone," Elizabeth replied. "The officer was here for an entirely different reason. We're going to take a ride to the hand quarters—hang tight," she said just before closing the tail gate. As she turned to head to the driver's side, Irving spoke up.

"Ms. Campbell?"

"Yes?" she said as she stopped in her tracks.

"He ain't comin' back, is he?"

"No. I would say he won't be coming back," she replied in a compassionate voice to ease his obvious concern. "That had something to do with intruding family members upset that they aren't inheriting this farm. No big deal. Nothing to do with you." Irving nodded his head and took a deep breath as his father patted his leg.

"You gonna be alright," he whispered to Irving.

After a bumpy ride to the hand quarters, the truck parked near the door just as Runt jumped out and hurried inside to light the lanterns. When Irving walked in, he looked around. Having been very familiar with hand quarters, he was impressed by the size. He nodded his head in approval as he looked over the small kitchen at the end of the large room. Irving's parents weren't so impressed.

"Where the bathroom at?" Mrs. Washington asked.

"Outside," Runt said.

"It's an outhouse?"

"Yes."

"Oh, I thought I was done with outhouses," Mr. Washington said with a look of disdain. "I hate getting my tired old body out of bed to go to the bathroom outside."

"Is that the kitchen?" Mrs. Washington asked as she pointed at the stove.

"Wood burning stove. Works great!" said Runt.

"I was hoping for similar accommodations to what we had in our rental house," she replied as she looked in Irving's direction.

"Momma," Irving started to tell her to keep her complaining to a minimum when Elizabeth interrupted. She looked at Irving's parents and spoke as if she was thinking out loud.

"There is a bedroom at the main house on the first floor. You are welcome to it, if you like."

"Oh, ma'am. I don't think that is appropriate," Irving said as he shook his head from side to side. Elizabeth put her hands on her hips. Claire watched her mother as she spoke, taking in her attitude and watching her facial expressions.

"Why, that room is just sitting there. Empty. There is a rest-room ten feet from the door and the kitchen has a refrigerator and a stove."

"I don't think this is a good idea. That officer comes back and sees black folk living with a white woman and her daughter, we gonna have to move on. We'll have to leave."

"I don't think he's coming back, Mr. Washington," Elizabeth said. She pointed at Claire as she continued. "My daughter and I sleep upstairs anyway," she explained before turning back toward his parents. "You won't bother us none. And if you don't take that room, I will be offended."

Suddenly, Elizabeth found herself entangled in four arms that had wrapped around her as Mr. and Mrs. Washington embraced her. Claire smiled.

"Sent from Heaven. We are in your debt, young lady." Millie said.

"If we gonna be livin' underneath her roof we better intro-duce ourselves, Millie." Once the embrace ended, the elderly man started first.

"My name is Karl Washington, but you just call me Captain.

Everybody else does."

"I noticed your hat. Were you in the Navy?" Elizabeth asked.

Millie held her hands up like she was trying to stop a train.

"Oh, lordy, it's too late in the night. Let's not get him started," Millie said.

"That's right. I was in the Navy during the Great War. I was a petty officer."

"It will never end if I don't jump in here. My name is Millie, and I am so glad to know both of you," she said as she held both of Elizabeth's hands and nodded at Claire.

The introductions continued until Elizabeth asked that Runt fill Irving in on the details of the farm and that they talk tomorrow. She drove back to the house with Claire in the front seat, and Captain and Millie rode in the bed of the truck as they dangled their feet off the tail gate looking at the stars above them.

Across town, Gordon Tyrell had just gotten Harold to sleep. He placed his hand on his sons' chest and felt him breathing as he slept. He prayed to God and was so thankful for the breaths he took and then continued his prayer to include the breathing machine Harold so desperately needed. He thought of what it would be like to take him to school and let him learn with the other kids. He so desperately wanted his son to live a better life outside the confined walls of their home. Gordon quietly left the room and walked down the hall and into the kitchen. It was late, and his wife was sleeping, but Gordon had been thinking all day about an item he had acquired earlier that morning. Once he had learned that Elizabeth was going to sell in June and the farm would be for sale, he visited the co-op and requested the farm division map for the Campbell Farm. The division map showed the lines of how the farm was divided into fields. Thaddeus Campbell had plotted many fields on the farm for more control over pests, blight, and to make crop rotation more efficient.

After paying a small fee, a carbon copy of the division map had been rolled up and handed to Gordon. He had kept the rolled-up copy in his truck and had left it there while he was at work. While he functioned at work and spoke with many people, his mind was in the truck, thinking about the division map.

He sat down at the kitchen table and removed the rubber band, unrolling the map. He removed a charcoal pencil from his back pocket that he used to write on burlap bags at the feed mill. *Where would T.C. have buried his money? The hand quarters? The barn? Could the money be buried in the barn?* He began looking at the areas where Mr. Campbell grew his crops. *The corners of a field would be a good place. You could easily find it. No one would question it if you left space between your crops and the corner. The dirt could even be tilled after burying the money.* Each field had four corners and there were twelve fields on the Campbell Farm. He recalled hearing the story about the milkman watching Gordon with the wheelbarrow full of glass jars. Thinking he may have just discovered the locations of the buried money, Gordon circled the corners and decided that he might try to dig before June. *What if I found the money before she even moved on? Then I wouldn't even have to buy the farm.*

Chapter 19

The morning after the Washingtons' arrival on the Campbell Farm, Irving had walked from the hand quarters to the main house carrying the large trunk by the leather handle. Unable to carry the load the entire way, he set it down on the soil and used it as a bench, resting his hands on his knees while he sat and took a few deep breaths. After several rest stops, he made it to the main house and set the trunk on the porch with a thud. He knocked on the back door just as his eyes focused through the window on his mother and father sitting at the kitchen table drinking coffee. He opened the door and stuck his head inside wearing an irritated expression.

"What ya'll doing?"

"Drinking coffee."

"Where'd you get it?"

"The cabinet." Captain said as he pointed toward the kitchen cabinets.

"You can't do that! This ain't your house!" Irving hissed as he entered the kitchen, keeping his voice to a near whisper.

"She told us we could."

"Mrs. Elizabeth did?"

"What's wrong?" Millie asked. She watched as Irving paced the floor between the backdoor and the refrigerator. His voice dipped to a low whisper once again.

"What is this? A white lady needs help, and she buys herself a farm hand?"

"Is that what she said?" Captain asked with deep wrinkles of concern setting into his face.

"No. But that's what this is, ain't it?"

"What she want you to do?"

"She wants 40 acres of tomatoes."

"That it?"

"I don't know, but I assume there's more."

The front door to the house opened and in walked Elizabeth and Claire with two men carrying a large sheet of wood. From the kitchen, Irving and his parents listened to Elizabeth speaking to the two men.

"Just bring that into the dining room." Elizabeth said. One man's voice was deep, and another was a little higher. "Yes, right here against the door," she added.

"Cover the door?" the man with the deeper voice asked. Millie mouthed her question to Irving in order to keep quiet, *what are they doing?* He shrugged and continued to listen.

"Yes, please, and if I could politely ask you both to help move the hutch here to block the door I would be very appreciative."

Not being able to see what was going on, Irving walked cautiously to get a better look. From around the corner, he peered into the dining room and watched two white men as they held a large sheet of wood over a green door. They each took out nails from their pockets and nailed the wood to the doorframe, completely blocking the door.

"Easy," Elizabeth said. "I wouldn't want the vibrations to break the glass."

Not knowing what was happening, Irving hurried back to the kitchen and motioned for his parents to stand up. They grabbed their ceramic mugs as their son hurried them out onto the back porch. Irving stood next to the trunk.

"What's going on?" Captain asked as he looked over his shoulder while the hammering in the dining room continued. Irving closed the back door.

"I don't know, but I'd say it's none of our business. I don't want no part of it," he said as he walked over to his father. He spoke quietly as he gestured to the trunk.

"I need you to keep this in the bedroom. That okay?" His dad nodded and said he would keep it by the bed.

"Let me help you move it inside."

Minutes later, Irving walked out of the house onto the back porch where he found Elizabeth waiting for him.

"Could you walk with me a moment?" she asked.

"Yes ma'am."

Elizabeth led him between rows of hardened dirt in the field behind the main house. Instead of walking, Elizabeth's pace slid into a stroll as her weight shifted from one hip to the other. She began the conversation by explaining that she would inherit the farm, but only if she could cultivate forty acres of tomatoes. During her explanation, she added that she had very little experience and was solely relying on him to help her. Irving stopped walking and turned toward her.

"Okay, first things first. I need the rotation book. Did Mr. Campbell have one?"

"He did. I have it."

"Good. Then we need to hire at least ten hands to help till, sow, and maybe a water truck depending on rain. You got enough money for that?" he asked like a parent speaking to a child, thinking she'd probably answer with a no.

"I do."

"We need to start tillin' tomorrow. Gonna need five men right away. That alright?"

"I will see what I can do. You just tell me what you need. My daughter and I will help, too," she added. It was the last thing she had said that caused Irving to look at her with an expression of an unhinged door.

"You going to be out here in these fields with us?"

"I need to learn too, right?"

"I don't know. Women in the field rarely work out."

"You don't have to worry about me not working out," she said with a confident and demanding tone. Irving turned toward her and slowly crossed his arms.

"Why you doing this?"

"What?"

"If you inherited this farm, can't you just sell it and live your life?"

"It isn't that easy. Plus, I want this farm. I want to live the rest of my life here."

"You mind if I speak frank, Miss Elizabeth?"

"Please."

"Women don't belong in the field. They don't own farms, and they don't know nothin' about tomatoes. Be best if you left this to me. Once things get going and your 40 acres is coming in, I'd appreciate it if you just let me go on about my business."

"That's pretty frank."

"I don't want to beat around the bush none. Growing a crop of tomatoes isn't easy. It's a difficult thing to do right. People could spend their whole life trying to grow a crop of tomatoes and never get it right. Spoilage. Insects. Droughts. Infertile soil. Blight. Improper crop rotation. Improper harvesting methods. And to just say that you're gonna learn is…"

"Offensive?"

"I was gonna say it's a 'difficult thing to do'. But I suppose offensive isn't far off. If someone thinks they can just do their best and come up with a sellable crop of tomatoes, most farmers fail right there. And this is Grainger County—it's different here. Farmers are held in high regard and growing tomatoes is more religion than agriculture," he paused as he looked at the ground. "I don't know. If anything, consider farming cucumbers or squash or carrots. Anything but tomatoes."

Elizabeth thought he sounded exactly like Norman and thought about what he had said as she gazed off into the empty fields. She had made up her mind. She turned toward him and crossed her arms. She looked up at him directly in the eye, like a friend handing out difficult advice.

"You're out of prison?" she asked him as she nodded her head as if to answer her own question.

"Yes, ma'am."

"In exchange I need to know the bare minimum, so I can do everything I can to make a life for me and my daughter. I ain't saying that I am going to grow tomatoes all by myself. I suppose I will have to hire someone with the knowledge of doing it right season after season, but how am I going to know if they are doing a good job?" Irving took his eyes off Elizabeth and looked back at the ground. He shook his head before looking up and seemingly giving in.

"I'm gonna need a lot of supplies and materials for forty acres. You have enough to pay for all of it?" he asked again as if he still didn't believe she had the means.

"I do. I will get it paid."

"Now, I am gonna fool proof this with fertilizer, seeds, earth-worms and labor. All that don't come cheap," he spoke once more as if he thought she didn't truly understand what she was getting into. While it took a few jabs, Elizabeth finally felt the subtle punch in her direction.

"No problem," she replied as she swatted a gnat in front of her face. "Let's move forward, Mr. Washington." She turned away from him and headed back toward the house. He watched her walk away as he shook his head. "Okay," he said under his breath. Shoving his hands into his pockets, he started back toward the hand quarters while gazing upon the fields.

Elizabeth walked back into the house, and leaned on a wall in the kitchen, biting the nail of her ring finger. Forty acres of tomatoes would be planted and once the farm was hers, she would then figure out what to do next.

Chapter 20

After the two men had completed boarding up the green door in the Campbell home, it didn't take long for them to start talking once they were back at the hardware store. Several of the customers had stuck around after their purchases to hear the story from the two handymen. They explained in detail the boarding up of a locked green door. Then moving the hutch to conceal its existence. The customers that listened scratched their heads and said things like, "*Wonder what's that all about?*" and "*She must have lost her mind.*"

While the weird tale circulated around town, another strange thing happened later that day. A couple farmers had gathered down at the local co-op while their supplies were being loaded into their trucks. Often times, the co-op would turn into an impromptu bar where jokes were told, and the occasional fight would break out among farm hands.

Miles Haley, 71, a third-generation farmer was standing outside near the loading bay with four other men. They all listened to a joke told by one of the younger farmers involving a midwife assisting a woman during childbirth. Miles listened with a slight grin until he saw a red truck park in front of the co-op and a black man hop out of the back. He watched him walk to the front door of the co-op and go inside. His grin slowly subsided, and his eyes widened. The others took notice.

"What's the matter, Miles? Looks like you seen a ghost."

"Who are you looking at?"

Without saying a word and stunned by what he saw, Miles took slow steps out of the loading bay. His leather boots with hard soles lightly scraped the dirt underneath his feet with each step. He looked at the red truck and saw a thin, white girl behind the wheel.

Miles approached the passenger side window and Elizabeth took notice. Miles watched as the thin, pretty girl reached across the seat and rolled down the window with an outstretched hand.

"Yes, sir?"

"Sorry to bother you. Was that Irving Washington that just walked inside?"

"Yes, sir, it was."

Inside the co-op, Irving had found a counter with two areas for service. On the far left was a sign that read *White* and on the far right the sign read *Colored*. Irving stood at the counter on the far right and waited until a black man in a white apron approached the counter.

"Can I help you?"

"I'm looking for some hands for the summer."

The man reached under the counter and pulled out a box of index cards. Each card had a name, an address and some even had a phone number.

"If you hire one, please take the notecard out of the box," the man said as he turned and walked into the back room. Irving reached in the box and pulled out the stack of cards. After a few minutes of flipping through the names, he took ten cards and walked outside. Irving looked up from the stack and saw a man in overalls and leather boots standing near the truck who seemed to be waiting on him.

"You Irving Washington?"

"Yes, sir," Irving said. He watched as the man extended his hand for a handshake. Irving shook his hand in confusion.

"I got about sixty acres of Sailor's Sunset a few years back with the irrigation channels you told me about. Remember me from about five years back? I couldn't get the water to my tomatoes?"

"Oh, yeah! You don't say! You got a full sixty, huh?"

"I did. I wasn't sure you knew what you were talking about, but I had my hands dig those channels like you said. Crop came in at ninety to ninety-five. Just wanted to thank ya."

"Of course. Sure! Glad to have helped."

"Where are you at now?"

"I'm over at the Campbell Farm."

"Campbell? He passed on recently," Miles said as he shifted his weight from one leg to the other. Irving pointed to Elizabeth sitting in the truck.

"The heir to the farm is right there. She takin' it over."

"Well, good. Good to see ya around. I might come by and see ya if that's ok. Been thinking about rotating from tomatoes to peas and beans."

"Well, five years ago I might have agreed with ya. Now I'm thinkin' lettuce, spinach, or cabbage. Then rotate to peas or beans. If you really want a perfect soil for something like Yellow Peak or say Green Valley, I'd go with a root crop like onions or carrots and then back to tomatoes. In that order or you could fert and worm. I'm doing that for the Campbell Farm now." Miles had followed Irving's explanation like a musician reading sheet music.

Elizabeth had witnessed the exchange and marveled at how the man didn't regard Irving as a field hand, rather another farmer. It had caught her off guard hearing the enthusiasm in the man's voice as he spoke to Irving. When their conversation ended, Irving walked over to the driver's side and showed Elizabeth the index cards.

"I got six cards here with phone numbers and four without. I will call the ones with numbers today to see if I can get them to the farm tomorrow. What are you paying?"

"I've heard forty-five dollars a week is a good wage, so that is what I will pay."

"Forty-five a week?" Irving said with a smile. "You can cover that?"

"Yes. What would you pay?"

"That is what I would call the going rate, but there aren't any farmers I know of that pays that right off the bat. You could start at thirty-five or forty and let them work their way up to it."

"I don't know. What if I paid forty-five and we make it known that if anyone falls behind then there are other workers waiting to take their place. I'm ok with forty-five, plus I know what it is like to be underpaid for good work." she said with a single nod. Irving shook his head and looked back at the cards.

"What?" Elizabeth asked.

"For forty-five a week," he smiled, "I bet we get every hand in this stack," he said as he held up the note cards with a big smile that showed his white teeth. "Makes my job that much easier."

"I like the sound of that." Elizabeth said as she turned the engine over while Irving jumped into the bed of the truck.

Chapter 21

Gordon Tyrell was sitting at his desk looking over the payables for the month. Outside his office door was the sound of the large industrial feed mill that made a racket like a freight train. When the phone rang, he answered—"Tyrell"—while still looking over an invoice wondering why it was so high.

"Honey! Harold can't breathe. I've already called the doctor."

Gordon jumped up from his desk and grabbed the door handle of his office and flung it open. The door smacked the wall behind it. A few workers filling up feedbags saw Gordon bolt out the bay door and run at full speed toward his truck.

Once on the roads, he floored the truck and pushed the engine to its limit. The tires screeched as he took corners at high speeds and the engine roared after each turn until his luck ran out. The right front tire ruptured causing Gordon to run off the road and into a ditch.

"No! No! Come on! Not now," Gordon screamed and beat the steering wheel as a passerby slowed his 1950 Crosley Station Wagon and stuck his head out the window.

"Need some help there?" Ed Meyers, 63, was a farm implement dealer and a deacon at the Baptist Church. When Ed pulled up with a smile, his face quickly took on an expression of concern as he watched Gordon turn his head with rage in his eyes. A man on the edge threw open the driver's side door of his truck and ran to Ed's driver side door and opened it. Ed scooted his rear end over to the passenger side.

"Gordon?"

"My son can't breathe," he yelled as he threw the car into drive and slammed on the gas.

The next four minutes were the scariest in years for Ed as he braced himself by placing both hands on the dashboard in front of him. The engine roared. The tires emitted sounds of stress around corners. Relief set in the second Tyrell stopped the car in front of his house. Gordon jumped out and ran into the house. Ed slowly started to inch toward the driver's side thinking he could take his abused car back home and call it a day. Before Ed could make good on his plan, Dr. Talbot burst out the front door carrying twelve-year-old Harold with Gordon supporting his son's head.

"Out Mr. Meyers. We need your car," Gordon shouted. Ed did as asked. A moment later, Harold was lying in the backseat with his mother. She soaked a thin sheet of gauze with Aerohalor liquid and held it over his mouth as Dr. Talbot had instructed. Breathing the medicinal fumes through the porous cloth would help to relax his airway. Dr. Talbot stood with Ed as they watched the car speed off down the road.

"Where they headed?"

"Knoxville General Hospital."

"Knoxville! That's my car!"

"I couldn't stabilize him. Your car might save that boy's life."

Gordon drove the car through tears that filled his eyes. He prayed to God that He would spare his son and give the doctors the ability to free Harold of his illness. As he made his way to the hospital, he listened to Harold gasp for air while Annie tried to get him to calm his breathing.

"Hurry, Gordon. Hurry."

Gordon cleared his eyes with the back of his hand and drove as fast as he could down Highway 11 W. He swerved around a cluster of vehicles, honked the horn, and flicked the high beams on and off.

"Hang on, Harold! We're going fast, buddy! Just hang on!" The 1950 Crosley Station Wagon passed a police officer who immediately turned on his lights and hit the gas.

"What in the world?" the officer said aloud as he wondered if maybe the gas pedal was stuck on the floor. Thinking it wasn't a teenager gone awry, he pulled up alongside the wagon. Upon seeing a woman tending to someone lying down, he looked at the driver who was furiously pointing down the road. Flooring his cruiser, the officer pulled in front of Gordon leaving his emergency light spinning.

With a police escort, vehicles on Highway 11 W parted biblically and the run to the hospital from Rutledge was unknowingly a state record. Dr. Talbot had called ahead and alerted the staff of Knoxville General Hospital to be on standby. Once the car arrived, a team of nurses rushed Harold into the Emergency Department.

Two general physicians and a pulmonologist tended to Harold and eventually concluded that he had indeed suffered a number of full respiratory failures even if for only seconds at a time. After a phone call to a pediatric pulmonologist physician in Atlanta, the doctors decided upon an oral dose of corticosteroids.

Once Harold was under an oxygen tent and stable, Gordon held his son's hand and cried while Harold lay motionless from sedatives. He continued to pray to God for nearly an hour before driving back to Grainger County, leaving Annie to care for their son in the hospital. As he drove on Highway 11 W, all he could think about was the shovel and flashlight that were in his shed behind his house. Gordon Tyrell was about to dig a few holes on ol' man Campbell's farm.

Irving had been on the phone all evening and began hiring hands for forty-five dollars a week. By the time seven o'clock in the evening had rolled around, he had a crew of eight ready to help till forty acres.

In the kitchen at the main house, Millie was standing at the sink with a large milk can on the counter. It was on its side with Millie scrubbing the interior of the can making a loud reverberating swishing sound. Captain was standing next to her giving her unnecessary instructions.

"Oh, stop it now. I don't need you telling me how to scrub the inside of the can," said Millie.

"You ain't got enough soap."

"I got more soap than I need. Quit tellin' me what to do." Millie's arm was only so long and couldn't reach the bottom of the metal can. She removed her hand and took a step back. "Get your arm to the back of the can and scrub it good. My arm won't reach," she said as she handed Captain her wet rag.

"I got it darlin'—just let me get some more soap in here."

"It don't need more soap! You crazier than a rabid dog."

By eight thirty, three milk cans had been cleaned, filled with water and sealed using the milk cap. Even though the sun had set long ago, their old, tired bodies kept pushing forward, and continued the food preparation. Captain had chopped up a pound of cooked corn while Millie had combined eggs, flour, butter and cornmeal into a large bowl. After a good five minutes of mixing the ingredients, Captain stood over Millie and looked down into the bowl.

"That good, now! Ain't no more mixing needed."

"Why don't you go out in the yard? I can't hear you out there."

"I can yell like the dickens! You'll hear me alright."

Captain set out five mason jars on the counter and held each one while Millie poured the mixture into each jar. Elizabeth walked in the kitchen and saw the milk jugs, the mason jars, and Millie and Captain fighting.

"You pouring it too fast."

"How it make any difference? Fast. Slow. It gets in the jar anyhow."

"Do y'all need any help?"

"Nah, we got it."

"What is all this for?"

"You all tillin' the fields tomorrow and you gonna need water and lunch," Millie explained. While Elizabeth stood in the kitchen with a confused look on her face, Claire walked past her carrying a tray with three bowls of food she prepared for Scout, Pepper, and Blue outside and set them on the porch.

"Come on, doggies! Dinner time! Come and get it!" She expected to hear their paws thumping on the dirt as they ran toward her and she would scratch their ears as they lapped up their food. Instead of paws, she heard nothing. Silence. Claire clapped her hands and whistled. "Scout! Come on and eat! Come on, doggies!" A light that wavered in the darkness had intrigued the coonhounds. It was far off in the distance, and their curiosity had gotten the best of them. As they approached, they found a car with the headlights off and a man with a flashlight. The dogs pawed at each other and playfully trotted over to the man who was digging a hole. The division map was laid out on the ground, and one of the dogs stepped on it.

"Aww, come on. Get! Get out of here!" Gordon said with a lowered voice. He had driven onto the farm from the backside to keep anyone from seeing him, still using the borrowed station wagon that he intended to drop off at Ed's house the next morning. With each shovel full of dirt being tossed to the side, the dust would plume up into the air, giving the car a coat of fine dust. The beam from the flashlight became more visible with each shovel full plopping onto the growing pile. The hounds had scampered off into the darkness, but their gnawing and pawing could still be heard nearby.

Chapter 22

Elizabeth had set her alarm clock for 4:45 A.M. but had been awake since a half hour before. She had been restless all night as her mind raced with thoughts of growing 40 acres of tomatoes. She kept thinking about Irving and the thought of him leaving the farm too early. What if he left while the tomatoes were coming in only to have the crop take a turn for the worse? She turned the alarm off before it rang and gently woke up Claire.

"Time to wake up, sweetheart."

Claire dragged herself out of bed and trudged into the bathroom. The sound of men laughing could be heard outside causing Elizabeth to look out the window. She saw nine black men including Runt standing around in the cold air. Most were wearing warm clothing and smoking rolled cigarettes while talking and laughing. They looked relaxed, but ready to take on the day of tilling soil. Once downstairs, she saw Irving and his mother in the kitchen. While he held open a burlap bag, Millie carefully put several mason jars inside. Her hair was in a nightcap and her tattered purple robe was cinched around her waist. Irving looked over at Elizabeth and spoke in a calm, quiet voice.

"I'm ordering eighty-nine dollars' worth of fertilizer and thirty-two dollars for worms. It'll guarantee your crop, but I won't do it unless you can afford it. It's a lot of money."

"Have them send me the bill. I'll pay it," she replied. Irving nodded. Elizabeth wanted to ask about the worms but opted not to.

"Come on outside with me. I will introduce you," he said as he gently hoisted the bag over his shoulder. The glass jars clanked in the bag without breaking. Elizabeth looked down at Claire.

"You listen to what Mr. Washington says, okay?"

"Okay, but Mom?"

"Yes."

"I'm a little cold."

"Get your sweater. Hurry now."

"Do you want yours?"

"I don't think so. I hope to be moving enough to keep me warm. Besides, the sun is shining."

Elizabeth followed Irving outside into the chilled air. She tugged at her tattered shirt for warmth, making the fabric hug her torso. The tractor had already been removed from the barn and a tilling attachment had been hitched on the back. The red truck had been parked close to the house on the back lawn and stocked with bags of fertilizer, sealed milk cans, sack cloth, rakes, hoes, and spades. Instead of tilling soil, it appeared they were going on a journey. Every worker seemed to have his place and looked relaxed, making Elizabeth and Claire seem even more out of place as if being white and female wasn't enough.

"Listen up!" Irving started in. The workers calmed down and gathered near him as he spoke. "We gonna run the tractor through the front forty. Behind the tractor we'll have several scuffles. Behind the scuffles, there'll be a few grub hoes. Runt will start the rotation in and out." Everyone seemed to be on board except Elizabeth and Claire. The lingo meant nothing to them. "Keep in mind we ain't turning the soil over. The tiller here is simply breaking ground and the scuffles are to break up the clods and the grub hoes break up the sections that split off the clods. Got it? Don't turn the soil. I ain't running this tiller deep." Irving said and then pointed to Elizabeth and Claire. "This here is Mrs. Campbell. She owns this farm, and she going to be learning from all of us. So, help her and her daughter when ya can. Just so ya know, she is the reason everyone is starting at forty-five a week." The hoots and hollers came before the clapping. The introduction was now a warm one. Elizabeth waved slightly as she spoke.

"Hi. Don't let us get in your way and don't be afraid to tell us what to do," she said with a smile. Irving yelled out as he began walking toward the tractor.

"We're only working the front forty so let's get goin'."

While everyone was ready to go, the work didn't begin for a full thirty-five minutes as it took time for the tractor and the truck to make their way along the edge of the field. Some men walked, some men rode in the bed of the truck. Some hung onto the tractor as it puttered along. Halfway to the forty, both the truck and tractor stopped. All of the men got out and huddled near a cluster of trees on the edge of the field. To Elizabeth and Claire's amazement, the men began to dig three deep holes under the shade of the tree. Once they were satisfied with their depth, the three cans of water were taken out of the bed of the truck and placed in the holes. Runt unrolled a large piece of sack cloth and used a knife to crudely cut large square pieces. He then took the three squares and laid a piece of cloth on top of each milk can. The men began covering the cans with dirt. Since everyone acted as if this was an everyday thing, Elizabeth didn't ask any questions. Soon enough, the tractor started up, and they were back on their way leaving the truck under the shade of the tree.

Once the tilling began, Irving drove the tractor carefully making sure the tires were in between the rows of dirt. The tiller was lowered and began disrupting the soil. Five men had grabbed long poles with a metal blade on the end in the shape of a diamond. This was what the workers referred to as a scuffle. Once the tiller broke the ground, the men used forceful, downward motions to break up dirt clods brought up out of the ground by the tiller.

Elizabeth and Claire kept their distance and watched as the men with scuffles were followed by four other men carrying grub hoes. Once the clods were broken, the four men next in line split up the chunks from the broken clods with the grub hoes.

"Mom, I think I can do that."

"I bet it is harder than it looks."

After about twenty minutes, Elizabeth and Claire were given an initiation that began with rotating in as they were each handed a scuffle. For the first ten minutes, it was fun hacking the dirt clods. They would slam and chop the clods with a smile, getting used to the motions. Soon into their initiation, their forearms began to burn. Their muscles became sore and ached, but Elizabeth pressed on. Claire rotated out and shook out her arms as if she were shaking water off her hands. As the hours went by, the air became warm and Claire removed her tattered sweater and tied it around their waist.

The morning was rough as the crew worked non-stop and kept their eyes on their shadows. Once their shadows were directly underneath them, they took a break to eat lunch. When the tractor shut off, the workers began heading for the tree line in the distance. It seemed they were headed back toward the buried milk cans. Claire spoke with her mother as the men rolled cigarettes and chatted about days gone by. Elizabeth noticed two of the men had brought their hoes with them and carried them over their shoulders.

Once at the tree line, the hoes were used to uncover the three milk cans and they were brought out from the earth. Two men began to build a fire while Irving brought over the burlap sack and removed the mason jars with the batter Millie and Captain had made the night before.

Elizabeth and Claire sat down in the grass and watched as the milk cans were uncapped. One of the men dipped an empty mason jar inside and came up with a clear glass of water. He began washing both of the grub hoes while tending to a cigarette in his mouth and talking with the other men. He would occasionally stop cleaning the grub hoe to laugh at what another man said, causing Claire to crack a smile even though she didn't understand what was so funny.

Elizabeth's attention was focused on the men who built a fire and reduced it to coals. The man that cleaned the grub hoes relinquished them to Irving who put them in the flames of the fire. Claire picked at the grass under her coiled legs as her mother poked her side.

"Look at what they are doing," she said as she looked on as Irving unscrewed the top of a mason jar and poured batter on the hot, flat surface of the grub hoe. The batter sizzled around the edges for half a minute. Elizabeth watched as Irving made a quick motion and flipped the hot cake over. After another thirty-seconds of cooking, Irving slid the cake off onto the lid of the milk can and began cooking another. Within fifteen minutes, fifteen corn cakes were stacked on the milk can lid.

Once the batter was gone, the men began taking the cakes off the lid and eating. Elizabeth looked up at Irving who motioned a quick snap of his head for her and Claire to join in. They each took a cake off the milk can lid and bit into the soft, circular sponge. The first bite offered an immediate texture of grit from the corn meal. Although cooked on a makeshift griddle, the cake was moist and had a hint of butter and salt in each bite. Irving walked over and bent down as the girls were eating.

"You ever had hoe cakes before?"

"Can't say that I have."

"Me, either," added Claire. "Why are they called hoe cakes?"

"Cause they cooked on the flat surface of a hoe rake. We have another jar of batter and we'll cook 'em up here in a few. Everybody should eat two hoe cakes and drink plenty of water. Just wash the batter out of a mason jar and drink from that," he said as he took a bite. His elbows rested on his knees and he looked out over the fields. He turned his head and looked at Claire as he spoke, "You doing good out there. Keep it up, ya hear?" Irving stood up and walked over to the group of men smoking, eating, and laughing. Claire reveled in the comment. When the lunch break was over they headed back out into the fields and continued their work.

When the sun had set and there was little light left, the tractor stopped, and the men retired to the hand quarters. The day proved to be very taxing on all, except Irving. Riding on the tractor only made him walk like a child with a bruised behind.

Claire took a quick bath and fell asleep on her side of the bed while re-reading her Nancy Drew book with missing pages. After Elizabeth had taken a bath and tried to relax her sore muscles, she put on comfortable clothes and went downstairs for a drink of water. Before she entered the kitchen, she could hear Irving talking to Millie. The tone of Irving's voice sounded as if he was telling her a secret.

"No, Momma. We gonna get our own place. This is just temporary."

"How you gonna do that?"

"There's a furnish merchant in Kingsport who will work with me."

"Kingsport? You certain they'll work with you?"

"I can get by on my name. People know me 'round these parts. They know what I can do."

"Why you wanna do that?"

"I want my own farm. I'm tired of workin' for other people."

"When you gonna do this?"

"This crop will break around the last week of May then we're gone."

"You gonna leave her high and dry? She busted you out of that slave camp," said Millie. "Ain't no son of mine gonna up and leave nobody like that." Elizabeth had shifted her weight while standing as quietly as possible. The ball of her foot applied pressure on the floor beneath her and caused a pop. Elizabeth shut her eyes tight and clenched her teeth. Irving turned his head, but Elizabeth was out of view. He cautiously spoke at a much lower pitch.

"I ain't leavin' her high and dry. She'll be fine once the crop breaks ground. Besides, I got plans for my seeds. I need my own place." Elizabeth quietly crept up the stairs, opting to drink from the tap in the bathroom.

The next morning, she awoke with the thought in her head that she should consider finding a farm hand like Irving who would stay on after the crop broke ground. She thought about how much knowledge Irving had and wondered if she could she find someone similar. In mid-thought there was a knock at the front door. Elizabeth went downstairs and found Norman Werthan standing on her porch.

"Can I see you for a moment?" he asked.

Chapter 23

A warm rush of disappointment came over her as she stepped out onto the front porch and closed the door behind her. She felt ashamed and embarrassed that she hadn't listened to Norman.
"I heard a rumor in town, and I wanted to come over to see if it was true."

Elizabeth broke eye contact. Tears started to form in her eyes, and her hand subconsciously went to her mouth.

"I'm so sorry, Mr. Werthan. I am so sorry. I know you told me to not even try, but I had to. I just had to. Please don't be mad." Norman held up his hand to stop her.

"You cry all the time?" he asked as his face scrunched together. "Let me ask you, do you know Irving Washington?"

"I do," she replied as she wiped her runny nose and swept the tears off her cheeks.

"Is he here?" he asked as Elizabeth looked him in his eyes.

"He's in the kitchen. Why?" she asked.

"How in the world do you know Irving Washington?"

"Well," she started to say as she wiped her nose with her sleeve. "I didn't know him until a few days ago. A farm hand that lives in the hand quarters told me about him."

"And you got him to come here?"

"I did," Elizabeth replied. Norman put his right hand on his hip and his other hand scratched his forehead. He exhaled a shallow breath and then looked at Elizabeth.

"Could I meet him? Could you bring him out here?"

"I can. Why?"

"I would just like to meet him."

"You want to come in?"

"Nah. I don't want to step in this house if I can help it."

"Ok. Just give me a second," she said, now regaining her dignity.

Norman waited on the front porch with the front door cracked for a moment before Elizabeth reopened the door. A tall black man of 48 years stood behind her. Elizabeth made the introduction.

"Mr. Werthan, this is Irving Washington. Mr. Washington, this is Norman Werthan."

"Hello," Norman said as he reached out his hand. Irving shook it cautiously.

"Sir, do I know you?" Irving asked hoping that this man wasn't affiliated with the Sugar Creek Prison Farm.

"No. Can't say I have ever met ya. I have heard about you for a decade now. Just wanted to come by and say hello."

"You farm tomatoes?"

"Heirloom, Big Rainbow. Some seasons I'll do Hillstacker, Sunrise Streak or Red Bliss. I used to have a few acres of Northern Lights, but the aphids invaded. They ate those first."

While the two men spoke, Elizabeth watched Norman's eyes and his mannerisms. He acted as if he was slightly nervous. She hadn't seen him smile in the limited time she had known him, but she did get to see him crack a smile while talking to Irving.

"Over the past several years, I have been having a real issue with aphids, hornworms, and caterpillars." Norman explained.

"Aphids, huh? I seem to remember last time I was working in

Grainger County aphids caused a lot of problems."

"Yes, sir. I wasn't able to salvage any Northern Lights."

"I see," Irving said as he crossed his arms and appeared to think of a solution. "Have you seen any praying mantis bugs around? The ones that look evil with the weird eyes?"

"Not lately."

"You know the mantis is a friend to tomatoes. They don't eat plants. They eat bugs."

"They do?"

"Yep. Trick is to hang the eggs on the vine 'bout three feet off the ground. We got lucky one year and found a bunch of mantis eggs in a nearby wooded area and we carried them to the fields. Took several hours, but the time spent was well worth it," he explained. He then held up his right hand and made gestures as he spoke. "The eggs look like a delicate shell, kinda like a cicada shell. Once they hatched, a lot flew away, but enough remained behind that they ate most of the plant eaters."

"You hang them on the vines?"

"Yes sir."

"When do you do this?"

"First flowering stage."

"It works?"

"It seemed to," Irving replied.

"I have heard of farmers buying live ladybugs. Never a praying mantis though."

"If there was a way to buy mantis eggs, that would be something to look into. Bet you get your Northern Lights!"

"That's a good idea. I'll look in the annual catalogue down at the co-op. If it's cheaper than pest killer, I might give it a go."

"Yeah, pest killer is expensive. Be interesting to see how much a case of mantis eggs runs, that is if they sell them at all."

"If I find out, I'll come back with some news," Norman said

as he reached out his hand and shook Irving's. "It was nice meeting you."

Irving smiled and nodded his head as he spoke.

"Nice meetin' you as well." Walking back in the house, he left Elizabeth and Norman alone on the front porch. Norman slowly turned to go to his truck and she walked next to him.

"So, you're not mad?"

"Naw, I'm not mad. I am in awe."

"In awe?" she asked. Norman stopped and looked at her.

"Where'd you find him?"

"In prison," said Elizabeth. Norman stopped in his tracks.

"In prison?"

Norman made her tell him the whole story, not leaving anything out. When she was done, he looked her in the eye and nodded his head as he spoke.

"I can tell you that if you want to keep this farm, you sure found the best way to do it."

"Really?"

"He's known around here. Knows more than most about tomatoes."

"So, I've heard."

"I don't think you have to worry about not getting the farm," Norman said. The tears in Elizabeth's eyes began to show again. "This is ridiculous. Every time I am around you, you cry."

"I'm sorry. I just want this more than anything," she replied. Norman walked over to his truck and opened the door.

"Evidently. You got the best farm hand working for you. I wouldn't worry about a thing."

The morning had started off in the best way possible with

Norman confirming Irving's ability and knowledge. The fact that he had certainty in his voice as he told her *"I don't think you have to worry about not getting the farm"* made the soreness and aching in her muscles all but disappear.

Elizabeth and Claire were ready for day two on the farm. They walked near the field behind the main house and saw Irving out among the rows of dirt by himself. He was standing about an acre away and was bending down, running his fingers through the dirt.

"What's he doing?" Claire whispered.

"I don't know." They watched as he picked up a handful of dirt and let it fall between his hands. The workers were nowhere to be found. The air was cool and the silence was almost deafening. Then the sound of a truck could be heard in the distance. The sound grew louder and louder until two trucks came into view. Following the farm truck was a flatbed delivery truck with eighty-nine dollars' worth of fertilizer on the back. As the truck approached the field, Elizabeth could see that a worker was driving. She didn't remember his name, and he appeared to be having a good time behind the wheel with a cigarette dangling from his mouth.

"They took the truck?" Claire asked.

"I guess so," Elizabeth replied.

"Should they have done that?"

"I don't know. Who are we to say at this point?"

The workers had returned although there seemed to be a few more. They rolled cigarettes and told jokes in one big group. The laughter and carrying on receded as Irving made his way into the middle of the crowd.

"Listen up! Today we loosen the dirt the tractor tires compacted yesterday. I'll be doing a lot of that. The truck will be close by on the edge of the field. We also have buckets of earthworms and bags of fertilizer to tend to. I will instruct you on how to spread them in the field, so don't go thinkin' you do it how other farmers taught you before. I need four by four scuffles and grubs with worm and fert spreaders and two rotators. Runt and Harris, ya'll go bury the water cans. My ma and pa are cookin' green beans and potatoes for lunch. We're doing 40 acres without a tractor today so we got to move! Let's get to work," Irving walked over to Elizabeth and Claire. "Need you to both scuffle and grub until you rotate out. Then watch the fertilizer and worm spreaders. They will show you how to do both," he said before bending down and looking at Claire in the eye. "You gonna be handling red wigglers today. Tons of them. Don't think they are gross," he said with the tone of an educator. His eyes narrowed and his expression was sincere as he spoke. "They help the soil. We need them. Don't make 'em feel bad by thinking they are gross and slimy. Watch the others. When they rotate out of spreading worms they wash their hands in the dirt."

"Wash in the dirt?" Claire asked as she smiled.

"You'll see," he said as he stood up and patted her on the shoulder before turning his attention to Elizabeth. He spoke softly as he gazed out over the field.

"This is overkill, but this is a fool proof method. Worms and fertilizer is the best way. That's why we're doing this and we'll put this in the rotation book. For now just go along and know that the added expense and time all but guarantee that the forty come in."

The day for Elizabeth and Claire began with using their already sore neck, arms, shoulders, and back muscles to chop and break up the clods of dirt that came up from the compacted soil. Their eyes would shoot over to those spreading fertilizer and worms every few paces in a conservative manner. When the worm spreaders would rotate out, Claire watched as they avoided stepping on any red wigglers. The workers would bend down and rub the palm of their hands in the dirt as puffs of dust scattered in the air. The workers appeared to make similar motions with the dirt as if they were washing their hands in water.

The group moved slower than the tractor moved the day before and the rotating in and out gave them ample time to take a break and rotate back in. Elizabeth would look up and see Irving who was on the tractor the day before, now on his feet and sweating profusely as he worked harder and faster than the others. When it finally came time to spread fertilizer, Claire worked beside her mother and eyed the worm spreaders the entire time.

The farm hands would reach in the bucket and spread a handful of worms every fifteen seconds or so. Remembering what Irving had said, *Don't think they are gross. They help the soil. We need them.* Claire tried her best to think of the worms differently. When it came time to take over the worm bucket, she willingly reached in and grabbed a handful of squirmy, slimy, squishy red earthworms. Without making a face, and thinking that Nancy Drew would do this with fervor, Claire cracked a smile as she spread the worms on the ground. Without her knowing it, Irving had turned his head slightly and watched as she did her job. He nodded his head in approval and went back to breaking up clods of dirt.

Later that evening when the sun disappeared over the horizon, a truck with the headlights turned off, crept onto the backside of the Campbell farm. Using the last moment of twilight, the truck stopped at a corner of the field. Gordon had picked up his truck from Neary's Garage just off Main Street. Unable to foot the bill for a brand-new tire, he asked Roy Neary to repair the tire with tar and a temporary rubber patch.

He got out of the driver's side and removed his flashlight and shovel from the back. Using the flashlight, he looked over the division map on the ground finding where he was. The previous corner proved to be unfruitful. Thinking he was on the right track, he plunged the shovel into the dirt in a new corner.

Chapter 24

Norman Werthan had put in a full day's work with his farm hands out in the field. They sowed Sunrise Streak tomatoes in one field and carrots in another. When the sun went down, he put the tools in the barn and sent the farm hands to their quarters. Norman took a much-needed shower and shuffled into the kitchen with the intention of making a sandwich until he heard a knock at the front door. Upon answering it, he found Elizabeth standing on his porch.

"Good evening, Norman."

"Hello, young lady."

"Are you busy?" she asked. Norman didn't like visitors, but if he were to be forced to do so, a petite, strawberry blonde was considered acceptable.

"I suppose not. Come on in."

When she entered, she found a desolate living room in need of dusting and sweeping. Ignoring it, she turned her attention to Norman.

"Am I interrupting anything?" she asked as he closed the door.

"No. I was just about to make myself a sandwich."

"Oh. Could I sit with you in the kitchen then?" she asked with a smile. His eyes squinted while he thought it through.

"Ok, but I have a rule."

"Alright. What is it?"

"No crying."

"No crying. Got it," she replied with a grin. He headed toward the kitchen with Elizabeth following closely behind. She took a seat at a small table by a window. Norman opened his refrigerator and removed items for making a sandwich as he spoke.

"I've been thinking about Irving working at your farm."

"You have?"

"A lot of farmers around here don't share their secrets, and they never offer any tips or advice to one another."

"Really?"

"It's also hard to find good help these days," he added as he spread mustard onto a slice of bread with a knife. "I'd appreciate it if you wouldn't let Irving go without asking me first. I'd like to offer him a job."

"He knows that much, huh?" she asked. Norman got quiet as he continued assembling his sandwich. Elizabeth could feel the awkward silence getting thicker. Her mind drifted to previous conversations with him and recalled that he seemed to ignore the normal pattern of conversation and conversed to the beat of his own drum. As abrupt as the conversation stalled, it picked up again.

"Years ago there was a farmer here in Grainger County outside of Rutledge. He had suffered in the drought that year."

"There was a drought?"

"Yep. He couldn't afford to pay the water truck to come by. Anyway, a drought can take a year or more to recover from and even then you usually do not get an acceptable yield."

"I didn't realize a drought was that bad," she admitted. Norman stopped in his tracks and looked at her.

"Always have money ready for a water truck. That's the best tip I can give ya," he replied as he placed a thick slice of ham on a piece of bread. "So, this farmer hires ol' Irving on the premise that he could help. Irving tilled that man's land and sowed him right into going broke," Norman looked up while holding a silver-plated knife and pointed at Elizabeth, "I mean, not one red cent was left in this man's account," he explained as he went back to fixing his sandwich.

"That's awful!"

"So, a couple weeks pass and the crop broke ground and everyone told him how lucky he was. Then when the harvest came, it was one of the highest yields we had ever seen."

"Wow!"

"Saved that farmer's life. If you catch him in a diner, he will tell stories of Irving. Tell you how the man took soil from one field and mixed it with another. Doing strange things like digging channels and if you'll recall from our conversation earlier, he would hang praying mantis eggs on tomato vines."

"Is that what that was about?"

"I had heard about it, but I thought it was a story. Turns out that was real. So, let me ask you, what is Irving sowing?"

"Not sure, but we've been tilling, spreading fertilizer and worms."

"Worms and fertilizer? That's costly."

"He says it will ensure a crop and right now that's all I need."

"He would know. Sounds like overkill though."

"Funny. That's exactly the word he used. Overkill."

After pouring two glasses of tea from a glass pitcher, Norman sat at the small table with his sandwich. Elizabeth grabbed her glass, took a sip, and sat back in the chair.

"So, you live all by yourself, Norman?"

"I do," he grabbed his sandwich off his plate and held it with both hands as he spoke. "My wife passed about four years ago. My daughter and son-in-law live over in Jackson, so it's just me. She married a guy with the last name Higginbottom. She went from Penelope Werthan to Penelope Higginbottom. Rather unfortunate if you ask me." He took a bite and set the sandwich down.

"Do you get lonely?" she asked. He nodded his head slightly as he reached for his glass of tea. After he swallowed, he answered as he continued to chew.

"From time to time, but it ain't so bad."

"Does your daughter come over and see you?"

"She has kids so it's hard to travel when you live six hours away."

"You have grandkids?"

"I do."

"You get to see them any?"

"Not really. A few years ago they all came here around Christmas. They were babies then."

"You should go there for a visit."

"I did once. This was while she was pregnant with her first child. I felt like I was intruding. They were busy since they both work."

"She works too?"

"She's a nurse."

"Oh. That's very admirable."

"She is very smart. I'd like to see them more, but I'm busy here, too."

"I see," she replied as he took another bite. Feeling a break in the conversation, she started it back up to avoid another uncomfortable silence. "Norman, I need some business advice. I have a lot of questions actually, but I am wondering if you might be someone who would know such things and be willing to help me with some advice." Norman moved the food he was chewing to one side of his mouth as he answered.

"Oh, well. Have you come to the wrong place!" he said with a smile. "And I'm not kidding. We farmers know how to make money by growing the best tomatoes, and we know how to get paid, but that's about it. We are more savers than anything."

"I see."

"If you need money help, try talking to that treasury fella. Mr. Humes said his name, but I can't quite remember."

"Mr. Collins?"

"That's it. Did you go visit him yet?"

"No. Not yet."

"He's the guy to go to, and if he can't answer your questions, he would know who could."

"Alright. Well, thanks for your honesty."

"Of course."

"Norman, would you mind if I came back here for a visit?"

"No. Not at all. But why do you want to? I don't want any pity with you thinking I'm lonely and need someone to…"

"I need a friend," she said quickly, cutting him off. "I like you, and you're nice, and so far, outside of my husband, no one has ever been so good to me."

Norman took a moment to soak up her compliment.

"Do you remember me telling you that you remind me of my daughter?" he asked.

"I remember you saying that."

"Well it's true. My apologies for sounding rude a minute ago. I suppose I would like it if you stopped by once in a while. That would be nice." Elizabeth then pantomimed the motions of wiping a tear from her eye as she acted like she was beginning to cry. "Now you stop that!" Norman said as he pointed his finger and raised his voice. Elizabeth started to giggle. When it dawned on Norman that she was joking, he smiled. "Ha. Ha. You're so funny," he said as he took another bite.

Chapter 25

Warm air had come up during the night from the gulf continuing the unusually warm weather the *Farmer's Almanac* had predicted. Just as the sun had started to rise, Elizabeth put on a skirt and a blouse that was missing a button at the very bottom. She arrived at the hand quarters just as Irving had finished shaving his face. After knocking on the door and asking one of the farm hands to see Irving, he eventually appeared with bits of shaving cream on his face and a towel over his shoulder.

"Yes, Missus Campbell?"

"I have to go into town to see a man about some bills."

"Okay."

"I don't want you to think that I am skipping out from working."

"I don't think that," Irving said as he used the towel to clean off his face.

"Okay. I just wanted you to know. I will be back shortly," Elizabeth said as she turned around. Irving took a few steps toward her as she walked away, making sure the door closed behind him. "You know you don't have to tell me anything." As he spoke, he lowered his voice. Elizabeth turned around and faced him. "You could just not show up. I would just assume you had something else to do."

"I know, but you mentioned that a woman has no place on a farm. I don't want you to think I couldn't take it and quit."

"I see. Well, I wouldn't think that."

"I also don't want you upset with me."

"How's that?"

"I don't want you to leave. I am grateful for you being here."

"Now, hang on," Irving said as he took another step closer and looked into her eyes. "I don't think you realize that I am grateful for you. I guess that's my fault for not showing you my gratitude. You got me out of that place. You gave me a new life. I ain't leavin'. I ain't goin' no where until you got a full crop comin' in you hear? You don't need to tell me anything. I am not your boss. You treatin' me like I am your boss comin' out here and saying you have somewhere to be. Don't be doin' that. You and I have an arrangement, and I will not leave before fulfilling my end."

"Okay."

"Alright? You got it? You are my boss. You tell me what to do, and I listen."

"I know. I understand."

"Uh huh."

"If you leave while the crop is still comin' in and then there is a problem, what do I do then?"

"I will give you a way to reach me. I'm gonna try to get my own place up in Kingsport. If you need me, I will come down and believe me, I will come down. You got me out of prison and whatever you need for years to come, I will try to help you in any way I can."

The conversation drifted to Irving getting his own farm which involved utilizing a furnish merchant. He explained he was looking to buy twelve acres and growing his tomatoes his way.

Long after they ended their conversation, Elizabeth thought about Irving on the way back to the main house. When she first met him, he seemed harsh and unreasonably upset. Now he seemed different. While he was still harsh and very direct, his voice contained a subtle tone of compassion and kindness she hadn't yet experienced with him.

Once back at the main house, Elizabeth found Millie and Captain cooking in the kitchen, getting food ready for lunch.

"Stop cuttin' them scallions so thick."

"I ain't cuttin'em thick. Mind your own business."

Instead of getting in the middle of it, Elizabeth smiled to herself and ran up the steps to her room. Claire was up and getting ready.

"You remember me telling you that I had to go into town today?"

"Yeah."

"You can sleep in."

"I thought I would help in the fields."

"You want to work in the fields?"

"I don't mind it. Gives me something to do until the Nancy Drew books arrive."

"You like Irving?"

"Yeah. He really knows what he's doing. He takes charge and orders everyone around and no one questions him."

"That's for sure," Elizabeth replied as she put her hair up in a ponytail. "I'll be back soon, okay?"

"Okay. See ya when you get back."

After stepping off the front porch, Elizabeth saw a man in a dirty truck pull up in the driveway. She stopped and watched as the man squeezed himself out of the cab with a grunt and walked toward her. He was plump and wore a straw hat that was as tattered as his overalls.

"Miss? Do you know where I might find Irving Washington?"

"I do. He's out in the fields."

"Thank you." The man said as he started toward the back of the house.

"Excuse me, may I ask what this is about?"

"Oh, sorry, Ma'am. I'm Willy Shaw. My back forty crop has first signs of blight," he replied as he removed his hat in a gentlemanly manner. At first, she hadn't noticed he was upset and jittery, but during his explanation she could easily see his anxiety. "I am looking for advice, and someone tol' me that Irving was back in town. I thought I would look him up. I need some help in a bad way."

"I see. Sorry to hear about your crop."

"Yes, Ma'am," he responded before putting his hat back on and headed toward the fields. She watched him as he walked away, reveling in the fact that farmers were seeking advice from Irving. The thought of owning the farm and feeling like it was a certainty caused a warm sensation in her stomach. The sensation crawled up her spine and tingled the skin behind her ears. While excitement surged through her body, she made her way to the truck and sat in the driver's seat, recalling what Norman had said. "You got the best tomato farmer working for you. Don't worry about a thing."

Once on the square, she parked near the courthouse and applied the parking brake. A quick glance in the side mirror made sure that she looked half decent. Seeing her reflection, she noticed more freckles on her nose and cheeks. After walking inside the city offices, she found a receptionist.

"Hi. I'm looking for Mr. Collins's office." The directions she was given led her down a dark hallway to a door that read *City Treasurer*. After opening the door, she saw two large windows with a big desk in front of them. Mr. Collins, 52, was sitting at his desk holding a mason jar that contained scrambled eggs and his fork clanged around the inside of the jar. Just as Elizabeth entered, she saw him pierce a few chunks of scrambled eggs. He had just taken a bite when he looked up and saw a young woman in a floral print dress and strawberry blonde hair. Mr. Collins stood up. Elizabeth took notice of his crooked tie and old button up shirt. He seemed nervous, and his eyeglasses magnified his anxiety.

"Mr. Collins?"

"Yes, Ma'am," he replied as he chewed.

"I'm Elizabeth Campbell. I am supposed to see you concerning the estate of Mr. Thaddeus Campbell."

"Oh, yes," he said as he set down his mason jar breakfast on his desk. "For a second I thought you had the wrong office."

"Oh? Why is that?"

"They are interviewing for an assistant clerk down the hall. Thought you might be lost."

"Oh, I see," she said as she closed the door behind her.

"Please have a seat. I have already received a few bills from the co-op," he said as he reached for a small stack of papers on his desk, "and I got one from Wade and Son's Seed Company and... some kind of worm farm," he continued as he looked at the invoices through his thick glasses.

"Yes. I was told to have them sent here. Is that correct?"

"Oh sure. You bet. I can take care of all of these. Is that why you're here?"

"Sort of. I also have a fertilizer bill that was mailed to the house," she said as she placed it on his desk. He smiled and nodded as he took the bill and laid it on top of a stack. Having a difficult time making eye contact with her, he attempted to straighten his tie.

"I'll take care of all of these. Strange thing about this account though."

"How's that?"

"Well, mostly I appropriate funds from a bank account. Upon Mr. Campbell's death, I received hundreds of dollars in cash. Apparently, Mr. Campbell was terrified of another depression."

"Rightfully so. Very understandable."

"No problem, though. I will pay all of these bills for you. Glad to do it."

"Thank you, Mr. Collins."

"Everything going okay at the farm?" he asked before forcing himself to make eye contact.

"It is. Have you heard of Irving Washington?"

"I have not."

"Oh. Well, he is the farm hand helping me with sowing the tomato seeds."

"Speaking of farm hands, I am able to help you with your payroll. Just send them here, and I will have their check ready. How much are you paying?"

"Forty-five a week per hand."

"Ok, let me make a note here," he said as he wrote down a note to himself on a scrap piece of paper. "You can always call if you have one not work a day or two out of the week, and I will prorate it."

"Well, I must say I haven't ever had to manage payroll, so your help in the matter would be very much appreciated."

She spoke with Mr. Collins at length and found him to be sweet and very kind. After some time, he appeared to be more comfortable and had made certain that she understood that he could help her with all of her financial matters. Then Elizabeth asked the question that ultimately brought her to his office.

"Mr. Collins, I have some questions about business and handling operations and personnel. Would you be someone who could help me in these matters?"

"Oh, I don't think so," he smiled and shook his head. "I can help with financial matters, but that is about it."

"I see. Well, is there anyone around here I could ask?"

"You can, but if you're looking for real business advice I wouldn't ask around Rutledge. Don't get me wrong. They're great folks, but they aren't too business savvy—well except for one guy."

"Who's that?"

"Your uncle."

"Mr. Campbell?" she replied. Mr. Collins nodded his head as he closed his eyes.

"He had a knack for it, that's for sure. But even then, if he were still alive, I would tell you to steer clear. Not the nicest man, your husband's uncle." Mr. Collins explained until he realized he may have just insulted her. "Oh, sorry! I didn't mean…"

"No, no. That's okay. I've heard stories."

After a moment of awkward silence, she could tell he was thinking of something. As if a lamp was turned on in a dark room, he looked back at her.

"I seem to remember seeing a story in the newspaper. An article about four fellas in Knoxville," he said as he leaned to one side and hollered toward an open doorway near his desk. "Debbie? Could you come here a moment?" The sound of footsteps could be heard growing louder with each step. A petite woman much too young to have a chain connected to her glasses leaned inside the office door while holding onto the painted doorframe.

"Yes?"

"Could you bring me the stack of newspapers we read through?"

"We certainly have a stack. It's pretty big. Do you want all of them?"

"Yeah but get Mrs. Stovall and bring the papers in here. We'll all look through them really quick."

After Debbie left the room, Mr. Collins explained that if she needed business advice, one of the men in the article would be worth tracking down. When Debbie returned, she brought Mrs. Stovall with her. Mrs. Stovall wore her hair in a beehive configuration and the wrinkles around her lips advertised her 20-year smoking habit. She and Debbie entered the office with an arm full of *Knoxville News-Sentinel* newspapers, they set them down on the desk and looked at Mr. Collins.

"Either of you remember the article about the guys in Knoxville? They ate breakfast at the same coffee shop?" he asked. Neither appeared to have remembered it. "There were four guys, but I think one was a real estate guy, the other was a funeral home director or something?"

"Oh! Yes," said Mrs. Stovall.

"That's what we're looking for," Mr. Collins explained.

"I don't remember reading it," Debbie replied.

"It would have been last week, or maybe even the week before," Mr. Collins added as he began to rifle through the stack of newspapers. Debbie jumped in and took a small stack in her arms and began flipping pages. Elizabeth watched as Mr. Collins and the two secretaries flipped and turned pages looking for the article. Feeling like she should help, she took a few papers and began her own search.

"Was it a front-page story?" Elizabeth asked. Mrs. Stovall quickly replied.

"No. It was inside somewhere. Maybe it was in the Around Town section." The search continued while Elizabeth felt a hint of guilt as her question prompted a frenzy of rifling through pages of old newspapers and taking up their time.

"Oh! It was the Sunday paper!" snapped Mrs. Stovall. Elizabeth took notice of her nicotine stained fingers. "I know it was. It had a photo on the front page of a car that hit a fire hy-

drant." Her recollection redirected their efforts. Debbie slid a
newspaper out from a stack and found the photo.

"Fire hydrant! Got it!" she hollered as she handed it to Mr.
Collins. Using his thick glasses to glance over the pages, he
quickly found the Around Town section and then the article.

"This is it! Right here!" he said as he then folded it back up
and handed it to Elizabeth. "That's all yours. Could be a good re-
source for you."

"Oh! Thank you! I really do appreciate all of you helping me.
I do have a few more questions about the payroll. Do you have
another minute?"

"Of course."

She asked questions about paying the farm hands which Mr.
Collins explained in detail. She borrowed a scrap piece of paper
and pencil and took notes. Before leaving the office, she thanked
Mr. Collins and his two assistants and hurried home with the
newspaper in hand. After setting it on the bed, she quickly
jumped out of her nicest clothes and threw on her worst.

Her feet pounded the dirt as she ran through the field, her
tattered skirt flapped in the wind as she hurried out to the cluster
of workers, and she quickly rotated into the fray. Plunging her
hands into the fertilizer, she began spreading the nutrients, while
keeping an eye on her daughter who was focused on mixing the
fert with a scuffle. While sliding into the rhythm, Elizabeth's
mind drifted to the Sunday paper that had a photo of a car that
had hit a fire hydrant. She mostly wondered *what could be in that
article that made Mr. Collins remember it?*

Just before the sun had set, Gordon Tyrell drove out onto the
backside of the field. He parked his truck near another corner,

and he started to dig. Harold was still in the hospital, and money was becoming scarce. With each shovel full of dirt, he became angrier and full of hate for the situation his son was in. Gordon's blood pressure was increasing, and his heart was pounding. He plunged the shovel into the ground as hard as he could, trying to hurry up the hunt. *There has to be money buried here somewhere,* he thought. *I need it. My son needs the money.*

Twenty minutes later, the head of the shovel hit something that sounded like glass. It was a high-pitched sound. He grabbed his flashlight and knelt by the hole. Digging with his hands he uncovered smooth glass. After freeing the glass from the soil, he saw that it was a mason jar. The outside was dirty, and he couldn't tell what was inside. Unable to turn the lid, he raised the mason jar up above his head and then smashed it against the head of his steel shovel. The glass broke and rolls of ten-dollar bills spilled out onto the dirt.

Chapter 26

Gordon set aside the broken jar and stuffed the cash in his hip pocket as sweat dripped off his brow. He grabbed the shovel and dug another six inches before hitting another glass jar. This time the jar was packed with twenty-dollar bills. Stuffing the cash in his pockets, he dug until he found another jar. Now finding a fat roll of five-dollar bills, he continued to dig deeper and wider to no avail. The hole eventually became so wide and deep, he surrendered thinking that old man Campbell had only buried three jars in that corner.

Gordon sat next to the flashlight with his back up against the front of the truck. *I was right. There is money buried on this farm. I was right about the corners.* With the myth now confirmed a reality, Gordon jumped up and ran to the cab of his truck and turned off the headlights. He shut off his flashlight and looked around in the moonlight. Now paranoid someone would catch on, he began filling the dirt into the hole using his hands. He coughed from the dust and reached into his back pocket and shoved part of a red bandana into his mouth. On his knees, he made wide sweeping motions with his arms to gather the dirt. A shard of glass punctured his hand and blood began to flow and soaked the dirt. He spat the bandana out of his mouth.

"Ow! Dang it!" he recoiled his hand to his stomach and bent

over. The blood soaked into his shirt and felt warm on his skin. He turned on the flashlight and looked at his hand. "Oh no!" Gordon wrapped the bandana around his hand and jumped into the truck. "No! No!" He started the truck and sped off headed for Dr. Talbot's house.

After a hot bath, Elizabeth brushed her teeth before climbing into bed. Claire was reading a Nancy Drew book and trying not to fall asleep.

"You okay, Claire?"

"Yeah, just tired. My shoulders are sore."

"Mine too. I'll turn this light out in a few minutes," she said while unfolding the newspaper.

"Okay."

After finding the *Around Town* section, she flipped the pages and found a headline.

FOUR FOR BREAKFAST– A STUDY IN BUSINESS.

BY MIKE MCARA

At a time when a business in Knoxville seemingly opens only to close six months later, four men with four different businesses have persevered through a recession and a world war. Some years ago, Larry Keaton and Chuck Gates formed a morning breakfast meeting at Tate's Coffee Shop with two other notable business owners.

Elizabeth continued to read the article about the two men who also invited a local attorney named Burt Owens and a real estate investor named Greg Carter to join their breakfast. Describing how their relationships affected their businesses, the article continued:

When a resident of Knoxville passes away, Keaton informs Carter, the local real estate investor. Mr. Carter then attempts to either list the property of the deceased or purchase the deed. Upon a successful trans-action to another party, Mr. Carter then refers insurance matters to Chuck Gates. Then comes Burt Owens. All three men refer legal matters to Mr. Owens while Mr. Owens refers all insurance, funeral and real estate matters to the other three.

Elizabeth looked at the black-and-white photo of the men sitting in a booth at a coffee shop. They looked professional, yet relaxed. One man in the photo was holding a cup of coffee and about to take a drink. She folded up the newspaper and set it on the nightstand before turning out the light. As she slid down and pulled the soft covers over her sore and aching body, she thanked Norman Werthan for getting her and Claire out of the Harris Clay Mining Camp. While she drifted off to sleep, she wondered how long it would take to drive to Tate's Coffee shop.

With his son and wife in Knoxville at the hospital, Gordon came home to an empty house. His hand had been stitched and bandaged up by Dr. Talbot after he made up a story about cutting it at the mill on a bag cutter.

Bringing in the rolled-up money, he set the bills on the table and began counting. Unrolling the bills and trying to lay them flat proved to be a problem. Gordon grabbed a few glass vases and set them on the stacks to keep the money from rolling up.

Once the money was laid out, he began counting. The stack of five-dollar bills added up to $125 and the stack of twenties added up to $400. After counting a few stacks of fives, tens and twenties, he added up the take and found he had dug up $670.

A far cry from twenty thousand dollars, but he had more corners to dig up. His mind raced to think of the other sections of the farm while he grabbed his division map. With a marker, he made a large X to mark the spot.

Gordon began circling every corner of every field on the farm, ending up with sixteen more possible locations.

Chapter 27

The next morning, Gordon jumped in his truck and headed toward the highway to Knoxville. On the seat next to him was the envelope that contained the information on the breathing machine for Harold. After arriving at Knoxville General, he grabbed the envelope and hurried to his son's room where he found his son under the oxygen tent and Annie by his side. For more than an hour, he spoke quietly with his wife while he held his son's hand as he slept.

Dr. Patterson was sitting in his office looking over a patient's chart and eating a sandwich with lettuce and tomato. He was a bulky man with thick cheeks that caused his speech to rumble and roll like a dog with a chew toy. When he heard the rap of a knuckle on his wooden door, his head spun toward the knock and his thick cheeks shook from the sudden movement. At the door was a thin man holding a manila envelope.

"Yes, sir?" he said to Gordon who quickly introduced himself and took a seat in front of his desk. Removing the information packet from the manila envelope, he slid the papers toward Dr. Patterson.

"My son is the one who came in with the severe asthma attack. This is a breathing machine that is built by a medical company in Chicago."

"Okay."

"I want to purchase this to help my son."

Dr. Patterson held the packet in his hands. He flipped through the pages, not really reading them until he came to the last page.

"It says here this machine is twenty-thousand dollars."

"Correct."

"You have that much?"

"Not yet, but that brings me to why I am here," said Gordon. Dr. Patterson returned his attention to the packet and raised his hand to keep Gordon from speaking as he read further. Once he finished a paragraph, he set the packet down and removed his glasses.

"Mr. Tyrell, we see devices like this often. They promise results with high price tags."

"What do you mean? The machine won't even work?"

"No, no. I didn't say that. I just mean don't pin your hopes on a medical device. I see how this machine could work, sure," he nodded as he put his glasses back on and looked over the packet as if he were inspecting fruit at a supermarket.

"I wanted to ask if there is anyway this hospital could help me with the cost?"

"I don't know. May I keep this?"

"I'd like it back."

"Of course. Tell you what, I will look this over, make a few phone calls and verify this machine's function. Hopefully a study was completed on this. Who knows."

"Okay."

"If I think this will help, at the very least I could give you my opinion, but as far as splitting the cost...that I would have to leave up to the administrator. Understand?"

"I do."

"Okay, thanks for stopping by, and I will try to call you in a few days. Do I have your phone number?"

"You do. On the forms for Harold Tyrell."

"Good. I'll call you when I find something out," he said as he wrote Harold's name on the envelope.

Gordon thanked him profusely and promptly left his office. Tears filled his eyes as he thought about getting closer to buying the machine. While it wasn't a certainty, there was hope.

Chapter 28

On a Thursday morning, Elizabeth hopped into the truck and navigated south toward Knoxville. She passed by a tractor and three cars before the sun crested the horizon. After an hour on the road utilizing the worn and faded map in the glove compartment, Elizabeth found herself in front of Tate's Coffee Shop. It was a small brick structure with a bright blue awning over the front door. When she walked inside, she scanned the coffee shop and saw three older men sitting at a booth with steaming cups of coffee in front of them.

Walking toward their booth, she was forced to gather courage from unknown places. As she took the necessary steps toward them, one-by-one they noticed her approaching.

"Hello. Sorry to bother you. My name is Elizabeth Campbell, and I read about you gentlemen in the paper."

"You did, huh?" smiled one man wearing a white shirt and a thin black tie. His hair was shaped with an electric trimmer into a flat top hairstyle.

"We're pretty famous 'round here since that article came out," laughed another man with combed hair and a similar shirt, but no tie. His black comb was visibly seated in his shirt pocket.

"I recently inherited a farm from my uncle, and I desperately need business advice. I came here to ask a few questions."

The man with the black comb in his pocket scooted over to the far end to make room.

"Have a seat, little lady," the man said as he patted the red vinyl seat. "I'm Larry," he said with a smile. As she took a seat, she smiled a sigh of relief.

"You're Larry Keaton, and you own Keaton Funeral Home," she said as if she was verifying she had done her homework. The man seated directly across from her had a surprisingly deep voice.

"I'm Chuck Gates."

"Owner of Gates Insurance," Elizabeth replied with a grin.

"You got it," he replied as he smiled and took a sip of his coffee. The other man nodded a single nod of his head as he spoke.

"I'm Greg Carter."

"The real estate investor," Elizabeth added as the waitress came over and looked at her.

"Get you anything, hon?" she asked as she refilled a cup of coffee for Mr. Gates.

"No, thank you. I'm fine. I won't be here long." As the waitress left the table, Larry spoke up.

"We're glad to have you here this morning, but not sure how much help we can be."

"At this point I'll take any advice I can get. Now, I thought there were four of you?"

"Burt has business in Maryville. He's unavailable today. Happens sometimes. We can't always make it here every week."

"Oh, sure. I understand." Given the floor to speak, she explained her situation with the farm and how she needed to curate 40 acres of tomatoes. Greg, Larry, and Chuck hung on every word. When she got to Irving and told the story of how important he was to her success, the questions started firing her way.

Larry asked about replacing Irving just as Chuck started a string of questions about possibly paying the man a higher wage.

Then the conversation steered toward questions about how much revenue 40 acres brings in, what her monthly expenses were, and if she could find ways to save on labor costs. These were questions she didn't know the answers to and was surprised that her lack of knowledge was met with disappointed looks from all three.

Greg Carter put his hands on the table and interlaced his fingers as he spoke.

"Look, you admit that you don't have a grasp on your business. You admit that you don't have the knowledge to grow a crop of anything, but I might have a suggestion for you that will fix all of your problems."

"I do admit all of it. Your answers and advice is why I am here."

"I have a feeling of where this is going," Larry interjected as he looked at Greg. "You don't think that might cause a problem?"

"What's that?" Elizabeth asked, unable to catch on to what they were talking about.

"I think it'll be a problem in Rutledge," Chuck added.

"What problem?" she asked again. Greg turned to her and spoke softly.

"You know nothing about farming. You have at least one worker that does. Right?"

"Right."

"The heart of your farm is one single man. Right?"

"Right again."

"We would recommend that you create a partnership with him. Give him a portion of the farm."

"A partnership?"

"What is keeping him there? A wage? No wonder he wants to move on."

"How does this work?"

"An attorney can set it up."

"I'm sorry. Can you give me a few details? I am not sure I am following," her expression clearly communicated that she felt she was too inexperienced to understand. Greg Carter unlaced his fingers and crossed his arms and leaned his elbows on the table. As he spoke, he looked at her like her father used to.

"Let's say you both earn a wage of fifty dollars a week. At the end of the quarter, you add up your revenue. You get say, a certain percent and he gets a certain percent. After expenses of course."

"So, he shares the profit?"

"Yes, he owns a percent of the farm."

"I see."

"But you don't want to give away a large percentage."

"Why is that?"

"Let's say you gave him twenty-five percent. Let's say that after expenses, you sell tomatoes at four dollars a crate. At twenty-five percent ownership, he gets a dollar. Sell a hundred crates in a month, he earns a hundred dollars when he would've stayed for fifty. See what I mean?" Chuck explained.

"Consider ten percent or less."

"Yeah, but she needs him more than he needs her. I'd go fifteen."

"Yeah, fifteen sounds good," Greg said. "But you need to make sure that you have someone handling your finances. While it costs money to have an accountant, they usually pay for themselves by helping you avoid mistakes."

"Sure. But I also want to learn about growing tomatoes though. I don't want to just sit back and watch everyone work. That'll drive me crazy," she explained. Larry spoke up.

"You don't look like the kind of woman who would get her hands dirty. But you should know that there isn't a successful businessman on this earth who just sits back and lets people work for him," he explained. Chuck signaled the waitress for a refill as he asked Elizabeth a question.

"Let me ask you something, does this Irving that is in charge of the workers...does he sit back and watch others work?"

"Not at all. In fact, he is right there with the other workers, sweating and getting things done. Most of the time he works harder than the workers. You should see how other farmers react when they find out who he is. They forget he is a black man and look upon him as an equal or more," Larry looked back at Greg as he spoke. The waitress arrived with a fresh pot of coffee and filled Chuck's mug.

"I don't know," Greg said. "Fifteen percent. Maybe twenty."

"A black man owning part of a farm could cause a problem," Larry said as he sat back in the booth in a more relaxed posture as he looked at Elizabeth. "Now if you really want this, you have to outwork everyone. Every business we own was built on respect, and earning respect as an owner is only earned through outworking the others."

"Do you feel respected at this point?"

"I do. But only because I am paying a higher wage."

"That's the path to despair and misfortune," Chuck explained.

"He's right. Repeat that to yourself." Larry said as he nodded.

"You are on the right track, though. I will say that just getting your hands dirty isn't enough. You need to be first one there and the last to leave," Chuck added. Elizabeth looked out the window as she recited the advice under her breath.

"First one there and last to leave."

"You need to treat workers like they mean everything to you. Too many business owners get wrapped up in having employees. They should have relationships with those that work for them instead," Chuck said just as Larry began to speak.

"A ledger? Do you have a good ledger?"

The conversation then focused on the purchase of a ledger. One she would write in every day or every other day. The three men explained in great detail where they kept their ledgers and how they made time every day to give it attention. Larry even went as far to say that "the ledger is a living and breathing thing. It's the heart of any business."

Greg chimed in and went on to explain that on Sunday evenings he would listen to a ball game on the radio and drink a beer or two with the ledger opened up on his lap.

The information was too much to take in. While she already felt she was being too intrusive, she gathered the courage to ask if it would be alright if she returned should she need more advice.

"I could pay you by buying breakfast," she offered. Greg was the first to react.

"Well, we don't need free breakfast. You can come back, but on one condition," he replied as he held up a single finger. Larry spoke up and leaned toward her.

"Yeah, one condition." he said with squinting eyes, somehow, he knew exactly what Greg was going to say. The seriousness of the condition grew to profound heights as Chuck pointed at her as he spoke.

"This condition is unbreakable."

"Okay, name it," she said as she took a deep breath. Greg leaned in with very serious eyes and spoke softly.

"You bring us some of those tomatoes." A big smile stretched across his face. Elizabeth giggled.

"You got it!"

"So, this opportunity could change your life, right?"

"Absolutely," she replied.

"This was given to you?"

"Yes."

Greg leaned in once again and now appeared very serious. He drove the end of his index finger down onto the surface of the table, tapping as he spoke.

"No one just gives you something. If you don't earn it, you'll lose it."

The workers on the Campbell Farm were eating their lunch under a maple tree. Raw carrots, apples, and bologna sandwiches were on the menu, and while everyone was eating, Claire carried on a conversation with the workers.

"So, the bell rings and no one knows who is ringing it. It's in a cave, and you can't go inside, or you would drown."

"How does the bell ring?"

"No one knows. That's the mystery she is trying to solve."

"How does it end?"

"Not sure. My mother gave me the book, but it only has so many pages. The ending was torn out. I hope to know the end when the books arrive," Claire explained. Elizabeth returned from Knoxville, quickly changed clothes, and headed out to where the workers were eating lunch. Irving saw Elizabeth approaching and hollered out.

"Your daughter is earning her stripes out here," he said as he took a bite. The other workers nodded their heads in agreement. Irving spoke while chewing. "She been out here sweatin' and tillin' with the rest of us."

"I'm not surprised," Elizabeth responded as the feeling of motherly pride warmed her chest. One of the hands spoke up as he looked at Elizabeth.

"She been telling us about the tolling bell book."

"I bet. She's read it about a hundred times."

"That's for sure," Claire added.

The crew uprooted themselves from their shady spot under the tree and got back to work in the sun. The afternoon and evening comprised of readying the soil with more worms and fertilizer until the final row was completed. Elizabeth worked side by side with the workers and didn't give in to resting her aching muscles, even though she wanted to with every passing second. When they completed the final row, Irving hollered out.

"We gonna wrap up and call it a day. Be ready for tomorrow. We'll be sowing with the side-by-side method. If you have a side-by-side pole, bring it. If you can make one, do it before tomorrow morning. I haven't checked the barn for seed tubes yet. I'm sure I'll find 'em if I look hard enough." At this, Runt spoke up.

"He got 'em 'round here boss. I seen 'em around the barn I think." Irving patted and brushed the dirt off his hands by using the front of his pants while the workers disbanded and headed back to the hand quarters. Elizabeth walked up next to Irving and before she could say anything, he started speaking.

"We gonna be sowing Early Girl. It's a tough seed. Fends off disease and makes for a good yield.

"Why is it called Early Girl?"

"The Girl part of the name comes from the breeding. The Early part of the name has to do with the early maturity. A lot of tomatoes mature at ninety days or so, Early Girl matures at sixty. Two months' time from first seed, and you'll have juices running down your chin when you take a bite."

"So the crop will definitely be ready by judging time."

"Yep. That's why we're sowing 'em."

"Irving?" she said. Saying his first name was how she chose to start her question. Her tone and the way her arms were crossed caused him to stop in his tracks. "I need to meet with you tomorrow night in the kitchen," she said while looking at the ground. After the brief pause she looked up at him. "I have to speak with you about something, but it has to wait until tomorrow evening."

"Okay," he replied in a confused and curious tone.

"You have all the help you need at the moment?" she asked as she looked at him in the eye. Something was different, but he didn't know what. "Is there anything that you don't have that can keep you from moving forward?"

"No, ma'am. Everything is going like it should. In about fifteen to twenty days or so, the crop will break ground," he answered, but his mind was stuck on her request.

"Good. See you tomorrow morning," she said as she started to walk away and then turned around as if she had forgotten something. "Hey, what's a side-by-side pole?" she asked. Using his hands, he made elongated hand motions as he spoke.

"It's a long pole or stick usually made from wood. At the end are two prongs—exactly the depth a seed needs to be in the ground. I'm sure there's some around here somewhere. That and seed tubes."

"Seed tubes?"

"A long metal pole. Hollow. You stand up over the hole and put the tube above it and drop a seed in the top. Seed falls down the tube and into the hole. Saves your back."

"I see. Well, goodnight."

"G'night," he replied. Her back was turned as she walked toward the main house keeping her from being able to see the puzzled expression on his face.

Chapter 29

Irving ran his fingers through his unruly hair thinking he was overdue for a haircut. Ignoring his personal care, he put on a shirt and hummed a tune to himself as he walked to the sink at the end of the hand quarters. While brushing his teeth, he could hear the workers as they tossed, rolled, and forced themselves out of their bunks.

Once outside, puffs of smoke from rolled cigarettes, dragging feet, and the occasional cough could both be seen and heard as the rag-tag crew took steps over mounds of dirt between the rows of fertile soil.

Elizabeth had cleaned out a five-gallon pickle jar and filled it with water, sugar and thirty sliced lemons. As the workers approached the main house, they could see someone moving around in the darkness. After another fifteen steps, they could see it was Elizabeth standing over a tree stump, stirring the liquid in the big jar. Then, she spoke to all of them the way Irving did.

"Today at lunchtime we will be having lemonade. It'll sit in the sun and dissolve the sugar and Mrs. Washington will be coming out here to stir every half hour or so. When we break to eat, I will drop an ice block in the jar which will cool it down."

From behind Elizabeth, Claire came into view holding seed tubes and side-by-side poles cradled in her arms. She bent down and let them roll off her forearms and hands, spilling them onto the ground. Elizabeth looked at Irving.

"We found 'em in the loft of the barn. You been in there?"

"Not yet."

"Pretty well organized. There's also about fifty bundles of wooden stakes and rolls of string," Elizabeth said as she covered the top of the pickle jar with a cloth and stretched a rubber band around the lip. The same confused expression Irving had when Elizabeth walked away the night before appeared again. She was different, and he noticed her walk had even changed. She seemed more comfortable or maybe it was confidence. He couldn't decide.

When the rising sun gave enough light, Irving had two work-ers hoist seed bags purchased from the co-op onto their shoul-ders. The others grabbed seed tubes and side-by-side poles. Once out in the field, Irving held up his hand causing the jokes to stop and the commotion to cease.

"We gonna do two rows under my supervision. Once I feel like ya'll got it, I'll jump in. The order is obviously side poles first followed by seed tubes," he explained. Holding up two fingers, he continued. "Only two seeds per tube. Not three, not four. Two seeds only. Do not stray from my rule." Irving removed his two fingers from the air and added one more thing. "Raise your hand if an owner ever made you lemonade before." Elizabeth looked around, suddenly feeling foolish as if she might have done some-thing wrong. No hands were raised. Irving continued. "Raise your hand if you ever made forty-five dollars a week before?" again, no hands. "If you think you are in a better place than any other worker in Grainger County, I want you to act like it. So far, so good, I ain't got no reason to be sideways with any of ya. Let's keep it going and get this done."

The morning began with the first two rows under Irving's supervision. Claire rotated into poking the soil with a side-by-side pole. Irving showed her the proper way to force the stick into the soil and remove it.

"See that? It's perfect. Now watch them come in behind you and seed them," he explained as a worker stepped up to the hole and stuck the tube into the cavity. He reached into his pocket and removed two seeds and dropped them down the pipe. With the two seeds in the hole, the worker moved the topsoil with his foot, covering the hole.

Gordon headed toward the main square and parked his truck in front of Rutledge Savings and Loan and knocked on the locked door. Roger Landry answered and let his friend inside.

"You get it figured out yet?"

"No. Still trying to find a way to get the money. Problem is, I need it sooner than later," Gordon explained to Roger who dipped his head and looked back at his friend over the top of his eye glasses.

"What leverage do you have left?"

"I don't know." he replied, shaking his head in an irritated manner. Gordon began pacing the floor. "When does the bank open?"

"About forty minutes," Roger replied while looking at his watch. "Take your time." Gordon walked over to a chair in front of Roger's desk and sat down. When Roger took a seat, Gordon exhaled and ran his fingers through his thinning hair.

"If I came up with fifteen thousand cash, less than what I need, could I get a loan for the rest?"

"How much we talking?"

"Five thousand."

"I think so. It would give me some room to fix the paper work to make it happen."

"You won't get in trouble?"

"Nah. I'll just list your liquid assets as fifteen thousand, which wouldn't be a lie – it's just that you would have to make sure you paid on time to keep me out of hot water."

"Yeah, I understand."

"Think you can get fifteen thousand cash?"

"I don't know. My head is spinning. Who knows, maybe I can come up with twenty in cash. On the other hand, I might only need ten thousand if I can get this hospital to chip in."

"Sounds like you have a lot of angles."

"It's complicated."

"Well, I don't know what you're up to, but it doesn't sound good."

"I'm not doing anything illegal really, but I'm at the end of my rope."

"How is he?" Roger asked. Gordon bit the fingernail of his index finger as he answered.

"Not good."

Back at the main house, Captain and Millie were standing over a twelve-inch-deep hole they had dug after the workers left for the fields. They had placed charcoal and bits of wood inside the hole, reducing the contents to hot coals. A metal rack was placed on top of the hole followed by two plucked and prepped chickens. By 10:30 a.m. the chickens were browned with juices dripping onto the coals below. Salt and pepper were added before taking them off the grill and bringing them inside the kitchen.

Captain sliced the chicken meat off the bones while Millie collected the edible parts and placed them in a metal pan. After all the meat was cleaned off the bones, Millie covered the mound of fresh grilled chicken with a towel and watched as Captain took the pan outside and set it back on the metal rack.

When the shadows were directly underneath the workers in the fields, Irving hollered out for the workers to break, causing a resounding sigh of relief from everyone. Upon walking up to the main house, the aroma of grilled chicken grew stronger and stronger. While the crew was salivating and already beginning to form a line, Elizabeth grabbed Claire's hand and walked up to the house.

A previous conversation with both Captain and Mille had been held about the serving of the food the night before. Captain scrounged around the kitchen cabinets and had found as many bowls as possible. While most were mismatched and not all the same size, they were what Elizabeth requested. Millie had found cups, mugs, and drinking glasses and set them outside near the 5-gallon jar of lemonade. Elizabeth and Claire entered the house and grabbed two bricks of ice from the freezer. Using both hands, Elizabeth carried them outside while Claire opened the doors for her.

After dropping the bricks into the 5-gallon jar, Elizabeth headed over to the mound of juicy, browned, and sliced chicken. The workers lined up and watched as Elizabeth used tongs to grab a generous portion of chicken from the metal pan. After filling a bowl with chicken, she handed it to a worker. After leaving the line, the workers would walk over to the 5-gallon jar of lemonade where Claire used a ladle to pour a glass of sun lemonade.

While lounging underneath the shade of the massive willow tree, the workers talked, joked, and laughed until Claire and Elizabeth sat with them holding their own bowl and glass of lemonade. Many of the workers were quiet as if they were waiting for something. When Elizabeth's eyes connected with Irving's, he nodded his head before he spoke.

"They're hoping for more of the story."

"What story?"

"The tolling bell," he replied. Claire turned her head. "Claire? You got your books yet?"

"No. It's taking forever."

"What do you think is going to happen?" a worker asked as he bit into a chunk of seasoned chicken. Claire had come to know the worker as Winston. While most of the workers were thin and wore similar clothing, Winston wore an old baseball cap and was heavy set, which made him easy to pick out of a crowd.

"I think someone is in the cave, and there is a way into the cave from the outside. I don't know. Maybe."

"When you get the book, could you read it to us?" Another worker asked. When the question was asked, Claire had just taken a bite. The question caused her to stop chewing. She looked at the eyes of the workers that stared back at her. With a mouthful of food, she replied.

"Of course!"

After lunch, the workers walked back to the fields. Irving had kept his distance from Elizabeth for most of the morning as he was concerned as to what their meeting was about. After lunch, his thoughts had built up like a pressure cooker, and he couldn't take it anymore. He walked up alongside Elizabeth and spoke softly. He aimed at trying to get more information as to what she had in mind.

"Mrs. Campbell, you up early, making lemonade, and getting tools together, and then serving us at lunch. Is there anything I should know?" he asked.

"I am just making sure that I give this everything I have. I will not lose this farm," she replied. Her eyes looked around the landscape as she spoke. Irving noticed that her eyes used to dart around, and her brow would wrinkle with stress. Now her eyes were sharp. She looked focused and in control.

"As far as I know, there hasn't been an owner that has ever served their workers lunch."

"Maybe they should. Who is really helping who? If there weren't any workers around, a farmer would be on their own. A farmer should be grateful that there are workers to help out."

"Well…" Irving started to say as they continued walking toward the middle of the field. The other workers were carrying on and smoking while Claire picked up rocks she found along the way and put them in her pocket. Irving was about to respond with a line about workers needing money, but it didn't sound right in his head. He then thought about workers not working at a particular farm, because the owners were cruel or mean. It was rare when a worker turned down a job, but it did happen. Now he was walking with an owner who did the opposite. Instead of cruelty, she served the workers food.

"Well, what?" Elizabeth asked. Irving snapped out of his deep thought.

"Nothin'. I suppose you're right."

Gordon drove his truck into the parking lot of his feed mill and saw a brand-new, shiny Cadillac Coupe De Ville parked near the office entrance. Because the color of the paint was a deep, dark blue, the chrome accents popped and made everyone turn their head as it drove by. Wondering who it belonged to, he walked inside his office and found Hunter Stevenson, the owner of Stevenson Poultry. Hunter stood in the office wearing a white suit and carried his cowboy hat in his left hand.

"Hey, Hunter, good to see you!" Gordon said as he smiled and hurried up to Hunter in an enthusiastic manner. He reached out for a handshake.

"Hey, Gordon," he replied with an expression that didn't return the enthusiasm. He shook Gordon's hand and tried his best to return the smile.

"You doin' okay?"

"I am actually. I just sold my business and I'm headed to Florida."

"Florida?" replied Gordon as a lump in his throat grew and it suddenly felt like he had a fever. "Good to hear," he added. With everything Gordon had been going through, his smile wasn't genuine. It was forced and a complete fabrication.

"Dyer Feed and Hatchery bought me out, and I wasn't certain that they were going to contact you, but they won't be utilizing your feed services. I hate to tell you that, but it didn't seem fair for no one to let you know."

"I see. Well that is disappointing, but such is life."

"I tried to get them to understand how helpful you are."

"What did they say?"

"They are building their own feed mill to service their hatchery and will also be selling to farmers in the area. I am so sorry to bring you this news.

"No, no. Don't you worry about it. I am just glad to hear you are moving on to better things. You worked hard and you've earned it. Now, the only thing we have left to talk about is that fantastic car you have out there. How does it drive?" Gordon put on a show for Hunter as he pretended that losing his biggest client didn't bother him.

After the tour of the Cadillac and a departing handshake, Gordon went back inside the main office and sat down at his desk. He unrolled the division map and looked at the corners of the fields. With his biggest client gone for good, the payroll would pile up as would the payroll taxes. If things weren't difficult before, his situation now felt like he couldn't breathe. *Harold. Harold can't breathe. Harold can't breathe.* Gordon couldn't stop thinking about Harold, the trouble his business was facing and that he was about to be behind on his mortgage.

Getting up from his desk, Gordon walked over to a window where he could see the workers on the floor. They were filling burlap bags and shouting over the bucket elevator, the loudest piece of equipment in the mill. The bay doors were open, and a truck backed up to the door. Sunshine blasted down onto the concrete and created an orange hue throughout the mill while the workers filled bags and hoisted them onto their shoulders. Gordon watched as the men walked to the truck and flung them off their shoulders onto the bed of the truck.

Gordon hired the McGurn brothers in 1948 even though they had a reputation in Rutledge for fighting and drinking. They were tough men that could get any job done no matter how strenuous or hot or cold it was outside. Despite the fact that they had served time in jail together and would sometimes give each other a knuckle sandwich, they were great employees. Gordon stuck his head out of his office window and shouted.

"Wesley! Dalton!" He waved them over once they both looked his way. Dalton set down a feedbag, and Wesley took his rawhide gloves off and stuck them in his back pocket. They hurried up to the office and closed the door behind them.

"Yeah, boss?" Wesley asked. He was tall and two years older than Dalton. Wesley had big shoulders and always looked ready for a fight. Gordon sat down in his chair and leaned on his desk. His hand was still bandaged, and while most people would wonder what had happened, a bandaged hand was commonplace at the McGurn house.

"I need some help with a project, and it would require the utmost secrecy and would involve an incredible amount of money for both of you," he said as he looked both of them in the eyes. "I want your word that if I give this opportunity to you that you will continue to work here. No matter the amount of money you receive."

"We'd sure appreciate the opportunity. You can count on us," said Dalton. At five foot six, he was the shortest worker at the mill. His sandy blonde hair was so thick that his haircut resembled the head of a matchstick. Stories of Dalton were told in bars and poker games around Grainger County. One autumn evening, after a community barn dance he was seen jumping up and slugging his taller brother in the jaw with a wiry left hook, knocking him out cold. Conversations about which brother was tougher never lasted long.

"The fact that I can count on you is the sole reason why you're in my office right now, but I also know that when you two get liquored up all bets are off. So, if I could please ask you to give up the hooch for the time being, it would help me sleep at night. I don't want people knowing what we are up to. Got it?"

"Yeah, Boss," said Wesley.

"How much we talkin' here?"

"I don't really know, maybe one thousand dollars each?"

"Each?"

"Maybe more."

"What do we gotta do?" asked Wesley. Gordon stood up and unrolled the division map on top of his desk.

Chapter 30

There was only one postman for Rutledge, Tennessee in 1951. Every Christmas, Mr. Billingsley would threaten to quit if he didn't get seasonal help. Many people in Rutledge had to order their gifts from a massive Sears catalogue, which wreaked havoc on Mr. Billingsley between Thanksgiving and Christmas Eve. His requests were in vain as his superior in Knoxville ignored his threats of quitting his job, never really believing that his only postman in Rutledge would ever up and quit.

Mr. Billingsley drove his mail truck along Dishman Lane while he looked over at a package in his mail bucket. It was his only package of the day, but he resented it as the package reminded him of Christmas. He delivered the mail along his route until lunch time. Unable, any longer, to bear the thought of the package waiting for him in the mail bucket, he drove over to T.C.'s home, walked up to the front door and knocked three times. When a black lady answered, he thought that the new owner of the Campbell Farm had a wait staff.

"Delivery!" Mr. Billingsley said with a smile.

"Oh, I will see that Miss Campbell gets it. Thank you!"

"Thank you!" he said as he turned around hoping that was the last package until November.

Claire was out in the field when she heard the bell ring. Millie had rung the dinner bell near the back porch, and Claire knew exactly why it was ringing. She shouted at her mother and Irving that she would return as she bolted off for the main house. Her feet landed in between rows of dirt with each stride.

Upon reaching the back porch, Millie handed the package to a smiling and joyful Claire whose eyes sparkled with delight. After removing brown paper and string, she found six, small hardback books. Each were finished in yellow with a printed photo of an oil painting on the cover. She sifted through the titles and found *The Mystery of the Tolling Bell!*

Out in the fields, Irving could see that their shadows were underneath them and called out for lunch. After Claire and Elizabeth served the workers mashed potatoes and carrots, the tired crew sought shade underneath the willow tree while Claire held up the book for everyone to see. Hoots and hollers commenced upon the sight of the brand-new copy of *The Mystery of the Tolling Bell.* For the entire lunch break, the workers listened to Claire as she picked up from where her book left off. Elizabeth watched as her daughter commanded an audience. Even Irving had gotten caught up in the story.

When the lunch break was over, and everyone was back in the fields, the workers and Claire had gotten to talking about the book. Elizabeth watched as her daughter had taken to working in the fields and had earned respect on her own. Claire hadn't heard what Larry, Greg, and Chuck had said. She was doing it without guidance. Feeling pride for her daughter, Elizabeth continued using the side-by-side poles and seed tubes until the light in the sky had faded and the stars were beginning to take over. Irving stopped the crew and explained they would continue seeding tomorrow. Elizabeth walked up to Irving and spoke with a polite, but authoritative tone.

"I'll see you around seven-thirty. That okay?"

"Seven-thirty, it is," he replied. Elizabeth turned around and headed for the main house while Irving walked with the workers back to the hand quarters.

Gordon found a few grain crates outside the mill and brought them into his office. He overturned them so that Dalton and Wesley could sit down. After taking a seat at his desk, he opened a drawer and pulled out a photo of his son. In the photo, Harold had just gotten out of the bath and was allowed to go outside for a brief moment. He didn't get to go outside much and when he did it was a treat. The photo showed Harold holding a small ice cream cone and his hair was wet. Gordon held the photo so that the McGurn brothers could see it.

"This is my son, Harold. He can't breathe."

"We know. We hear things around the mill. Sorry to hear about your boy." Wesley offered. Gordon set the photo down.

"I have learned of a machine that will give Harold breathable air and could really help him. This medical device costs twenty thousand dollars."

"Geez. That much?"

"It is a fortune," Gordon replied as he held up the division map. "Now, this here is a sort of treasure map. I need to uncover twenty thousand dollars that is buried right here on a farm in Grainger County."

"Twenty thousand? You serious?"

"Assuming this farmer made four thousand dollars a year from 1930 to 1950, twenty years times four is eighty thousand. I figure he saved a quarter of that money, and it's in the ground. But who knows? Could be more."

"More?" Wesley asked. Gordon leaned forward and looked at both of them in their eyes.

"I don't care about anything but getting twenty thousand."

"Yeah, but what if there is only twenty?" Dalton asked.

"We would do all that work for nothing," Wesley added.

"I will guarantee you both one thousand each."

"Two thousand guaranteed?"

"Yep."

"Okay, so how does this work?"

Gordon unrolled the division map on his desk.

"You sure there is money buried on this farm?" Dalton asked. Gordon put his hands on the desk and leaned over the map. He placed his index finger on an X marked on the map.

"Already found some."

Elizabeth had taken a bath and put on her floral print dress after putting her hair up in an effort to appear more business-like. She walked from the bathroom to the dresser where three papers were paper-clipped together. She held them in her hands, handling them delicately and reviewed the words that were typed on each page. Satisfied with the documents, she went downstairs and sat at the kitchen table.

Irving had already arrived in clean clothes and combed hair. He was talking to his parents in the living room while his father listened to the radio. When Irving heard Elizabeth's feet on the tile floor, he excused himself and walked out of the living room and into the kitchen.

"You ready for me?" Irving asked. Elizabeth's eyes appeared bothersome. "Something wrong?"

"Actually, would it be okay if you and I spoke alone?"

"We are."

"I meant, would it be rude of me to ask your parents to vacate the living room until we are done?"

"No problem," he said. Irving, acted as if it wasn't a problem, but in his head, it made him even more curious and puzzled. When he approached his father, Irving reached over and turned off the radio.

"What you doin' here? I was listening to that."

"Mrs. Campbell and I have business to discuss in the kitchen."

"Oh, I see."

"Could you take momma into the bedroom and close the door? Mrs. Campbell needs privacy."

"The bedroom? Why?"

"Just do it. Come on!" Irving said in a whisper.

"Oh, alright. Mille! Come with me."

"Where we goin'?" asked Millie.

"Just come on," retorted Captain.

"Sorry, Dad."

"Ain't no sorry 'bout it. Don't you worry. We movin'."

Irving returned to the kitchen and found Elizabeth with papers in front of her. They were face down. When he sat across from her, she looked him in the eye with a slight smile.

Chapter 31

"My husband was a good man. He was kind to others, and he loved growing crops. He loved to spend time with me, and he was a good father to Claire. I loved him more than anything," she said. Irving nodded his head as a sign that he was listening. "After he died, me and Claire moved to a mining camp where we were given food, shelter, and I was given a job. The living conditions were horrible, the food was scarce, and we couldn't leave because we couldn't save enough money. We were trapped."

"Sounds familiar."

"Norman Werthan got us out of there. He used some of his money to help us leave and then he helped me get to where I could stay here."

"Still sounds familiar."

"I went to see an attorney a few days ago. I asked him to make a legally binding contract. Some things had to be done in order to get this together which is why it took a while for this meeting to happen."

"I see." At first Irving couldn't think of where the conversation was going. The mention of a contract confused him, but the kindness in her eyes eased his concerns. Still wondering where she was headed, he continued to listen. She turned over the document and then looked at him directly in his eyes.

"I want to give you half of this farm." Inside Irving's head, the sound of a car smacking another car at high speed could be heard. Blindsided. Dumbfounded. He sat motionless as she continued to speak. "I want to be your business partner and I want you to consider this farm your home and let Claire and me help you in your efforts to grow tomatoes."

Irving looked like he was keeping it together. He looked at her until little by little she could see small changes in his expression. His lips pursed and his chin began to subtly quiver. He broke eye contact for a brief moment. When he regained eye contact with her, she saw that his eyes were watering. What once was a man sitting across from her now resembled a child. His breathing had quickened as his shoulders moved slightly with each breath. His fingers picked at his bottom lip, a nervous tick that hadn't showed up in decades. With tears in his eyes, he asked.

"Why you doing this?"

"You can help me, and I can help you," she said as if she had rehearsed the response over and over in her head. Irving couldn't sit still. He repositioned himself in the chair and stopped picking at his bottom lip just before he quickly wiped tears off his cheeks. Elizabeth broke eye contact as she spoke. "I haven't slept very well the past few nights. Mostly because I have been thinking this through. My only fear is that you say no and move on to Kingsport," she explained as she looked back at him with an expression that conveyed the highest level of sincerity.

"I don't deserve this. One hundred and sixty acres is more than I could ever dream of. I've never owned anything," he said as he choked back tears. Elizabeth stood up and moved her chair beside his. She took a seat and leaned forward and grabbed his hands. Holding his hands in hers, she spoke softly.

"I don't deserve this either. If it weren't for Norman, I would still be in that mining camp."

"If it weren't for you, I'd still be in that slave camp."

"This is a big step for both of us. We can manage the farming; we can handle the business side of things and you and I will both call this farm home."

"If you have thought this through, and you really want to do this, I will accept. I'd be a fool not to."

"You will bring so much to this farm." At this, Irving looked at her with a strange expression that she couldn't place. He stood up. "What's wrong?" Elizabeth asked. He seemed to be in deep thought as if he was trying to find the words. Then,

"I need to tell you something. Something I've never told anyone before. No one else knows."

"What?" she asked. Irving paused briefly before speaking again.

"I don't know. I can't tell you as much as show you. Can you wait here a moment?" he said as he held up his index finger.

"Of course."

He quickly left the room and hurried toward his parents' small bedroom and opened the door without knocking. His father was lying on the bed reading a book while his mother was threading a needle as she sat on the corner of the mattress. Irving looked around the room and saw his wooden trunk in the corner.

"Everything okay?" Captain asked as he saw a glazed look in his son's eyes. Irving grabbed the leather handle on the trunk.

"Everything's fine, Dad." Irving closed the door and lugged the trunk into the kitchen. Using his strength, he set the trunk on the table with a thud in front of Elizabeth. Instead of it laying on the table horizontally, Irving had set it on the table vertically. Confused and bewildered, she watched as he unlatched three latches and opened the trunk like an armoire. Inside were drawers. Hundreds of drawers. Most were around the size of a business card and about forty of the drawers were labeled. Elizabeth read a few of the names written on the labels.

First Rain

Peppercorn Gold

Chambered Moon

Red Barn

"What is this?" she asked. Her eyes followed Irving's hand as he reached out and pulled on a tiny knob of a tiny drawer labeled *Juliet Wine*. Unable to see the inside, Elizabeth watched as he removed a small, clear bottle with the tiniest cork she had ever seen keeping the contents inside. Instead of liquid, the tiny jar held about twenty seeds.

"Several years ago, I was in a movie theater in Chattanooga and saw a newsreel about a man crossbreeding grapefruits and oranges. I got a few books from the library and started learning how to cross two breeds of tomatoes to get a better flavor. I have been experimenting ever since."

"Wait. These drawers, all of them hold seeds? Tomato seeds?"

"These are all tomato seeds. I cross breed the plants and invent different types of tomatoes."

"I had no idea. I didn't know this was even possible."

"Evidently people have been cross breeding for centuries. Someone wrote a book about it. There are hundreds and hundreds of different varieties of tomatoes."

"If that's the case, then why continue? Aren't there enough tomatoes for farmers to grow?" she asked. Irving took a deep breath and thought a moment before he spoke.

"Tomato farmers want to grow better, longer lasting tomatoes, but I want to grow more flavorful tomatoes. I want to breed for flavor."

"I don't think I have ever heard of anyone breeding a more flavorful type of crop."

"Well, it's not just breeding," he replied. Irving slid toward the edge of his seat. She could see the intensity in his eyes as he looked at her. "You remember the rotation book?" he asked, Elizabeth nodded her head. "A lot of farmers will simply rotate their crops with lima beans, cabbage or cucumbers. There are far better rotation crops that further benefit the soil. Far better rotation crops that will ultimately result in a better tasting tomato."

"Have you worked out all of this on your own?"

"Not all of it. When I was twenty-eight, I taught myself how to read. I wanted to learn so that I could read books on agriculture. By the time I was thirty-eight, I was reading every book I could get my hands on and came across a sentence that changed my life and I wrote it down," he explained as he leaned to one side and removed a billfold from his back pocket. He unfolded the wallet and carefully removed a small piece of paper with words written in pencil. He read it aloud.

"*You have to have a crop following its most suitable predecessor. During World War II, we grew food in the name of efficiency and convenience, ignoring the need to farm for flavor.*"

"So that rotation book is really important then," she said as he placed the paper carefully back into his billfold.

"That rotation book is everything," he replied. "It seems Mr. Campbell was already doing some of what I have been reading about," he explained. Elizabeth looked at the tiny drawers in the trunk. She reached out and pulled on a small drawer labeled *Ozark Sour*. Inside was another bottle filled with seeds. "What about my parents?"

"As far as I am concerned, they can stay as long as they like," she said as she pushed the small drawer closed having never removed the bottle.

"What do I have to do?" he asked. Elizabeth glanced down at the legal document, and then looked back at him.

"All you have to do is sign it. It gives you fifty percent of the farm if the agricultural judges approve the crop. Upon their approval, I will be given the deed to the farm and this document here makes it so that you own half of it," she explained as she slid the papers and a pen in front of Irving. He signed his name, set the pen down and looked up at Elizabeth.

"Is that it?" he asked.

"That's it," she said with subtle laugh. "Do you feel different? Do you feel like you own a farm?"

"What was it like for you when you found out you were inheriting a farm?"

"It didn't feel real. It still doesn't."

"That sounds about right," he grinned as he looked back down at his signature.

Chapter 32

The McGurn brothers met Gordon on the backside of the Campbell Farm just after sunset. Using a flashlight, he illuminated the map as he spread it out on the bed of his truck.

"Here is where I found the jars. I suspect that there might be more here and here," he said as he pointed to the corners of different fields. "The corners are the safest place to bury something since no one tills the corners. This is where we dig."

"How far down?"

"I found the other jars at a little more than two feet deep."

"What do we do when we find something?" Wesley asked.

"Drop your shovel and come find me. If I am nearby, whistle and I'll hurry your way."

After lighting their lanterns, Wesley and Dalton hoisted their shovels over their shoulders and trekked about six hundred feet, each taking an untouched corner of a field. Gordon got back in the truck and drove up toward the main house but stayed out of sight by keeping behind a small hill. Once he found a corner, he got out of his truck and grabbed a shovel and a lantern. He started loosening the dirt by piercing the soil with his shovel in several places before he started digging. After about twenty-five minutes, he deemed the hole to be barren and put the shovel and lantern back in the bed of his truck. After looking around for Wesley and

Dalton, he saw that they had each advanced to other corners. Their speed reassured Gordon that he made the right move in recruiting them. The money would be dug up in no time.

After being out in the fields for over an hour, Gordon heard something. A whistle. He quickly looked up and saw a lantern waving side to side. Dropping his shovel, he ran through rows of packed dirt unable to see if it was Wesley or Dalton. As he got closer with each stride, he could see another lantern running toward the whistler.

Dalton was standing over a hole when Wesley and Gordon arrived. Just as Gordon stopped and began to catch his breath, he looked down at the ground where a single glass jar could be seen in the hole.

"I was digging and heard a strange noise. I tossed my shovel to the side and used my hands to uncover that," he said as he pointed at a hole about two feet deep. "It's glass and I can see money inside," Dalton added. Gordon reached down into the hole and pried the jar out of the packed soil. Once he freed the treasure, he took the shovel from Dalton's hands, smashed the spade into the glass, shattering the jar.

After fishing out the wad of money, he unrolled five- and ten-dollar bills.

"Man, how much you think that is?" Wesley asked.

"We'll count these rolls back at the office. Not enough time to be counting cash out here, besides, I think there is another jar in the hole."

The Feed Mill in Grainger County was just outside the Rutledge city limits on Highway 11. Sitting back off the road, it provided a better cover for the nighttime activities of Gordon and the McGurn brothers. After digging up five jars in one night, they retreated to Gordon's office thinking that if anyone saw them, they could simply say they were repairing the hopper as it was often out of order.

Gordon's office was dark. Normally, the light from the windows illuminated the room, but since it was eleven at night, the pendant dome lamp above his desk was the only light in the office. The desk was well lit, but every corner of the room was dark, looking more like a detective's office from the gumshoe movies of the 1940s.

Two unopened jars sat on the desk. Next to the jars were rolls of cash they had already freed. Wesley and Dalton each took a jar and unscrewed the lids with force and dumped out the bills. After twenty minutes of unrolling and counting, they discovered they had dug up over six hundred dollars.

"This guy was crazy to be burying this much money," Dalton said.

"I would never do that. Why did this 'ol coot not put it in the bank?" Wesley said.

"Be glad he didn't. The Great Depression did something to people. It changed how people thought about banks."

"Yeah, I'm glad he didn't," Dalton replied. Gordon could see that his mentioning of the Great Depression went through one ear and out the other.

"Me too. How much do we got right now?" Wesley asked.

"Let me divide this out. We'll keep it fair and adhere to our agreed upon split."

"We going back tomorrow?"

"You bet we are. Meet me at the same spot and same time. Don't talk to me about this during business hours. Keep this quiet and no drinking until we are done here. Got it?"

"Yep."

"Got it," Wesley replied as he nodded his head.

Chapter 33

The sun hadn't risen yet, and the stars could still be seen in the sky as Irving walked up to the main house. He could see that the kitchen light was on and there was movement inside, but he couldn't tell who it was. The workers wouldn't be waking up for at least another hour, and Irving had been tossing in his bunk for most of the night. The thought of owning a farm sent waves of sleep-killing scenarios through his head.

He thought mostly about the rotation book and how he could improve upon what Mr. Campbell had laid out. Irving had kept it underneath his worn and ripped mattress. At one point in the middle of the night, he took it out and used the moonlight to read a few dimly lit pages. When he decided to go ahead and get up, he put on his overalls and stuck the book into his back pocket.

When he arrived at the main house, he could see it was Elizabeth moving around in the kitchen. After knocking lightly on the back door in an attempt to not startle her, he entered when she turned her head to see who it was.

"Mornin'."

"Good morning."

"This the third time in three days you been up early," he said as the unmistakable aroma of fresh baked goods permeated the air. First to arrive, last to leave, she repeated in her head. "What ya doing? Smells good."

"Biscuits. I am baking twenty-eight of them for us to eat at lunch."

"I would call you crazy for going to so much trouble for farm hands, but I happen to know that the fellas would run back here when you need them. Not many hands will be at a farm's beck and call like that."

"Yeah? Do you think that they respect me?"

"I think you shown enough respect their way for you to earn theirs. They like you, and they like Claire."

"Why would you call me crazy?"

"No owner goes out of their way for hands. But seeing you do it and get loyalty and respect in return makes it not a bad idea. But if you continue to pay hands forty-five dollars a week and make lemonade and biscuits everyday, you might go broke."

"We might go broke," she said in a corrective tone. "I don't know. Maybe. Lemonade and biscuits are inexpensive. Just takes more effort than money."

"Can I ask you somethin'?"

"You can ask me anything," she replied as she shifted her weight to one foot. Flour on her cheek, wisps of hair floating around her face, she waited for the question with her hand on her hip.

"Well, I can't really ask you anything personal. A black man asking a white woman a question like this can get him in trouble," he explained in a serious tone. Elizabeth tried not to smile, but she couldn't help it.

"Now you've got me very curious, but in no way can you get in trouble for asking me anything – especially when no one else is around."

"Okay. Well, I was thinking last night, you mentioned something about your husband and that he was deceased. What happens if you marry someone in the future and he doesn't want me for a business partner?"

"Hmmm...good question. But first why is that something a black man can't ask a white woman?"

"Men have been lynched for less. Asking a white lady a personal and private question can cause problems. Always has."

"I see. Well, being that we are business partners," she said as she took a seat across from him, "I feel that we have to be open with each other, and if that must be done without others around to avoid conflict, that's fine. To answer your question, I still see myself as being married and always will. I can't marry anyone else as I already have a husband. I have been told that is an unhealthy way to look at it, but I suppose I won't have it any other way. My focus is Claire and this farm. Nothing else."

"I noticed you still wear your wedding ring."

"I do. Every time I look at it, it reminds me of Samuel. What about you?"

"Me? Getting married? Well, I have chased off a few. Mostly because I have been so focused on growing tomatoes, and I have had to move a lot. Go where the work was. Then a year ago I was thrown into a prison farm for a crime I didn't commit. Who knows? Maybe someday."

They heard the door to the downstairs bedroom open and the shuffling of feet. Soon, Millie appeared while tying the belt around her robe.

"What smells so good?"

"Miss Elizabeth made biscuits."

"Oh. I could have done that for ya. No need to put yourself out none," said Millie.

"Not at all. I don't mind," Elizabeth said with a smile.

"You sure are up early. I came out here to see if you needed help. Not much can wake me from a sleep except the smell of food cooking," she said with a laugh.

"I figured biscuits could go with whatever you and Captain prepare for lunch."

"I'm sure it will go nicely with our food," she said before turning to Irving. "Did you ask her about the jubilee?"

Irving's face turned to an expression of forgetfulness. He turned toward Elizabeth.

"After seeds are in the ground, we have a little reward dinner. Folks around here call it 'jubilee'. Lotta farms let the hands have a little fun at their quarters before they move on."

"Really? What's involved?"

"Just food. Usually done outside with all the farmhands. We all chip in and cook. Mama wanted me to ask you 'bout getting some food to cook since we ain't got no money right now," he explained. Elizabeth crooked her mouth as she stared off into the distance. She then looked back at Irving and spoke under her breath.

"You gonna tell her?"

"I don't know."

"Why not?" Elizabeth asked. Millie furrowed her brow, wondering what they were talking about.

"Superstitious. The second I say something to someone, I feel like it might go away."

"It won't go away," Elizabeth said with sincerity and a look of kindness in her eyes.

"I hope not."

"Can I see you outside?" she asked. Irving nodded.

"Mamma, hang tight. We be right back."

Once outside in the damp cold air, Elizabeth told Irving how much money she was given to raise forty acres. She further explained that after labor, supplies, seed, and a small legal bill for drawing up the partnership document, there was nearly nine hundred dollars in the account, half of which was his. His bottom lip started to shake. Tears started to form in his eyes. He covered his face with his left hand. Through a quivering voice, he did his best to speak.

"I don't deserve this. I didn't do anything to deserve..."

Inside the kitchen, Millie had started scrubbing the mixing bowls and wooden spoons Elizabeth had used to make the biscuits. When she turned her head, she saw Elizabeth through the window release an embrace from Irving. She watched as they spoke, and Irving appeared to wipe away tears. When he turned to come back inside, Millie, mouth agape, quickly turned her head back toward the mixing bowls.

Elizabeth decided to stay outside and enjoy the sunrise while Irving spoke to his mother. While taking in the orange glow of the sky, she heard a scream followed by yelling.

"Oh, no! Oh my goodness! Oh, no! Oh, no!" Millie hollered as she burst out of the back door, her robe dragged on the dirt and wet grass, and she waddled with outstretched arms ready to deliver the greatest hug an elderly woman could bestow. Elizabeth watched as she approached, still carrying on. "Oh, no! The Lord is working in our lives!" Elizabeth smiled as Millie's arms wrapped around her and squeezed.

Sidney Kroll, 44 years of age moved to Knoxville after World War II. He served in the army with the judge advocate general in the capacity of an attorney and was stationed in Hawaii after the Japanese bombed Pearl Harbor. His duties were administrative in nature, requiring him to attend many meetings with commanders and generals. Sidney was part of a legal team that offered legal insight concerning the Hague Convention and international standard law in times of war.

With dignity and integrity, he served the United States in wartime. Unfortunately, seven years later he found himself in Knoxville, Tennessee working for gold diggers, greedy corn-fed mountain folk, and unscrupulous businessmen.

Sleeves sat in a chair directly across from Sidney and watched him review six signed affidavits. Each affidavit was signed by the husbands and wives stating that they believed Thaddeus Campbell was not of sound mind when he signed his Last Will and Testament. They cited many fabricated examples in which T.C. spoke and acted like an elderly man afflicted with dementia. While Sleeves sat in a chair, the other husbands stood with their wives and children. The children played as if they were in a daycare center, which grated on the nerves of Sidney Kroll. He had considered saying something to get the wives to keep their children quiet, however he had already siphoned off nearly five hundred dollars from his gold-digging clients thus far. After reviewing the affidavits, he looked up and spoke to Sleeves.

"I can confirm that the woman staying in the house is Mr. Samuel Campbell's widow."

"Is that good or bad?" Sleeves asked.

"I suppose in our case, it's good. Better fighting a widow than the intended party."

"So, what's the plan?"

"Well, these documents I am preparing will help make a case against the Last Will and Testament of Mr. Thaddeus Campbell," he said as he racked the papers and slid them into a folder. He then pulled out a document that was typed on draft paper. "This document here will attest that the will was only intended for Mr. Samuel Campbell and is considered null and void upon Samuel's death," he added as he returned the draft to the folder. One of the

children playing near the bookcase threw a toy at another, causing it to cry. The wives were too entranced in the explanation to
do anything about it. They continued to listen as Sidney removed
another document from a separate folder and held it up. "This
quitclaim deed has already been filled out. We will require that
Arthur Humes sign it as he is Mr. Campbell's executor of the estate and give the deed to you in the presence of a judge who will
then sign as a witness upon receiving the deed. Understand?"

"I think so. Do you think this will work?" asked Sleeves. He
had been chewing on the same toothpick since breakfast.

"Judge Murphy is going to have to take a hard look at the first
two documents, and if the affidavits don't make him lean our way,
the death of Samuel Campbell should be enough to void the en-
tirety of the will," he explained. The laughter of two children
erupted behind the wives.

Sleeves turned his head and looked back at his wife. "Shut
them up, will ya?"

Sidney continued. "If this judge doesn't rule in our favor, I
am certain we can find one that will. For now, I am going to make
a formal request for a copy of the Last Will and Testament."

Chapter 34

Norman Werthan sat on a tree stump behind his house with a wire brush in one hand while holding a rusty side-by-side pole in the other. He saw movement from the corner of his eye and looked up to see Elizabeth and Claire walking toward him. They were each holding a covered dish and wearing a smile.

"Good evening, Norman."

"Hello there, ladies."

"We brought you dinner and good conversation," Elizabeth said as Norman stood up and brushed the dirt off his pants.

"No crying?" he asked as he pointed his index finger.

"No crying," she replied with a nod. Norman pointed his wrinkled finger at Claire.

"That goes for you, too," he said although Claire couldn't tell he was joking.

Both Norman and Claire set the table while Elizabeth spooned out heaps of a chicken casserole onto plates.

"You know, I'm glad to see you. I almost called you the other day," Norman said.

"You did? Why?"

"Well, let's get situated here, and I'll explain. It's something I heard down at the co-op. Not sure what to think about it," he explained. Elizabeth had thought that she and Claire were coming over for dinner and light conversation until Norman's tone made her nervous. She suddenly lost her appetite. Once they were seated and a few bites were consumed, Norman began.

"A man down at the co-op was talking about the Campbell Farm and mentioned the green door."

"He did?"

"Apparently everyone around town knows about it."

"How?"

"I don't know, but I didn't think much of it when Arthur Humes told us about it, but now I wonder what is in there."

"No idea."

"I do," Claire said. Her mother froze as did Norman. Norman looked like he was waiting for her to continue, but Claire was unable to move or talk due to the gaze her mother was burning into her soul. "I didn't go in. I didn't. I promise."

"You better start making sense."

"Remember when those people walked into the house, back when you brought Irving to the farm?"

"Go on."

"I was under the house looking up through the floor boards."

"Claire Lynn Campbell! Those books are going to get you in trouble, young lady."

"Wait. What books?" Norman asked, but was ignored. The attention was on Claire.

"Mom! I didn't do anything, I just looked up through the floorboards with a flashlight."

"What did you see?" Noman asked in vain. Elizabeth continued to scold her.

"What did I tell you? It's part of the rules that we can't mess with that room, and I told you! I explained how important it is to me, and you disobeyed me!"

"What's in the room?" Norman tried again.

"I should take those books away as a punishment. You did not listen to me."

"What books?" Norman asked again. Claire hung her head.

"Nancy Drew. She reads them over and over."

"The girl detective novels?"

"Yes," Elizabeth answered.

"I don't blame you," Norman said to Claire.

"What?" Elizabeth asked. Claire looked up and grinned.

"You give a girl Nancy Drew books and then tell her not to go near a green door?"

"What do you mean?"

"It's like showing a coonhound a raccoon bounding into a forest and then telling it not to go chase it."

"I didn't go near the door after you told me not to," Claire said trying to make her case.

"That's not the point, and you know it," Elizabeth said trying to ignore Norman's involvement. She turned to him and casually apologized for the scene. He waved it off and looked at Claire.

"So what's in the room?"

"Jars," she answered before her mother could keep her from answering.

"Jars?" Elizabeth replied.

"What kind of jars?" Norman asked.

"I don't know. It was hard to see through the cracks and all I could see was what looked like a shelf with a few glass jars. I couldn't really see much."

"We need to stop talking about this now," Elizabeth said. She then pointed at both of them. "No one talk about this, I am serious." Norman raised his hands as if he was being held up at gunpoint. Claire copied his movements.

"Not a word," he said.

"Not a word," Claire echoed.

Chapter 35

Shepard and Stowe Mercantile opened their doors at seven-thirty every morning except Sunday. When Millie and Captain entered the store at 7:32 A.M., a clerk wearing a buttoned shirt and a pencil behind his ear looked them over. From time to time he would watch them from the corner of his eye.

Captain browsed the aisles wearing his captain's hat while Millie looked at canned goods on a wooden shelf. She looked at the condition of the fruits and vegetables through the glass of each jar, focusing on the peaches, green beans, carrots and corn.

"Now, we need a lot of buttermilk," Captain whispered to Millie.

"I know what we need. You don't need to tell me what we need," she whispered back.

"You gonna need flour too."

"Will you stop it? It's on my list. You see this list in my hand or are you too blind to see this in front of your face?" she whispered as she flapped a piece of paper in front of his eyes.

"You might as well get a broom too if you keep that up," he muttered. Millie hit him in the shoulder, causing Captain to laugh.

When Millie and Captain left the general store, they visited a nearby farm and purchased three live chickens before heading back. After entering the kitchen, pots of water were placed on the stove, spices, and seasoning were laid out and canned vegetables were unsealed.

Captain went out back with a meat cleaver in hand and walked toward the chickens. The kill was quick. Three chickens were plucked and butchered inside twenty minutes. He placed the meat into a bucket while Millie poured a gallon of buttermilk over the raw drumsticks, necks, thighs and breasts. Using all of the strength in his back and arms, Captain placed the soup pot in the canary yellow refrigerator.

He then focused his efforts on making a small fire out back using chopped maple and hickory he found stacked against in the barn. Once the fire was going, he situated a cast iron pot over the flames and simmered green beans and a ham hock. Captain tended to the fire and stirred the beans throughout the day, caring for the slow cooked food like a nurse caring for a patient.

While they were preparing food for dinner, the workers in the field lived off of Elizabeth's biscuits and water the entire day as to save their stomachs for the feast they would have that evening. Each seed sowed and every side-by-side pole plunged into the ground meant they were that much closer to dinnertime.

Irving sidled up to Claire as they neared the end of the day. He continued to poke holes with a side-by-side as he spoke.

"You ever heard of a jubilee?"

"I haven't."

"When we done sowing, we celebrate it. When we done harvesting, we celebrate that. We call it 'jubilee' like in the Bible. Normally we do this out behind the hand quarters of whatever farm we workin'. Instead, your mamma gonna let us have it behind the main house."

"Is it fun?"

"It is. It can get rowdy sometimes if the boys get into the hooch."

"I bet," she smiled.

"You ever hear of somthin' called *In The Round*."

"No. What's that?"

"Folks get up in front of everyone and share somethin' with the others."

"What do they do?"

"Some sing, some tell a story, or show everyone somethin' they made, or somethin' they found. Could be anything."

"Sounds fun."

"I was kinda hoping you could be part of it."

"How?"

"Tell that story of the tolling bell again, and then read the last of it to us. We didn't get to hear the last part"

"You want me to read?"

"Yeah. But tell the story to us up until the part you haven't read yet. Can you do that for us?"

"Okay. I can do that."

"Alright. Good to hear."

Late in the afternoon when Captain and Millie heard hoots and hollers from the field, they looked out the window and saw the lighting up of rolled cigarettes. Smiling faces and pats on the back signaled that the workers finished sowing the forty acres. Millie looked at Captain.

"We be eatin' soon. Gonna need the chicken right about now," Millie said as she bent down and removed a cast iron skillet from a cupboard. Just as Elizabeth and Claire entered through the backdoor and headed upstairs to clean up, Millie was busy seasoning and dredging raw, buttermilk soaked chicken through flour before placing the chicken into a hot pan of vegetable shortening.

Just before sundown, the workers had followed Irving into the barn and helped him move a long workbench. They carried the bench and set it down next to a tree behind the main house.

Corn, green beans, carrots, peach cobbler, mashed potatoes, and a pile of fried chicken graced the work bench.

"Thank you all for your help sowing the forty," Elizabeth said. "It is my hope that you all come back once we decide on the next 120 acres," she said with a smile. A voice from the back row of hungry workers spoke out.

"You keep treatin' us like this, we ain't never gonna leave Mrs. Campbell!" Laughter erupted among the small crowd.

"Thank you to Millie and Captain for fixing us the delicious dinner! Let's eat!" Elizabeth hollered.

The line went quickly. Plates were piled high with food. Everyone took a seat in the grass and ate with conversations that continued under the stars. After everyone had stuffed themselves, a few of the workers broke out jars of a clear liquid they had been brewing behind the hand quarters. Once the moon was out and the stars twinkled over their heads, a harmonica was removed from a worker's pocket. A bucket was overturned and used as a drum. The jubilee began to take a turn toward entertainment as a few workers began to sing a song:

Running through the swamp and hoppin' over logs
Dodging low limbs and chased by dogs
Man with a lantern and a long gun
Over train tracks oh run boy run

The sounds of singing and music were being overheard from a distance. Gordon saw the crowd gathered around a glowing fire. He laid in the dirt to keep from being noticed in the moonlight. Wesley and Dalton stayed back as Gordon watched for a brief moment. When he came back, he relayed his findings.

"A celebration of some sort. Keep your lanterns off. Use the moonlight."

After the music settled down, one of the workers got up and told a scary story about a pumpkin man on Halloween. Then three workers stood up and harmonized *Amazing Grace*. Next up was Claire. She had her new book with her, and she stood up to her mother's surprise. She spoke with a hint of nervousness.

"Tonight, we find out the end of the *Mystery of the Tolling Bell.*" The crowd cheered as they got closer by sliding their bottoms toward their storyteller. While she told the tale aloud, her finger marked her place in the book near the end where she would read. After she finished the recap of the story, she used the light of the fire to read the ending while her audience hung on every word.

Chapter 36

The Law Office of Arthur Humes received an envelope in the mail. It was very thin as it contained a single sheet of folded paper. In the upper left-hand corner was a return address for *Sidney Kroll, Attorney at Law.* Arthur used a pocket knife to open the top of the envelope and removed the typed, double spaced letter. Upon reading it, he wasn't surprised by the request. In fact, he was wondering what was taking so long. The formal request for a copy of the Last Will and Testament of Mr. Thaddeus Edward Campbell, Jr. was short and to the point.

Two days later, Sidney Kroll sat in his leather chair in Knoxville and opened a legal envelope with a gold-plated letter opener. He slid the document out and tossed the envelope in the trash. Leaning back in his chair, he reviewed the last will and testament, and read the section and paragraphs pertaining to proving one's worth. He read through the raising of forty acres of tomatoes. He read through the names of the agricultural judges in Nashville who were to be summoned when the crop was fruitful. Sidney sat forward and leaned his forearms on his desk.

"What is this nonsense?" he said under his breath.

A few days after the jubilee, all of the workers, including Runt, had moved on to another farm. While Claire took time to read, Elizabeth had purchased a brand-new ledger from Shepard and Stowe Mercantile. After her purchase, she checked out a book from the library, entitled: *Carter's Accounting and Finance*. She sat at the kitchen table and began filling out the columns in the ledger. While her self-education in accounting began, across town at Rutledge Savings and Loan, a rumor was brewing.

Roger Landry had gotten word of something unusual, a story about the last will and testament of Thaddeus Campbell. Upon hearing the gossip from one of the bank managers, Roger headed to his desk and picked up the phone.

Ring.

"Hello?" Gordon answered as he held a stack of invoices in his right hand and stood next to his desk. In his left was a clipboard. With his hands full, he used his shoulder and right ear to hold the phone in place as he began to sift through the invoices.

"Hey. It's me," said Roger.

"Oh. I'm not late on anything, am I?"

"No, no. Nothing like that. I heard something, and I wondered if you could clear it up?"

"Okay. What?"

"Seems that Old Man Campbell had a will and in it he made certain that a room in his house was to remain locked."

"A room?"

"It's not supposed to be opened until the deed is transferred," Roger explained. Gordon set the invoices down and took a seat. "So, is that the reason you wanted to buy the house and then sell it? Do you think there is money in there?"

"No."

"Did you know about the room?"

"I didn't."

"Very strange. Lot of people are talking about it," Roger said. Gordon's mind exploded with worry and fear. People are talking about it? What if other people catch on and start digging alongside him? What was in the locked room? Was the rest of the money in the room?

"Huh. It is strange. Guess that woman knows what's inside," Gordon said trying to sound casual.

"Well, I heard she doesn't own the farm."

"No?"

"In the will, it also states that she has to grow a crop of tomatoes, and apparently if they net a yield, she gets the farm."

"Wait. So, she doesn't own it yet?"

"Not yet."

"The room is still locked?"

"The room is locked until the deed is transferred. You sure you know nothing about what's in that room?"

"I'm sure. This is the first I am hearing of it. Look, I gotta go. I'll come see you soon."

Click.

He quickly closed the door to his office and locked it. He then reached between the wall and the cabinet and removed the rolled-up map. After unrolling it, he looked at the areas where they had dug up the jars. A few of the locations had yet to be marked. Thinking back to where the last three dig sites were that produced money, he made an X and then noticed something. His breathing stopped. He turned the map clockwise on his desk. The X's on the map made a line.

Using a marker, he connected the X's together. The line was headed toward the main house and he could see that there were four corners yet to be dug up.

Once the orders at the mill were filled for the day, Gordon closed early. Sending all but two workers home, he called a private meeting in his office. With the map unrolled on his desk, he explained the theory to Dalton and Wesley.

"I believe the bulk of Campbell's money is in a locked room in this house. Old Man Campbell was taking jars every so often from this room and burying them out away from his house in a straight line. Like this," he explained as he traced his finger across the survey map.

"If he started from his house, then it looks like we got four corners left to dig up," Dalton said as Gordon put his left hand on the map and leaned his weight on his palm as he spoke.

"If we can somehow get into this house, we can get the money before this woman does."

"I don't understand. Wouldn't she already have the money?"

"The Last Will and Testament of this old coot said she can't even open the door to the room until she grows a crop of tomatoes."

"What?" Wesley said with a smirk. "That old man was crazy!"

"We need to get inside this house and get that money," Gordon explained. He stood upright thinking of how he could get inside that room. Wesley and Dalton came up with ideas that involved watching the house until she left to run errands. Gordon began pacing back and forth, biting on a fingernail while their conversation drifted toward scaring Mrs. Campbell out of the house. Wesley then mentioned sneaking underneath the house and breaking a few floorboards. As he explained using hand motions, his hand hit the pendant dome lamp. With the lamp swinging, Gordon stopped pacing and looked at both as he spoke.

"You mentioned scaring her," said Gordon.

"Yeah. When they leave to go get help, we sneak inside."

"No. We might not have to. Scaring her could be enough," Gordon explained.

"What do you mean?"

"We make it seem that her life is in danger, she gets frightened and leaves. By the looks of her, she couldn't grow a thorn bush in a briar patch."

"Think it'll work?"

"I think she's biding her time anyway. We just need to give her a push."

Chapter 37

Irving walked into the main house at sunrise and hurried over to the door where his parents slept. After knocking, he opened the door and stuck his head inside.

"Dad," he whispered. Captain tossed under the sheets and reared his head, looking at Irving. "You still got your eyepiece?" Irving asked.

"My what?"

"The spyglass?"

"Yeah. Whatchya want it for?"

"Get it and bring it out back," Irving said just before he closed the door. Captain could be roused out of bed for pancakes and sausage, but not much else. The only other thing that could rouse him out of bed was anything related to performing any of his wartime duties as a sailor. Hurrying up out of bed and grabbing a spyglass was on that list. After slipping into his boots, he grabbed a long wooden case and snuck out of the bedroom. Trotting in his jammies and black boots, Captain made his way to Irving who was standing at the edge of the fields.

"What you see when you look out yonder?" Irving asked as he pointed toward the open field. Captain gleefully extended the spyglass and peered down the long tube and saw a hole dug out in the ground more than 200 yards away.

"A hole."

"Yep. Look a little beyond that."

"A few more holes," he replied, still looking through the optics.

"Keep going."

"More and more holes."

The sound of a screen door hitting the frame came from behind them. Elizabeth crossed her arms from the cool air and approached Irving and Captain.

"Any warships on the horizon?" she said with a grin. Irving looked at her as if there was. Before he spoke, she could see trouble in his eyes.

"Someone is digging holes in the fields."

Moments later, Irving stood at the corner of a barren field and looked down into a hole as Captain picked up a shard of glass. Elizabeth stood beside Claire who was searching the ground for clues.

"This looks to be a few days old," Irving said. "There are footprints all around here." Captain held up the piece of glass to the sky and examined it.

"Any of the workers been out here?" Elizabeth asked.

"Not that I know of. It takes time to dig all these," he said as he looked over his shoulder at the holes that had been dug out behind him. Claire started walking toward one of the other holes nearby.

"I bet they are digging up some kind of glass. There's quite a few shards around this hole," Captain said as he bent over and began collecting the shards and placing them in the middle of his handkerchief. "Looks to be glass from a mason jar."

"Mom?" Claire shouted from a few paces away. Elizabeth and Irving looked her way. She waved them over as she squatted and looked down at the dirt. When they came upon her, Claire pointed at tire tracks. "A truck was here."

The dinner bell back at the house began to ring repeatedly. Irving stood up and saw his mother waving, appearing to be in distress. He ran in her direction with Elizabeth and Claire following closely behind.

Even though Sidney Kroll had advised his senseless and reckless clients to steer clear of the Campbell Farm, there was nothing he could do once they left his office. Sleeves and his gang of wives and husbands arrived on the farm and entered the main house holding papers in their hands as if the documents were weapons. Once they demanded that Millie pack up and leave, she rang the dinner bell and summoned Irving and Elizabeth. Claire stayed outside and peered through a window on the side of the house. Upon seeing Irving, Sleeves began to yell while the other husbands and wives kept their distance behind him, opting to stay by the front door.

"Why is the help in my house? You must vacate this property!" he yelled while pointing at Irving and his mother.

"How is this your house, mister?" Irving asked.

"These court documents say this is my house and I want you all out of here now!" he yelled as he waved the papers in the air.

While Sleeves continued to yell, Elizabeth had just hung up the phone from telling the operator to send the police. When she walked into the room, Sleeves couldn't see her behind Irving but could hear her voice.

"Excuse me," she said in a pleasant tone. Irving moved out of the way, and Elizabeth came into view.

"Excuse me! Why don't you and your help get out of my house!" shouted Sleeves.

"I have already had this conversation with you before. If you say that we must vacate this house, then I need documentation. Otherwise we will not be leaving."

Sleeves shoved the documents through the air and invaded Elizabeth's personal space. Instead of reacting to his intimidating tactic, she calmly took the papers and began to read through them.

"Now get out!" he yelled. Elizabeth kept her cool and replied melodiously.

"I haven't had time to read through these, please give me a moment." She read the document and expected to see paltry and petty lines of demands and claims. Instead, she read a line about Mr. Campbell's state of mind when signing his Last Will and Testament. She also read a line concerning witnesses that claimed he was not of sound mind before he died. She then saw a sentence stating that the wife of a deceased heir was not eligible to receive the farm.

The document took her breath away. When the police arrived, Sleeves walked to the window and looked outside.

"Good! Pack your things."

The officer that arrived was the same one that had been present the previous time Sleeves had invaded the Campbell Farm. Officer Flynn escorted him outside and made him stay on the front porch. Only after reviewing the document and making a quick phone call did he discover that the husbands and wives were, in fact, involved in a legal dispute over the farm. After he hung up the phone, he walked over to Elizabeth.

"Look, I'm gonna make him go away, but you need to start locking your doors from now on, or he's just gonna come back inside. If he does, call us and we'll hurry over. I made it clear to him that he can't do anything until the dispute is resolved."

"Thank you," said Elizabeth.

When Sidney Kroll got word of his clients not heeding his advice, he shook his head in disapproval, yet hoped it would cause problems and induce additional fees from his ignorant clients.

Days after Officer Flynn escorted Sleeves from the farm,

Elizabeth walked to the mailbox and retrieved a few envelopes. She opened the thickest envelope first and found that her worst fears were confirmed. While she wasn't being forced to pack up immediately, the document stated she had twenty days to respond. Within twenty minutes of opening the letter, she was sitting in front of Arthur Humes.

"I received the same letter. The one sent to your address is a copy. I am shocked by the use of six witnesses that attest to his state of mind."

"Am I going to lose the farm?"

"Well, I know if I can get six people here in town to attest to his state of mind, a judge would have to throw out that part of the complaint. The eligibility of a wife of a deceased heir does cause me concern. In the state of Tennessee, a direct descendant of the deceased is concrete and very hard to overturn. The spouse of a direct descendant however, has caused problems. The laws are a little different in this state."

"Tell me straight. Have I have lost the farm?"

"No, no. Certainly not. I have a lot of ammunition to fight this. Also, consider that your daughter is a direct descendant and could inherit the farm. While this is a card I can play, the smart move is to leave it as a last resort."

"So, what do I do?"

"Nothing. Let me look this over and consult with a few people. I'll get back to you."

Elizabeth held off going into detail with Irving about the man claiming he owned the farm. She explained the legal document and what Arthur Humes had said. Irving thought a moment before speaking.

"Mama would say, 'No reason to worry if you don't know what to worry about'. We'll just keep moving forward."

That night Elizabeth couldn't sleep. The bed that was once comfortable with soft sheets no longer felt good on her skin. The bed felt hot and confining. Claire was asleep next to her, and the fear of losing it all wouldn't let up. Her thoughts were interrupted by the sound of dogs crying out in pain just beneath her bedroom window. Claire opened her eyes and sat up.

"Is that Scout? What's wrong, mom?" The sound of dogs coming to the end of their lives filled her ears. "Mom? What's happening?" she asked as the yelping and crying suddenly ended. Elizabeth wondered if she had locked all the doors.

Chapter 38

Irving was disturbed in his sleep just after 1:30 A.M. He sat up and heard Elizabeth's voice coming from outside.

"Irving?"

"Yeah, I hear you," he said, speaking out into darkness. He could see that the door was cracked, and her head was peering inside.

"Please get dressed. Something has happened."

Elizabeth had told Claire to stay inside, which she obeyed until she could stand it no longer. After throwing on pants and a shirt, she grabbed her flashlight and walked outside. Reaching the side of the house, where the upstairs bedroom window looked out, she saw a pile of coonhounds. Scout wasn't moving. A pool of blood soaked into the dirt. Her flashlight illuminated Pepper's lifeless face; she could only see Blue's body underneath. On the side of the house, written in the canines' blood were the words MOVE OUT NOW. Using her flashlight, she looked down at the ground, illuminating footprints and tire tracks.

"I told you to stay inside!" Elizabeth yelled from the darkness. Claire turned her head and saw her mother approaching with Irving in tow. Unable to process everything fully, she didn't reply. She looked back down at the tire tracks. Elizabeth snapped her finger and pointed to the back porch.

"Get inside now!"

Claire was startled by the anger in her mother's voice. Knowing she would lose any argument, she hurried inside. Irving surveyed the scene, taking note of the message written in blood. Irving put his hands on his knees as he bent down and looked at the dogs. Their throats were cut and the blood had soaked the fur on their chests. Irving righted himself and looked around.

"What we gonna do?"

"Call the police in the morning."

"Who you think done it?"

"I bet I have a good idea."

As the sun came over the horizon, Elizabeth made the phone call and fixed a pot of coffee. When Officer Flynn arrived, Elizabeth came out onto the porch and waved him over to the side of the house. He stood over the dogs with his hands on his utility belt.

"Are you kidding me? I can't believe they would go this far! Were these your dogs or Mr. Campbell's?"

"His."

"This makes me sick!"

"What are you going to do?"

"I'm gonna have to take a photo and fill out an incident report. Sheriff is gonna want to see this!"

"Will he come out here?"

"You bet. He loves coonhounds too. He ain't gonna like this." Flynn looked at Elizabeth with a squint in his eye "You call Mister Humes yet?"

"I haven't."

"Well, he will want to see this for himself."

When the call came into Arthur's office, he was opening a package mailed from a shoe store in New York City that sold men's dress shoes. The package was wrapped in brown paper and tied up with twine. After freeing the wrapping from the box, he excitedly opened the lid revealing white tissue paper and the slightest glimpse of a brand-new pair of Florsheim shoes with tan colored mesh vents. Just as he reached into the box, his secretary hollered from the front room, flattening his smile.

"Phone for you, Mr. Humes." He put the lid back on as he exhaled and picked up the phone.

"Hello, this is Mr. Humes."

The call prompted him to get up and quickly drive over to the Campbell Farm where he found Claire and Elizabeth standing at the side of the house. As he approached the scene, he pulled out a handkerchief and cover his nose as he spoke.

"Aw, what a shame! Who did this?"

"I only have one guess."

"Well, there's motive for sure. What did Officer Flynn say?"

"He said he's filling out papers."

"Yeah, an incident report. I'll go get a copy and see what I can do. Call you soon," he said as he quickly left. Claire turned to her mother.

"Mom? Where do these people live?"

"I don't know. I don't think they live in this town."

"Any idea who dug those holes?"

"Not exactly sure but I'm guessing it's the same people. Why?"

"Well, whoever dug those holes also killed the dogs."

"How do you know?" Elizabeth asked. Claire pointed at the ground.

"The tire tracks here are the same as the ones out in the field. Both have a small section of the tire missing."

Paying attention to tire tracks was something Claire had learned from *The Mystery of the Tolling Bell*. Nancy Drew had examined tire tracks with her flashlight after an encounter with a threatening stranger. While living at Harris Clay Mining Camp, Claire paid close attention to tire tracks, observing their unique pattern and trying to discern between a truck tire and a car tire.

"The guy that was in the house yesterday drove a car, right?" Claire asked.

"I believe so."

After a lengthy stay at Knoxville General Hospital, Harold Tyrell overcame his most recent asthma attack. The attending physician requested that Harold attempt a light activity, so he could administer a lung function test. To Annie's surprise, Harold then asked to speak to his father on the phone. When Annie finally got Gordon on the line, she handed the receiver to Harold.

"Dad!"

"How you doin' buddy?" Gordon asked, stopping in his tracks, his mind racing.

"Doctor Patterson wants to test my lungs while doing an activity!"

"He does?" Gordon said with a confused tone.

"He mentioned walking up and down a hallway or lifting a weight."

"Really?" he replied, still perplexed.

"Dad?" Harold started to say, his voice sounded much clearer and lively. Gordon felt a form of relief attempting to set in, but Harold's medical history prevented it.

"Yeah?"

"I asked Doctor Patterson if my activity could be throwing a ball. They said I could in the cafeteria. Could you bring the baseball and our gloves?" Harold asked. Gordon's throat tightened, and his face became warm.

"Yes. I will be there as fast..." he said, trying to calm himself down, clearing his throat... "as fast as I can, buddy."

Chapter 39

Gordon arrived at Knoxville General Hospital at 5:30 P.M. with two gloves and a baseball. His glove was worn and flexible. The leather had dried and cracked where the glove flexed, each crack seemingly begging for a drop of oil. The laces that held the leather fingers together had slit and frayed over the years. Harold's appeared brand new and was a little stiff even though it had been purchased over three years ago.

Gordon's arrival was greeted with a big smile and hug from Harold and a kiss from Annie. When the doctor came into the room, he explained they would have to wait until the cafeteria closed at eight o'clock to use it as a venue for Harold's breathing test.

At 8:00 P.M., two nurses entered the dark cafeteria, pushing a Spirometer on a cart and unraveling extension cords toward an outlet on the wall. One of the nurses turned on half of the lights in the large space and the cafeteria was ready to host a game of catch.

Annie pushed Harold's wheelchair into the cafeteria while Gordon and Dr. Patterson followed closely behind. Once Harold was in the middle the room, the nurses helped him stand up, pushing the wheelchair out of the way. Dr. Patterson looked over the spirometer and then supervised the nurses as they attached a hose to the machine and flipped a few switches. The subtle hum of a motor started up. Once the doctor saw that the setup was to his liking, he began to explain through the rumble and roll of his thick cheeks.

"So, we will do an initial test. This will measure pre-activity, and then we will throw the ball for about three to five minutes under my constant supervision. Understand?" he asked. Harold nodded. The test was performed by placing a tube in Harold's mouth while being given instructions to take in a breath and blow out until all of the air was purged from his lungs. After another two rounds of breathing out, the doctor listened to Harold's heart and lungs while Gordon and Annie watched.

"Okay, now you may throw the ball and this activity will last a maximum of five minutes," Dr. Patterson explained. Gordon walked up to Harold and handed him his glove with a smile that had been a long time coming.

"You ready?"

"Yeah, Dad," Harold said with a big grin. Gordon gripped the ball. The first toss was under-handed and a short distance. As the tosses became more and more controlled, Gordon stepped back a few paces until he felt comfortable with the distance. Then the overhand throws commenced. On the second overhand throw, Harold caught the ball and then attempted to throw the ball over-hand. A wayward throw hit the cafeteria floor and rolled behind Gordon.

"I got it," Gordon said as he hurried and scooped the ball into his glove. Quickly returning to his spot, he continued to throw and catch the ball only to become overwhelmed with the thought of Harold getting better. Tears flowed from Gordon's cheeks, which he attempted to hide after each lob into the air, wiping the streams with the back of his ungloved hand.

The killing of three coonhounds in Grainger County didn't sit well with Sheriff Dan Keller. His weapon of choice wasn't a gun rather it was a typewriter. Filling out forms and reports put people in the county jail. Some forms launched investigations. Some reports caused lives to change.

For the murder of three coonhounds, both a report and a state form launched an investigation and caused issues in Mr. Sidney Kroll's office. The husbands' and wives' case contesting the will of Thaddeus Campbell was officially halted until a police investigation was completed. When a copy of the report fell into the hands of Sleeves, the wives, and husbands, they were surprised to find that in addition to being named a suspect in the death of three canines, they were also being investigated for a series of holes dug on Mr. Campbell's property.

Back on the Campbell Farm, Irving and his father used a hay bale tarp to roll up Scout, Pepper, and Blue before they dragged them to the side of the barn. After an hour of digging, they buried them and then rested underneath the shade of a nearby tree after Millie had brought them a glass of lemonade. While they sipped their drinks and wiped sweat from their brows, they watched as Claire came into view, having walked around the side of the barn. She stopped and knelt beside the coonhounds' grave. Just as she had once pet one of their heads, she did so on top of the mound of dirt. Captain spoke softly to Irving,

"Sure is a shame. To do something like that to dogs."

Claire could hear something but wasn't sure what it was. At first it sounded like a bird. Maybe a crow in the distance. She stood up and saw Irving and Captain hurry out from underneath the tree towards the house. The sound she heard was yelling coming from inside the house. As she approached, Captain and Irving

GRAINGER COUNTY TOMATOES

stopped outside the backdoor. Claire hurried past them and went inside.

"I didn't kill no dogs, and you know it! You probably killed them yourselves just to get back at me! Get outta my house!"

"I didn't say you killed our dogs," Elizabeth said. While Sleeves carried on, Claire carefully looked around the corner seeing her mother keeping the door half closed while talking to the man on the porch. Seeing an opportunity, Claire spun around and ran out the back door, around the house, and hurried toward the car. She ducked down out of sight and looked at the tires. The tread was different than the tire tracks in the field and on the side of the house. She continued to crouch as she hurried to the back porch and through the back door, ending up at her mother's side where Sleeves was still ranting.

"You probably killed your own dogs just to stall the case!"

"That is quite a stretch, Mister!" Elizabeth yelled. Sleeves removed the copy of the investigation report from his back pocket and held it in the air as he continued to yell.

"And what is this digging holes business? You know we ain't out here digging no holes on this property! Why on earth would we do that for?"

Before Elizabeth could reply, Claire pushed past her and stood in the doorway.

"Mister, do you own a truck?"

"No," he replied with a puzzled expression.

"Any of your kin own a truck?"

"What?"

"Where were you on the night of May 23rd between the hours of ten and midnight?"

Sleeves transferred his attention from Claire to Elizabeth. "Is this little girl interrogating me? I don't believe this!" he shouted as he raised both arms, letting them slap the sides of his thighs.

Elizabeth pushed Claire behind her ready to close the door. "I have had enough of this. Please leave or I will call the law," she said as she closed and locked the door. Through the window, she saw the man head to his car. Elizabeth turned to Claire.

"He didn't do it, Mom."

"Easy, Nancy Drew. You don't know that."

"He is a well-dressed man. Pants. Button up shirt. Doesn't own a truck. Those tracks by the holes and by the side of the house belong to a truck. I checked his car tires. They don't match! You think a guy like that is out there digging holes?" she asked as she pointed toward the man walking away.

"How do you know a relative of his doesn't own a truck? He could have paid someone."

"Nancy Drew looks for people who don't answer clearly or look away as they speak. He didn't. I believe him."

"Nancy Drew isn't real, and she can't get hurt. You can. Stay out of this," Elizabeth said with a tone that abruptly ended the conversation. Claire peered out the window and watched the man back out into the road and drive away.

The next morning at Knoxville General Hospital, Gordon rose out of an uncomfortable cot and struggled to stand up straight. The first thing that hit him was the length of time he had been away from work. Instead of worrying about it, he simply hoped that every order was getting filled. While Annie cleaned up in the women's restroom in the hallway, Gordon waited with Harold until she returned. He then took his toothbrush out of his pocket and started toward the hallway as Annie looked at her watch.

"Sorry, I took so long, but you should hurry. Doctor will be here shortly with the results."

Gordon entered the men's restroom and brushed his teeth without the luxury of toothpaste. After splashing water on his face, he ran his wet fingers through his hair. He tucked his toothbrush into his back pocket, left the men's room and turned the corner. The hallway now appeared to be a tunnel with an oncoming train. Why did the doctor pull Annie out of the room? He hurried up to them as his shoes squeaked on the polished tile floor. The loudest squeak came when he stopped suddenly and stood next to Annie.

"Mr. Tyrell, I was just telling your wife that the test has given me and other physicians some concerns. Now that you are both here, let me first say that your son's lung capacity is shrinking. Going back over previous test results, at age eight his capacity was greater, and now it is less. Much less."

"Shrinking? He seemed to be doing better last night. He threw the ball!"

"The test was about his lung capacity, not if he could perform the activity. The concern is, what happens if he has another asthma attack a few weeks or months down the road. If his lung capacity continues to shrink the risk of surviving an attack decreases dramatically."

"Okay. How do we stop his lung capacity from shrinking?"

"I'd like to keep him here for about six more days. I need to run a few more tests," Dr. Patterson explained. Gordon crossed his arms and exhaled. Annie began to cry as she leaned into her husband. He wrapped his arm around her and held her close. Gordon watched Dr. Patterson as he pulled out the familiar manila envelope with the packet peeking out from the opening. "I have good news and bad news about this device," Dr. Patterson said as he looked at Gordon.

"Okay. I guess I am ready."

"This machine will not increase your son's lung capacity, but it could keep him where he's at, meaning it could stop his lungs from shrinking further."

"Really?"

"And the bad news, is that this hospital just cancelled an order of two X-Ray machines. We really needed them, but we are forced to wait until next year. Not sure that the administrator could even find funds in the budget for something like this," Dr. Patterson said as he handed Gordon the envelope. "Just keep in mind that this kind of treatment might not help. There is no guarantee. Some patients respond to aggressive treatments, some don't. It may not work for your son."

Annie wiped the tears from her eyes as Dr. Patterson left them alone. She looked up at her husband.

"I still don't see how you're going to get the money. It's just too much."

Gordon embraced her without answering and thought about the room locked behind a green door.

Chapter 40

On the other side of Rutledge, Norman Werthan had spent his day working out in the fields with his farm hands, and when daylight started to fade, he ended the work day, placed the tools in the barn, and took a much-needed shower. While making a sandwich in the kitchen, his knees buckled at the sudden, severe pain in his chest. Falling to the floor, he clutched his heart.

Norman thought about T.C. Campbell doing the same and wondered if he was meeting the same end. Instead of screaming and letting the chest pains get the better of him, he crawled to the wall where the telephone hung five feet high up from the floor. *Would T.C. be holding the gates of heaven closed?* The pain continued. Placing himself up against the wall, still clutching his chest, he sat underneath the phone and began to scoot up the wall. Once he gained enough height, he reached up and unhooked the phone off the receiver and sat back down. A female voice came on the line.

"Operator."

"My heart is giving out. I need an ambulance."

Claire read one of her books on the back porch while her mother sat nearby as she sorted through invoices and payroll slips. With the ledger opened on her lap, she used a pencil and wrote a series of numbers in a column while dismissing the thought that the farm could go to Mr. Campbell's nieces and nephews. Instead, she repeated the words she learned in the coffee shop, "The ledger is a living and breathing thing. It's the heart of any business."

Elizabeth heard the phone ring and stood up. Thinking it might be Arthur Humes, she hurried to the kitchen. Instead of Arthur's voice, it was Irving's on the other end of the line. Still at the co-op, he had used the pay phone outside.

"I have bad news."

"What is it."

"Norman was taken to the hospital over in Morristown."

"What happened?"

"Some kind of heart trouble. The fellas 'round the co-op were talking about it."

"I'm on my way." Elizabeth hung up and shouted at the top of her lungs. "Claire!"

Elizabeth grabbed the truck keys and started out the back door toward the barn. Claire walked alongside.

"What is it?"

"Mr. Werthan is in the hospital."

Morristown was a little closer to Rutledge than Knoxville and while the hospital wasn't as big, it had a good reputation. When Elizabeth and Claire arrived, they parked near the entrance and rushed inside. Coming to a receptionist desk they asked for Norman's room number. Seeing that they were in a hurry, the nurse flipped feverishly through the book and found his name.

"Room 143."

Elizabeth hurried down the hallway with Claire following, nearly coming to a jog. Norman was sitting in the hospital bed reading a newspaper and wearing reading glasses. When they appeared in the doorway, he rolled his eyes.

"Oh no," he said to himself, thinking they were going to start crying.

"Norman! What happened?" Elizabeth asked.

"How'd you know I was here?"

The McGurn brothers swept the wooden floor boards of the mill and stuffed burlap bags into a burn barrel. When the last employee left, they knocked on the office door.

"Come in," hollered Gordon. They entered and closed the door behind them. "Everyone else gone?" Gordon's feet were on his desk and he was biting the fingernail of his index finger.

"Yep," Dalton replied.

"Were you able to do anything to scare her off?"

"We killed their dogs."

"What?" Gordon said as he swung his feet off his desk and onto the floor. He stopped biting his fingernail.

"They had three coonhounds. We killed them with a knife." Wesley said in a matter-of-fact manner as if he had just completed a menial task.

"You killed their dogs? I didn't mean for you to do that!" he said as he raised his voice. Gordon stood up. "I meant burn a cross in their front yard, or leave a message in paint on their front door!"

"We did leave a message." Dalton said.

"We wrote the words *MOVE OUT* on the side of the house in blood," Wesley explained.

"In blood?"

"The dog's blood," said Dalton with a nod. Gordon ran his fingers through his hair as he shook his head in disbelief and mumbled expletives under his breath. Being cruel and vicious wasn't something Gordon was used to. Killing a dog went beyond his comprehension. His hand covered his mouth as he thought about them using a knife to bring a dog to its end. He then looked up at them with a hopeful look, removing his hand from his mouth before he spoke.

"Did it work?"

"We been driving by there. It looks like business as usual," Dalton answered. Gordon looked deflated.

"Okay, from now on I will be clear in my instructions and no more killing anything."

"Alright," Wesley said.

"Sure," Dalton added as he hung his head. He picked chunks of mud off his boot while he asked about the next move. "So, what do we do now?" Gordon paced the floor for a moment before coming to a stop.

"We get inside that room."

Chapter 41

Norman didn't feel like he was going to die. While his body ached from lying on his back in an uncomfortable hospital bed, he kept his spirits up whenever a nurse walked into the room. He made light of his condition in an effort to go home as he hated the hospital and didn't like Elizabeth and Claire fussing over him.

Elizabeth would wet a wash cloth in a nearby sink and place it on Norman's forehead. He would complain, but it did feel good. Claire took to reading in a chair next to the bed while keeping an eye on Norman's drinking glass. When it would get low, she would fill it up and bring it back.

"You don't really need to be here. I'm fine."

"If you keep it up, I'll start crying again," Elizabeth said with a smile.

A curtain to the hallway was parted, and a nurse came into his room. Instead of looking at Norman, she looked at Elizabeth.

"There is an Arthur Humes on the phone, and he is trying to reach you."

She followed the nurse out to the nurse's station and was handed the telephone.

"Hello?"

"I heard about Norman. Figured you'd be there at the hospital. How's he doing?"

"Good, I guess. He keeps telling me to go home."

"That sounds about right. I needed to reach you to give you an update on Mr. Campbell's family."

"Okay."

"The Sheriff is conducting an investigation into the Campbell family and has filed a report that lists them as suspects in both the murder of the canines and the holes dug on the property. This gives me the ability to file a temporary injunction against the case of the Last Will and Testament of your uncle."

"What's an injunction?"

"Ehhh...don't worry about that. Just know the whole thing is at a screeching halt until the sheriff's department completes the investigation."

Elizabeth's memory went back to Claire when she said that the man on their porch couldn't have dug those holes or killed their dogs.

"Mr. Humes, what if this family is found guilty? Is there a possibility that the farm would be out of their reach?"

"Well, it gives me more ammunition to fight the case, so in a way it might. I have to get down to the courthouse to file this thing. I will keep you updated as this progresses."

"Thank you for calling me."

When Elizabeth hung up, she looked around finding that she was alone as the nurses were on their rounds. She quickly dialed the operator. Upon finding the right Penelope in Jackson, Tennessee, the line clicked and then rang until the phone was answered.

"Hello?"

"Hello, is this Penelope?"

"It is."

"My name is Elizabeth Campbell, and I am a friend of your father's," she said before going into the explanation of his health scare. Penelope started in with specific questions and sounded calm.

"What are his cholesterol levels?"

"Oh. Um…I'm not sure," she replied before leaning over the nurse's station and grabbing a pencil and a piece of paper. While cradling the phone between her shoulder and ear, she wrote down *cholesterol level*. "I'm writing this down, and I can call you back when I get the answers. By the end of the conversation, Elizabeth had also written down *triglyceride levels and blood pressure*.

Gordon had made the trip back to Knoxville General while thinking about the green door in Mr. Campbell's house. The more he thought about it, the more he convinced himself that there was a fortune inside. When he arrived at the hospital, he hurried to his son's room and sat on the edge of Harold's hospital bed. He caressed his son's face with his right hand and looked into Harold's sleepy eyes.

Before entering the room, Annie had explained that they had given Harold a heavy dose of antihistamine and that he was sleepy from the side effects.

"Am I getting better dad?"

"I think so."

"I got to listen to a baseball game today."

"You did?"

"Stan Musial hit a home run with two men on base."

"You hear the crack of the bat?"

"Yeah," Harold smiled. Gordon recalled seeing several boys playing stick ball in the street a few days prior. How lucky they are, he thought. On the packet of information for the asthma breathing machine, was a paragraph that contained a sentence that Gordon hung onto. *For asthma patients to breathe normally in a controlled environment.*

Anytime Harold coughed, he thought about that sentence. Gordon reached down and held his son's hand as Harold drifted off to sleep. He placed his other hand on Harold's chest and felt him breathing shallow breaths.

Gordon stayed for nearly an hour and soaked up the time with his son by his side. When he finally stood up, he let Annie take his seat, and he left the hospital and found a nearby phone booth. After depositing a nickel, he dialed a phone number and asked for Dalton. When Dalton came on the line, Gordon kept it short.

"Bring two shotguns and meet me at the office at eleven."

"Tonight?"

"Tonight."

"How much do you think is in there?"

"Plenty."

After speaking with a nurse, Elizabeth had gathered the answers to Penelope's questions and called her back.

"His triglycerides are one hundred and twenty."

"Hmm…that's borderline. How about blood pressure?"

"One hundred and thirty over ninety."

"Okay. He must have had a spike in blood pressure and triglycerides if his chest was hurting."

"The nurse didn't have cholesterol levels yet."

"That's okay. How's he doing at the moment? I mean, is he alert, is he sitting up, or is he lethargic?"

"Oh, he's definitely alert," Elizabeth replied. As the conversation continued, she envied that Penelope sounded so confident and intelligent. Her replies were seemingly instantaneous, and her follow-up questions were quick. One day at the mining camp, she had stood near a radio and listened to Harry S. Truman speak about the war in Korea. She compared Penelope's vigor to the President and wished she sounded as bold and confident.

"Do you think his hospital stay will be long?" asked Penelope.

"I think he will be out tomorrow, if he has his way."

"Could you please keep me updated, and have him call me?"

"I will most certainly do that, but let me ask you first. I am thinking that if I were to arrange a lunch in Rutledge, you could come see your father, and eat here and then leave in the late afternoon. Does that sound like something you could do? I know it is a lengthy drive."

"Ooooh!" Penelope said as the idea settled in her mind. "I like that! Let me speak with my husband. Do you think a Sunday would work? It's the only day he has off."

"Of course!"

"This is a great idea!"

"I will have a full lunch prepared at his house and, on the table, when you arrive. This way you can visit longer."

"Elizabeth, this would be so great! I can't wait to speak to Heywood about this," Penelope continued to talk, but all Elizabeth could think about was the name Heywood Higginbottom. *Who were his parents? And why were they so cruel?*

"Let me give you my home phone number, and we will work this out."

Chapter 42

Just before midnight, Gordon turned the headlights off and parked the truck on the side of the road near the Campbell house. The limited light from the crescent moon above them helped conceal Dalton and Wesley as they hopped out of the truck bed with shotguns in hand and hurried to the side of the house with Gordon.

They sat beneath the window while Gordon removed a flashlight. Shining the beam of light through the window pane, he looked through the window and saw a dining room before turning the flashlight off and ducking beneath the window.

"This is it. We'll go in here," he whispered before removing a tool from his back pocket.

"Thought we were going in through the floorboards?" Dalton whispered.

"We need to know where the room is first," replied Gordon.

Dalton and Wesley watched as Gordon stood up and slid the tool between the two windows and quickly unlatched the interior lock. Gordon quietly lifted the heavy window. Wesley, the smaller of the three, squirmed up on the sill and slithered inside the dining room while trying to make as little noise as possible.

"Here," Gordon whispered as he handed Wesley the flashlight. "Find the green door, and then come back. Don't wake anyone.

Keep quiet." Wesley nodded, turned around, and snuck into the darkness.

"God, please let there be a fortune," Gordon said under his breath as he lowered the window and propped it open with the tool. If he had looked at his watch when Wesley went inside, he would have noticed that he was only gone for five minutes although it felt like twenty.

"Where is he?" Dalton asked. Gordon simply shook his head with a concerned expression. Finally, Wesley popped his head through the open window.

"You find it okay?" Gordon whispered.

"I didn't. No idea where it is," Wesley responded. Gordon rolled his eyes and helped Wesley back out through the window. He grabbed the flashlight and hoisted himself inside.

Upstairs Elizabeth woke to a noise. She listened while her head rested on her pillow. *Was Millie up and about? What time was it?* She considered for brief moment of getting up and looking outside for a hint of sunlight but succumbed to the euphoric fall into sleep.

Gordon used his flashlight and saw a radio, a rocking chair and lace curtains. He moved to the kitchen and saw nothing resembling a green door. He walked down a hallway finding a small bathroom, and then a floor board popped underneath his right foot.

Elizabeth's eyes snapped open. She sat up in bed causing Claire to wake.

"Did you hear that?" she whispered to Claire.

"No."

Elizabeth got out of bed as she held a finger to keep Claire silent. As she walked out of the room and stood out in the hallway at the top of the stairs, Elizabeth saw a figure walk past the staircase on the first floor. She ducked around the corner out of sight.

Claire could barely see her but could tell she was frightened. Thinking quickly, Elizabeth reached inside the bedroom and grabbed an old chamber pot water pitcher.

Just before Elizabeth discovered a trespasser in the house, Gordon was wondering where the green door was. It wasn't in the kitchen. It wasn't in the living room, and it wasn't in the dining room.

When the green door was boarded up, the dining room hutch had been moved to the left to cover up the plywood board. Just when Gordon was wondering where the door could be, the porcelain pitcher tumbled on the wooden steps, making loud, thunderous sounds as it cracked and broke coming to a rest in pieces on the first floor. Gordon hurried to the window and shimmied through the opening.

Upstairs, Claire had crawled through a window and onto the roof. She watched as three men, one shorter than the other two, ran to a vehicle parked in the distance. She squinted to see better in the dark as the engine turned over and the headlights turned on. In the darkness it was difficult to see, but it appeared that they had jumped into a truck with a flatbed.

Millie had woken up to the sound of what sounded like thousands of glass jars shattering inside the house. Captain was still asleep and snoring.

"Wake up!" she whispered loudly as she pushed him and rocked his body awake.

"What you want now?" he grumbled.

"Get up! Get up! Something has happened," she continued to whisper as she stood up and searched for her robe.

Once Claire had told her mother about the men running off, Elizabeth told Captain and Millie to stay put as she grabbed a flashlight off the top of the refrigerator.

"I'm going to get Irving," she hollered as she ran out the back door and through the fields. Her feet punched the dirt with each stride as she gave it her all, running as fast as she could possibly run between the rows of soil. Using the limited light from the crescent moon above, she held the flashlight without turning it on to save the batteries. Each stride tugged at her brain in the way that she thought something wasn't right. Something was causing her to look down as she slowed her pace and then came to a stop. Trying to catch her breath and thinking that something was strange about the field, she turned on her flashlight and saw sprouts of tomato leaves breaking the soil. Her breath caught in her chest for a moment. Waving the beam of the flashlight revealed sprouts as far as the light would let her see.

It took longer to get to the hand quarters as she ceased cutting through the field. Keeping her stride, she ran between the rows and around the forty acres, keeping her flashlight on and admiring the beautiful sprouts as she ran.

After being woken up, Irving followed Elizabeth to the main house. Once inside, they found an opened window in the dining room. Claire spoke of what she saw out on the roof. Millie fanned herself with her hand.

"Well, what do they want? Why they breakin' in here?" Millie asked. The explanation of the will and the green door commenced. Irving jumped in a few times making sure his mother and father knew to never mention it in public.

"Well, I think it'd be best if we just forgot about it, Millie," said Captain.

"Well," Millie asked as she looked at Irving. "What do you think is in there?"

"I don't care. Just do what dad says and forget you ever heard about it."

"Now that we all know," Elizabeth said, "we will make sure the windows are locked. I will have a deadbolt installed on all the doors." As she spoke, Captain nodded his head.

"Good idea," Captain added. "You buy the locks and I'll see to it that they installed."

Elizabeth thanked him and walked over to an end table where she had set down the flashlight. She picked it up.

"Now, I have to call the sheriff's office. This may further help our case against Mr. Campbell's family who are trying to take this farm away."

"I know what that means," Captain said as he headed toward the back bedroom. "Come on, Millie. We sleepin' in the hand quarters tonight."

"Hang on," Elizabeth said. "It'll be easier on you both if we take the truck, but on the way there, I want to show Claire something."

Millie and Captain's toiletries and clothes for the next day were packed in a small suitcase. Irving helped his mother and father up onto the truck bed while Claire and Elizabeth rode in the cab.

"What are you going to show me?" Claire asked.

"You'll see."

The truck drove around the forty acres and toward the hand quarters only to stop half way in between. Irving hopped off the back of the truck while Millie and Captain remained. Elizabeth and Claire exited the truck and stood next to the field. Once the flashlight illuminated the rows, Claire's eyes widened. She had been expecting another hole in the ground or a tire track but was floored when she saw the rows and rows of tomato sprouts.

Irving bent down to take a closer look. Elizabeth handed him the flashlight. As he spoke, they all gathered around.

"Breaking ground is the hard part. We gonna need to use stakes every six feet with string."

"We need to call back a few hands for that?" Elizabeth asked. Claire was still in shock. She looked out as far as the flashlight would let her, seeing the tomato plants cresting the soil.

"Nah," Irving said. "Three people can stake about five acres a day. Have it done in no time. Save on labor. Looks good though," he said as he stood up. "I'll come out here in the morning. Give it a once over to see if there are any trouble spots. Shouldn't be though. This here is 40 acres of rich soil with worms." When they got back in the truck, Claire sat in the passenger seat and recalled when they first arrived at the Campbell Farm. The dogs had greeted them at the truck when Norman dropped them off.

"These dogs are crazy!" Elizabeth had laughed just before she closed the driver side door. The dogs had jumped and pawed at the new arrivals all the way to the back porch.

Norman waited for a light to come on in the house to ensure they got in okay. Once he saw the light, he had backed out into the street and headed for home.

Elizabeth and Claire left the playful dogs outside and walked in through the backdoor into a dark room. A light switch was quickly found after Elizabeth had swept the walls with her hand. Elizabeth pushed the button and illuminated the kitchen.

"Wow!" said Claire. Elizabeth covered her mouth in disbelief. "It looks brand new!" They took their shoes off to ensure that they kept the white tile clean.

"Mom?"

"Yes?"

"Is this ours?"

At the time, her mother had said no. It was later that Claire found out about the growing of the forty acres and the Last Will and Testament of Mr. Campbell. Driving back to the hand quarters and helping Millie and Captain get situated, she thought about what her mother had done. While Irving had done most of the work, it was her mother who made it happen. Claire recalled her mother being out in the field, rolling soil with a scuffle. She re-played in her head when her mother was spreading fertilizer and worms with her bare hands. Her memory went back further, even before Harris Clay Mining Company and thought of her dad and the day he passed away. Her appreciation for her mother slowly churned into admiration. Tears started flowing down her cheeks. It took only a few seconds for Elizabeth to notice.

"Claire? Are you crying? What's wrong?"

Claire's hands were loosely clasped in her lap. Without wip-ing her tears, she turned her head and looked at her mother.

"I miss Dad. I miss him so much."

"Oh, honey," Elizabeth replied as she slowed the truck and ap-plied the parking brake.

"When I saw the field and the sprouts, I couldn't believe it. I guess it just sort of hit me all at once."

Elizabeth embraced her daughter and held her tight. Claire continued. "All I could think was that dad would be very proud of you. You did this. You made this happen."

Elizabeth's heart swelled, and she began to cry. She hadn't thought of what her husband would think. It hadn't crossed her mind. Simultaneously, she felt prideful and guilty.

"We did. We made it happen. I wasn't out there in the fields alone."

Elizabeth embraced her daughter while the truck remained parked and the engine ran. The deep throaty rumble of the engine filled Claire's ears. She thought about the farm and the men who were there sneaking around the house. While her mother held her, Claire remembered the man with the rolled-up sleeves on the front porch. She recalled the tire tracks in the dirt and the mur-dered dogs at the side of the house. Someone was trying to take the farm away from them, but who?

Chapter 43

Sidney Kroll sat in his office with Sleeves sitting in a chair in front of his desk. Their conversation had begun with unsavory talk of having to come up with a check for Mr. Kroll's legal services. When the dollar amount left the lips of the attorney and travelled to the ears of his client, the weight of a hundred elephants fell onto Sleeve's chest.

"What? Why so much?"

"Well, if you recall the number of hours spent on your case has been significant, and if I am to continue, I will need funds today."

Sleeves had every intention of speaking with Mr. Kroll about the investigation concerning the holes dug on Mr. Campbell's property and the three dead coondogs found next to the main house. Instead, the conversation began with money. After Sleeves excused himself, he left the office, folded himself into a phone booth, and deposited a nickel. He phoned his relatives and explained the situation only to be given the runaround. "I'll pay you back," said one brother-in-law. "Can I just take it out of the inheritance?" a sister asked. After four phone calls, he came up dry and was forced to pay the exuberant sum himself. As he wrote out the check, he frowned and grumbled, berating himself for going into the dry-cleaning business instead of becoming an attorney. He slid the check across the desk and watched as Mr. Kroll's fingers applied pressure to the other side and began sliding it toward him. Sleeves watched the check leave like a child looking at him through the back window of a car.

"Excellent. Now that our financial matters have been cleared up, I have some news."

"Good news?"

"I'm sorry. This is bad news."

"Bad news?"

"There is a warrant out for your arrest issued by the Grainger County Sheriff's Department."

"A what?" Sleeves yelled as he stood up.

From time-to-time in the world of Nancy Drew, she would need a bicycle to get around town to solve the mysteries she would encounter. It occurred to Claire that she, too, would need a bicycle if she were to investigate the mystery of the tire tracks around the Campbell Farm.

The morning after the men had invaded the main house, she was out by the road where she had watched them jump into a truck. Kneeling in the grass and dirt, she looked for signs of tire tracks that might look like the ones found out in the field. While she did find tracks, they weren't clear as there was too much grass and not enough dirt to give a distinct impression. She stood up and headed toward the house thinking that it was time to ask for a bicycle and permission to go into town.

Gordon sat in his office biting his fingernail while the sounds of the grain belt could be heard outside his office. Anger had been surging through his body all morning wondering why the green door wasn't there. He briefly considered that it was a small-town rumor. He shook off the thought and picked up the phone.

"Rutledge Savings and Loan this is Mr. Landry. How may I help you?"

"It's me."

"Hey, Buddy! How are you? So great to hear from you! Can you by any chance come meet me at the bank? I'd certainly like to get some brunch from the mercantile if you have time. Weather is nice, and I thought we could walk."

Something was wrong. Roger didn't talk like this. Maybe a customer was sitting at his desk, and he couldn't talk.

"Uh, sure."

"Great! Come on over, and we'll leave from here!"

Click. In a state of confusion and curiosity, Gordon left the mill and drove over to the bank. Before he reached the entrance, Roger hurried out and walked up next to Gordon. As they headed toward the town square, Roger spoke just above a whisper.

"Sheriff Keller is investigating a break-in last night."

"Where?"

"Campbell Farms. Was that you?" Roger asked as he stopped walking. Gordon looked away without answering. "Good news is that they are looking at Mr. Campbell's kin down in Knoxville," Roger explained. Gordon started biting his fingernail.

"I see."

"So, what was in there?"

"What?"

"What was in the room with the green door?"

"There isn't a green door."

"What?"

"It wasn't there."

"How's that possible? Wasn't there a big 'ol piece of plywood nailed to the wall? That's what the two guys from the hardware store said."

"I don't know. I was only on the first floor. Maybe it is on the second."

"Stay off the phones. I was trying to get you to not say anything on the phone, because a few years ago they caught a thief in Elm Springs talking about cattle he stole from a farm. Operator heard it and turned him in."

"Yeah, I heard they listen in from time to time."

"Be careful. How's your boy?"

"Could be better."

"Still think the machine will help?"

"I do. But if something happened to him and I was unable to even find out if…" Gordon said until he was unable to continue. Tears formed in his eyes. Roger gave him a single pat on the back.

"You'll get the money," he said as he turned back toward the bank.

"I dug up more than five thousand already," Gordon muttered as he wiped a tear from his eye.

"Five?" Roger said as he spun around.

"Yeah, but I had to split it with the McGurn brothers."

"Okay, look. You get ten in cash. I will get you the rest."

"Ten?"

"Yep. Ten. Get it, and I'll get you the other half. I'll have to complete the loan and ask for forgiveness later, but the first thing I'm gonna do is find out about that door. I'll ask that guy Ben at the hardware store. He borrows money from us from time to time. He's not that friendly, but I'll ask and see if we get anything from him."

"I don't know if I can go back there. Their guard is raised."

"I'm sure you'll think of something."

Chapter 44

The morning Norman was to be released from the hospital, Elizabeth and Claire took Millie and Captain to Norman's house. They brought pots, pans, a roast purchased from Kirby and Son's Butcher shop on the square, and bags of carrots, green beans, ham hocks, and potatoes. By ten o'clock they had a roast in the oven, and a big pot of seasoned vegetables simmering on the stove.

When Elizabeth and Claire left Norman's house, the aroma seemed to follow them briefly on the way out to the truck. Once on the road to Morristown, Claire started in on her mother.

"Mom, I have something to ask you, and I don't want you to say 'no' right away."

"Where is this going?"

"I need you to hear me out and not rush to say 'no'."

"Don't I always listen to you? Don't I always hear you out?"

"No."

"No? What do you mean 'no'?"

"Can you just let me talk?"

"This is an interesting way to begin asking for something."

"I wanted to ask you about the possibility of getting a bicycle."

"You want a bicycle?"

"Well, I also want permission to be able to ride into town."

"On the road? Don't you know how fast these trucks drive on these roads?"

"I do. But I can get off into the grass if I hear a car coming."

"I don't know."

"Come on! I'm old enough!"

The conversation continued until they reached Morristown Hospital. Claire didn't get an immediate no, but it didn't look promising.

Once inside the hospital, they found the door to Norman's hospital room closed. Before knocking, they walked over to the nurse's station.

"Excuse me, we are here to pick up Mr. Werthan."

"Oh, he's getting dressed. He'll be out shortly."

Gordon sat at his desk, and signed checks he could barely cover. The invoices were plentiful, and the revenue was not. One invoice was 90 days past due. So he paid it first and set a few on the back burner. The phone rang, and he quickly answered.

"Hey, Gordon. How's it going?" Roger said in an overly polite tone.

"Fine."

"Do you have a hutch in your dining room?"

"No. We have a rack."

"A rack?"

"Yes, we keep our nice dishes in a rack. Can't really afford a hutch."

"Well, suppose you had a hutch, and you didn't like where it was, maybe you would move it."

Gordon felt as if he had gotten slapped. His mind transported him back to the dining room in Mr. Campbell's home. There was a hutch along the wall. He remembered seeing it as his flashlight passed over the front.

"Yes," Gordon answered and then continued in a tone that made it very clear that he was following. "But I wouldn't want to scratch the floor."

"I see. Well, I hope you have a great rest of your day."

Gordon hung up the phone and picked at his fingernail with his teeth. His thoughts came together while thinking of how to get back in the house. He stood up, pulled a drawer out from his desk, and removed a set of keys before walking out of his office. The mill was grinding away while the McGurn brothers filled burlap bags. They watched from the corner of their eyes as Gordon walked out of his office and through the large open bay door.

Behind the mill, Gordon walked up to a storage shed and unlocked it with a key. He opened the double doors finding two metal barrels of gasoline. He wrapped his arms around one of the barrels and tried to move it. It wouldn't budge. He then wrapped his arms around the second barrel and was able to slightly move it. He nodded his head as if the barrel of gasoline was now a part of the plan forming in his head.

When Sunday came, Penelope Higginbottom and her family began the trip to Rutledge. She sat in the passenger seat and calmed her children who were arguing over a toy. With her children appeased and her husband caught up in the music on the radio, she thought of her father while the wind from the cracked window sprung loose a few strands of her brunette hair. Her hair wisped around as she recalled being pushed in a tire swing that hung from a large tree behind the house. Her father would always push her up higher than her mother liked, but she loved the feeling in her stomach as she fell briefly before swinging back and forth.

When she was little, she rode through the house on a wooden horse her mother had purchased second hand from a neighbor. The horse would rock back and forth, and if she rocked hard enough, the wooden horse would scoot along the hardwood floors. One day the horse scooted too fast for Penelope. She fell off and hit the back of her head on the hardwood floor.

Penelope recalled the injury as the scenery outside the car seamlessly slid past. She leaned her head against her arm that was propped up on the window. She remembered her father rushing to her side and holding the back of her head as she cried. His arms cradled her, and yet he seemed angry at the same time. Whenever she was injured, it stung his heart to the point of anger. She faintly remembered her mother taking over and holding her as she cried while her dad picked up the wooden horse. For an unknown reason, when an object upset him or caused him grief, her dad would undoubtedly open the front door, and hurl the object out into the front yard. Over the years, a jar of marbles, a broom, an old radio, a mallet and a wooden horse had been ejected from the house. Even though he was upset in those moments, the memory of his unusual antics made her smile.

"What are you smiling about?" Heywood asked as he navigated a curve in the road.

"My dad. He used to throw things he didn't like out into the front yard."

"He did? Why?"

Penelope shifted in her seat as she began to explain her dad's eccentric behavior as best she could without making him seem deranged.

On the other side of town from the Campbell Farm, Captain taunted Millie in Norman's kitchen while she cut up potatoes. Standing over her shoulder, he spoke while he pointed at the cutting board.

"Them are too thick now. You gonna have these folks eatin' undercooked potatoes."

"They are fine. They will cook just fine."

"Uh huh. But you need to know that these potatoes gonna be off, and it'll cause problems."

"When I married you, your father told me the same thing about you."

"Don't be bringin' my daddy into this."

Chapter 45

Norman sat in the passenger side of the truck next to Claire, anxious to finally be home. Elizabeth steered the red truck on the highway and could see the sign for Rutledge. Unbeknownst to her, the Higginbottom family had already pulled into the driveway at Norman's house. They were already introducing themselves to Captain and Millie when Elizabeth told Norman of the surprise.

"Claire and I wanted to do something nice for you, so we have a little surprise when we get to your house."

"I don't like surprises. Unless it's cake. Is it cake?"

"Sort of. We thought you might not feel up to cooking something for dinner. So, we took care of that for you."

"That's fine. Doctor told me not to eat salt. Is it salty?"

"Hmmm…not sure."

"Well, what does he know…I think a lot of these doctors are shootin' from the hip anyway."

When the tires of the red truck rolled into the driveway at Norman's house, he could see the lights were on and there was a car in the driveway.

"You leave the lights on? Who else is here?"

"Well, let's just say our surprise comes with a few guests."

"Oh, great," Norman replied. Claire looked at her mother who

251

was wincing at the thought that this might not go over well. He walked to the front porch and opened the door to a nose full of aromas. Pot roast, green beans, carrots, and potatoes wafted in front of his face. Elizabeth and Claire stood behind him and remained on the front porch.

"Smells good," he said as he took a step inside. When he did, a figure standing in his living room caught his eye. When he turned his head, he saw Penelope.

"Dad," she muttered as tears started to collect in the corner of her eyes. Suddenly he was taken back to pushing this little girl on a tire swing in the backyard and holding her hand during the Spring Baptist Picnic as they walked through a crowd. Norman uttered her name as he took two steps toward her. Wrapping his arms around her, he held his daughter in a tight embrace. The feeling of almost losing her father enveloped her thoughts, causing her to squeeze him tighter. Norman spoke though trembling lips.

"I have missed you so."

Claire and Elizabeth decided to step quietly off the front porch and sneak in through the back door.

Heywood Higginbottom sat at the dining room table adjacent to the kitchen. He was a thin man with hair suitable for the military. Though he never served, people would often mistake him for a veteran. He sat with his two, grade-school kids and shushed them the second they got loud. When the back door opened and he saw Elizabeth step inside followed by her daughter, he stood up and nodded his head.

"Ma'am," he said.

"Hello."

They introduced themselves and waited quietly until Norman and Penelope finished talking.

Gordon and the McGurn brothers bided their time until the sun went down, then drove over to the backside of the Campbell property. They maneuvered painfully slow over uneven ground while the gasoline sloshed in the large drum in the back of the truck.

The dinner commenced with Elizabeth and Claire taking plates of food from the kitchen to the table, serving everyone including themselves. Sitting around the table and eating spoonfuls of hot carrots, potatoes, and pot roast, they listened to stories of Penelope's childhood from Norman and how they used to ride on the tractor together in the fields.

At one point, Elizabeth looked over at Norman as he laughed at something Penelope was saying. The crow's feet around his eyes flexed and retracted. He looked happy and thoroughly delighted throughout dinner and dessert.

Chocolate cake with a homemade sugar icing that both Captain and Millie prepared with a fair amount of bickering and goading. Slices were cut and placed on small plates and distributed to the table by both Claire and Elizabeth. Before anyone had a chance to bite into a piece, Norman tapped on his drinking glass with a silver knife and stood up. He looked awkward as he stood at the head of the table, but he appeared determined.

"I, uh, I want to thank both Elizabeth and Claire for tonight," Norman said as he shifted his weight to his right side. He appeared to be stressed and unsure of what he was doing and to help Norman along, Heywood tapped his knife on his glass as if to encourage Norman.

"Here here," Heywood said as he nodded.

"I guess I want to say," he continued. His hands shook slightly from nerves and his voice wavered. "I don't know. I just want to say…" Norman seemed lost in thought and now appeared to be embarrassed and rested his weight on his hands as he leaned on the table. Penelope reached out and put her hand on top of her father's.

"Dad, it's ok. I understand."

"I'm sorry."

"No. No need to say you're sorry," she added as he took his seat.

"I just don't know what to say. I wanted to…," he added before he leapt up out of his seat once again. "I know. I want to say that I would like to do this again. All of you. Let's do this again," he said with confidence and knocked a single knock with his knuckle on the table.

Norman hadn't ever been to an occasion in which a toast was made. He understood the idea of it, and in his effort made that night at the dinner table, he had gotten it wrong. Elizabeth smiled to herself thinking that he was sweet and was probably a very charming man in his younger days. Penelope looked up at her father who was still standing at the head of the table.

"When would you like to do this again?" she asked. Norman's lip trembled and fell into a frown as his eyes poured.

"As soon as possible," he said as he failed at choking back tears. The weight of missing out on parts of his daughter's life fell upon him suddenly. He had missed out on getting to know his grandchildren. The weight felt a lot like guilt that transformed into the tears that fell down his face. Penelope stood up and embraced her father as he wrapped his arms around her.

"We'll stop here," Gordon said as he applied the parking brake. The moonlight was bright enough to cast shadows of the tomato sprouts that stretched far into the forty acres of darkness. Dalton and Wesley walked a few paces from the truck and took a seat in the grass. Both lit up cigarettes while Gordon leaned against the hood of the truck and looked at the main house far off in the distance.

Heywood got into the driver's side of his car while the kids climbed in the back as Norman held the door open. He spoke with Heywood while Penelope gathered her things and walked out the front door where Elizabeth was leaning against the porch railing. She grabbed Elizabeth's hand and looked into her eyes.

"You have no idea what you have done for me. Words can't even begin to express how thankful I am for you."

"Well, Norman had me worried there when he was in the hospital, and your calm voice and the information you provided helped me through it. So I am thankful for you."

"I feel like you were there when I couldn't be, and you arranged and planned all of this. You have done so much for us."

"I'm glad to do it. If it wasn't for Norman, I wouldn't be here. I would be in a very bad place. He's very important to me," Elizabeth explained. "I think it was good for him to see you and your family again."

"It is good for me, too," Penelope hugged Elizabeth and spoke softly. "If Dad comes to Jackson to visit, you make sure you and your daughter come with him."

"Thank you. You're so kind."

Penelope left Elizabeth and headed toward the car. She set her things in the front seat and then hugged her father. Elizabeth watched briefly from the front porch before heading inside.

Chapter 46

The orange light from the fields was so bright, Claire thought the sun had already risen. The sound of a paper bag being wadded up came from downstairs. Claire could see stars in the sky and sat up in bed. She nudged her mother, then she stood up and walked to the window. The fields were on fire!

"Mom! Mom! Wake up!" she yelled.

The sound of beating fists on the walls downstairs coupled with Captain's booming voice, overpowered the faint sound of the crackling.

"Elizabeth! Hurry down, Elizabeth! The fields, the fields!" Captain yelled. Within seconds, Elizabeth, Claire, Captain, and Millie stood behind the main house looking at the flames burning the sprouts. Even the soil was on fire.

Irving ran out of the hand quarters and headed toward the flames. His bare feet thumped the soil with each stride, running around the field that was on fire until he made it to the main house.

A string of phone calls woke Arthur Humes, the Rutledge Fire Department, the County Sheriff, and two deputies. By the time they all arrived on the scene, the fire had died and smoke was wisping up into the air from the soil. After statements were written down, an examination of the soil and crops were examined with flashlights. The sheriff was the first to notice that burlap cloth soaked in an accelerant had covered the crops.

"Gasoline most likely," Sheriff said as his flashlight illuminated a piece of burned burlap.

"I got tire tracks. All throughout here," a deputy yelled as he hovered over the soil with a flashlight.

Elizabeth could see Irving surveying the damage. Arthur had arrived at about the same time as the sheriff. Strangely, he was dressed in a fine tweed suit and was wearing a bowler hat. He watched with interest and kept quiet. When Elizabeth approached him, her arms were crossed to keep warm from the chilled air. He removed his bowler hat before Elizabeth spoke.

"My friend Irving said that it looks to be about fifteen to twenty acres that burned. Somebody did this. This isn't my fault and I need to know if my time can be extended. I am certainly not going to meet the deadline."

"I don't know yet. I'll be speaking with the sheriff about this immediately. I will contact the attorney in Knoxville and I'll see if an arrangement can't be made. These people are shooting themselves in the foot."

At 7 A.M. in the morning in Knoxville, TN, a man by the name of Edward Campbell was eating breakfast with his two children. It was the last week of school, and they were particularly excited to begin summer vacation. Edward's hair was slick with pomade. He had on a button-up shirt with his sport coat slung over the back of his chair.

"Will you rugrats calm down? I can barely hear myself think!" he said before taking a sip of hot coffee. His wife stood in the kitchen buttering a piece of toast and looked up at her kids and motioned for them to not make their father yell. Edward Campbell currently had his sleeves rolled down and buttoned, but as soon as the stress of the day would grab ahold of him, his sleeves would surely be rolled up. He flapped the newspaper as he turned the page and took another sip of his coffee. Outside his home, a police car parked in front of his house. Sleeves' attention was immediately locked on the car as he read the words *Grainger County Sheriff's Department.*

"What is a Grainger County Sheriff doing in Knox County?" he asked himself aloud. Sleeves set down his cup of coffee as he watched a Knox County Sheriff park his car beside the other squad car. When four deputies exited two cars, he folded his newspaper and stood up. The doorbell rang before he could get to it. After opening the door, one of the deputies from Grainger County spoke up.

"Mr. Edward Campbell?"

"Yes?"

"You are under arrest for arson in Rutledge, Tennessee, and we are to escort you to the Grainger County Jail."

"What?"

Back in Grainger County, Elizabeth sat in Arthur's office while he was on the phone with Sidney Kroll. As she could only hear one side of the conversation, she thought that things were going well.

"Well, it certainly seems to be a reasonable resolve to this matter, and I will discuss this with my client. Yes, sir. Okay, thank you." When Arthur hung up the phone, Elizabeth was on pins and needles. He shuffled a few papers and took a few notes before speaking. Even though she was anxious, she kept her calm. "Okay," he started as he looked over his glasses and set his fountain pen on his notepad. "Keep in mind that this is not set in stone, nor is it even at this point considered a resolution. However, Mr. Kroll will be advising his clients that they should sell the farm immediately for seventy percent of its value."

"Okay. Why seventy?"

"Well, it is complicated, but this is a number that Mr. Kroll and I feel works best for both parties involved. After what they have done, in no way would they get a full inheritance. Now, I know you want this farm, and I have a way for you to acquire it."

"I'm all ears."

"You would simply visit the bank and inquire about a mortgage. They will assess its value and you would simply take out a mortgage on seventy percent of its value. You would simply make monthly payments to the bank. The money will go to this irritating family, and it'll be over," he explained. He stopped talking and waited for Elizabeth to reply. When she didn't reply immediately, he cocked his head like a dog trying to understand a command.

"Is that it?" she asked.

"Yes. The Last Will and Testament of Mr. Thaddeus Campbell will be considered valid. The growing of 40 acres will still be needed to fulfill the wishes of Mr. Campbell, however an extension of the deadline will surely be made available to you. I'm willing to bet a lot of money that the family will want everything behind that green door too," he explained.

"Okay," Elizabeth replied with a shrug.

"Now, you'll be on the hook with the bank for the mortgaged amount, and you will be unable to press charges for killing your dogs, digging holes, breaking into your house, and setting your crops on fire."

"It sounds good to me, but what do you think?"

"Well, if we contest the will and lose, you get nothing."

"How do I not do this? This solves everything!"

"Yes, but you only technically inherit thirty percent of the farm. Is that okay with you?"

"It is," she said with a smile. "When would this happen?"

"It could take a while. Mr. Kroll and I are working on this, but don't get your hopes up until we have something in writing." Elizabeth stood up and hurried around the desk and hugged Arthur.

"Oh no. My suit," he said under his breath as the fabric was bunched from her embrace.

Chapter 47

The excitement and relief of finally owning the farm flowed through Elizabeth. Moments after she returned from Arthur's office, Claire unknowingly approached her at a good time with a newspaper opened to the classifieds section. She pointed to a description of a boy's bicycle for sale. After reading it, Elizabeth looked at Claire.

"That's a boy's bike."

"I know. I don't care. I just need one, and this one is cheap, and it has new tires. See?"

"If that is what you want, you can have it."

"Really?"

"Upstairs on the dresser is my billfold. You may open it and remove only what you need."

Gordon sat at his desk in the mill and read a newspaper with his feet propped up. He looked for a story on the fire at the Campbell Farm, but found nothing. The phone rang, and he quickly answered.

"Hello?"

"Gordon?" Annie replied in tears.

"What is it, honey?"

"They are releasing Harold today," she answered while sniffling and sobbing.

"Today? Why?"

"I don't know."

"Is he improving?"

"I don't know. They just said that he is being released."

"I'm on my way."

Gordon sped down the highway to Knoxville and made it to the hospital as fast as his truck would let him. He hurried to the third floor and found Annie in the doorway to Harold's room. Two nurses had already begun to wheel Harold out into the hallway. Over his mouth was a respiratory filter mask.

"Hey! What's the meaning of this?" Gordon asked as he stopped Harold's wheelchair by placing his foot in front of a wheel.

"Sir, we have discharge orders."

"Orders from who?"

"Dr. Patterson."

"Wait here!" Gordon scrambled down the hallway and found Dr. Patterson in his office filling out a medical chart.

"Doctor, what is the deal? I thought we were weighing options on his treatment?"

"Certainly, but we cannot do anything else for him here."

"What if he has another attack! I mean, it's better for him to be here than at home if that happens!"

"I'm afraid that isn't true. If he has another attack, he may not survive it no matter where he is located. Hospital or not."

"Well, can we have a week or two to figure out where we can transport him? I just don't think him being at home is the best option."

"I'm sorry. We need the room."

"Please, even a few days would help."

"I'm sorry but there are other patients we have to care for."

The argument continued. The nurses leaned up against the wall while they listened to Gordon yelling and pleading with Dr. Patterson. Annie wrapped her arm around Harold's head and covered both of his ears. She stroked his hair while her husband continued to yell.

Gordon put both of his hands on the desk and leaned over, getting closer to Dr. Patterson's face.

"You can't do this to me. You could kill him."

"Look, when I say that 'we cannot do anything else for him', I mean we can't do anything should he suffer from another attack. If you feel this machine will help him, you need to hurry up. Do you understand what I am saying?" said Dr. Patterson. Gordon didn't move. "Do you hear what I am telling you when I say 'hurry up'?"

"I do," Gordon replied. His head nodded. He took his hands off the desk and walked out into the hallway. As he walked up to Annie and Harold, his eyes focused on the respiratory filter mask, wondering if it really helped.

"Hurry up! Let's get him to the car."

The next morning, Claire purchased a Huffman Airflyte boys' bicycle from a fourteen-year-old boy who lived close to Norman's side of town. It was painted red and blue and had noticeably new tires. Brand new, the bike fetched $22.50. Claire paid $12.00 cash, then loaded it into the back of the truck with her mother's help.

On the way back to the house, Elizabeth explained to Claire about what Arthur had said. She went into detail about the Last Will and Testament and how the family might concede under certain circumstances. Claire thought about the tire tracks. She didn't think that the man on their front porch could have killed the dogs. *Where did the tires tracks come from?* Unable to let up, Claire took mental notes until she had her pencil and notepad. As they drove back to the farm, a police car came up behind them and passed on the left side. The man sitting in the back of the cruiser wasn't visible.

Sleeves was handcuffed and sitting in the middle of the back seat and listened to the deputies in the front of the cruiser talk about their wives.

"Does she make meatloaf?" the deputy behind the wheel asked.

"Yep. Does the whole thing with potatoes and peas too."

"Sounds good. I do like meatloaf," the deputy responded as he turned the wheel.

"Does your wife make meatloaf?"

"Yes, but she burns it. Every time."

"You still eat it?"

"Are you crazy? Of course, I eat it. Ask for seconds, too."

Sleeves rolled his eyes as he leaned to one side to keep the cuffs from digging into his wrists. To his dismay, the boring conversation continued between the officers. At one point when the driver looked back at him in his rearview mirror, Sleeves tried to time it perfectly so that he would see him roll his eyes. It didn't work.

There were only two cells in the Grainger County Jail, and both were unoccupied upon his arrival. As the iron door clanked shut, it was explained to him that he would be incarcerated until the judge could set his bond.

"Can someone call my family and explain this? I need to call my lawyer."

"One of the deputies remained behind and explained the situation to your wife."

"How long will this take?"

"Judge is out-of-town today. He will see you tomorrow morning."

"You're kidding me!"

"Good news is, Grainger County provides three squares a day to inmates. You won't go hungry. I'll go ahead and arrange your phone call. It'll be a minute or two," the deputy added as he hooked his thumbs into his belt and sauntered away.

Gordon and Annie walked Harold into the emergency room at Morristown Hospital. To get Harold admitted, they listed his symptoms to the attending physician. They explained the tests performed on their son and what treatments he was receiving. Their explanations paired with their persistence made them seem irrational and unsound. The nurses looked upon them with concern and did their best to distract Harold from his parents as if they were crazed and delirious.

Once Harold was under an oxygen tent, one of the nurses and attending physicians pulled Annie and Gordon aside.

"We called Knoxville General. They explained to us your situation."

"Why did you call them?" Gordon asked.

"Because we aren't equipped to handle severe asthmatic patients. We were inquiring about a patient transfer when they informed us that Harold Tyrell had just been discharged."

"So, you're telling us that you can't admit him?"

"No. We can't," the physician stated. Gordon ran his fingers through his hair. Annie held onto him as if to keep from fainting. Gordon looked at the doctor,

"What are we supposed to do now?"

One of the deputies in the sheriff's office went by the name Peck. His full name was Willard Peck, but no one called him by his first name. He was thin, and he had a good head of hair at the age of fifty-two. Anytime Officer Flynn was off work, Peck on was on-duty. It wasn't often that the county jail had an inmate, but when they did both Officer Flynn and Officer Peck would see to it that they were fed.

Food was often cooked by a few ladies from the Baptist church and brought over to the jail in pie tins. On the first night Sleeves was in his cell, Peck walked up holding a pie tin covered with foil, and a metal fork.

"Gotcha some chicken casserole with carrots and peas. Smells good."

"Yeah, thanks."

"Oh, and you got a biscuit comin' too, but I'll have to go back up front and get it. My mistake."

"Fine," Sleeves said as he watched Deputy Peck open the cell door and set the tin dish on his bed. He closed the door and disappeared around front. Sleeves then heard Deputy Peck talking to a female out front.

"Would it be okay if I asked him a few questions?"

"I don't think so. He's eating dinner and then it's lights out. Sorry."

"I have some questions that could prove his innocence. He might like to speak with me."

Sleeves' ears perked up and listened more closely.

"I don't think this is a good idea. I'll have to be with you the entire time. Uh, how long is this going to take?"

"Less than five minutes."

"Let me ask," Deputy Peck replied. Sleeves then heard foot-steps headed his direction and watched the Officer's shadow slide across the floor until he appeared around the corner.

"Mr. Campbell, I got a young girl out here that wants to ask you some questions. That be okay with you?"

"Wait. A young girl?"

"Yes, sir."

"How young?"

"Eleven or Twelve," Peck answered with a shrug.

"Hmmm...I suppose she can ask me some questions while I eat."

Peck disappeared back around the corner and soon reappeared with the young girl that interrogated him before.

"Mr. Campbell?"

"Yeah," Sleeves said as he peeled back the tin foil covering the casserole dish. He held the fork and dug inside. Peck reached his hands through the bars and handed him a biscuit.

"My name is Claire Campbell. I believe we might be related."

"Oh, yeah? Who's your Dad?"

"Samuel Campbell. He passed a while back."

"Sorry to hear that. I didn't know him. I knew your great uncle though."

"You mind if I ask you some questions?"

"Go ahead," he replied as he took a bite. He was dressed nice, and his shoes were shined. His hair had fallen from the slicked back, styled look as sharp strands pointed down over his fore-head.

"You remember me asking you about driving a truck?"

"Yeah. I was standing on the front porch."

"You don't own a truck?"

"I do not."

"Do you know anyone who does?"

"I do."

"And who is that?"

"My neighbor owns a truck. He also owns a furniture store."

"Has he been to Grainger County?"

"I wouldn't know. I don't like my neighbor, and I don't speak to him unless his dog is in my yard."

"I see."

"You think I did those things that I am accused of doing?"

"I don't," she said with a confident tone. Sleeves leaned forward and used his fork to point at her.

"Why not?"

"Because someone has been digging holes in the fields. They snuck into our house in the middle of the night, and they killed three coonhounds and just the other night, they set fire to the field behind the house. Each incident had tire tracks with a missing section of a tire."

"A what?" Deputy Peck asked.

"A missing section of the tire. I know there can't be a hole in a tire, but the tire track looks like it." Claire explained. Sleeves looked at her as he set his casserole dish back on the bed.

"Sheriff thinks I'm guilty. Your mother thinks I am guilty. Even my own dang attorney thinks I am guilty. I can hear it in his voice over the phone." he explained. He once again pointed his fork at her. "But you don't."

"You didn't do it."

"I know," he said with a smile as he sat back against the brick wall. A swell of accomplishment rose in Claire's chest making her feel warm causing her to lose focus. "So, what now?" He asked. *What would Nancy Drew say? What would Nancy Drew say?* She thought. Before she could formulate anything in her mind, Peck spoke up.

"If all you have to go on is a unique tire track, you need to

ask around at a garage that repairs tires. See if they know anything. At least that is what I would be doing."

"Are there any here in Rutledge?" Sleeves asked.

"One," replied Peck. "Neary's Garage."

Chapter 48

Gordon and Annie carried Harold into the house and set him underneath his oxygen tent. Gordon mixed a jar of *Aerohalor* medicine and knelt down beside Harold's bed.

"Just breathe easy."

"Do you have to leave?" asked Harold.

"What? Leave?"

"Can you stay with me?" Harold asked. Gordon slid his hand under the tent and held his son's hand.

"Of course. I'm not going anywhere."

"Can you get the book and read the Casey poem?" he asked. Gordon let go of his son's hand and walked over to his dresser where a book of poems lay next to stacks of baseball cards and coins. Gordon returned to his bedside and opened the book to *Casey at the Bat* – a favorite poem of Harold's who almost had it memorized.

While Gordon sat and read from the book, Annie stood outside his bedroom with her back against the wall. Neither Gordon or Harold could see her. She listened to her husband read from the book and could no longer hold in the stress. She began to sob and cupped her face with her hands. Wiping her tears from her face, she listened to Gordon finish the poem and could hear the book close.

"Dad, you think we could throw the ball again?"

"I don't know," he replied as he stroked his son's hair in an attempt to pat down the wild strands. "It's certainly possible."

"You think I will be able to play baseball soon?" he asked. It took Gordon a good while to answer. He knew if he answered right away, he would have had to choke back his emotions of having to lie to his son. He knew Harold wouldn't be able to soon. Only weeks ago, Gordon would have answered a quick yes as he thought it was a possibility. Before he answered, he thought it best to keep Harold's spirits up instead of crushing them with a negative answer.

"I think so."

The next morning, Claire rose out of bed with a to-do list. After brushing her teeth and putting her hair up into a ponytail, she went outside and got on her bicycle.

"Claire!" a voice yelled out. She turned around and saw Millie holding a biscuit. "I got you a warm biscuit!" she said as she waddled toward her. Claire set her bike down and met her halfway.

"Thank you!"

"You welcome. I got some pear preserves on it spread like butter."

"Smells delicious!"

"Can you ride and eat with one hand?"

"I think so."

"Don't be getting' in no bike wreck on account of my biscuit, ya hear?" Millie said as Claire laughed.

"I won't."

In 1951, Rutledge only had one service station, and it was owned by a man named Roy Neary. After World War II, he put in a second gas pump to help meet the demand for fuel after the GI's came back home and traveled about the state. The mayor of Rutledge even held a ribbon cutting for the second pump and somehow managed to get the service station mentioned in the *Rogersville Review* newspaper.

Roy was underneath a car when he heard a bicycle come to a stop by the single garage bay door. Claire had eaten the biscuit that Millie had handed her and accidentally got jelly preserve on her fingers. After vain attempts to lick off the sugary jelly, she saw a sink in Roy Neary's garage and wondered over to it as if she owned the place. Dirty rags hung on the edge of the filthy sink, and grease covered the white porcelain. Roy slid his plump body out from underneath the car and saw a young girl opening the faucet and scrubbing her hands under the running water. Roy mainly used the sink to wash grime off of auto parts. Before he could speak up and tell the young girl that there was a proper restroom in the back, he observed her extend her head under the faucet and cock her neck so that she could take in a mouthful of water. She took a big drink, turned the water off, and wiped her mouth with her shirt.

"Young lady, can I help ya?" he asked thinking maybe she just needed a drink before getting back on her bike and pedaling away. She turned her head and looked at him as he lay on the roller board.

"You, Mr. Neary?"

"I am," he replied in a surprised tone as he looked over his stomach with a rag in one hand and a screwdriver in the other.

"I am here to see you. I have a few questions about tire repair."

"Got somethin' wrong with your bicycle?"

"No. It's fine. I wanted to ask you about the repair of a truck tire."

"Oh," he replied as he grunted and sat up before standing. He stuffed the rag into his back pocket and looked at her as she removed a notepad and pencil from her back pocket. "Whatcha got there?" Roy asked.

"Just taking a few notes. Do you repair tires?"

"I do."

"How many have you repaired?"

"Since when?"

"I don't know. Say, in the last two years," she replied. Roy looked at her in a state of confusion. Her questions were forceful, and he hadn't ever seen her before.

What is going on? he asked himself. He walked closer to her with a confused look on his face. "What's your name?"

"Claire Campbell."

"You live around here?"

"At the Campbell Farm. I am the great niece of Mr. Campbell."

"Oh. Sorry to hear of his passing."

"Thanks."

"Now, you have a truck tire you need repaired?" he asked as he looked at her notepad.

"No. I just have some questions."

"Ok. Questions," he nodded.

Claire was caught off guard and felt uncomfortable. In the books, all of the character's answered Nancy's questions without fail. Here, standing in front of Roy Neary, she felt foolish.

"Let me ask you a question first, what is this all about?" he asked, taking control of the conversation.

"Well, three dogs were killed on our farm. Someone has taken to digging holes throughout our fields. The main house was broken into, and recently someone set fire to the fields and destroyed about twenty acres of tomatoes."

"You don't say," Roy replied as he scratched his head. He hadn't heard much about the goings on at the farm as he spent most of his days underneath broken vehicles. Now even more confused, he asked more questions. "So, what in the world does this have to do with tires? I'm not fully understanding."

"In all four instances, I found truck tire tracks and one thing that stands out is that one of the tire tracks has a missing section," she explained. Roy jolted as if hit by lightning.

"Oh! Okay! I get it now," he said with a smile.

Claire took note that she had just started asking questions and didn't give her interviewee context. She winced and took a few quick notes before Roy answered. "So, you want to know if I have repaired any truck tires, so you can try to find out who did these things to the farm?"

"Yes."

"Okay, so you're like a little investigator going around asking questions." His response now sounded patronizing to Claire, and her expression of resentment was clearly visible to Roy. He quickly changed his tone. "Right, so I would say I have repaired maybe thirty tires or so in the last two years, but when did this happen?"

"Everything I mentioned has happened in the last six weeks."

"Hmmmm…well, now that I think about it…"

"What?"

"Well, can you show me how big the missing section is? Could you draw the tire track, so I can see what it looks like?"

Claire walked outside of the garage to an area with loose dirt. Roy followed. Using her finger, she made a crude outline of a tire track and made a clean space where the missing section would be. Roy examined it as he rested his hands on both knees and looked at the ground. He then stood up and stroked his chubby face while in deep thought.

"Well, the thing is, a missing section that big would be a temporary patch. A patch that big isn't meant to be on there long. I mean, they don't last that long. So, it's only meant to be a temporary solution."

"Is that important?"

"If these events happened in the last six weeks, you wouldn't want to look for someone with a tire patch from two years ago. They would have already gotten a new tire."

"I see," she said as she took notes.

"You would need the names of the people who got a tire patch within the last two months really."

"Okay."

"But even then, they could have gotten a patch at any number of stations around the county, but I suppose it's worth a try."

"Sounds good."

"I guess there's three people I would question. First one is David Laughlin. I repaired a tire like the one you are describing about a month ago. He's a horse and cattle farmer here in town," he said as she took notes. "Next is Gordon Tyrell. I repaired a tire for him about six weeks ago. He owns the local feed mill. The last is Mrs. Butler, and I don't think you need to talk to her."

"Why not?"

"She's ninety and coughs a lot. Doesn't drive much."

"Good to know."

"You say these people killed your dogs?"

"My great uncle's dogs. Yeah."

"You want to just go up and talk to someone that might be killin' dogs? Sounds like they might be dangerous."

"Good point," she said as she continued to take notes.

"How'd you know to come here anyway?"

"Deputy Peck mentioned it." she answered. Roy laughed.

"You working with the police? You are a little investigator, aren't you?"

"I suppose. I thank you for the information."

"You be careful out there."

Chapter 49

About an hour before lunchtime, Elizabeth sat at the kitchen table with her head propped up with one hand while the other hand turned a page of her ledger. She looked at all of the numbers she had written down in the rows and boxes that were printed on the ledger. She had a column for wages that were paid to the farm hands. Another column for expenses showed the paid invoices of the fertilizer and the price she paid for buckets of worms.

The back door opened, and Irving walked inside. He looked at her as if something was wrong.

"Can you come out to the fields with me?"

"Certainly," she replied as she closed the ledger and left it on the kitchen table. She followed him out the back door and into the fields, walking on burnt burlap and soil before coming upon a hill. On the other side of the hill were more than twenty acres of unburned Early Girl. On the way, they had walked on black, burnt soil with no care taken of where they stepped, now they were carefully stepping over rows of lush green tomato plants and mounds of rich, brown soil. Suddenly Irving stopped in his tracks and knelt down. Elizabeth copied his movements.

"This right here," he said as he reached into a green, leafy tomato plant, "is the first tomato of this crop that I can find."

He picked the smooth-skinned, red tomato off the vine.

Elizabeth watched him remove a knife from his front pocket and begin to cut the tomato in half. The juices flowed out from the edges of the knife and dripped onto the soil. He handed her half of the tomato.

"This soil is perfect. It's rich with nutrients, and it's in the best possible condition. The juices you see dripping down here is because of the soil. The better the soil, the better the crop. Now Early Girl is a good tomato, not a great tomato. It's what my mama calls a 'table tomato'?"

"Why is that?" Elizabeth asked with a grin.

"Well, you pick it, and keep it in the sunlight on a kitchen table and slice it when you need it. Other tomatoes you keep on the vine until you're ready to eat or sell them," he explained as the juices from the tomato she was holding began to drip over and under her fingers. "Early Girl goes for $4.12 for a crate. If we grew a crop of Hillstaker Gold, we'd get almost $5.00 a crate, and if we grew something like, uh…I don't know… Sunset Ox Heart or even Alabama Rain, we'd get more than $6.00 a crate." Irving looked at her as she held the tomato in her hand. "Go ahead, take a bite. A big bite."

Elizabeth looked at the tomato and its smooth, bright red skin and juicy, soft interior. The seeds looked like a marching band on a high school football field as they were seemingly lined up around curves. She held it up to her mouth and took a big bite. The sensation of sweetness and tartness—blended with a hint of sourness—covered her taste buds. She made a joyful sound as she chewed and closed her eyes. Irving then took a bite as he looked off toward the horizon. Behind him were acres of burnt Early Girl and in front of him were rows and rows of leafy green plants with near red tomatoes on the vines. With a chunk of juicy tomato in his mouth, he spoke.

"Now imagine this flavor times a hundred. Some of the tomatoes I will grow in this field will feel like magic with every bite."

"I can't wait."

"You hear back from that lawyer fella?"

"I did. Mr. Humes said that the family might agree to forego the will and just get paid, which means we might have to take a loan out from a bank and pay them back overtime."

"Hmmm…," Irving said. "Sounds simple. Not as good as being handed the farm, but I bet it would be okay. That gonna work?"

"I don't know. I have been looking at the ledger, and it seems like it would work."

She looked at the tomato in her hand and took another bite. Her eyes squinted from the sun and he held up his hand to block the sunlight from her eyes. Elizabeth smiled as she wiped the juices from her chin.

Unable to let it go, Claire looked over her notes at her two leads. She went over scenarios in her head as to why either a feed mill operator or a cattle breeder would need to set a field on fire. Or why they would sneak into a house in the middle of the night? Who would murder coonhounds to try to get them to leave the farm?

While she tried to connect the few dots she had, one of her leads was sitting in his son's bedroom in tears. Harold couldn't stop coughing and the amount of blood startled Gordon.

When Dr. Burt Talbot arrived, he tended to his patient and noticed it took longer to subdue his attack. The breaths Harold took were too shallow which prompted Talbot to leave the bedroom and head toward the phone in the kitchen. Annie stayed with Harold while Gordon walked behind Dr. Talbot. He listened to the one-sided conversation.

"Dr. Odil, this is Dr. Burt Talbot in Rutledge. I have a twelve-year-old eosinophilic asthma patient in my care who is now therapy-resistant to heavy doses opium and steroids. I need to request a transfer to University of Colorado for advanced pulmonary care," Dr. Talbot explained. He had spoken so quickly that Gordon missed the part about Colorado. The words seemed to linger in the air until they seemingly rushed into his ear canal all at the same time. Gordon covered his mouth and took a few steps realizing he hadn't been paying attention to the rest of what Dr. Talbot was saying. While on the phone, Talbot noticed movement from the corner of his eye. He turned and saw Gordon. Talbot whispered out to him while making quick hand motions.

"Need a pencil and paper!"

Gordon sprang into action and handed Dr. Talbot an envelope and a pencil. Dr. Talbot took notes and asked several more questions. When he finally hung up the phone, he continued taking notes.

"Gordon, go get your wife. You'll both want to hear this," he said in a hurried voice.

Normally, Dr. Talbot was a friendly man with a lot of polite mannerisms and good-natured conversation. When he finally addressed Annie and Gordon, they could see a change in him. He was stiff and calculated. He seemed more professional and less friendly.

"Harold is at the point where I can no longer care for him. If he stays here, he will not survive. Now, previously his condition did not warrant what I am about to suggest, but if we don't act fast we will lose him, so here is the plan," he said as he looked down at his notes. Gordon and Annie hung on every word. "We will board a plane in Knoxville at McGhee Tyson airport. All four of us will fly to Denver and admit Harold to the University of Colorado Hospital. There, he will be treated by some of the top pulmonary physicians. The cost of the airfare will be significant I am afraid, but I will take care of my own. Now, the hospital, the treatments, and lodging for you both will be free of charge, so don't expect to have to pay out-of-pocket for any medical expenses or lodging but know that he could be there a month or more," Dr. Talbot said as he looked up from his notes.

"Why won't we have to pay?" Gordon asked.

"It's a teaching and research hospital."

"When do we leave?"

"Not sure, but it'll be on the next available flight. In the meantime, I am going to call one of the nurses I work with and have her come sit with me and Harold to watch over him until we leave for Denver, so expect two houseguests," he explained. Gordon looked at Annie.

"I'm going to have to make some arrangements at work before we leave."

"I know."

"We need to keep making the payments on the loan for the mill. I'll have to speak with Roger at the bank."

"You do what you need to do."

"I know it's going to be difficult, Harold may be there for months to come, but here's the thing," Dr. Talbot said as he took a step closer to them, "your son should feel a whole lot better once we are in the hands of the pulmonologists. Okay?"

Gordon's eyes filled with tears, and his lips began to shake. Annie wrapped her arms around her husband and held him tightly as he sobbed.

Chapter 50

David Laughlin was a well-respected cattle breeder in Grainger County and had been in business since WWII. Years ago, he had given up breeding horses, but his business was still called *Laughlin Horse and Cattle.* One day he had gotten up from his favorite chair in his office and walked outside when he heard someone moving about outside the barn. He first saw a blue and red painted bicycle on the ground and then a young girl looking around his '38 Chevy Pickup truck. She was kneeling down and looking at the right front tire as if she were judging it in a FFA competition.

"Can I help ya?" David asked. Claire had hoped to inspect the tire and be on her way without anyone noticing. Frightened, Claire jumped up.

"Oh! Sorry, I am just looking for my cat," she said with a smile. The pattern of David Laughlin's patched tire was now burned into her memory.

"You lost a cat?"

"I did, uh, just a tabby cat, but I don't see it here," she said trying to laugh it off. The tire patch was circular whereas the one she was looking for was elongated. Mr. Laughlin's truck was not the one she was looking for. David watched her head toward her bike.

"You want me to help you look for it?"

"Oh, no, that's fine. His name is 'Irving'. If you see him, tell him to come on home," she explained with a smile as she got on her bike.

"Where do you live?"

"Over yonder. Best be getting home now," she said as she pedaled off. David shook his head in confusion as Claire thought about what Mr. Neary had said about the people who killed the coonhounds possibly being dangerous. Even though she ruled out Mr. Laughlin, she was still scared when he spoke up out of nowhere.

Gordon and Annie had begun the process of packing for a long trip to Denver. With none of them having been on an airplane, there was an element of excitement of the trip mixed with an immeasurable amount of hope.

"Do you think I will be able to play baseball dad?"

"I do," Gordon replied. Now that there was even a remote chance of getting Harold to a better place, he counted on it like it was a certain thing.

Claire was pedaling down Highway 11 when a sheriff's cruiser pulled up beside her. Peck yelled out to her as she continued pedaling.

"Miss Campbell?"

"Hey!"

"You gotta second?" he asked as she slowed her bike to a stop.

"Yes, sir?"

"That fella at the jail—he keeps asking me if you found out anything yet, and really I'm kind of curious myself," Peck said as he leaned over and looked at Claire through the window.

"Well, I stopped by Neary's Garage. He gave me two names that I could ask," she replied as she slightly bent down to see him sitting in the driver's seat.

"You really went over there, huh?" he smiled.

"I did."

"What names did he give you?"

"Mr. Laughlin."

"Cattle breeder."

"Yep. His tires didn't match," she replied as she removed her notepad from her back pocket.

"I see. Who else?" he asked. She referred to her notes.

"Gordon Tyrell over at the feed mill."

"Hmmm…" Peck replied as he turned his head slightly and looked out the windshield. "His boy is sick. He lives over off of Knob Road, and the mill is located just off the highway outside Rutledge city limits. You going to the mill now?"

"I don't know. I don't think I want to ride my bike on the highway. My mom would kill me."

"If I give you a ride, you could check it out. And it might help to have a bonafide officer with ya!" he said. She recalled that Nancy Drew once rode in a police car with an officer to solve a crime and quickly agreed to take him up on his offer.

Her bike was placed in the trunk of the squad car and she sat up front in the passenger seat. Instead of asking questions, she answered them as the scenery outside flew by.

"You seem to know quite a bit about investigating. You do this often?"

"Nope. I read a lot, so I know a little. Not much really."

"How do you know about truck tires?"

"I read a book where a mysterious person drove away in a car, and all that was left were tire tracks. Then I started noticing them more."

"Well, let's see what you think of these," he said as he pulled into the dusty parking lot of Tyrell Feed Mill and parked near a light pole. As Claire got out, she noticed the parking lot was a fine dust, similar to dirt on a baseball field. There were tire tracks all over the parking lot crisscrossing over each other into a collage of undefinable lines.

The employees of the feed mill were too busy filling orders to look out and see a deputy and a young girl looking at the ground near the parked cars and trucks. Weeds and rocks were scattered about on the right side of the mill which is where Gordon would sometimes park his truck. Officer Peck had found what looked like a tire track with a missing section, but at first, he wasn't sure. He bent down and approximated where the tire would roll out in front of him. The missing section of the track repeated, and then he called out to Claire.

"Come see this," he hollered. "It's definitely a patched tire," he said as she hurried over and looked at the track. She recognized it almost immediately.

"That's it!"

"It is? This is the track you're looking for?"

"It's elongated, and the patch is on the right side," she explained. They both looked up, but didn't see where the truck was parked.

"Okay, let's get back to the car," he said. Claire began to have a feeling of impending doom again—exactly like when Mr. Laughlin walked up behind her.

"Whoever killed those dogs, was in that truck," she said quietly. Officer Peck heard her, but didn't answer. Once back on the road, he offered some advice.

"Since this was found at a place of business, you can't assume that the owner is the one involved."

"Why not?"

"It could be employees using the truck."

"I see," she replied as she took out her notebook and pencil. She scribbled quickly, but in detail.

"This needs to be handled carefully, and in a way as to not tip off whoever is the culprit which very well could be the McGurn Brothers. You ever heard of them?"

"No."

"You ever hear the term 'usual suspects'?"

"I don't think so."

"I bet a dollar and a rabbit pelt they're somehow involved. They're gonna need to be questioned. I happen to know they work there at that feed mill."

"How do I do that?" she asked. He smiled and shook his head.

"I have a little girl. She a bit older than you, but I wish she had your grit. You definitely got that—grit. You need to let the sheriff take over from here."

"Can I help?"

"You already have, but you can help me further by giving me a full statement at the police station."

"Why?"

"You got a lot rolling around in that head of yours, and your notes will help too. I need the full scope of what you know."

In the book where Nancy Drew rode in a police car, she also gave a detailed report to a police officer that ultimately led to the arrest of a thief who robbed a lake house. Claire felt as if she had done her part but couldn't relish in her achievement as she thought of her mother.

"You gonna release that man in jail?"

"I would say so, but it ain't up to me. I will file this report today, and we'll see what happens. I doubt he will stay in there much longer, and he has you to thank for it."

Claire held her head up with her hand as her elbow rested on the door. She thought of what her mom would say when she found out about the man getting out of jail. While she didn't understand the full circumstances, she knew his release would create yet another problem for her mom.

Chapter 51

Gordon had made arrangements for his uncle to come up from Chattanooga to help run the feed mill while he was out of town. When the phone rang, he thought it was his uncle calling to let him know when he would be arriving. Instead, it was one of the mill operators.

"Mr. Tyrell?"

"Yes?"

"Sorry to bother you, but I wanted to let you know that both McGurn brothers were picked up in a police car."

"What'd they do now? They liquored up?"

"No. They were working on the line and filling orders. Sheriff came and got 'em."

"Okay. No telling what they did. Just keep the orders filled, and if you need help, call Webber if you have to."

"Yes, sir."

The phone call ended, and Gordon thought nothing of it. It wasn't unusual for Dalton or Wesley to be locked up for a period of time.

Back at the sheriff's office, Dalton was kept separate from Wesley until it became clear that they were both giving up the same man. In exchange for a slap on the wrist, they explained the problems with Gordon's son, a situation that everyone was already aware of, and then came the details about digging the holes on the Campbell Farm.

The killing of the coonhounds and breaking into the house were confessed to, as well as setting the fields ablaze. Gordon was painted the mastermind which floored Sheriff Keller.

"Okay, so Mr. Tyrell plans all of this out, and you two are just paid employees."

"Exactly."

"Why would he need to do this?"

"He needs money for his son's treatments."

The explanation made enough sense to write up a report and the McGurn brothers were released once they signed a statement. A court appearance for their minor charges would be scheduled at a later date.

When Claire heard two car doors shut outside, she could only assume the worst. She thought that Officer Peck was about to explain to her mother that her daughter's superior detective work had foiled her goal of owning the farm. The sickening feeling rising from her stomach made her run upstairs and look out the second-floor window.

"Oh no," she said under her breath. She saw Sheriff Keller and Officer Peck walking up to the house. A few seconds later she heard a loud knock at the front door.

Elizabeth sat down at the kitchen table. The story was unfolded by the sheriff. He began with the medical condition that Gordon Tyrell's son suffered from and continued with the rumors around town about Ol' Man Campbell burying jars of money. The explanation concluded with the room in the house behind the green door.

"Out of complete curiosity," Sheriff said as he shifted his weight in the chair. "What is in that room?"

"I don't know. I was told not to go near it, so it is boarded up, and a hutch is blocking it."

"Why is that?"

"It's part of the condition of keeping the farm. I'm not allowed to open it until my name is on the deed."

"Condition of what?"

"Mr. Campbell's Last Will and Testament."

"I see. Well, we need to explain one last thing here," he said as he looked over at Officer Peck who took over the explanation. "We are going to arrest Mr. Tyrell as soon as we leave here. This is an emotional time for him as his boy is very sick. While he is certainly a threat, we know him as a good man."

"He's a good man at the end of his rope," Sheriff Keller chimed in as he stood up. Deputy Peck and Elizabeth followed suit.

"I do want to say that you have a very bright, young daughter. She is very smart, and this would not have happened without her," said Peck. Claire had snuck downstairs and was listening to the conversation from the hallway. When she heard the accolade, she cringed and quietly went back upstairs.

Sheriff Keller and Deputy Peck walked back to the cruiser and headed toward Gordon's house.

"So how do you want to do this?" Peck asked.

"No handcuffs. Just pull him aside and explain that we have some questions and, we need to take him to the station."

"When do we mention the McGurn brothers?"

"Don't say anything until we are back at the station."

"Got it."

"This is gonna be rough on him and his boy."

"On Annie too."

"Yep."

Sheriff Keller wore a noticeable frown as he pulled into the driveway of Gordon's house. As he parked the cruiser, he took notice that Doctor Talbot's car was parked next to Gordon's truck. As Deputy Peck exited the passenger side, he walked up to the truck and took notice of the patched tire. As they made their way to the front door, they heard screaming coming from inside. Sheriff Keller opened the front door, and Deputy Peck followed. Annie was screaming over the sound of gurgling as Sheriff Keller stood in the doorway of Harold's bedroom. Gordon was cradling Harold as blood gushed from his mouth as he choked and gasped for air. Gordon held his son still while Dr. Talbot injected him with a large dose of a pink fluid. Once the plunger injected the contents, Dr. Talbot stood up.

"Forget the airport! Knoxville General! As fast as we can! We'll have to get him stabilized on the way!" he yelled. Sheriff Keller ran to the squad car as Gordon carried Harold out his bedroom, down the hall, and through the family room. The cruiser was already started when Gordon ran outside while holding Harold with Deputy Peck keeping the front door wide open. Annie and Dr. Talbot followed.

With the siren wailing and the lights on the roof spinning, Annie and Gordon both cradled their son in the backseat. Harold whispered as he looked at his father and patted his chest.

"Dad! It hurts! Dad!"

Dr. Talbot had taken the passenger seat leaving Peck in the front yard as they sped away. Harold was turning blue while Annie couldn't control herself.

"OH GOD, NO! HAROLD!" she screamed. Harold, unable to breathe could only mouth his speech.

"Dad, I'm scared. I'm scared. I'm scared."

Sheriff Keller's heart was racing as he floored his car toward the direction of the hospital. Dr. Talbot spun around and leaned over the seat as he used his stethoscope to listen to Harold's heart.

"Stop! Stop the car! Pull over!" Dr. Talbot yelled. Both Annie and Gordon scrambled out of the backseat as the car stopped.

They looked on as Dr. Talbot hurried over the front seat and knelt over Harold as he began to perform chest compressions. With each compression, a loud gurgling sound resonated from the inside of the car. The red tail lights on the cruiser illuminated the faces of Annie and Gordon as Harold died in the backseat. He held his wife and sobbed into her shoulder as she screamed in agony.

Sydney Kroll called Arthur once he heard the news that his client was innocent of all charges which changed things for the greedy Campbell family.

"We can no longer entertain the idea of an agreement and my clients will be filing to revoke the Last Will and Testament," Mr. Kroll explained.

"Okay, how shall we proceed?"

"I will file within 48 hours or so, and I will be applying maximum pressure here. How about you?"

"We will be refuting and gathering evidence to support our case. I'll be prepared for the argument."

"If there is even the slightest chance of a settlement, I'll ring you."

"That's appreciated. Thank you."

The call ended with Arthur immediately replaying the conversation in his head and feared Elizabeth would lose the farm.

Chapter 52

Gordon and Annie sat in the blood-spattered back seat of the Sheriff's squad car and held their son until the coroner arrived. Sheriff Keller kept his distance as his heart couldn't take the sound of the uncontrollable sobbing. He nearly lost it when he heard Gordon speaking to his deceased son. Dr. Talbot walked away from the car and sat down on the edge of the road as he looked out over a field, the sunlight fading. He picked at the wild flowers and wondered if he had done everything he could to help little Harold.

When the coroner arrived, Harold's body was placed on a stretcher and slid into the back of a black 1948 Hudson hearse. Once on the road, Sheriff Keller followed behind the hearse with Gordon and Annie in the backseat. Dr. Talbot rode in the passenger seat with his eyes closed, mourning the death of his longtime patient. When they arrived at the Morristown Hospital, Sheriff Keller walked to the nurses' station and fixed himself a cup of coffee. Extra cream. Extra sugar. Stirring the cup as he walked down the hallway, he could hear Gordon and Annie arguing. Gordon's voice grew louder and louder until he was yelling. Annie was crying. Sheriff Keller did nothing to stop it, instead he opted to look down at the light brown color of his coffee as he stirred. Annie attempted to calm Gordon down and didn't speak as loud. Looking up from his cup of coffee, now thoroughly stirred, he saw that Annie's hands were on Gordon's shoulders briefly until he smacked them away. She cupped her mouth as Gordon kicked the wall in anger and walked away as Annie sat down on a bench and cried. More stirring.

Back at the Campbell Farm, Elizabeth was in the kitchen stirring a pot of green beans that were steaming on the stove while Millie and Captain tended to a bowl of mashed potatoes on the counter. Irving and Claire were sitting at the kitchen table with a glass plate and a small cutting board. Claire watched as Irving held a ripe Early Girl and sliced it into five slices.

Once dinner commenced, dishes were passed around and each plate was filled with hot food and one sliced tomato.

"It's been a long time since I had one of your tomatoes, Irving," said Millie with an expression that radiated pride.

"It'll be good. I just wish I had a Painted Sun or a Cherokee Purple. Now those would be something to talk about."

While dinner was underway at the Campbell Farm, Sheriff Keller had thrown away his coffee without taking a single sip. Walking outside of the hospital he shuffled over to his squad car as he removed his hat. Leaving the driver's side door open, he sat down behind the wheel and took a deep breath while trying to think of something else other than little Harold taking his last breath in the backseat. He looked out the windshield and did a double take when he saw Gordon exit the hospital. He watched from the driver's seat as Gordon approached the cruiser.

"I need a ride back to my house. Annie is staying here," he said in a gravelly voice as he got in the front seat. Sheriff Keller turned the engine over and put the car into gear.

"I am so sorry about your boy," he offered. Keller looked at Gordon who started to tear up—wiping his right eye and uttered in a shaken voice,

"Can we just get to my house, please?"

Once Sheriff Keller drove out onto the highway, he reached down and toggled the switch for the roof light. The red light on top of the car spun as they headed toward Rutledge. The ride was completely silent except for the sound of the engine, the wind that rushed past the cruiser and the occasional squawk of the CB radio.

Sheriff Keller pulled into the Tyrell driveway. Gordon didn't say a word as he opened the passenger side door and got out. After he closed the door and walked inside his house, Keller knew it would be a while before he could go back and place Gordon under arrest.

Perhaps after the funeral, he thought to himself as he backed out of the driveway.

At the Campbell Farm, Millie and Claire cleared the table after dinner while Elizabeth began slicing pieces of a peach pie. She cut through the lattice butter crust, sliding a warm piece of pie onto small glass plates. Captain and Irving talked at the table while everyone else listened.

"Now why you wanna spend your time crossing tomatoes? Don't we have enough varieties?" asked Captain.

"Sure we do, Pop. We have more than enough varieties, but some of them lack flavor. Only a few of those varieties are good enough to serve up. That's what I am after. I want the tomato with the most flavor," explained Irving. Captain used his fork to cut off a small piece of pie down to the crust and had to use a little extra effort to cut through it. The fork hit the glass plate with a *clink*. He scooped up the piece and held it over the plate as he asked another question.

"How many have you crossed to date?" Captain asked before he ate a bite.

"Eighteen or so."

"Any of them turn out?"

"About half of them did. I kept the seeds from those, but I also keep seeds from other varieties I come across. Got about forty different seeds right now," explained Irving. Claire had been listening and spoke up when there was a slight lull in the conversation.

"Where do you keep all these seeds?"

"In a big box with a bunch of drawers. My folks kept it with them while I was at the prison farm."

"Show her, Irving. Bring it on out here," Millie said as she chewed on a bite of peach cobbler. Claire watched as Irving stood up and took the napkin from his lap and set it on the table. He walked to the bedroom where his parents were staying and soon came out with a big wooden trunk with a small leather handle. Elizabeth smiled as she took a bite and watched Claire as she followed Irving's movements. He hoisted the trunk and set it on its end on the large kitchen table. *Thud.* Claire watched as the brass latches were opened and the trunk spread apart like a book. Instead of pages of a book, small labeled drawers were inside. Some drawers were as big as a business card, some were smaller, some bigger. Claire followed Irving's hand as he reached out and pulled on a tiny knob of a small drawer labeled *Peppercorn Gold.* He pulled the drawer open and reached inside and pulled out a tiny bottle with a tiny cork at the top. Inside, she could see about thirty seeds.

"How do you cross them?" Claire asked.

"Well, I brush pollen from one plant onto the bud of another tomato plant. At least that is the easiest way to explain it."

Claire looked at the drawers and read a few of the labels.

Copper Omaha
Peppercorn Gold
Huckleberry Sweet
Honey Dollar

Elizabeth and Claire finished their peach cobbler as they listened to Irving talk about the different varieties of tomatoes. The enthusiasm that emanated from Irving was contagious, and Claire absorbed it like a sponge. She asked more questions about the breeding of tomatoes which required in-depth answers. Irving was excited to answer her questions and reveled in her interest. He spoke of Brandywine and Sun Gold tomatoes and how he wanted to cross them to get a super sweet and super acidic tomato.

"Is it that easy?" Claire asked.

"Well, I wish it was. The success of crossing tomatoes depends on many factors," he said as he handed her the tiny jar of Peppercorn Gold. She held it up to the light. "Depends on rain, time of year they are sown and how much care they receive, but most importantly, it comes down to the soil."

As Claire held up a small clear bottle and looked at the seeds, she heard the roar of an engine coming from outside just before the wall of the kitchen exploded and collapsed as a truck crashed through it, nearly hitting the large, wooden kitchen table. Plumes of dried plaster billowed through the air as the roaring of the engine grinded and clanked to a stop. Elizabeth and Irving stood up from the table as they waved the white powder away in front of their faces in an attempt to breathe clean air. As they coughed and used articles of their own clothing to breathe through, every light flickered as if the house were about to lose power. The front tires of the truck were on the hardwood floor while the back tires were on the grass outside. Millie stood up and grabbed Claire, pulling her away from the wreckage and dust while Captain sat stunned in his chair. Irving and Elizabeth walked around the truck.

"Mom!" Claire hollered.

"Stay put!" Elizabeth shouted. Lumber had splintered and snapped, covering the truck in broken pieces of wood and chunks of plaster. The driver's side door opened. Irving couldn't see anyone in the vehicle until some of the dust swirled away. As the air cleared, Irving could see a man standing with a shotgun in his hands, aiming to the left. Then the man spoke.

"Move the hutch and open the door to the room with the green door or she dies," the voice said. Unclear as to what he meant, Irving followed the barrel as to where it was pointing. Elizabeth was the target. He looked back at the man holding the gun.

"Okay. I'll do it. Just stay calm," Irving replied as he held out his hands in a compliant manner. When the man spoke again, it sounded like he was speaking through his teeth with enough anger to boil a kettle.

"I'm pretty far from calm. Just do as I say, or I will kill her!"

Still seated in his chair, Captain could see that he was slightly out of the man's view. Using the opportunity, he slowly stood up and walked toward his bedroom.

Irving had moved over to the hutch and used his weight to push the cabinet to the side. The feet of the hutch scraped and rubbed the hardwood floor, making a sound that resonated throughout the room. Elizabeth watched as the hutch revealed the sheet of plywood that boarded up the green door. The lights continued to flicker. Irving looked at the plywood sheet blocking the door and then back at Gordon.

"I'll need a hammer," said Irving in an apologetic tone. Gordon looked at Elizabeth.

"Don't move!" Gordon yelled as he kept the shotgun trained on her. With his free hand, he reached into the bed of his truck keeping his eyes on his target. Finding a lantern, he set it on the roof of the truck and went back finding a flat pry bar.

Gordon threw the pry bar to the right side of Irving who picked it up just as the lights went completely out, only to come back on a second later. While Irving went to work on the plywood, Gordon fished a lighter out of his pocket and lit the lantern with one hand while the other aimed the shotgun. Out of Gordon's view, Captain quietly walked out of the bedroom holding a Springfield .30-06 Bolt Action Rifle. He had already loaded it with rounds and cycled one in the chamber. Taking careful steps, he kept out of sight.

Once Irving removed the nails from the plywood, he tossed the pry bar to the floor and gripped both sides of the wooden sheet. He walked backward several steps before tossing the board to the side as the lights continued to flicker throughout the house. The green door was now visible, and Gordon took his first step away from the truck as he held the lantern. He quickly aimed the shotgun at the glass in the green door and fired a shot. The glass shattered. Elizabeth screamed. Gordon racked another shell into the chamber and continued to aim it at Elizabeth.

"Open the door and step inside." Elizabeth did as asked while Gordon followed her. She opened the door and stepped inside. Finding a light switch, she pushed the button and the light above her flickered on, illuminating the glass jars on the white shelves. Her eyes grew large as she took in the sight. In a state of shock, she turned her head slowly looking dumfounded as she locked eyes with Irving.

Seeing his chance, Captain raised his rifle and fired a round at

Gordon, hitting him in the right hip. As he fell to the ground in front of the green door, Gordon let go of the lantern. Shards of glass, fuel and fire splashed onto the pile of lumber and plaster. In one quick movement, Irving grabbed the shotgun from Gordon and pointed it at him. Elizabeth spun on her heels and hurried toward Millie and Claire guiding them outside the house. Standing in the front yard, Elizabeth and Claire stood next to Millie. Captain hurried out of the house and waited for Irving to exit.

"Where he at?" asked Captain.

Inside the house, the fire crawled up the sides of the walls as the plaster and broken boards from the crash served as kindling for the blaze that quickly grew into a raging furnace. Irving stood over Gordon next to the green door and was forced to yell above the loud crackling and popping of the fire.

"You better get up and get movin' if you want to live," said Irving. Gordon didn't respond. With the blaze now coming to a full-on structure fire, plaster and wood fell near Irving causing him to turn his attention to the ceiling. With one swipe of his arm, Gordon knocked the shotgun out of Irving's hand.

Just when Elizabeth and Captain ran back inside to see if Irving was okay, Gordon grabbed the stock, aimed the barrel at Captain and pulled the trigger. Buckshot entered Captain's stomach and shredded his intestines. Before Gordon could rack another shell, Irving pounced on him and grabbed the gun and twisted it out of Gordon's hands. Irving fell backward and landed halfway inside the room with the green door. Black smoke and flames rolled along the ceiling.

Elizabeth bent down and cradled Captain's head in her arms. The fire now engulfed the dining room and the thick black smoke made it difficult to breath. Elizabeth looked down at Captain's stomach as blood gushed a very dark shade of purple from his wound.

"I have to get you outside," she said as she moved his arm around her shoulders to lift him up. Captain wasn't having it.

"Leave me be. You get Irving out of here. Save my boy."

Near the green door, a wooden support beam had fallen next to Gordon. The sound of crackling and popping grew very loud. As Elizabeth turned her head toward the sound of the collapsing roof, she saw Irving standing up in the room with the green door.

"Irving! No! Get out of there!" she yelled as she righted herself. "Irving! Don't look! Don't look at the jars!" she shouted as she ducked around the black smoke wafting through the burning house.

Unaware of his father's injury, Irving looked at the mason jars on the white shelves. Each jar looked as though they held seeds. Masking tape had been used to affix a label on each jar wherein a name was written.

Roma Sungold
Juliet Stripe
Missouri Giant
Indian Plum I
Indian Plum II
Indian Plum Trial
Red Racer
Southern Glacier
Sungreen Garden
Sweet Ranger Zebra

"Oh God no!" he said aloud as the sound of cracking wood caused by heat could be heard above him. Irving started reaching for jars until he felt a hand on his arm, pulling him.

"We need to get out of here!" Elizabeth yelled. He pulled away from her and grabbed three jars off the shelves before reaching for more.

"Help me! Grab as many jars as you can!" he ordered as he let the shotgun fall to the floor. Elizabeth got between him and the shelves and screamed in his face.

"We're going to die if we don't leave now! Your father is going to die!" she screamed, pointing to Captain who was on the floor. The fire was now on all four side of the dining room, and the ceiling was close to fully collapsing.

"Dad!" Irving yelled as he dropped the jars and ran to his father's side. Elizabeth stepped over plaster and lumber before feeling a hand around her ankle. Gordon was still on the ground, and he yanked on her leg, toppling her. Irving carried his father outside thinking that Elizabeth was right behind him. The fire had reached the gas tank of Gordon's truck and it exploded. A wave of liquid fire splashed on both Gordon and Elizabeth. Her hair was now on fire and she screamed. Gordon grabbed the shotgun and smashed the stock of the gun into Elizabeth's head, knocking her out. His clothes were on fire and his left ear was sizzling from the flames burning his skin.

"How much was there? I don't even want the money! How much was there!" Gordon screamed as blood flowed from Elizabeth's open head wound. She was unconscious, and Gordon's state of mind couldn't grasp that she couldn't hear him as he continued to scream in her face. Her clothes were on fire and her entire right arm was bubbling and blistering as it charred. "How much money was there?" screamed Gordon. She couldn't feel anything as he once again raised the stock of the gun above his head and slam it down onto her neck, shattering her collarbone.

After setting his father down in the front yard, Irving raced back inside the house and hurried to find Elizabeth. Running past flames and ducking under the black smoke, he saw Elizabeth unconscious on the floor, her hair and clothes were on fire. Gordon was screaming and crying as he held the shotgun just before Irving kicked the barrel knocking the gun from Gordon's hands.

Standing over Elizabeth, Irving removed his own shirt and beat down the flames on Elizabeth's clothes, skin and hair. Using both arms, he cradled Elizabeth's body and lifted her up off the floor as the house began to collapse around them. Gordon screamed Harold's name as the flames began to consume him.

Outside, Claire watched as Irving carried her mother's beaten and burned body out of the blazing house and set her on the cool grass.

Chapter 53

Elizabeth was brought to Morristown Hospital at 10:05 P.M. When she arrived, nurses began using scissors to cut around the burns where the fibers of her clothes had fused inside her second and third-degree burns. On the right side of her head, her hair had been burned leaving her scalp bright red and oozing blood. The burns extended down her neck where her clavicle had been broken by the stock of the shotgun. Down along her arm were the worst burns with black, brown and yellow blisters cascading down from her shoulders and toward her wrist. Down the hall from the ER, Claire waited in a reception area nearby.

When the ambulance had arrived on the Campbell Farm, it was quickly deemed that they would transport the young female before the older man. Twenty minutes after the first ambulance arrived, the second one parked in the front yard and quickly transported Captain. By the time they got to the hospital, Captain succumbed to his injuries.

Taking the farm truck, Irving and Millie parked outside the hospital and went in the main entrance. Thinking they would be directed to a hospital room, they both broke down in tears when they learned they were to go to the basement where the morgue was located. Moments later, Irving sat outside a room and held his head in his hands as he looked down at a concrete floor. His mother had gone into the identification room by herself to speak to her husband as he lay on the cold table with a white sheet draped over his body. Irving had covered his ears so that he couldn't hear her wailing, but his efforts were in vain. When she exited the room, she sat down in a chair near Irving and sobbed. Irving stood up and put his hand on her shoulder before going into the room to see his father for the last time. He closed the door behind him and stood next to the metal table. Looking down, Irving saw his father's fingers just beneath the white sheet. Moving the sheet back, he uncovered Captain's hand and held it like he did when he was a child.

"We were dealt a difficult hand, Dad. You sure did make the most of it though," he said as he began to cry. "I miss you already, and I would give anything to hear your laugh one more time. I wish I had made you laugh more," he said as his tears dropped off his face and onto the white sheet. "I'm gonna remember your stories. I'll tell 'em to anyone who will listen."

Irving spent nearly a half hour talking with his father, and he held his hand the entire time. When he finally exited the room, he sat next to his mother and put his hand on her back and prayed. Leaving the morgue, Irving made his way to the Emergency Department where he found a short brunette woman wearing a white nurses cap sitting behind the intake desk.

"Miss? Where do people wait to hear about a patient in the ER?" he asked.

"Right here. Who are you waiting on?"

"Mrs. Elizabeth Campbell."

"Oh. She was transported to another hospital."

"She was? Was it the hospital in Knoxville?"

"I don't know, but I think she had a daughter with her? Is that right?"

"Yes. Her name is Claire," responded Irving in confusion.

"Hang on. Let me ask," she replied. Before she could pick up the phone, she heard a door open behind her. An older nurse with gray hair exited a door that led back into the Emergency Department. She was holding an unlit cigarette and a brown paper bag lunch. Before she could get outside, the nurse at the intake desk stopped her.

"Phyllis? Did Elizabeth Campbell get transported?" she asked. Irving waited with a confused look.

"She and her daughter were transferred to Chicago."

"Chicago?" Irving replied. The nurse could see that the man was in distress and took pity on him. She slid her unlit cigarette above her ear and set her sack lunch on the intake desk.

"You know her?" the nurse asked.

"She is my friend."

"Well, her burns are so severe that she wouldn't survive here or in Knoxville. They dressed her wounds and sent her on an ambulance chain to Chicago that has a burn unit. If she's going to make it, that is the only place that can help her."

"Her daughter went with her?" asked Irving.

"She did."

Irving looked down at his feet and tried his best not to cry. He thanked the nurse and took a seat while taking deep breaths.

Claire sat on the left side of the ambulance and held her mother's hand. A medic sat on the right side and monitored Elizabeth's vitals. The nine-hour drive was broken up by switching ambulances in Louisville and again in Indianapolis. At one point, Claire had fallen asleep and was dreaming of sitting on the back porch reading a Nancy Drew book when the ambulance hit a pothole and shook the interior. Claire rubbed her eyes and looked down at her unconscious mother covered in bandages. The back doors opened, and a team of nurses and medics began to pull the stretcher out of the ambulance.

Chapter 54

The small town of Rutledge awoke the next day with news of Harold's and Gordon's deaths followed by the fire that engulfed the Campbell farmhouse. The details of the deaths weren't yet known, and while the town didn't consider Harold's passing to be unexpected, Gordon's death was both confusing and difficult to understand. The confusion arose when it was discovered that Gordon's body was found inside the Campbell farmhouse and that the fire and his death were not coincidental—rather they were connected.

It would be another week before the McGurn brothers would set people straight on what happened. Roger Landry took a few days off from work thinking about what he could have done to help. A few drinks made him think he had dug Gordon's and Harold's graves himself. After he finished a bottle on his own, he knew he was at fault and cried for hours until the back of his eyes hurt.

Sydney Kroll prepared estate documents for his clients, billing them his full hourly rate. Only a few houses in Grainger County were insured, and the Campbell house wasn't one of them. The value of the property plunged significantly after the house had gone up in flames. At the time of Thaddeus Campbell's death, the value of the estate was estimated at $22,000. With the house burned to the ground and no insurance policy to speak of, the value plummeted to $12,000. It brought $10,900 at auction, and Sleeves picked up the check the day after the sale had taken place.

The new owner of the Campbell Farm sold half of the acreage to another farm for $6,000 soon after. The people of Rutledge thought it was shameful to break up T.C.'s farm that way.

Irving took a job at the Meacham Farm off Highway 92 where he and his mother lived in the hand quarters. A few of the hands didn't want Millie living with them as she was female, but the food she cooked for them kept them quiet. During the day, Irving would sow seeds and at night he would cry himself to sleep thinking that Elizabeth had died. He would also think about his wooden case with the seeds he had collected over the years and how he would never see it again. One image that stayed with him was the room with the green door and how it went up in flames. He would close his eyes and try to read the names on the jars, but his memory was too fuzzy. He would think about Mr. Campbell's effort and wondered how long he had stored seeds and wondered if he cross bred the tomatoes himself or if he had purchased them.

For more than a month, Irving thought non-stop about Claire, Elizabeth, and the tomato seeds. On a Saturday morning, Irving rose early and walked down to the town square and used the only pay phone in town. With a roll of dimes in hand, he nervously dialed zero and asked to be connected to the hospital.

"Morristown Hospital, may I help you?"

"Hi. About a month ago there was a woman brought in with severe burns, and she was transported to Illinois. I am trying to find out which hospital she was taken to."

The woman who answered the phone asked him to hold. Irving looked out the booth and saw a blue sky, clouds, and birds flying lazily above the trees. After watching them circle around and fly off, the woman came back on the line.

"That would be Cook County Hospital."

Irving ended the call and paid for the call to Chicago.

"Hi, uh, I am looking to speak with Mrs. Elizabeth Campbell."

"Is she a patient or staff?"

"Patient."

"One moment," the voice said. Irving waited thinking Elizabeth would be the next voice he would hear. "Sir, this patient is in the ICU and is unable to take phone calls."

Irving thanked the woman and hung up the phone. A few days after the call, Irving was working in the Meacham fields when an old white lady approached the hands while crossing her arms and looking out-of-sorts. The old lady stumbled over the uneven rows and hollered out as she approached.

"Irving Washington!" Irving looked at the old lady and walked toward her as he carried a scuffle in his right hand.

"Yes, Ma'am?" he hollered back as he walked toward her.

"Someone is here to see you," she yelled out as she turned around and headed back to the house. *Is it Elizabeth?* he thought. He held onto his scuffle as he ran toward the Meacham farmhouse and blazed past the old lady. At the edge of the field, he dropped the scuffle and hurried to the front of the house where he found a man wearing an old button up shirt and a crooked tie. Standing next to his car, the man looked up with his thick glasses when he heard someone approaching.

"Sir?" Irving said as he slowed his run to a walk and stopped in front of Mr. Collins.

"Mr. Irving?"

"Yes, sir."

"I'm Mr. Collins, Mrs. Campbell's accountant."

"Oh yes, sir."

"Sorry about how things turned out. I am the one that helped her with payroll and her uncle's bank account."

"I see."

"I found you through the co-op, and they said you were working here, and I have an envelope with your final wages. I thought I would deliver them personally," he explained as he held out the envelope. "I had to settle some invoices and balance the account. This is the last thing I had to do. Uh, when is she coming back?" Irving took the envelope.

"I don't rightly know."

"I see. I do wish things would have turned out better."

"I called the hospital in Chicago," said Irving. "They told me she was unable to talk on the phone. I'm not sure how bad it is."

"Well, please keep me in mind if you hear from her."

"Will do. Thanks, again."

Irving went back to work and finished up the day by cleaning mud off his boots and sharpening a few scuffles. Before going to bed, he said 'goodnight' to his mamma who slept on the far end of the hand quarters. He got comfortable in his cot with his hands behind his head thinking about Elizabeth. The thing that bothered him the most was not knowing how she was doing. He considered calling again—just as a fleeting thought flashed past his mind. Like the truck that entered the dining room that evening, the thought entered his mind and turned into a plan. He sat up in bed and considered the idea once more. He flipped the thin blanket off and set his feet on the cold floor and quickly walked to the other side of the hand quarters and woke up his mother.

Chapter 55

The next morning, the other men in the hand quarters came together to fit Irving into some proper clothes. A pair of dark brown pants was loaned to him by a similarly tall man. Another farm hand lent him a button-up shirt, and another let him borrow a nice pair of shoes and a brown Fedora.

Looking dapper and somewhat fashionable, Irving hitched a ride to Knoxville and was dropped off on North Central Street. After walking a few miles to the bus station, he approached the ticketing window and opened the envelope that Mr. Collins had given him.

"Where to, fella?" a man behind the window asked. He was chewing gum as if he was in a contest for the most chewing. He wore a blue hat with the word Greyhound on the front, and his shirt looked pressed.

"Round trip to Chicago please," Irving said as he removed the Fedora and set it on the ledge in front of him. The ticketing agent turned to a big machine and chewed ferociously as he punched big, white mechanical buttons. He then reached for a long arm like a slot machine and gave it a long pull as if it would help him win a jackpot. Gears inside the machine made a racket along with clanking and winding and whirring. When the machine stopped, the chewing stopped for a brief second as he looked at the total.

"That'll be $22.13."

Once his ticket was punched, Irving climbed aboard a Greyhound bus and sat in the colored section with several other black men and women. The ride was rough enough to make Irving think the bus needed new tires, but he soon got lost in his thoughts and forgot about the jolting. When the bus arrived at a truck stop in Evansville, Indiana, everyone on board exited and used the restroom and purchased snacks. When Irving got back on the bus, the colored seating area, previously designated by a sign, had been removed. Turning to a black woman wearing glasses, he asked her a question in a hushed tone.

"Where we sit at?"

"We above the Mason-Dixon line, so anywhere we want."

Irving turned back and once again looked for the sign and found it to be missing. Not wanting to look like a first timer, he quickly took a seat by the window.

It took more than seven hours to get to Chicago and when they finally arrived, it was 10:19 P.M. Irving walked from the bus station to a motel and paid $6.10 for a single bed room and map of Chicago.

Spending the night in the big city of Chicago proved to be difficult. Sirens from police cars and fire trucks kept Irving awake and made him long for the sound of cicada's buzzing in the trees. With a pillow over his head, Irving found moments of rest during the night until the sun came up. Rubbing his eyes with the back of his hands, he stood up and began to get dressed.

Once on the streets of Chicago, he kept to the map and kept to himself. The sheer size of the buildings intimidated him and made him wonder if it was safe to walk between them. He watched the sea of people navigate in and out of revolving doors. Some people were granted entry into buildings by men in uniforms with white gloves. Irving saw these well-dressed men opening wooden double doors for well-dressed people. Looking down at his map, he found Cook County Hospital to be seven blocks away.

The sounds of the street were unknown to him, and his senses overloaded with the smell of food from the hot dog carts, and the odor of sewage that ran in streams under the sidewalk. The noises came from street cars and automobiles, and the wind whooshing past his head that nearly knocked off his fedora. For seven blocks, he kept his focus on the streets and the map in his hand. Upon entering Cook County Hospital, relief set in as if he had found shelter from a storm. Irving approached a main desk with two black women working behind it. As one spoke, he removed his Fedora.

"Can I help you?" the lady asked. Irving found comfort in the familiarity of speaking with another person of color.

"I am looking for a patient named Mrs. Elizabeth Campbell."

The lady looked through a book with many rows and columns. Irving thought the book looked similar to the one Elizabeth had carried around with her. The rows were written in pencil and a large rubber eraser sat next to the book.

"Here, Mrs. Elizabeth Campbell is in room 336. That's the Intensive Care Unit on the third floor. Not sure they'll let you see her."

"Oh? Why is that?"

"Visitors are kept at a minimum in ICU."

"May I go up there and see?"

"Of course. It'll be up to the charge nurse if she can have visitors. Elevators are by the water fountains," she said as she pointed.

"Thank you."

Irving hurried to the elevators and found one packed with people. Although he had never been inside an elevator, he'd seen a few in the movies. He boarded and followed suit as to what everyone else was doing. He looked ahead and said nothing while people got on and off until it reached the third floor. He exited and finally pocketed the map he'd been carrying. Irving walked toward a nurse's station and saw three women in white uniforms buzzing about with towels and napkins.

"Oh gosh! I'm so sorry," said a nurse.

"It's fine. Let's just get this cleaned up."

"It was my first cup of the day too!"

"Someone call a janitor."

The ruckus continued and Irving stood back waiting to inquire about Elizabeth. He looked around and saw a hallway on his left with doors and could see numbers painted on them. He wondered if Elizabeth was in one of them and looked closer to see if he could spot number 336. As the nurses finished cleaning the desk, they pulled their chairs away as a black man in a blue jumpsuit began mopping underneath.

"Spilling a perfectly good cup of coffee is almost unforgivable!" a nurse said as she smiled. Irving saw another hallway to his right and saw the number 336. He looked back at the nurse's station thinking if they weren't looking at him, he could stroll on over to the room.

"Can I help you?" one of the nurses asked as she sat back down in her chair. The janitor put the mop back in the bucket and rolled it out from behind the desk.

"Yes Ma'am. I am here to see Mrs. Campbell in room 336."

"She's a burn patient. No visitors until she is out of this unit."

"But, I'm from Tennessee. I came all the way to see her."

"I don't make the rules," said the nurse.

"Uh…ok. How about Claire? Her daughter?"

"I don't know, sir. You will not be able to see this patient. She's going to be here a while."

"Her daughter is young. Is she around here? Have you seen her? Her name is Claire?"

"Sir, I don't keep up with such things. I'm sorry. You'll have to leave."

Irving hung his head, and he felt sick. He turned toward room 336 and thought if he could at least get a glimpse of her. He wanted to see if she was okay. "Don't even think about it," the nurse said as she looked over the top of her glasses.

Irving turned around and headed toward the elevators and got on as soon as the doors opened. He spent the ride down to the lobby thinking of how close he was to seeing her. *What if I had gotten there at the exact moment the coffee spilled?* The distraction would have given him enough time to slip away and into Room 336.

"Hey," a voice said as he exited into the lobby. Irving turned around and saw the janitor. "You want to get into Room 336?" he asked in a hushed tone.

"Yes, I do," whispered Irving.

"Be here at 3, and bring five dollars. I'll get you in the room. Can't promise for how long, but I'll get you in there."

"In the lobby. 3," Irving replied to confirm.

"Yep," the janitor said as he put his hands in his pockets and strolled away, trying to not look suspicious.

Out on the city sidewalk, Irving bought a hot dog from a vendor for fifteen cents and walked down the street and found a bench. He sat in the sun and ate the hot dog thinking of what he was going to say to Elizabeth. *Should I tell her that the farm sold?* The hot dog was the best he'd ever had in his entire life, but his situation prevented him from truly enjoying it. *How is this janitor going to get me inside?* After finishing the hot dog, he reached into his pocket and removed a five-dollar bill from the envelope. He placed it into his other pocket, ready to pay the man.

Irving had several hours to burn off, and he spent all of it
wandering the streets and looking at clocks in diners and asking
strangers for the time. He saw a little boy standing on a stack of
newspapers and selling them for four cents. An alleyway to his
right was occupied by women smoking cigarettes and beating
rugs with broom handles. On the corner of Ashland Avenue, a
man hollered out to anyone who would listen "Shoe Shine! Get
your shoes shined here! Make 'em like mirrors. Wingtip special!
Impress your boss! Get a raise! Like mirrors!"

The hours seemed to drag on until 3:00 arrived. Irving walked
back to the hospital and stood in the lobby until he saw the janitor. He made a small motion with his head that implied that
Irving should follow him. He walked behind the blue jumpsuit
and watched as the man opened a door in the hallway. Once inside
and the door was closed, he could see that he was in a room with
shelves, a wash basin and buckets of bleach. The odor in the room
was industrial and offensive, but easy to ignore under the circumstances.

"You got the money?" the janitor asked. Irving reached into his
pocket and removed a five-dollar bill. Once he handed it over, the
janitor began the plan by removing a blue jumpsuit from a shelf.
"Put this on, and you'll follow me up to the third floor. The shift
change just happened, and the nurses won't know anything as long
as you're with me. I'll have you push the mop bucket, so you'll look
bonafide. Then I'll slip away as you enter room 336. Got it?"

"Got it. Thanks for doing this."

"Thanks for the five."

Irving slid into the jumpsuit and zipped it up the front.

"When you're done, just come back in here and throw the
jumpsuit on any shelf. On the way up to the third floor, I'll carry
your hat and hand it to you when you go in room 336. How long
you gonna be?"

"I don't know."

"Just be prepared to get kicked out at any moment."

Irving followed the man down another hallway and stepped into a cargo elevator. He waited while the janitor pulled a large door down and used a lever to operate the lift. Within moments, they were on the third floor and walking toward room 336. The nurses weren't even paying attention when Irving walked inside the room in custodial attire holding a Fedora. The janitor had taken over the mop bucket and went on his way.

Inside the room, Irving saw a motionless Elizabeth laying on the hospital bed. The right side of her head, face, and neck were bandaged. Some of the bruising could be seen where her flesh was exposed. He winced as he looked at the elastic bandages that were wrapped around her right shoulder and entire arm. Her eyes were closed, and she looked to be asleep. Irving sat in a chair that was next to the bed and kept as quiet as possible and could only hear sounds of the street faintly through the window pane. Elizabeth had been in and out of consciousness since her arrival. Sometimes she would see nurses standing over her bed before fading out. Other times she would open her eyes and see the hand of her daughter holding hers or Claire would be asleep in the chair with her head resting uncomfortably on her own shoulder. Some moments seemed like being underwater and her consciousness would bob up above the surface momentarily only to bob back down into the murky water. The morphine was wearing off and her eyes slowly opened. She believed she wasn't awake but dreaming instead. Irving Washington was sitting in the chair where Claire would usually sit. Irving thought she looked to be in severe pain. Her brow wrinkled, and her eyes winced.

"Hey," he whispered. "I came here to see you." His face wore a slight grin. "I just had to see you. I wanted to make sure you were doing okay." Elizabeth closed her eyes as if she didn't want to see him. He began to tell Elizabeth about the job he found at the Meacham Farm.

"We planting beets right now. The acreage is about a third smaller than…"

"I can't do this." Elizabeth mumbled as she looked up at the ceiling. Tears formed in her eyes. "Please leave, Irving," she uttered through trembling lips. His expression fell and his mouth was left open in a state of confusion.

"Did I say something?"

"Everything. I just can't do this. Please don't say anymore. Just leave."

He stood up as she began sobbing. Unable to move her burned arm, she covered her mouth with her other hand. Stunned and speechless, Irving watched her sob thinking she would calm down. He didn't want to leave and thought she might change her mind. He continued to stand by her bed until she opened her red, watery eyes and looked at him. "Get out!" Elizabeth said, raising her voice. She tried to turn her head away from him but couldn't as the pain from the burns and her broken collar bone was too much.

Dazed and shocked by her words, he turned and walked out into the hallway.

While Irving was sitting with Elizabeth, Claire had been out in the city near the park. She had quickly figured out how to use public transportation and ways to get food. Without having any money, she would wait in the back of restaurants and chat with cooks smoking cigarettes. She would approach a group of cooks talking and laughing and ask for a dinner roll and sometimes they would reach inside the kitchen and pull out a roll or two and if she was lucky, they would go inside and fix her a plate.

The day that Irving walked into Elizabeth's hospital room, Claire was checking the alleys for cooks but found the alleys to

be empty and decided to go back to the hospital. Sometimes patients would be transported from one room to another, or the patient might pass away or even be released. Claire discovered that
if she hung around empty rooms when meals were being delivered, she could sometimes grab a free tray if the food service department didn't get word of the patient's departure.

She walked into the lobby and toward the elevators, past a
black man in dress pants and button up shirt. As they passed each
other, Claire thought he resembled Irving Washington. She had
turned her head and saw a nicely dressed man wearing a Fedora
and quickly dismissed the thought and got on the elevator.

Walking into her mother's room, she saw Elizabeth awake and
sobbing with nurses on either side.

"Mom! What's wrong?" she asked.

"She's in pain, honey. Just keep your distance, okay?" said the
nurse as she injected morphine into Elizabeth's IV. "The doctors
will be meeting with her tomorrow," she added. Claire watched her
mother's eyes roll back into her head as the medicine kicked in.

Irving had walked out of the hospital wiping the tears from
his eyes. Confused and hurt, he walked unconsciously past other
pedestrians on his way to the bus station.

Chapter 56

Just after nine o'clock in the morning, two men in white lab coats sat in chairs next to Elizabeth's hospital bed as a nurse gently woke her from a deep sleep. The sounds of sirens and trucks could be faintly heard outside.

"Mrs. Campbell? Honey, can you wake up for me?" a nurse said. "This is Dr. Garner and Dr. Rawlins. They need to speak with you. I'm gonna sit you up and it will cause a little discomfort. You have been off painkillers for more than 12 hours so I'm not gonna lie. This will hurt a bit." Elizabeth then discovered that the nurse's grating voice was irritating even without having to listen to her through a cloud of morphine.

"Where's my daughter?"

"She comes in and out. I suspect she'll be around shortly. For now, answer a few questions for me. Who's the president?" the nurse asked as she pulled on sheets and tucked them in before reaching behind the bed and began winding the crank.

"Uh, President Truman," Elizabeth answered as she rubbed her eyes. The bed was moving slowly as the nurse turned the crank. Elizabeth could feel herself starting to sit up and the pain in her neck and shoulder began to throb.

"What's five plus five?"

"Ten," Elizabeth answered as she winced from the sharp pain.

The cranking stopped. Thank God she stopped. The nurse walked around the bed and spoke before she left the room.

"I'll be back in a few."

Elizabeth's focus was still hazy. One physician had dark brown hair, the other black. The brown-haired doctor spoke first.

"Mrs. Campbell, I'm Dr. Garner, you have suffered considerable second-degree burns which have affected the epidermis and the dermis layers…" While much of it was medical jargon that she wasn't familiar with, her low energy level kept her from asking questions. She just listened. When the doctor with the brown hair was finished, the black-haired man spoke.

"The skin graft is doing quite well, and because of that, we need to move you to a different floor of the hospital. There you will receive tub baths, exercise and…," Elizabeth felt coherent until the doctors voice began to sound like the droning of a tractor engine puttering along.

Outside in the city of Chicago, the back alleys were filled with undesirables. Claire had come to like the cooks who hung out in the alleyways and smoked cigarettes and told dirty jokes. It reminded her when the farm hands would gather and tell jokes before and after a day's work. If she had a favorite alley, it was one that had multiple dryer vents that smelled of clean clothes. Often times when hanging out in the alley and petting a stray cat, a door would open on the opposite side of the alley, which usually meant a cook from one of the restaurants was coming out for a smoke break.

One day while petting a tabby cat, Claire heard the back door open across the alley and saw three cooks pour out and light up their cigarettes. Leaving the friendly cat, she walked up to one of the cooks who had given her food before. As he listened to a story told by one of his co-workers, he glanced at Claire and then nodded as he took a drag from the cigarette. He disappeared back inside the restaurant and re-appeared in seconds with two garlic rolls. He tossed them to her and she caught them.

"Thanks!"

"Hey, kid, you homeless?"

"Kind of."

"You wanna job?" the cook asked as he took another drag.

"Of course."

"Come back at five. I'll give you cash at the end of the day," he said before going back to the conversation. Claire nodded at him even though it seemed he was no longer paying her any attention. She hurried out of the alley as she took a bite out of one of the dinner rolls. Back at the hospital, Claire walked into her mother's room and found her awake and sitting up. Her bandages had been changed, and her hair was now in a ponytail.

"Mom? You're awake," said Claire as she hurried to her bedside. "How are you feeling?" Elizabeth answered as if she was going to fall asleep at any minute.

"I'm in a good deal of pain. The nurses are keeping me off painkillers for now. They are moving me to another floor," she explained as she closed her eyes, but continued the conversation.

"Is that good?"

"It is. They're going to give me baths and get me to exercise," she added, keeping her eyes closed.

"What did the doctors say?"

"They said I am improving," she replied. Claire didn't respond and was very quiet. When Elizabeth opened her eyes, she saw her daughter in tears. Her nose was running, and she didn't use her shirt nor did she reach for a tissue. "Oh, honey. What's wrong?" As Claire responded to her tired mother, Elizabeth strained to understand Claire as she spoke while she sobbed.

"The nurses wouldn't tell me anything. I didn't know if you were going to survive. Sometimes I would be too afraid to come back and see you." Elizabeth reached out her hand.

"I am so sorry this happened. I wish I could hug you." Claire gently held her mother's hand and finally wiped her nose and tears.

"I just want you to be okay. I don't want you to be in pain."

"It will take time, but we will get there."

"What are we going to do?"

"I don't know. I suppose we will do what we always do. We will carve out a place for ourselves."

"I was in the lobby yesterday, and I thought I saw Irving. I keep thinking about the farm," Claire said. Her mother loosened her grip and let go of her hand.

"Claire. He was here."

"He was? What did he say?"

"The pain I am experiencing from my injuries is nothing. It's nothing compared to losing the farm, and I want to make it clear that we will never talk about the farm or Irving again. It hurts too much. Do you understand?"

"We will never go back there?"

"Never."

"But what did Irving say?"

"He wished us well."

Claire had been thinking that Grainger County was home. Even though she had spent very little time there, it was the place that seemed like home more than any place she had been. When her mother explained her feelings, Claire became angry. She wanted to push back at her mother's remarks but couldn't bring herself to argue with her mother in her condition. Elizabeth had taken in a deep breath and closed her eyes. When she opened them again, she reached out for Claire's hand. Unable to bring herself to accept that Grainger County was a lost cause, Claire turned around and walked out of the room.

Chapter 57

THREE YEARS LATER.

The Holman Building in downtown Chicago featured four floors of one-bedroom apartments. The superintendent of the building was an old man with a pot belly and a raspy voice. If the tenants were unlucky, they would catch him wondering around the building while wearing an old undershirt. Women and children were subjected to his unsightly shoulder and back hair that made veterans of foreign wars wince.

Elizabeth considered herself fortunate to be able to rent a one-bedroom apartment as there wasn't much available in the city that was affordable. When the superintendent wasn't lurking in the hallways while jangling his keys, he was pestering Elizabeth and the other tenants about their rent. In her rental agreement, it listed the amount of $105 if paid by the 5th of the month and $5 was added every day she was late. The apartment was grimy, and the walls were thin, but she and Claire made it work, often taking an entire Sunday to clean their little space in the giant city.

For three years, Claire had been working at Gauloise, a French restaurant three blocks from where she lived. Every day after school she would walk to the restaurant and begin whatever task they had set aside for her. She would peel potatoes, de-spot glassware, scrub floors, and other menial jobs. Her favorite part of working there was being able to hang out in the back alley with the cooks while they told jokes and smoked cigarettes. The jokes were dirty, but so were the cooks. Some smelled of body odor, especially the cooks that were from France. She liked their accent but preferred to listen to them from a distance. During dinner service, the kitchen was blanketed in chaos. With lots of yelling and pots banging, cooks would scream from being burned or getting angry at wait staff. Claire loved it.

When Elizabeth got out of the hospital, she arranged a very small line of credit with a department store. After purchasing a discounted dress that covered her scars, she would sit at the tiny kitchen table in her tiny apartment and take a pain pill before rehearsing her upcoming interviews. Elizabeth quickly found work as the assistant manager of a coffee shop just a block from the Holman Building. Mick's Coffee shop served eggs, toast, and bacon in the mornings. Sandwiches were served for lunch and dinner plates after five. Elizabeth handled scheduling of employees and counting drawers at the end of her shift as well as taking orders, filling coffee mugs, and serving customers plates of food. While working, she would often get questions about what happened to her arm and neck. The scars were quite visible even though she would always wear long sleeves. The worst scar was on the left side of her head where her hair had caught fire. With creative hairstyling, she had found a way to hide the bald spot and minimize the questions.

Most of her customers were men in hats and trench coats coming in to eat a quick bite and read a stray newspaper they'd find on the lunch counter. Some customers were regulars and came to know her by name. One of the many coats and hats that patronized the coffee shop had become very friendly with Elizabeth. He walked in polished shoes and wore pinstripe suits.

His name was Luke Cavell, and he worked in one of the massive buildings nearby. She came to know him as an executive for a shoe company. He came in with tales of traveling to Texas, California and Nevada. She lived vicariously through his stories as she knew that such travel for her and Claire was impossible.

On rainy days, Elizabeth would roll out a mat by the front door to allow customers to wipe their feet. One rainy day, she pulled the heavy mat out from behind the counter and set it in front of the door just as it opened, and two polished shoes walked in and stood on the mat. She looked up, and there was Luke.

"I'm sorry, sir."

"Hey, there! I was coming here to see you."

"You were?"

"Here, can you talk for a minute?" he asked as he motioned towards a booth along the wall. Elizabeth sat down on one side, and Luke on the other. The beaded rain on his shoulders rolled off as he spoke, but Elizabeth didn't notice. She suddenly became self-conscious of her bald spot and had hoped her hair was staying in place.

"I wanted to stop by and ask if you would be okay with me taking you out to dinner? I know you mentioned that you aren't married, and I thought it might be nice to get out and have someone serve you for once," he explained. Elizabeth thought he was very nice and handsome, but she still saw herself as married to her husband. She touched the place on her finger where her wedding ring once was. Ever since waking up in Chicago, it had been missing.

"I don't know. I don't think I can."

"What do you mean? You have Sundays off. Right?"

"Right."

"Then what's the harm?"

"It's not the time off."

"What is it? Is it me?" Luke asked with a smile. It had been a long time since a man had shown interest, not since the mining camp anyway. Thinking about the last time she had fun took too long, and now Luke began to think she was stalling.

"I'd go to dinner, but only if we could go to a movie too."

"Done."

"With my daughter."

"What?"

"My daughter will come with us."

"She will?"

It wasn't the date Luke had intended, but he agreed as he thought it might lead to another date. For three days, Elizabeth thought about the upcoming Sunday night and hoped for one night of forgetting about her rent. She and Claire could act like families do when they go out on the town. While she wasn't looking for a relationship, a single night of normality was something she needed. The days leading up to Sunday night included nervousness, daydreaming, butterflies, and excitement.

Elizabeth and Claire were picked up in a taxi cab in front of the Holman Building. Luke rode in the front seat, giving Claire and Elizabeth room in the backseat. Mother and daughter were dressed as nice as their budget would allow, while Luke wore his usual business attire with polished shoes.

"So, ladies, do you have a recommendation for a restaurant or a place you'd like to eat?"

"Gauloise," said Claire without hesitating.

"Gauloise," Luke repeated. He took a moment to himself as he knew the place and what it might cost him.

"It's just three blocks from here," Claire added.

"Yeah, I know. I know the place," Luke said with a smile. This is gonna cost me, he thought as he looked back at Elizabeth. He smiled, and she shrugged her shoulders while returning the smile. The cab driver could feel the hesitation as Luke confirmed their destination. "Okay. Gauloise, it is."

Once at the restaurant, Claire held her mother's hand and soaked up the moment of going in the front door of Gauloise as a customer. Elizabeth had been to the restaurant from time to time, although she had experienced the same as Claire. The back alley was their entrance. The maitre d' recognized Claire and approached her with a surprised look on his face.

"Now, Miss Clair'ee, I didn't recognize you at first. You look lovely tonight."

"Why, thank you. This is my mother, Elizabeth Campbell."

"I haven't had the pleasure," said the maitre d' while taking notice of the confused look on Luke's face.

"Come here often?" Luke asked Elizabeth. She whispered back.

"Claire works here. She works in the back."

"Oh, I see."

Once the introductions were completed, the bread basket was set on the table. Claire reached in and grabbed a dinner roll and stood up.

"Excuse me. I am going to see some friends." Luke briefly rose from his seat as she walked away. Elizabeth took notice of his gentlemanly actions.

"Have you eaten here before?" he asked.

"Not here inside the restaurant, but Claire brings home food from time to time."

"Can you recommend anything?"

"There's this dish that has a steak with these cracked peppercorns. It's my favorite one that Claire brings home."

Back in the kitchen, Claire received compliments from the kitchen staff on her appearance. Some of the cook's French accents made her laugh as they commented on her appearance.

"Oooh la la! You ready for zee magazine cover, eh' Miss Clair'ee?"

"We in the presence of royalty I think, eh?"

"Shut up," she said with a smile. "Who's smoking?" she asked as she went out back in the alley. A few of the cooks followed. Apple crates were turned over, and some cooks sat down while some stood up.

"You dining with us tonight?" a cook asked as he lit a rolled cigarette.

"My mom is on a date."

"You come here on your night off?"

"I've never been a customer," she said as she shrugged her shoulders.

"You come in as a customer, but you end up the alley," one of the cooks said. She took a bite of the dinner roll and chewed on one side of her mouth while she spoke.

"What can I say? I miss you degenerates."

While Claire spent her time cutting up in the alley, Luke asked Elizabeth questions about how she arrived in Chicago. She spoke about her husband's death and working at Harris Clay Mining Company but skipped over her time spent in Tennessee.

"So, I have always wanted to ask you, and forgive me for prying, but I was wondering how you came to acquire your injuries? That is, if you don't mind me asking."

"Well, I think this night is off to a great start and answering such questions would surely bring the evening down, so why don't we talk about better things?"

"Like what?"

"What movie are we going to see?"

Claire exited the kitchen and walked into the dining room holding a plate of hot croissants. She set them on the table and took her seat. Luke was wondering how much it was going to cost him and he had forgotten to stand when she arrived.

"On the house," said Claire.

"Ooooh. They are still warm," said Elizabeth as she took one and put it in front of her on a small plate.

"Just came out of the oven."

Soon after eating the warm croissants, their orders were fulfilled, and the dinner commenced. To keep the cost of dinner to a minimum, Luke told a white lie that he wasn't very hungry and confined his dinner to a bowl of soup. Elizabeth and Claire ate their favorite dishes and reveled being out of their apartment and inside a real restaurant. When it was time for dessert, Claire disappeared back into the kitchen and materialized a large slice of chocolate cake. Setting it in the middle of the table, she looked over at Luke.

"Relax. This one is on me," she said with a smile.

"Oh, good," Luke replied as he grabbed his spoon. The three of them took bites out of the slice while Claire regaled them in how the pastry chef created the chocolate wonder before them.

Once the bill came to the table, Luke looked it over as if he were ripping off a Band-Aid. The amount wasn't as high as he had thought it was going to be. The croissants were free as was the dessert. *I'm glad I got soup,* he thought.

The evening continued at the Clark Movie Theater where Luke purchased tickets to see the movie, *Rear Window* by Alfred Hitchcock. During the cab ride home, it was all they could talk about.

"Did you think Thorwald did it? I mean, before he came into the apartment?" Elizabeth asked.

"I wasn't sure, but I kept closing my eyes when I thought the flash bulb would go off," said Claire.

"I did too!" exclaimed Elizabeth.

Luke listened to his date speak excitedly with her daughter in the backseat. They carried on all the way to the front of the Holman Building. Once parked, Luke noticed the cab driver's relief as he exited the front seat and opened the back door.

Chapter 58

Over the next few days, Elizabeth reflected back to their night
out on the town. She used the memory to escape from her daily
routine of scheduling employees, refilling mugs with hot coffee,
and serving eggs, sandwiches, and dinner plates. She would think
about that night as she walked into the restaurant, talking with
Claire and Luke over dinner and her favorite part— she decided,
was getting out of the cab and walking up to the box office of the
movie theater. The anticipation of seeing a movie and not worrying about anything else was a relief she hadn't experienced in
a very long time.

Luke had been back once since that Sunday to say hello, but
he didn't stick around to be served. Elizabeth was glad he didn't
take a seat at the counter as it would have been awkward serving
him. She thought of Samuel, and looked down where her wedding
ring used to be. When she was discharged from the hospital, the
nurses explained that her clothes were too burnt to keep and
store. When she inquired about her wedding ring and where it
might be, the nurses had no explanation.

Deciding that she would consider a second date with Luke,
she did think of Samuel and how she had slowly started to forget
him. It hurt inside, but she could also feel the pull of needing to
move on and maybe explore other possibilities. On a rainy after-

noon, Claire entered the coffee shop and sat at the counter.

"Coffee please!" she said out loud so her mother could hear her. When Elizabeth turned around, she saw her daughter sitting at the counter with a big smile.

"What are you up to?"

"Well, I need some help."

"With what?"

"A dress."

"A what? You actually want to wear a dress?"

"For homecoming, I do."

"Homecoming?"

"My school is putting on a dance and there is a football game. It's a big thing and I was asked by a boy to go to the dance."

"Hmmm…okay. How old is he?"

"He's a junior."

"I don't know. Sounds too old for you."

"It's just a dance, and he's nice. He is my partner in home economics. He can't cook with a darn, but he's nice."

"I don't know. We don't have enough money for a new dress," Elizabeth explained. Claire pulled out a ten-dollar bill from her pocket and slapped it on the counter.

"I've been saving," she said with a smile.

When Elizabeth got off work, the two hopped on a bus to Marshall Field and Company Department Store. The entrance to the building looked like an entrance to the Roman Pantheon. The columns were massive and made customers look like ants. Once inside, they walked on polished marble floors and underneath grand chandeliers hanging above their heads. They strolled past waist-high counters that contained jewelry with nicely dressed female clerks tending to customers.

After a quick escalator ride, they found the young women's department in the back corner on the second floor. Elizabeth

watched from a chair as her daughter walked in and out of a fit-
ting room trying on several dresses.

"How 'bout this one?" Claire would ask. After forty minutes,
she decided on a light blue dress with a blooming skirt. Elizabeth
watched as her daughter paid for it with her own money and took
the bag from the clerk behind the register. It caught her off guard
at how fast her daughter was growing up. Elizabeth asked Claire
questions as they walked toward the escalators.

"You still want to go to college?"

"I don't know. I'm not exactly sure what I want to do."

"Remember when you wanted to be a detective?"

"I don't think there are any women detectives."

"You could be the first."

"I was thinking about cooking in a restaurant. Maybe going
to school to learn to be a cook."

"I don't know of any women working in the back of the
restaurant."

"I could be the first," Claire replied with a smile. Elizabeth
stopped and looked at her daughter.

"Do you seriously think that is something you might be interested in? Cooking?" she asked. Claire noticed her mother
looked interested and intrigued.

"Yeah. I think so."

"You don't want to be a detective? You used to say that you
wanted to be like Nancy Drew. Has that changed?"

"Well, being a detective seems slow and silent. When I work
in the kitchen, it's loud and fast and crazy."

"And you like that?"

"It's fun," Claire replied with a shrug. "One time I was asked
to chop onions, and the chef yelled at me. He got in my face and
yelled in his stupid French accent 'you chop onions like a moron.
You have no business in this kitchen. Get out of here, you sissy!'

and later that night after service he walked over to me and showed me how to chop an onion. Then it was, I don't know, maybe a week later when I had chopped up an onion and he put me on his shoulders in the middle of service and screamed to everyone in the kitchen 'This young lady can chop onions! She is one of us!' and the kitchen went crazy and I felt like I belonged."

"Why didn't you tell me this?"

"This was back when you were still in the hospital."

"Well, now you're gonna have to come back in the kitchen at the coffee shop and show me how you can chop onions. Also, I can't believe the chef yelled at you. That's not nice at all!"

"They're crazy. All of them."

"But you like them?"

"I do. Very much."

Elizabeth smiled. They took an escalator down to the next floor continuing to talk about why Claire liked working in the kitchen. After stepping off the escalator, they turned a corner and saw Luke Cavell holding a toddler. The toddler looked to be about two years of age, and the sight caught Elizabeth by surprise. Claire was confused. Before Elizabeth could say anything, a woman holding the hand of a seven-year-old boy came into view. Luke looked terrified as he saw both Elizabeth and Claire. He quickly ignored them as he and his wife walked toward the exit of the department store. Elizabeth's face turned white as a sheet.

"Mom...?" Claire started to ask.

"Don't say anything. Don't say a word," Elizabeth replied as she put her hand on a jewelry counter for balance. She closed her eyes and breathed through her nose. Claire looked up and saw Luke quickly hail a taxi while holding his daughter. When a cab stopped, he opened the backdoor while his wife and son got in. He put his daughter in the seat next to his son and closed the door. Once Luke got in the passenger seat, the cab drove off. Claire grabbed her mother's hand and they headed outside.

Back at the apartment, Elizabeth and Claire discovered that the entire building had been sprayed for bugs. The odor of the pesticide was nearly intolerable. They got ready for bed while making every effort to block off their sense of smell by breathing through their mouth while opening every window and turning on the one fan they had in the apartment. Once they were laying down on their mattresses, Elizabeth couldn't help but think of Luke and how nice he seemed. She didn't understand how a man could do something like that—which made her think of Samuel. He would never do anything like that, she thought. Tears started to form as she remembered that she considered going on another date with that man which in turn meant that she would be moving on from her husband. She apologized profusely in her thoughts and asked for her husband's forgiveness. *I will never forget you. I will never forget you. I am so very sorry.*

The next day, her co-workers could easily tell that something was wrong. At first, they asked if she was ill. She explained she was simply unhappy and that she wasn't sick. The more she thought about Luke, the more she felt foolish and stupid. She cleaned up a booth after patrons had left the coffee shop, wadding up napkins in her hands, and piling bowls, and stacking mugs to take back to the dishwasher. She thought of the way he briefly stood up when Claire excused herself from the table. How could a man act like a gentleman, but be so deceptive? Removing a ticket pad from her apron, she approached a table and asked what they wanted to drink.

"Coffee and some milk and sugar please."

Elizabeth became lost in her work and focused on the dinner crowd that was starting to come inside. She tried to forget Luke, and she continued to think about her husband when something caught her eye. A man walked through the front door by himself and walked toward the back where the payphone was located. He wasn't dressed like the rest of the working class that came and went. His suit looked exquisite and perfectly tailored to his frame. She looked away as she poured a cup of coffee for the customers at the lunch counter.

"What can I get you to eat?" she asked her customers while keeping the dapper man in her peripheral vision. Instead of using the payphone in the back of the coffee shop, he had taken a seat in the back corner. Her customers at the counter rattled off their requests.

"Meatloaf, mashed potatoes, and sweet peas, and I'd like a glass of water, please."

She wrote down the orders and casually glanced at the man in the back corner. He looked so familiar. After placing the ticket on the stainless-steel ticket wheel, she grabbed a pot of coffee and a mug and headed back to the far end of the coffee shop. As she approached, she could see the man had set his bowler hat on the table and had placed a monocle in his eye socket so that he could read the menu. When he looked up, she could see that it was Arthur Humes. Instead of setting the mug on the table and pouring a cup, she sat across from him.

"What are you doing here, Mr. Humes?" she asked as she set the hot pot of coffee on the table. Her eyes conveyed that she was upset with his presence.

"Mrs. Campbell, I am here on business."

"Oh, you are? In Chicago?"

"Yes."

"Oh. I see," she said as she set the mug on the table and poured him a cup.

"You looked upset when you sat down. What, may I ask changed?"

"It's not something that I wish to remember."

"What isn't?"

"The farm. Grainger County."

"I see. May I ask why that is?" he asked as he took a sip of his hot coffee. He watched as Elizabeth thought about it before answering.

"It hurts too much," she finally replied.

"I see. Well, would you like to go over this here or do you have another place in mind?"

"Go over what?"

"Your tax returns listed you as being an employee here, and I am charged with locating you."

"Mr. Humes, you told me you were here on business."

"I am. My client instructed me to find you," he answered. Elizabeth stood up. Her expression wasn't pleasant.

"And who is your client, Mr. Humes?" she asked as she took the coffee pot off the table, ready to walk away.

"I can understand that you want to forget about the Campbell Farm, especially after what happened to you, but you should know that what I am about to tell you begins with sad news."

"It does?"

"Norman Werthan passed a little more than a month ago," Mr. Humes explained. Elizabeth sat back down. The coffee pot remained in her hand.

"Norman," she said under her breath. She hadn't thought about him in years. A sudden emotion of sadness came over her, and her body seemed to deflate as Arthur continued to speak.

"I am sorry to be the bearer of bad news, but I have been instructed to read you his Last Will and Testament," he explained as he raised the lid off of the briefcase that was sitting next to him in the booth. He reached inside and removed a large envelope, setting it on the table. Elizabeth said nothing and set the coffee pot back on the table. Arthur removed a letter from the envelope, unfolded it and began to read.

Hey Kiddo, as we all do, my time has come, and I have passed away. I wanted to come see you after you were transported to Chicago, but Irving explained to me that it wasn't a good time. Just when I thought that enough time had passed, and you might be doing better, I considered making the trip, but I became ill and now you know that I never fully recovered. Arthur stopped reading and looked over the letter at Elizabeth. Her hand was propping up her head and she was looking right at him. "Still okay? Want me to continue?" he asked. She simply closed her eyes and nodded her head. She felt shame as she thought about Norman and how she should have reached out to him. *My life took a turn for the worse when my wife passed, and I suppose I let the grief from her loss impact me in an unhealthy way. When I was reunited with my daughter, something happened to me, and it was a good change. Suddenly my feelings returned, and my happiness flourished. I could enjoy the sunshine again, and I could taste tomatoes as if I was eating them for the first time. My life was forever changed by your actions and kindness. More than a year ago, I was approached by my neighbor who inquired about purchasing nearly half of my acreage and after little negotiating, I did alright. My daughter and son-in-law have inherited my nest egg, but I did find myself in the same boat as Mr. Campbell. I just don't want to see my tomato farm go to someone who cares little for tomatoes. My house isn't as big as Mr. Campbell's and after the sale of almost half of my land, I now only have 90 acres, but it is sufficient. My daughter and son-in-law want nothing to do with farming, and so I thought I would leave it to the most persistent tomato farmer I know. She is smart, a lot of fun to be around and she makes people smile. The farm is yours, Kiddo. You gave me a gift, so let me give you one. Call my daughter every once in a while, and remind her that I love her. I love her so very much and maybe give her a basket of tomatoes from time to time.*

Mr. Humes ended the letter and looked at Elizabeth. With her head still propped up, the tears streamed down her face and onto her hand and arm.

"Do you need a hug?" he asked. Elizabeth nodded, still propping her head up on the table. Mr. Humes stood up and removed his coat and folded it over the back of his seat. She stood up and embraced him and sobbed into his white button up shirt and clung to his bulky frame. Her breathing sounded like she was drowning, gasping for air. Diners were staring as they stirred and sipped their coffee. A few of the waitresses looked at Elizabeth hugging an old man who was dressed in nice clothes. As Elizabeth's mind drifted to Irving, she recalled that she yelled at him and told him to leave. She sobbed loud enough to cause the entire coffee shop to look. They had stopped stirring, sipping and talking, making Elizabeth's voice seem much louder.

"I don't deserve this!" she cried. Arthur continued to hold her as all eyes focused on them.

Chapter 59

When Arthur Humes held Elizabeth as she sobbed, he did his best to calm her down, although in the end, it just took time. She apologized for getting his white button up shirt wet and grabbed a few napkins from a dispenser on the table. He hadn't really seen the scars from the burns. As she reached for the napkins, he saw them on her arm and on her neck. She caught him looking.

"I'm so sorry. I didn't know it was that bad," he said. His expression quickly changed from lawyerly to that of a concerned father.

"Well, it was. I have moved on from it. It only hurts when I am in the sun. I have to keep it covered up."

"I understand."

Elizabeth excused herself and grabbed an empty coffee cup and quickly returned. She poured herself a cup from the coffee pot while Arthur removed a few documents and a pen.

At two-thirty in the afternoon, Claire entered Gauloise through the back door and stood in the kitchen with a somber look in her eyes. One of the cooks turned, saw her, and stopped what he was doing.

"What is zee matter, mon amie?"

"I'm leaving and heading south."

"When?"

"Now. Right now."

The explanation commenced while other cooks slowly abandoned their stations to listen to Claire. Several of the smelly French cooks hugged Claire; some patted her on the back. Before she left, the cooks took to the alley with her one last time. She listened to their jokes and told a few herself. Before she left, they gave her a sendoff with a sip of French wine from a ramekin. She smiled and wiped a tear as she left the alley and met up with her mother at the Holman Building. After they packed everything into a large bag, they closed the door to their little apartment and left for good, gladly breaking their lease. Once they arrived at the bus station, they purchased two tickets to Knoxville, Tennessee.

Once she and Claire were headed to Knoxville, she handed the document to her daughter.

"So, it's real now?"

"It's real. We own a farm."

Claire looked down at the document. It was complicated to read, but it looked very serious and official. After she and her mother reviewed the document, Elizabeth spoke to her daughter like a parishioner confessing to a priest.

"I know that when I was a kid, I always looked up to adults and whatever they said, I took it as gospel. I thought that grownups could do no wrong, and I suppose that I thought this way because I never saw them make mistakes."

"I saw a lot of cooks make a lot of mistakes."

"You did?"

"Uh huh."

"Have you ever seen me make a mistake?" she asked. Claire thought about it for a moment.

"I don't know. Not really."

"The Mining Camp was a mistake. I still regret ever going there," Elizabeth said as she looked down and picked at her index fingernail. "I also made a mistake several years ago, back when I was in the hospital."

"You did? How?"

"When Irving came to see me. He said he wanted to make sure that I was okay, and I yelled at him and told him to leave," she explained. Claire cocked her head in confusion.

"You did? Why?"

"I was in pain, but not from the burns. Not from the injuries. I couldn't bear to think of what I had lost. It was all I ever wanted for me and for you and if I didn't think about it, I could somehow move on."

"You wouldn't even let me mention the farm."

"The biggest mistake I ever made was talking to Irving that way."

"You were on medication. You weren't thinking straight."

"I knew what I was doing. I just thought I had it all under control and I gave my hopes up and when it all came crashing down…" she said as the bus drove over several potholes and caused the bus to rattle and shake.

"I was selfish. I couldn't handle thinking about what I had lost, and never even considered what he'd lost," Elizabeth added.

Claire watched her stare off into the distance in thought for a brief moment before her mother said, "Just don't think adults are always right."

The next day, after a long bus ride and many stops, they arrived in Knoxville, Tennessee, at three in the afternoon. After hitching a ride to Rutledge, they finally stood on the back porch of Norman's main house. They entered the kitchen with their luggage in hand and turned on the lights. Elizabeth dropped her suitcase on the floor and cupped her hand over her mouth. The loss she carried with her since leaving Grainger County dissipated, and she felt a comfort she hadn't known. She felt like a child being swept up by her father, holding her tight. Claire hugged her mother as she rambled.

"I feel like I need to find Norman and hug him and tell him thank you, and I still can't believe that I yelled at Irving, and it hurts me so bad to think he went back home all that way thinking that I hate him. I just don't feel worthy. I don't deserve this!"

"I don't know. Norman seems to think different," Claire said. Her mother nodded her head as she released her daughter. "So, what are we going to do?" asked Claire.

"The first thing we do is get Irving back here. Half of this is his too. Then I need to buy a ledger and begin filling it out and organize the columns and rows. We also need to enroll you in school. I'm gonna need to scrounge up our money though," Elizabeth added. Claire reached into her front pocket of her pants and pulled out two twenty-dollar bills and handed it to her mother.

"What's this?"

"It's forty dollars. That's my savings from working in the restaurant. I want you to have it. I kept five dollars to buy a few Agatha Christie books. The thing I missed most was sitting on the back porch and reading. For now, that's all I really need."

"I'll pay you back."

"You don't have to."

Elizabeth's chest warmed with pride standing with her daughter as she wrapped her arm around her shoulders.

"When are you going to go get Irving?"

"Now."

"Right now?"

"Yes, and I need you to stay here. I'll be back in an hour or so."

Chapter 60

The inheritance of Werthan Farms included the land, a barn, the house, and the hand quarters. A vehicle wasn't included which meant Elizabeth would have to hitch a ride into town. After grabbing a lantern off the back porch, she lit the wick and headed toward town. The first truck that drove by slowed to a stop behind her, and she hurried to the driver's side.

"Need a ride?" a man asked from inside the cab. He looked to be in his sixties but was only fifty-two.

"Yes, sir."

In the passenger seat was his wife of thirty years. She wore a permanent frown, but Elizabeth didn't have this information and thought her disdain was due to picking up a hitchhiker.

"Where ya headed?"

"Co-op."

"Hmmm…we better hurry. Closes soon."

Jumping in the back, Elizabeth put the flame out on the lantern. The truck took off and headed toward the co-op. After a bumpy ride, she thanked the man and the frown in the passenger seat. Upon entering the co-op, she looked at the long counter with two areas for service. On the far left was a sign that read *White* and on the far right was another sign that read *Colored*. She stood at the counter on the far left and waited until a black man in a white apron came out from the back room.

"Help ya, ma'am?"

"I'm looking for the whereabouts of Irving Washington."

"You an everybody else."

"How do you mean?"

"Plenty of farmers looking for him. Come in here every month or two asking where he is."

"Is he not around?"

"Nope. Last I heard, he was at the Deckard Farm, but that was two years ago."

"Hmmm…where might that be?"

"Out Highway 11 towards Tate Springs, but like I said, he ain't even been around these parts since '52."

"Thank you," Elizabeth replied as she turned around and headed out the door. After hitching another ride, she stood at the mailbox of the Deckard Farm. Striking a match, she lit the wick of her lantern and used its light to make her way to the front door of the main house.

Knock. Knock.

Elizabeth could hear footsteps approach the door. A creak sounded as it opened.

"Hello. I'm looking for Irving Washington. I was wondering if you might know of his whereabouts?" she asked. The man who answered was a small fella that looked as if he could barely break clods with a scuffle.

"This late at night? What's this all about?"

"It is an urgent matter."

"Well, I don't know of his whereabouts. He worked for me a few years back, but if you really need to know in a hurry, you might ask the farmhands out back. They know him."

"Thank you," Elizabeth replied and hurried off the front porch. The small man, confused and bewildered, shut the door.

The hands working the Deckard Farm had only been there a

few days. They had already plowed fifteen acres and sown ten. They were tired and washing up before getting ready for a card game and cornbread when they heard a knock on the door.

Willard Poe walked past a few of his co-workers and opened the door, finding a strawberry blonde-haired white girl holding a lantern.

"Hi," she said. "I'm looking for the whereabouts of Irving Washington."

"He ain't here this season."

"Do you know where he went?" she asked.

"I don't."

"Would anyone else know? It is very important that I find him."

"Step inside here," said Willard as he made way for Elizabeth to enter while he held the door open. The men inside the hand quarters were getting cards ready and rolling cigarettes and setting jars of hooch on the table. They were talking loudly and hurling curse words as they pulled up chairs and readied themselves for a night of joke telling, laughter, drinking, smoking, and poker. The ruckus was difficult to calm down when Willard began hollering out.

"Hey! Quiet! Listen up!" he hollered out in vain. When one of the hands sitting at the table saw a glimpse of Elizabeth, he stopped dealing cards and stood up as if he was a private in the presence of a general. His sudden change in demeanor caused the others to turn and look. The hands quieted down as three other men stood up as they saw Elizabeth.

"That's her," one worker said.

"Who?" a man asked, still seated at the table. He turned his head and saw the woman holding a lantern.

"She's the one we tol' you 'bout," another man said from his standing position next to the table. Four men walked toward her.

"Miss Elizabeth?" one man asked as he walked closer. She nodded her head. "We worked your farm some years back. We heard what happened," he added as the group stopped in front of her. They could now see the burns that had scarred her flesh. Another worker spoke.

"Glad you are okay."

"Thank you," she replied. "I'm looking for Irving." One of the four workers wearing an undershirt and a towel around his neck spoke up. He had a somber look on his face, and Elizabeth held her breath.

"A few years back, his mama passed. She buried up here at the cemetery with his pops. Irving worked here some time ago and then we was supposed to go work another farm here in Grainger County, but he didn't show up."

"He didn't?"

"We don't know where he went. We got farmers asking us all the time where he is, and none of us knows."

"Is there any way to find out? Is there anyone who would know?"

"I can't think of nothing right now."

"Miss Elizabeth?" one man said. She looked at him as he spoke. "Are you back at the old Campbell Farm?"

"I am not. I am the new owner of the Werthan Farm."

"Well, if we hear of anything, we will come see you at the Werthan Farm, and let you know."

"Thank you. I would greatly appreciate it," she said as she turned around and headed for the door.

"Miss Elizabeth? If you hirin' again, post it at the co-op. When you post the job, we'll come a runnin'" one of the men said with a smile. She put her hand on the door, pushing it open and stopped in the doorway.

"Is anyone committed to another farm after this one?" she

asked. A few hands went up in the back. "How much longer are you all here?"

"About two weeks."

"As soon as you finish here, set up at Werthan Farms and we'll get started," she said as she walked outside.

"How much you payin'?" a man asked. From outside, they faintly heard the reply.

"Forty-five a week," she said. As she walked between the rows in the soil, from outside the hand quarters, Elizabeth could hear hoots and hollers come from inside. She smiled to herself as she held the lantern just above her head and walked back to the main road.

Chapter 61

The next morning Elizabeth made arrangements to borrow a truck from a neighboring farm. She removed the two twenty-dollar bills from her coin purse and handed a twenty to Claire.

"On my way out of town, I'm going to drop you off on Main Street. You need to buy a newspaper and find a bicycle to buy."

"Really?"

"You'll need to get around town. Just remember to watch out for traffic."

"Thank you, but Mom?"

"Yes?"

"Do you think it would be okay if I applied for a job at the diner?"

"Doing what?"

"Working in the kitchen of course."

"Well, they'd be foolish not to hire you. Just don't forget about school coming up."

"I know," Claire replied. They hopped in the borrowed truck and drove into town. Once Claire was on her way, Elizabeth drove to the law office of Arthur Humes.

"Mr. Humes will be available in a few moments if you care to wait here," his secretary explained. Elizabeth took a seat, while the secretary turned her chair toward the typewriter and began striking the keys as she composed a letter. The letters clacked against the paper while Mr. Humes' voice could be heard on the phone. In between the clacking, his secretary would listen for the sound of his phone hanging up. She paused. Clang.

"You may go in now."

Elizabeth walked inside his office. Upon seeing her, Arthur stood up and gestured toward the chair in front of his desk.

"How was your trip back here?"

"Fine. We took the bus."

"I see. Glad you made it safely. Now, what can I do for you?"

"Well, I need to find the man who was to be my business part-ner."

"The gentlemen known for tomatoes."

"Yes."

"I see. How can I help?"

"Well, you mentioned that you found me through tax filings and I was wondering if you could do the same to find Mr. Washington."

"Do you know of his whereabouts? A city or an area?"

"I do not."

"Not even a state where he might be located?"

"I'm afraid not."

"Well, I had to pay a small fee to the Cook County Treasury Office to receive information on your tax filings. I only knew where to call because of what hospital you were transferred to and even then, I didn't know if you still lived in Cook County. Had you moved, I wouldn't have found you."

"I feel lucky to not have moved."

"You are very lucky. Now, if I were you, I would be finding a way to make it known that you are looking for him."

"How would I do that?"

"Post notices at the co-op and even co-ops in surrounding counties."

Chapter 62

The notices had the words: *MISSING* at the top and at the bottom was the word: *REWARD*. In the middle of the notice, the following words were printed, *SEARCHING FOR A BLACK MAN NAMED IRVING WASHINGTON. PLEASE CONTACT ELIZABETH CAMP-BELL in RUTLEDGE, TN.* In smaller letters at the bottom there were conditions of the reward. *FIFTY DOLLARS WILL BE PAID UPON MR. WASHINGTON'S VERIFIED WHEREABOUTS.*

Elizabeth and Claire traveled together to co-op offices and post offices in different counties. They hung a notice wherever they could until they used every notice they had. After two weeks, she hadn't gotten a single phone call which prompted her to call the operator.

"Hello, my name is Elizabeth Campbell, and I need to make certain that if someone needs to speak with me, that operators know that I am located at the Werthan farm."

"Yes, Ma'am, we have that information. If we are connected to anyone who needs to speak with you, the phone from which you are calling will ring," the operator explained. Elizabeth caught a glimpse of a black man walking past the dining room window.

"Thank you so very much," she said as she hung the phone in the cradle. She walked out the back door and saw several black men walking with sacks over their shoulder and heading back to the hand quarters. Upon realizing that the hands were coming to work, Elizabeth hurried to Rutledge Savings and Loan to meet with a man named Roger Landry. Roger immediately knew who she was and could see the results of what Gordon did to her. It pained him to see the scars on her arm and neck so he focused on her eyes the entire time. Elizabeth was unaware of his affiliation to Gordon and considered his full-on attention to be professional. After the introductions, she started the conversation.

"I need help with my first round of payroll expenses."

"We do that all the time. We will need records, a plan of repayment that includes a financial forecast, and if you don't have these things, we can…," he was interrupted by a ledger that she set down in front of him on his desk.

"I have it all," she said with a prideful smile.

"Even a plan of repayment?"

"I do. Please look at the loose paper tucked in the back. I have 90 acres. We are sowing 10 acres of lettuce, 10 acres of squash and 15 acres of cabbage. That's 35 acres of leaf vegetables, and I'm planning on 85% yield at $3.75 cents a crate. 70 crates an acre brings in $262.50, but keep in mind that's just leaf vegetables. I also have legumes listed here," she explained as she pointed to the paper. "Combined that's $573.97, and we haven't even gotten to the tomatoes yet."

"Your expenses?" he asked but could already tell a tidal wave of explanation was about to befall him.

"Look in the front of the ledger, I have it all broken out by machinery, labor, supplies, and I even have a row that budgets for a water truck in the event of a drought. However The *Farmer's Almanac* doesn't have one predicted for this year."

No one in Grainger County had such a clean ledger except for the president of Rutledge Savings and Loan. Each number was legible. Each column was labeled clearly. Totals were bold and pronounced.

"And how much is your payroll for 90 acres?" he asked. She reached across his desk and pointed at a row. He followed the row to the end and saw the total. "Okay. Just a second please," he said, never taking his eyes off the ledger. Elizabeth watched him walk across the other side of the bank and into the office of a man wearing a button up vest and eye glasses. She could see them converse briefly until Roger exited the office and sat back down at his desk. He closed the ledger and handed it back to her.

"No problem. Let me get some paperwork. I'll have you on your way."

The inheritance of the farm didn't include a truck; however it did include a 1939 Farmall tractor and a harvesting attachment. With years of rolling over uneven ground and being shaken by a bulky, rumbling engine, the tractor had endured years of vibration and stress. It creaked when it turned. It moaned when it pulled anything, and many of the parts had been repaired instead of replaced. The tires had been patched multiple times, and the steering wheel had baked and cracked under the sun. It was a rolling monument to the frugal Grainger County farmer. When it was started up and rolled out of the barn, the workers patted it like a dog.

"You gonna give us one more season?" one worker asked the red rolling heap. The first morning of working the Werthan Farm, the farm hands gathered around the back of the main house. Elizabeth had brewed a giant, clear glass jug of sweet tea and placed it out on the stump where Norman used to sit and clean his tools. Claire stood next to her mother as Elizabeth began to speak to the workers.

"Since Irving isn't here yet, we are going by Mr. Werthan's rotation book," she explained as she held the small notebook above her head. "We are simply doing what he had planned. He is our guide. Now, as you can see I am brewing all of us a jug of sun tea here on the stump. We are working the front forty today, and we will eat here close to the house as I have a block of ice in the freezer to chip off into our glasses. Nothing better than a cold drink in the hot sun," she said. Hoots and hollers followed. "The four of you that have worked with me before, please, run the scuffle and grub rotation for me. You know what to do. Those of you who haven't yet worked with me, I will be right alongside you in these fields. Not to keep an eye on you or make sure you work, but to give this everything I have. Me and my daughter will be rotating in and out with you. Now, I have batter in the ice box back in the kitchen so that means hoe cakes for lunch. Once soil preparation is completed, we're sowing lettuce, squash, and cabbage on the front. We are not sowing tomatoes yet on the hopes that Irving gets back here soon. If too much time passes, I'll have to get some help from a neighbor. Let's get to work."

More hooting from the workers could be heard before the tractor started back up, and the work commenced. The tractor puttered along with a worker sitting atop and keeping it straight up and down the rows. Both Claire and Elizabeth rotated in and out while the workers kept quiet as they felt unsure of how to act around their employer. The four that had worked for her before brought up a few questions for Claire.

"Are you still readin' them mystery books?"

"I lost them all in the fire a few years back. I haven't been able to read any since, but I did just order some more yesterday," said Claire as she hacked a dirt clod with a scuffle.

"Last time you told us the story of the ringing bell."

"That's right. I remember."

"Do you remember any more stories?"

"I do. Ya'll wanna hear more?" Claire asked as she broke up a clod, sending a plume of dirt into the air. When the workers all but begged her to tell the story, Claire started in. Her mother listened to every word with a smile.

"There's this one book called *Secret of the Old Clock*. Has to do with these rich people that Nancy Drew doesn't like. They're snobs. Anyway, there's this family that isn't doing too well, and they're nice and believe that something is wrong after one of their relatives passes away," she began to explain. The story made the work go by quickly. Sometimes the workers would have questions, and Claire would gladly answer them.

Over the next few weeks, Elizabeth would serve the workers lunch and retreat inside the house to make phone calls to surrounding counties. She phoned co-ops, sheriff's offices, prisons, and sometimes random farms to ask about Irving to whoever would answer the phone. The pain of hard work settled into both Claire's and Elizabeth's sore muscles. Their shoulders ached. Their forearms burned. At night when Elizabeth would curl up in bed, the soreness in her tight muscles made her smile as she fell asleep. The feeling of working hard was more than welcome, and it overpowered the stress of making the payments back to Rutledge Savings and Loan.

It took three weeks to sow sixty acres, and a day of rest was needed to continue the work. Though the farm hands felt the immense pain of working in the fields for 21 days straight, Elizabeth and Claire felt it even worse, but kept their complaints to themselves. After the sun would set, sometimes the hands would build a campfire. Claire loved to be around the workers anytime they would sit around the fire and play cards, drink from a mason jar, tell jokes, smoke cigarettes, and chew on beef jerky. While she didn't drink or smoke, she loved the smell of lit cigarettes and the sour aroma of whiskey being passed around. The hands came to think of Claire as more of a worker than an employer. When it would get too late, Elizabeth would peek out from the kitchen and holler.

"That's enough, Claire!"

Sometimes the fun would end too early for her, but Claire always abided by her mother's wishes. Hanging out with the hands reminded her of working in the restaurant and sitting on an apple crate in the back alley and cutting up with the cooks. The work on the farm continued until the lettuce, squash, and cabbage had been sowed. The hands left to find work on another farm, leaving Elizabeth and Claire to fret over the rain, seeds, and soil.

Chapter 63

The daylight hours on the Werthan Farm were spent cultivating crops, praying for rain, balancing the ledger, and paying Rutledge Savings and Loan. Before the sun set, Claire and Elizabeth would spend their time calling every county co-op in the state of Georgia as they had already exhausted Tennessee. When one state was completed, they simply moved on to Alabama, North Carolina, South Carolina, Louisiana, and even Arkansas and Mississippi. When they had a little extra money, they spent it on more flyers and postage stamps.

"I am looking for a black man named Irving Washington who might be working on a farm in your county. Do you happen to recognize that name? No? If I mail a notice to you, would you mind posting it there in your co-op?"

Two months crawled by and Elizabeth resorted to calling a few neighboring farms to consult on her crops. She pleaded for help, and most were kind and considerate of her situation. They would stand among the rows in her fields and inspect the crops with an intensity and purpose she didn't yet possess. She explained that she had a loan to pay and had hoped Irving would have gotten word to come back to Rutledge in time to begin sowing what he wanted. Since she hadn't yet sowed tomatoes, she knew it was time to get moving. She explained she wanted to sow a seed that would ripen quickly like Early Girl but pay more per crate. One of the farmers had an option. He was a plump man with male-pattern baldness and a bulbous nose. Every time he spoke, he sounded like a bulldog struggling to breathe.

"Yeah, Early Girl price is dropping. Usually does, but there is a 75-day tomato called Golden Nugget. Sweet in flavor when its mature. Problem is that you're never sure how many other farmers are bringin' in the same and drivin' the price down."

Some of the other farmers who came for a quick visit told her to sow Sun Gold or Pale Reds, but after a visit to the co-op, she discovered that very few farmers had purchased Golden Nugget seeds. After posting a job notice at the co-op for a weeks' worth of work, the hands were back at the Werthan Farm. They tilled a large section of the back forty and sowed the tomato seeds. Every hand could see the stress in Elizabeth's face with each seed sown as she second guessed her decision.

The final night of sowing Golden Nugget, a campfire was built in the back of the main house with mason jars of hooch and dirty jokes being dealt out like playing cards. Claire was in heaven. Elizabeth stayed by her side worrying about the seeds that were now in the ground. One of the men had a banjo with three strings and could play it like it had five strings. Music and singing continued until Elizabeth decided it was time to turn in and took Claire with her. Some hands went back to the hand quarters. Some passed out in the backyard underneath the stars.

While Elizabeth and Claire counted the days and prayed for rain, they waited for the lettuce and squash to break ground. In the meantime, they took to reading the owner's manual for the *Farmall Harvesting Attachment.* The jumbled wording in the manual and the use of agriculture jargon confused them to no end. Opting to ignore the manual, they decided to attach the harvester to the tractor to get a better idea of how it would work. As they attempted to make heads or tails of the complex machine, three black men appeared over by the main house. They were walking around the back and started knocking on the back door. Elizabeth heard the knocking and stood up from a crouched position.

"Hey! Over here!" she hollered as she waved. Dusting her hands off, she wiped the sweat off her brow and met them halfway. Claire followed closely behind. Two of the men she knew as farm hands but didn't recognize the other one.

"Miss Elizabeth! We met this man at the farm we workin' at. He got some news for ya!"

"News about what?"

"He knows where Irving might be," the man added. "We brought him to you as soon as he tol' us."

"Irving Washington?" she asked as she looked into the man's eyes. "You know Irving Washington?" She could tell he was nervous and filled with anxiety as he could barely make eye contact and stuttered slightly as he spoke.

"Well, I suppose I don't know him, but I have met him, and I have an idea where he might be," he explained. Elizabeth reached out and held the man's right hand in both of hers.

"It's okay. You can talk to me. He is a dear friend of mine and I have to find him," she explained in an effort to comfort him. Using her shoulder, she cocked her neck and wiped the sweat that continued to form on her brow. "Where do you think he might be?"

"See, I come from Florida. Near the ocean."

"Florida?"

"Yes, Ma'am. He in Florida workin' at a factory."

"A factory? What kind of factory?"

"Makin' steel parts."

"Steel? What's he doing there?"

"He talk about savin' up, and one day buying his own land.

That factory pays a hundred and fifty dollars a week."

"When did you last see him?"

"About six, eight months ago. I left. It gets so hot in that factory I about passed out many times from the heat."

"What's the name of this place?"

"Norville something."

"Norville? What city is it located in?"

"Pensacola. In Florida. We worked in a harbor," he explained as he finally made eye contact with Elizabeth. She had been holding his hand in both of hers until she maneuvered his right hand and shook it as if an agreement was reached.

"What's your name?"

"My name Grady."

"Grady, are you looking for work in Rutledge?"

"I am."

"You know these men?" she asked as she gestured to the two men at his side.

"No, ma'am. I am new to these parts."

"I see. Grady, I am going to see if I can't get Mr. Washington back here, and if I do, I'll give you a reward, and I will give you a job every time there is work here, you understand?" she said with a smile as she continued to shake his hand.

"Yes, Ma'am," said Grady with a grin as he began to make more eye contact.

"Now, you make sure you come back here when we harvest these ninety acres, ya hear?"

"Yes, Ma'am."

Over the years, Claire had watched how her mother interacted with the workers. More often than not, black men would seem timid around white women. Her mother could somehow make them calm and understand that she cared for them unlike most white women. Claire would often see her mother pat the workers on the back and shake their hands. The respect she received in return was greater than any white man would give her. After her meeting with Grady and profusely thanking the two men that brought him to visit with her, she pulled Claire into the house and dialed the operator.

"Norville Factory in Pensacola, please."

"One moment," the operator said with a brief pause. "Connecting you to Norville Industries."

Click. Ring.

The low rumbling of machinery could be heard on the line, but it sounded muffled and the man who answered came through clearly.

"Yes."

"Hello, I am looking for a worker by the name of Irving Washington."

"Ma'am, are you lookin' for a laborer?"

"I am."

"We have six hundred employees. No telling if we got an Irving from an Ernest. We probably got twenty Irvings."

"He's a black man and stands about six-foot-two."

"We hire all kinds. Truth be told it'd be easier to find a Mexican. Got only a handful of Mexican workers right now."

"This is an emergency. I really need your help."

"What's the name?"

"Irving Washington."

"Washington. Okay. Hang on," he said as he put the phone down. Elizabeth waited on pins and needles before the phone was picked up again. "I got a black fella working here with the last name Washington. My paper work here says the initial of his first name is the letter 'I'. You think that might be him?"

"I don't know."

"Well, that's all I got. Sorry, I couldn't be of more assistance.

I gotta go."

Click.

Elizabeth hung up the phone.

"What are you gonna do, Mom?"

"I'm gonna go find a truck I can borrow and get down there."

"When?"

"Right now."

Chapter 64

Back in 1952, a worker came into the hand quarters of the Meacham Farm holding a paper bill he had ripped off a community bulletin board. At the top of the bill, it read:

Work For Your Country! Below the bold text was a black and white photograph of the USS Indianapolis cruiser prominently displayed with five lines beneath the powerful image.

Top paying jobs
Housing is provided
Work by the ocean
$150 a week or more
Walk to grocery and restaurants

The bill circulated around the quarters until it made its way into the hands of Irving Washington. His thoughts focused less on the naval ship and more on the money that was promised. He turned the paper over and wrote out the math on the back with a pencil before hollering out to the other hands.

"$150 times fifty-two weeks is $7800 a year," he said aloud. The workers had just come in from sowing ten acres and were wiping the sweat from their faces with rags and small towels.

"Sounds too good to be true," one worker added as he headed toward the shower with a rag around his neck. "Besides, Florida is hot! The weather here ain't nuthin' I guarantee you that!"

Irving recalled that a 25-acre farm in Blount County had recently sold for $6,250. Another farm in Union County sold for $7,600 that included a house, a tractor, and seventy acres. Over the next few days, he thought about the words *Work by the ocean: $150 a week or more.* He thought about working for a year and having enough money to purchase his own land. Is it too good to be true? Nine days after first seeing the advertisement for the job in Florida, the workers left the hand quarters at the Meachamn Farm and headed to the co-op to find out which farm to go to next. Instead of working at another farm in Tennessee, Irving hitched rides and snuck onto dirty rail cars filled with filthy people to get to Florida. Three days after leaving Grainger County, he found his way into an employment line at Norville Industries in Pensacola. Twelve-foot high fencing surrounded a building that looked to be as big as Chicago. Never before had his eyes laid on such a massive structure. Irving could see towering steel cranes perched on concrete behind the factory with battleships out in the harbor. After waiting more than two hours outside under the hot sun, he made it to the front of the line and found a long table with Norville employees sweating and explaining the working conditions to candidates. Irving was handed an employment card by a thin-lipped white lady who then directed him to another line where men waited to be examined by a medical doctor.

After three more hours of waiting and a quick physical examination, Irving was cleared to work. It took another six days of unpaid training until he began earning $150 a week. Irving felt he was on his way to owning his own farm. The heat inside the factory was almost unbearable and to combat the heat, Norville Industries set up water stations. The stations were comprised of metal containers that held 20 gallons. Each container had a spout and was set on a high pedestal where workers could operate the spout and catch the stream of water in their mouths. White men in white button-up shirts thought of this as a good plan but keeping the water cool was difficult to do in the factory. Irving often found the water to be warm after ten o'clock in the morning and downright hot after five in the afternoon.

His first job at Norville was working on Rivet Row. Buckets with molten steel were poured, while workers hammered the steel into rivets. For two months, Irving's forearms burned from hammering steel as did his entire body whenever he went near the furnace. At night after work, Irving would walk a quarter mile to a large brick building that housed Norville workers. Aside from being four-stories tall, it was no different than staying in the hand quarters of any farm in Tennessee. Irving kept to himself mostly, refusing to join in on late night card games and jars of hooch. Instead he would rest on his bunk and write notes in a tiny notebook he purchased at a truck stop outside of Pensacola. His notes included a list of tomatoes he wanted to try crossing to increase the flavor or possibly invent a new flavor. He drew a forty-acre tract and made boxes inside the acreage where he would sow cucumbers, squash, onions, carrots and tomatoes. Sometimes workers would look over at Irving who would be lying in his bunk and smiling as he wrote in his notebook.

"Whatcha smilin' about Washington?"

"Oh nuthin'," he would say. It would have been too complicated to explain that he was imagining harvesting rotation crops such as broccoli and cabbage before sowing tomato seeds on his own farm.

On the third month of employment at Norville, Irving had saved $1,200 after taxes and was feeling great until he was told to report to his supervisor. The only time he ever saw his boss was from the corner of his eye while working amongst the heat and steel. Hard to miss, his supervisor was a portly white man who wore a white button-up shirt and always had a glare in his eye. When Irving finally located him standing with a clipboard near a loading dock, Irving approached him hoping his job wasn't in jeopardy.

"I was told to report to you, Sir."

"Washington?"

"Yes, Sir."

"We're cutting workers. After today you're done here," he said as he walked away from the loading dock and toward another section of the factory. Irving followed him.

"I'm done?" Irving asked as he pointed at his own chest. His face wrinkled, and stress emanated from his expression. "How can that be? I'm a great worker."

"Collect your final pay when you wrap up. You'll find your check at the front office," his supervisor added while continuing to walk with Irving following him.

"But I work hard!" Irving yelled. His supervisor stopped and tapped Irving's chest with the clipboard.

"Hey! Norville no longer requires your services. That's the end of it, or I won't let you finish this shift!" he yelled as he walked away. Irving stood motionless and in shock.

It was a few days later that Irving found out he could reapply to Norville, and after six days of unpaid training and a physical, he was back at work. Instead of working on Rivet Row, he was given a job in a section that machined rods and pins, but paid ten dollars less per week. His days were spent grinding and cutting metal with big machinery that had gotten men killed just weeks before Irving began. It wasn't as hot as working on Rivet Row, and the water in the nearest metal drinking station didn't get warm until one o'clock. While the conditions were a little better, the pay wasn't.

After one month of fabricating rods and pins, Irving was fired again for no reason and was forced to reapply. Supervisors firing employees was a common occurrence at Norville that the workers later discovered was a practice of preventing a union from being formed. Irving's original plan of working a full year and then leave for Tennessee to purchase a farm proved to be a lofty goal. Instead of only working a year, three years later he found himself still working in Pensacola in December of 1955. He had only been able to save two thousand dollars which was a direct result of Norville firing workers at any given time. Irving would usually be employed for 30 to 60 days only to be fired. After six days of unpaid training, he would be back on the payroll, and he didn't always earn $150 a week. Sometimes the job he was assigned to paid less—much less.

On one particular day when deliveries were behind, a young man of twenty-two years turned a forklift too quickly causing the cargo on top of the lift to tip and fall off, pinning Irving against a concrete divider. Screaming in pain, Irving yelled out.

"Get it off me!" Blood trickled down the wall and onto the floor. The workers quickly pulled the crate of engine components off Irving and his broken leg. He was laid down upon a tarp while the workers grabbed the corners and dragged him to the infirmary with Irving screaming the entire way.

After the doctors set Irving's tibia bone, he lay on a bed in the infirmary with a cast on his leg for four weeks. With nothing else to do, he memorized the water stains in the ceiling tile above him and even gave some of them names. One stain looked like a lamp, and another resembled grizzly bear. For four weeks, Irving was fed oatmeal, oranges, and bread. The oatmeal was thick and flavorless, and the bread needed more of everything. Just after his fourth week, the attending physician in the infirmary needed more room due to newly injured patients from Norville Industries. A man in a white coat approached Irving's bed and told him he would be discharged that morning. Even before he could be served the bland oatmeal for breakfast, Irving was wheeled outside by a nurse who got him to stand up, handed him a wooden crutch, and sent him on his way.

"You need to come back in two months to get your cast off," the nurse stated before turning around and walking back inside. Irving shook his head as he placed the crutch underneath his shoulder.

Hobbling along, he made his way toward the dormitory hoping he could collect his belongings and possibly find an empty bunk. In every step he took, the pain in his leg radiated and caused him to stop and take frequent breaks. He would lean against a wall or a tree and close his eyes wishing he was back in Grainger County working the fields. Once inside the dormitory building, he discovered that the workers had absorbed all of his belongings, and his bunk was occupied by another Norville employee. The only thing Irving wanted was his notebook that he shoved under the mattress. Half of the bunks in the dormitory were occupied by sleeping workers, while the other half were working their shifts. The man sleeping on Irving's bunk had three hours left until his shift began.

Thinking the notebook was still under the mattress, Irving wanted desperately to get down on his knees and look up underneath. If the book was there, he would see it between the mattress and the metal springs. Instead of causing himself great pain to get down on the floor, Irving decided to try and wake the sleeping man. Using the crutch, he poked the man's arm.

"Excuse me," Irving said softly. Without any movement, he poked the man again. "Excuse me."

"Leave me alone," replied the man without opening his eyes. Irving spoke a little louder.

"There is something I need under your mattress."

"Go on! Leave me alone!"

"This used to be my bunk. It would only take a second," he pleaded like a preacher begging the congregation to repent their sins. The man opened his eyes and looked at Irving.

"Get out of here, old man! I'm trying to sleep."

"If you could just check…," Irving started to say until the man reached out and grabbed his crutch.

"Leave now, or I'll beat you with your own crutch." The man released his grasp and closed his eyes. Irving could tell he was serious. Instead of enduring another injury, Irving thought it best to let the notebook go as there wasn't any assurance that the book was still there.

Irving took a cab ride to the bank and withdrew $2,024.97 and placed his funds in a bank envelope. He paid for the cab ride after he was dropped off at a motel close to Norville Industries. At a rate of $7.50 a night, he checked into a room and found great relief lying down on a comfortable bed.

For two months, Irving lived in the motel while keeping his leg elevated. He spent his time watching the black and white television in his room and eating as cheaply as possible. On the day he was to have his cast removed, Irving returned to the infirmary where his cast was cut off by a nurse. To his surprise, she used a hand saw, pliers and scissors to free him from the restricting plaster. Unable to walk without a lot of pain, he continued to use the crutch as he hobbled back outside.

By the time Irving had fully recovered he missed out on more than four months of work and had to spend more money than usual for food, shelter, and medicine. Two months after getting his cast removed, he could walk without the aid of the crutch, and he was finally able to re-apply to Norville Industries. He was assigned to the machine and weld section and was forced to endure five days of unpaid training to learn how to grind down mounting brackets for massive marine engines. The pay was so low in the machine and weld section of the factory that after taxes, he was only bringing home eighty dollars a week. Every month or so, Irving would be fired and rehired and was always forced to work a lower paying job since he had a difficult time supporting his own weight and walked with a limp.

One evening, a short man in a blue jumpsuit, using a glue bucket and a roller, posted notices on the walls inside the entrance of the the dormitory. Workers gathered as he rolled them on and they read the words *Demolition Notice* at the top. As the workers read the details, it became clear that Norville was going to demolish the dormitory in four weeks and in its place build another factory floor. At the bottom of the notice were the words, *Workers will be responsible for their own housing.* Irving had been working his shift when the notice was posted, and by the time he limped back to the entrance of the dorm, the workers were at the maximum level of outrage.

Chapter 65

After borrowing a 1946 Ford short-bed pickup truck from the neighboring farm down the road, Elizabeth packed crackers, biscuits, a canteen full of water, and two boxes of Cracker Jacks. She began the long drive to the Alabama border leaving Claire to look after the farm.

The five-hour drive to Huntsville went by quickly although she had already eaten a pack of crackers and a biscuit and washed them down with half of her canteen. She drove to the downtown square in Huntsville and found a courthouse. Once inside, she found a water fountain for *Whites* and another fountain for *Coloreds.* Using the White water fountain, she filled up her canteen and got back in the truck and was on her way. Two hours later she found herself in Birmingham needing fuel. After a quick stop at a gas station and another fill up of her canteen, she was again on her way.

It was another five hours before she made it to Pensacola and it had been dark for more than six hours. After using a folding map, she found her way to Norville Industries—a mammoth-sized building with massive battleships behind it in the harbor. Welding sparks could be seen on the sides of the battleships as the moon reflected the sunlight above them without a cloud in the sky. A guard shack sat outside the factory and after pulling the truck up to the gate, a man walked out of the shack holding a clipboard.

"Hello, I am from Tennessee, and I'm looking for a worker here at this factory."

"Sorry Ma'am. You'll have to come back at seven in the morning. Shifts run from seven to seven."

"I see. Would you be able to tell me if you have a certain worker that is employed here?"

"No Ma'am. This gate is for brass. Colonels, generals, and elected officials. Workers go through another gate on the harbor side."

"I see. How would I get over there?"

"You can't. Guards won't let in non-employees."

"Oh. How would I find out if a worker works in the factory?" she asked. The guard leaned against the door of the truck and spoke at a lower tone.

"You can't. This is a factory that builds vessels for the United States Navy. It's under tight security. Now, I am not supposed to tell you that if you're looking to find a worker, you might find him at the Norville Shuttle Station about a half mile from here. All workers are bused in to the factory."

"Oh. I see," Elizabeth responded as she smiled. "If one weren't going to give me directions, what might they not say?"

"West Chase Street and…," he said as he pointed his finger at her, "you didn't hear it from me."

Finding an empty parking lot near the factory, she pulled into the lot and cut the engine. Sleeping in the cab of a truck was uncomfortable enough to prevent Elizabeth from falling into a deep sleep. Tossing and turning on a firm truck seat was accompanied by random industrial noises that a closed-up truck cabin couldn't keep out. When the sun rose, she sat up and did her best to fix her wiry hair back into a ponytail. Once she started the truck, she drove to a gas station and asked for directions to West Chase Street. After navigating the truck to the correct stretch of road, she found more than a hundred workers standing around smoking cigarettes while holding metal lunchboxes and thermoses. It looked very familiar. She got out of the truck and started making her way through the crowd.

"Irving Washington!" she hollered. "Irving Washington!" she continued as she made her way through the crowd of whites, blacks, a few women, and Hispanics. "Irving Washington!" she yelled out until a hand grabbed her shoulder. A black man with gray patches in his hair stood in front of her. The skin around his eyes were wrinkled, and his cheeks had dropped to jowls long ago.

"Ma'am, I know him. In fact, he just left on that bus right there," the man said as he pointed off in the distance at a green and white bus driving away.

"Would you be able to tell him I am out here when you get inside?"

"I am on the other side of the plant, so I won't see him. I won't be much help until after seven tonight when we all get off. All these workers here go to the other side of the plant. Irving works in section one right now. I work in section three."

"How can I get word to him?"

"Well, I got a cousin workin' at the front office. That's where people come on their first day. You take this next bus and when they stop at the office, you get off and go inside. Ask for Tully. He is my cousin, and you tell him I said to help you."

"What's your name?"

"Lucius Evans," he replied with a big smile as he gestured tipping an invisible hat. Three green and white buses arrived on West Chase Street and while the workers boarded, she looked at Lucius.

"They just gonna let me on board?"

"If anyone asks, just tell them you applyin' for a job," he said with a shrug.

"Thank you for your help, Lucius."

"Glad to help. Remember to ask for Tully."

Elizabeth boarded and found the driver to be an older white man wearing a worn naval uniform except for the white hat. On his belt was a gun in a holster. He smiled at everyone stepping up into the bus.

"It's a great day today, gonna be a hot one though," he looked at Elizabeth and without missing a beat, he added, "applicants and new employees sit at the front of the bus, please." After passing the first seat, she sat down next to a burly white man with a beard.

As the bus shifted into gear, the motor whined. They headed down West Chase Street and turned toward a closed gate protected by guards. She watched as the gate opened, and the bus headed toward the massive factory building. The size of the factory that spanned more than five football fields didn't impress Elizabeth as she had once thought that the Harris Clay Mining camp was impressive. She thought of the mines as a prison and had already passed judgement on Norville Industries. The entrance Lucius spoke about was designated by hand painted lettering that read *Office and Orientation Entrance* with a brown painted double door beneath the sign. When the bus came to a stop, the driver yelled out.

"Applicants and employees with office business get off here!" As she stepped down off the bus, she didn't see a train, but the sound of a steam engine coming to life could be heard coming from somewhere near the factory.

She walked to the brown double doors and stood for a moment after entering and took in the large room with fluorescent lighting, concrete floors, and cement block walls. On the opposite side of the room were two double doors that had been painted blue. A sign to the left and right of the doors read, *All Workers Must Wear Hard Hats.* Farther to the right was a massive, tall counter that reminded her of a drugstore that filled prescriptions.

"Help you, Miss?" a young white man asked from atop the counter.

"I'm looking for Tully." The young man pointed at a black man across the room wearing brown pants and a short sleeve, white button-up shirt. He was holding a clip board and collecting paper work from people sitting on long wooden benches.

"Thank you," she said to the young man and walked toward Tully. The benches were arranged as if they were for a small church service, looking more like pews than park benches. When it became evident to Tully that a woman was coming to speak with him, he perked up. "Excuse me, your cousin Lucius told me to come find you. He said you might be able to help me."

"Okay. Help with what?"

"I'm looking for a man named Irving Washington."

"Hmmm…don't know him, but we have hundreds of employees. Not sure I can help."

"He works in section one."

"That's through them blue doors right there. My boss won't let me go out onto the plant floor though."

"Oh."

"If you wanna speak to an employee, best be waitin' out on West Chase Street when the buses off load," Tully explained as he took applications from those who were seated in the church pews. Back at the tall drugstore counter, an older white man was talking to the younger man while looking and pointing at Elizabeth as if she might be a problem. In an effort to not get Tully in trouble, she took a seat amongst the congregation so she did not look out of place.

After taking a seat, she would watch Tully as he collected paper work from people and answered their questions. Anytime the blue double doors opened, the muffled sound of machinery became unmuffled and a wave of heat flowed into the office area. The loud droning, hammering, yelling, whirring of belts, and grinding of gears poured out through the double doors until they closed again. The thought of Irving working around loud machinery and laboring over steel concerned her greatly. Just like working in the mines, she knew what a place like Norville Industries could do to people.

As she sat thinking about Irving and what to do next, her thoughts were often interrupted by the blue doors opening and workers going in and out. The two white men at the drug store counter didn't seem to be paying her any attention and now, Tully looked very busy. Elizabeth couldn't stop thinking that Irving no longer had to endure his situation, and he wasn't aware. He was laboring under the impression that she was angry at him. The last thing he would've remembered was her yelling for him to leave. The blue doors opened once again. Droning, hammering, and yelling poured through. Unable to endure her thoughts for another second, she slipped through the closing blue doors and found herself on the factory floor. The ceiling was fifty feet high, and the space inside was massive. The concrete floor had two yellow lines that stretched down the length of the plant as if it were a designated walkway. All of the heavy machinery was behind the yellow line near the walls on both sides. Workers operating the deafening machinery didn't even notice a female had just entered through the blue doors. Covering her ears, she started down the middle of the factory, staying between the yellow lines and jogging at a slow pace. She looked at the workers faces trying to find Irving.

As she hurried along, she looked at the faces of fat men, thin men, tall and short men. Some white, some black, very few were Hispanic. As she continued to jog, a grime-covered white man in a white button-up shirt and hard hat saw her moving quickly down the aisle.

"You need a hard hat!" he yelled as he tapped his on his helmet. She yelled back.

"What?"

"YOU NEED A HARD HAT!"

"I NEED TO FIND IRVING WASHINGTON."

"I DON'T KNOW WHO THAT IS! HERE, TAKE MINE. I'LL GO GET ANOTHER ONE!" he yelled as he handed her his hard hat. Placing it on her head, she used one hand to hold it on her head as she jogged and scanned the faces of the men working around the machines.

Irving had been assigned the job of grinding down brackets that were used in a ship's engine compartment. He was given boxes of brackets every fifteen minutes, and he was to keep up by grinding down the edges and making them smooth. He removed a bracket from the current box he was working out of and touching the edges to the belt grinder. Sparks flew.

Elizabeth heard yelling coming from behind her, and she turned to look. The two men from the drug store counter were running after her. Picking up the pace, she began to run faster and let the hard hat fall to the floor as she used her arms to make longer strides. She looked at the faces of black men and skipped over the white workers who looked her way. A few of the employees started to abandon their stations, and hollered out, and clapped for her, cheering her on while being chased by management. In an effort to help find him, she began yelling out his name.

"IRVING WASHINGTON!"

The men started to gain on her. Tears flowed from her eyes

and streak back toward her ears as the rush of air pushed them backward. "IRVING WASHINGTON!"

More workers started to take notice as she ran down the aisle between the two yellow lines. Hooting and hollering could be barely heard over the loud machinery. From the corner of her eye, a figure came out from between two towering machines and ran up to her. A black man who heard her yell out for Irving ran alongside her.

"You looking for Irving?" he yelled out.

"You know where he is?" she yelled back. They spoke while management closed in.

"Yes, Ma'am! Follow me!" he said as he took off like a sprinter after the crack of a starter pistol. Unable to keep up, she used every ounce of strength to pull away from the men behind her.

Irving couldn't hear anything other than the grinding of the metal. A hand on his shoulder prompted him to turn around.

"Marvin? What's the matter?" Irving asked as he could see he was out of breath. Marvin simply pointed. Irving followed his finger and saw Elizabeth running with two white men chasing her down. Irving dropped the bracket in his hand and limped out in between the yellow lines and came into her view.

"IRVING!" she yelled as more tears streamed. Stunned and unable to comprehend the sight in front of him. He stood in disbelief as she ran toward him. Just as she got close, he opened his arms and embraced his friend. She cried in his arms, and he held her tightly. She yelled over the loud machines.

"I am so sorry!" she sobbed. The feeling of regret and misery she had been carrying for years surfaced in an uncontrollable flood of emotions. The men chasing Elizabeth finally caught up to them and scolded her for running into the factory. Elizabeth couldn't hear them over the sound of her heartbeat surging through her ears. Ignoring both men in button up shirts, Irving walked with Elizabeth toward the blue doors while the workers cheered and clapped. While it looked like they were being es-corted out, in truth, Elizabeth was pulling Irving toward the exit.

"GET BACK TO WORK!" the men yelled at the employees as they walked behind Irving and Elizabeth.

"Norman Werthan passed away," yelled Elizabeth.

"He did?" Irving hollered back.

"He left me his farm!"

"His farm? You own it?" asked Irving. They had walked past an incredibly loud machine when she replied.

"We own it!" she said although Irving didn't hear her.

"What's that?"

"WE OWN IT! YOU AND ME! 90 ACRES!" she yelled with a huge smile.

Chapter 66

It took time for life on the farm to fall into a comfortable rhythm, but the small surplus of cash Irving had saved up made things easier. Elizabeth paid off the payroll loan in one lump sum walking into Rutledge Savings and Loan and paying Roger Landry in cash. Changes made to the process of farming were controlled by Irving, while the ledger was left up to Elizabeth.

When they received their first check, her first act of spending their revenue was to make the hand quarters more livable for Irving. He insisted on living there, so Elizabeth purchased and installed insulation and a pot-belly stove that would keep the cinder block building warm during the winter. She might have overdone it with the number of ceiling fans that were installed to keep Irving and everyone else cool during the summer heat.

In 1957, Elizabeth and Claire erected a sign out in front of the main house by the road which read *Werthan, Washington and Campbell Farms.* It was a mouthful, but everyone in the community knew where it came from. It came to be known in Grainger County as the farm of Irving Washington, and it wasn't uncommon for a knock to rap on the hand quarters with a local farmer standing outside. They would ask for Irving so that they could inquire about agricultural problems they were facing. Inevitably, he had answers and had become revered in the community for having the heart of a teacher, sharing his knowledge. Claire found her place in Rutledge by attending the local high school and working the farm during the summer days and her nights were spent in the kitchen at the diner on the square. Strangely, a new item appeared on the diner menu that was a big hit. For an additional fifty cents, diners were treated to a plate of buttery croissants.

Elizabeth had found one of her favorite things to be working in the field sowing seeds or breaking clods with a scuffle alongside the farm hands. She came to know each of them by name (especially Grady), and when it was time for weeks of work to be done, the hands came running. The night before working in the field, Elizabeth would be up mixing cornmeal or brewing tea in a large jug. The next day, she would fix lunch and she and Claire along with Irving would serve the workers. Sometimes the hands would ask,

"Mrs. Campbell, would you like me to do that for ya?"

"No, sir, you just sit back and rest! I'm serving y'all today," she would say with a smile. Elizabeth carried with her a sense of gratitude for everything the workers did, and they came to love her for her kindness and the profound level in which she respected and cared for them.

While being in the fields was one of her favorite things, she also loved getting up one day a week and grabbing her ledger before heading out the door. She would travel to Knoxville on Thursdays and enter Tate's Coffee Shop to have breakfast with three men. In 1954, Greg Carter passed away and his seat wasn't filled until Elizabeth contacted the group and asked if she could join in on their breakfast meetings. Without ever saying it out loud, she called them her "grandfathers" as they dished out advice that surpassed business. Over the years, they had the pleasure of meeting Irving and Claire and were frequently brought incredibly flavorful, fresh tomatoes—the best they had ever eaten.

An amazing thing happened to Elizabeth a few years later in 1959. A large manila envelope reached the Werthan, Washington and Campbell Farm that was sent from New Haven, Connecticut. She opened the envelope and found a newspaper inside. She hadn't expected mail from Claire, so it was a surprise when she saw the return address. Inside the envelope was *The Register* newspaper and a note had been taped to the front which read: *Mom, page 7.*

Elizabeth opened to page seven and found an article with Claire holding a basket of Grainger County Tomatoes while wearing a white coat and a chef's hat. The headline read, *Female Culinary Student Wins Annual Prize With Produce From Family Farm.* Before reading the article, Elizabeth burst out the back door and tore through the field. Her stride missed the rows of tomatoes and beets as she hurried to the hand quarters.

Knock. Knock.

"Come in."

Elizabeth hurried through the door and found Irving by himself standing over crop rotation sketches that were spread out on a table. He was wearing reading glasses that sat on the end of his nose. He looked up from the sketches as she held out the newspaper.

"Look at this! You remember the tomatoes we sent Claire? The large basket of Brandywine and Caspian Pinks?" Elizabeth asked as she stood beside him.

"Yeah, I remember," he replied. When he looked at the photo and headline, his eyes widened, and he smiled. "Well, look at this!"

"I haven't even read it yet." Irving and Elizabeth continued standing and read the article that reported how culinary student, Claire Campbell, used tomatoes grown on her family's farm in Rutledge, Tennessee. She had prepared a dish called *Tomatoes Provencal* that was made with garlic, shallots, olive oil, and breadcrumbs. The article mentioned that every year, the instructors at The Culinary Institute of America would select one dish in a contest to be added to the menu at *La Espadon*, a French restaurant on the coast in New Haven. When the article concluded, they looked at the photo of Claire holding the basket of tomatoes. Elizabeth was smiling ear to ear until a tear from Irving's eyes fell onto the newspaper. She looked up at him and could see the pride radiating from his expression. His lips quivered as he wiped his eyes and spoke.

"She looks so happy," he said with a nod.

Elizabeth began to tear up at both her daughter's accomplishment and Irving's feelings for Claire. She embraced Irving as he added, "I feel like I have a part in that."

"In what?"

"Her happiness."

"You do. You absolutely do."